A Fool's Pilgrimage

David Frazer Wray

SPARSILE BOOKS LTD

To Kjersti and Owen

At Calais

On Saint Lambert's Day, in the third year of the reign
of King Henry, the fifth of that name.
(Tuesday 17th September 1415)

Meum est propositum in taberna mori
Vinum sit appositum morientis ori
Ut dicant cum venerit angelorum chori
Harry sit propitius huic potatori.

There.
At last.
This pen has finally held a line of ink.

And so it should! With five of its brothers, a pot of clotted ink and a bound book of—so I am assured—VIRGIN paper, it cost me three florins! So let the first entry in this daybook be a complaint against shopkeepers. Or at least this pen-monger in particular, for he knew full well that his wares could not be had elsewhere in Calais and asked five times the common price. Whoreson plague sore! He should be hanged in his own purse-strings!

It is many a long year since last I wrote at any length. Not since my days at Thomas Mowbray's[1] house and, may God preserve me, I truly wrote but little then, being rather more inclined to riot and debauchery. Aye, it was then began that slow-descending gradient of vice that has led me to my present sorry state.

I am sitting in a private upper room in an inn called *Le Père Abailard* in the town of Calais. My apartment is divided from the main body of the loft by a partition of wattle and daub which permits me a small degree of privacy. Sadly, it is no barrier against the snores and farts of my fellow guests.

The window of this room affords me a good enough view of the church of Saint Nicholas, who is the patron saint of children and thieves.

The innkeeper, a little man from Maidstone who has the King's Evil, has told me that on a clear day I may see the headland of Dover from my room. If ever there *was* a clear day here, which I much doubt, then I dare say he may be right. For myself, I saw the headland of Dover passing well when I toured the Cinque Ports with Hal[2] when he was Prince of Wales. We had been drinking deep in Dover Castle and he puked over it. The headland, I mean, not the castle. Though valorous enough in his fashion, Hal has never confronted a great height gladly and any elevation above that of a horse's back is wont to reveal the makings of his last meal.

This is the first time I ever was in France. In truth, it does not seem greatly different from England. The French language I know well enough, though till now I have had little occasion to use it. I say "well enough" for it is the French of Stratford atte Bowe and a tongue largely unknown to the French themselves. This is not the disadvantage it may appear. In the environs of Calais, Flemish is the common tongue. Besides that, you have your Breton, your Occitan, your Provençal, your Lingua Romana, your Limousin, your Basque and doubtless others. And I speak not of dialects here but of complete separate tongues. Your dialects are another matter. Harry Percy[3] spoke a dialect. For the most part he could be understood without undue difficulty, yet his frequent excesses of excitement bred unintelligibility in him. It is said that when he addressed his soldiery before the battle of Shrewsbury[4] a good half of them thought the rebellion over and started for home. The other half considered it a stirring and bloodthirsty speech—or at least what little they understood of it.

You may smell France long before you see it. Now it is well known that we English are uncommon fond of garlic. Wherever you go, from the Marches to the Weald of Kent, you may find your garlic seller and there is not a housewife in the land who does not count it in her larder. With good reason too, for it is a herb of great potency which elevates the flavours of meats, soups and other delicacies. Yet your Englishman, being essentially a creature of moderation, will add garlic to his soup rather than soup to his garlic. Not so the French. By so much are they enamoured of this herb that it seems they apply it to their very bodies and wallow therein like sows in a midden, so great is the stink thereof.

Nor is your Frenchman cleanly in his habits. I never yet saw one wash hands and face in the three days I have been here. In place of removing the dirt that defiles them, they prefer to mask its odour with scents and perfumes. Perhaps this explains their fondness for garlic. I wonder that any mariner should lose his way in the English Channel when his nose alone may tell him where lies the coast of France.

The inn at which I lie, *Le Père Abailard*, stinks worst of all. The Maidstone man with the King's Evil had it from his grandfather. The inn, not the Evil. His grandfather, for his part, had it from King Edward himself who slept here when he took Calais some seventy years ago. I doubt it has been swept out since.

Besides the stink, I am nettled with lice and bedbugs and this, so I am told, in the best inn and ordinary[5] in Calais. May Heaven help the worst.

At Calais

On the fifty-ninth anniversary of our glorious victory at Poitiers.
(Thursday 19th September 1415)

I was constrained to end my writing on Tuesday last through excess of drunkenness. To what an evil pass have I come!

I have read again what I wrote, and it seems a very boiling-bag of vanities and an unconscionable waste of damnably expensive paper. That I should have sat thus in my room, wearing pilgrim's clothes to boot, a man of seventy summers, grey-haired and grim-visaged, and quaffed off cups of wine[6] and indulged my choler in such irreverent wise is a source of great shame to me.

The end and purpose of this daybook is that it shall be firstly a penance, of sorts, secondly a meditation and thirdly a record of my pilgrimage to the Holy Land. Or to the shrine of St James at Compostella—I have not yet decided which. Thus have I vowed to write herein my thoughts and doings of each day—whether I be at my ease in some comfortable and LOUSE-FREE inn or faced with the trials of the open road. So, though today be a Thursday and my last entry that of Tuesday last, my next entry shall be tomorrow. Friday. This I most solemnly vow before God and all the saints.

As a meditation, I shall write down my sins past and present, that, being set in ink and no longer the flitting phantoms of cloudy memory, they shall better serve to correct my future conduct.

As a record, I shall put down the hours travelled, the leagues covered, the people met upon the way, *et cetera*.

To the meditation then.

I am Sir John Falstaff, knight banneret!

Nay, that lacks the proper tone of modesty, for all that it is true. In truth, I am unworthy of that rank. I claimed to be the vanquisher of Harry Percy, surnamed "Hotspur", at Shrewsbury field but it was not me who killed him. It was Hal. Sliced him neatly through the neck-piece of his bascinet and strolled off as calmly as you please. Left him as dead as some whoreson church-tomb effigy.

As for myself, I had feigned death to escape the murderous intentions of the Earl of Douglas and others, and seeing myself alone with the dead rebel I pulled myself up, stabbed him in the thigh, threw him over my back and wended straightway to the rear to claim the victory for myself. Stabbed him in the thigh! If you stab a sparrow in the thigh he will up and fly off, and Harry Percy was no sparrow. I dare say he had more scars on his thighs than *Le Père Abailard* has fleas. I gave a good account of myself. I lied. Hal, damn him, did not so much as blink as I mouthed my nothings. He counterfeited credulity as well as I had counterfeited death.

Later, when the fourth Henry was in the foggy evening of his years and foul rebellion raised its head again, and I had once more misused the press—as many a captain has—to line my pockets with silver and the army's ranks with dross, the same fortune attended me. It was at Gaultree Forest[7] when, the combat being already won, I bravely advanced to do battle with whosoever should be fleeing. I met up with one John Colville, knight, a valorous though misguided gentleman who, recognising in me the slayer of Harry Percy, gave himself up without a fight. From this courageous action did further honour accrue. I thought myself the very budding flower of chivalry, waiting only on Hal's light to blossom into nobility and wealth.

I was an old fool. Hal was not the man to reward fawning flattery and base cowardice. What favours he could bestow on me had already been bestowed. When no longer Hal but King Henry, the fifth of that name, he banished Jack Falstaff. Banished him! Took away his whore and his page. Forbade him to come within ten miles of his person till repentance and reformation had wrought change.

I had set much store by my future preferment and obtained great credit thereby. It is in the nature of things that those who advanced me money and goods should expect repayment, and that I could not do for the money was spent—aye, and the goods sold.

Short-winded and short-changed, I sought a space of time to pant for breath and so I amplified my true discomfiture and counterfeited heartbreak. I took to my bed in the upper room of the Boar's Head,[8] with much groaning and pulling of my hair.

I lay abed for a good two months and kept Nell Quickly[9] busy on the stairs, bringing me tasty morsels to tempt my appetite or a cup of hot broth or a few thimble-fulls of wine, and shouted for the Jordan to be emptied or for my linen to be changed and sundry other sickbed whimsies. I would have much liked to have enjoyed the generous favours of my sweet, lewd Doll Tearsheet,[10] but she had been whipped and imprisoned for whoring and, since her release, had departed for *Terra Incognita*, or Southwark as it is generally known.

When, at length, I tired of lying thus, I tottered downstairs and sat in the inglenook and terrorised the taproom like a peevish old crone, whilst claiming that only wine sweetened with sugar could quicken my recovery.

In truth, I had to endure extreme discomforts in the cause of sickness. The good Doctor Monks, as big a quack as ever left a duck, visited me twice at Nell Quickly's behest and bled me and purged me and pronounced me like as not to die and pocketed his florin and went his way. Never did a physick do better service, for his visitations left me paler than before and none could gainsay the gravity of my afflictions.

Around Christmastide, I rallied enough to join in the festivities but suffered an immediate relapse following Twelfth Night. After taking to my bed for a further two months, I graduated once more to the inglenook and had a merry enough time until Lady Day when, to mark the Feast of the Annunciation with an excess of tickle-brained folly, Nell Quickly proclaimed her betrothal to that swaggering, foul-mouthed ancient[11] Pistol.

I knew straightway how the land would lie thereafter. Pistol, as choleric a braggart as ever trailed a pike, had always envied me my loftier rank and thus, as the future proprietor of the Boar's Head, would lose no time in playing the tyrant to his sometime captain. Not only that: he knew full well how I had staved off my hour of reckonings with Hostess Quickly by promises of marriage and sundry other devices and, covetous rascal that he is, was ever deriding her for her simple-hearted pity in lodging me *gratis* during my infirmity. Thus I saw fit to make a second recovery. I prevailed upon John Bardolph[12] to borrow a cart and we set off for Gloucestershire.

At Calais

On Saint Matthew's Eve.
(Friday 20th September 1415)

I wrote so much yesterday that my hand was gripped by vile cramps and I almost missed supper. That would have been a great pity for I bespoke it with some difficulty and *Le Père Abailard*, for all its stink, prepares the food tolerably well. I supped on pease soup, roast mutton, roast duckling and pigeons, pastries and English cheese; this complemented with several draughts of the good red wine of Saintonge.

Now that I see this set down on paper, I perceive that I am in mortal danger of falling into the SIN OF GLUTTONY. Such is the effectiveness of this exercise of writing as a means of corrective meditation. Tonight I shall eat as a pilgrim should.

Yesterday, before I was seized so with the cramps, I had begun to write of my stay in Gloucestershire.

In truth, when I set out on that long journey, I little knew what welcome I might find. My host-to-be, Robert Shallow, was an aged, hare-brained Justice of the Peace from whom I had borrowed a thousand pounds against the prospects of my advancement, and who I had last seen as a fellow prisoner in the Fleet.[13] On that occasion he had been so sorely affrighted he was like to befoul himself and made such a clamour, with his *habeus corpus* this and his *nolo contendere* that, that the Lord Chief Justice had him released within a day, at which he scurried back to Gloucestershire as though the Scottish horde were at his heels. Since that day I had not set eyes on him. Nor he on his thousand pounds.

It was a slow and comfortless journey. Bardolph drove and I sat in the rear of the cart, reeling and bouncing about like a sack of turnips. It rained without cease. The cart was often axle-deep in mud and Bardolph would have to descend and wallow about in the mire in his efforts to free us. Yet little by little we progressed. Bardolph has ever had a way with horses, owing, I believe, to the extraordinary virtues of his face. It is of such a glowing, carbuncle ruddiness, especially when well-stoked with ale, that the most brutish dobbin would strive to get away from it as if it was a branding-iron. Thus, although our progress was not of the swiftest, we were seldom stuck fast, and arrived, at length, in Bushley where Robert Shallow has his house.

My reception was as cold as the journey thither. Such is the frailty of men that they flatter and cozen when they see advantage but, seeing none, will not trouble themselves to treat you civilly.

So was it with Shallow. On beholding me he grew so pale I thought him like to faint away. Then followed such a tirade of abuse that common modesty forbids I should set it down in ink. He threatened to have me whipped, to set his dogs upon me, to have me arraigned for theft and much besides. For my part, I remained aloof and, though I colour with shame to recall it, embarked on such a tangled skein of falsehoods as I doubt I could have unravelled myself.

The substance of my argument was thus: after securing my release from the Fleet, Hal had sent for me and granted me a private audience. He had made light of my rejection, assuring me that it was mere counterfeit and served but to convince the sanctimonious of his reformation. I would shortly be restored to favour and, in the meantime, I was to live quietly and draw no further attention upon myself. This I had done for over a year when, struck down by an excess of melancholia, I had been advised by the good Doctor Monks to repair to the country that the balance of my humours be restored. Thus did I present myself to him as an old friend in need of hospitality.

I had little trouble in persuading him. I have often noted that a man will believe what he wants to believe. Faced, on the one hand, with the prospect of never recovering his thousand pounds and, on the other, with eventually gaining much profit—and all of this presented with the correct air of wounded dignity—Shallow welcomed me into the bosom of his family with many an abject protestation of apology.

I shall not dwell overlong on the details of my sojourn. Only let it be said that as I had behaved in Eastcheap, so I continued to behave in Gloucestershire. Justice Shallow vouchsafed me hospitality for two months. I stayed a year.

At Calais

On the day after Saint Maurice's Day.
(Monday 23rd September 1415)

I shall leave off wine. On Friday night last I fell into the company of one Thomas Bettles, a wool merchant of Canterbury, who is also sleeping at *Le Père Abailard*. This Bettles is a man of some fifty years who, as a boy, fought in the third Edward's army and yet bears the marks to prove it.

We supped together and the talk turned to military matters. I told him of my exploits at Shrewsbury and Gaultree Forest, which he toasted roundly. He told me of his deeds in France, which I toasted roundly. We both toasted Hal roundly who is, at this moment, besieging Harfleur and, from what I hear, may still be at it come Christmastide.

Bettles took up an old besom and demonstrated the proper management of the pike, at which, I think, he is a trifle unpractised. Not to be outdone, I showed him how a good pilgrim may yet wield the sword, for which I substituted a loaf of dry bread. These manoeuvres were much applauded by the assembled company, who toasted us both and we them.

At midnight, or thereabouts, Bettles slipped gently from his bench and went to sleep on the rushes, but by this time the debate had long passed him by and the ten or so of us who remained were too deeply embroiled in charting Hal's strategy to pay him much heed. I cannot say with much certainty when the company broke up, but I well remember being helped to my bed by our host and falling asleep with the stench of garlic in my nose.

It was dark when I awoke and Mephistopheles and Beelzebub and a dozen or so lesser demons were cutting a caper in my head. I puked out the window and made my way down to the taproom for breakfast, much like a sheep with the staggers, only to find the hostess cleaning away the remnants of supper. I had slept all day.

Bettles was there. I think he was in a worse condition than myself. Indeed there were several present who bore the aspect of having freshly alighted from a winter Channel crossing. I had but little appetite, yet forced down some cold capon and felt the better for it. It has been said, by the Authorities, that all animals are sad after copulation. Much the same can be said after a bout of drunkenness. I have never been sad after copulation.

And so did we survivors of Friday night survey each other like a dock-full of Lollards and, after a deal of mutual commiseration, we agreed that the only sure remedy for such melancholy was a cup of wine.

It behoves me not to recount the minutiae of what followed. Only let it be said that as much as we had drunk on Friday night did we surpass on Saturday night.

I awoke on Sunday night feeling much as Lazarus may have felt when he awoke from death. I do not recall what Lazarus ate when he awoke thus. I doubt not that he had breakfast of some sort—loaves or fishes or somesuch. I do not believe he ate cabbage soup. I wished I had not eaten cabbage soup for it sent me straightway out the tavern door to puke in the kennel[14]. I was so sickened that I had no further appetite for carousing but betook myself to bed and lay there, half in slumber and half in fever, till morning.

This evening I feel much recovered and set down this debauchery as a cautionary memento of THE EVIL EFFECTS OF INDULGENCE. This being duly recorded, I shall continue my narrative of my last months in England.

It was after the second Christmas of Hal's reign that I began to outstay my welcome in Gloucestershire. The summer and the autumn had been pleasant enough, though they meant enduring the tiresome companionship of Justice Shallow, which I contrived to escape as often as courtesy would permit. I struck up a friendship with his god-daughter Ellen, a broad-hipped young lass who is the daughter of Shallow's colleague, Justice Silence. Nell readily took the part of nurse and escorted her invalid on several lengthy walks, during which she entertained me wonderfully with her quick conversation. We had many a happy hour together.

Alas we live in a mistrustful world. Since the fall of Adam, all men have seen in others a mirror of their own sins. Call me a liar and box my ears but I swear before God and His Saints that no commerce of an impure nature passed between Nell and myself. God's wounds, she was young enough to be my granddaughter! Yet thus was honest friendship misrepresented. I dare say that not a few false rumours were spread abroad when we departed to the hay-loft during the Twelfth Night revels. I dare say also that lasses have been taken to hay-lofts for reasons other than that they might show an honest gentleman where they oftimes played in infancy. I shall merely state, with dignity and the befitting gravity of my years, that I was the innocent inspector of her youthful playground.

Nonetheless, a cold wind blew from Justice Shallow thereafter. Silence had his ear. Silence in name, yet I never knew him to suffer in it! I was not with a woman of the household but there was another man present; Ellen was forbidden my company. I endured this for another two months before I could stand it no longer and said my farewells. Bardolph hitched Dobbin to the cart and we set forth for London.

As I bounced along, I set to devising a strategy that would provide me with food and lodgings once we arrived. Yet I was sick at heart. In this evil world there are few things sadder than a knight without lord or retinue.

After many a long hour spent in melancholy conjecture, only one course of action presented itself. Thus, when our rude chariot drew up on the cobbles before the Boar's Head, I sent in Bardolph, cap in hand, to plead his master's cause to Hostess Quickly. I had instructed him to say that I had returned from Gloucestershire at the King's behest; that I had returned immediately despite ill-health and that, in a private audience, Hal had said that no honours were to be bestowed upon me and that our friendship was at an end. Consequent on this, I had suffered an attack of apoplexy and he, Bardolph, knowing of no other place, had brought me to the Boar's Head that those nearest and dearest should nurse me in what would surely be a mortal affliction.

Bardolph is without rival in delivering this sort of message for his damson cheeks and bunion eyes lend him all the semblance of panic and confusion before he has uttered a word. Add to which, he had conned his part well and, within the space of time it takes to down a pint of wine, he had returned with my hostess Nell, Pistol, Nym and sundry others.

For myself, I lay spreadeagled in the cart like a beached rhinoceros—eyes closed and sighing and groaning from time to time - whilst those present formed a ring about me. I saw at once that little had changed in Eastcheap for they straightway began to argue.

First it was that base rascal Pistol who, in his usual hectoring tones, swollen with undigested erudition and half-chewed quotes, spoke much to the effect that I was a whoreson grey-haired villain counterfeiting sickness, and he would no more have me under his roof—*his* roof, mark you—as invite the kites and crows of fallen Troy to share supper with him.

At this I groaned a little. Truth to tell, my impulse was to seize my cudgel and stop his mouth with it, but a true man must control his passions, and so I groaned.

Then good Nym sprang to my defence, saying that this was a pretty way for Pistol to recompense the merry times he had had in my company and that Christian charity alone ordained that I should receive bed and board, be I truly sick or not. Though he has light fingers and a heavy wit, Nym has a heart worth gold.

On the other hand, Pistol has a heart worth kennel-scrapings and said that his tavern had not become a hospital and that I must fend for myself, whereupon my good Widow Quickly answered that, as she was a true woman—a point much open to debate—she would not see gentility cast upon the streets, and that Nym was right in what he had said about Christian chariots, and that besides her tavern was not yet become Pistol's tavern and that he had best remember that and there's an end on it. Nym also added that he had best remember it, whereupon Pistol cuffed him and they fell to blows till separated by Bardolph and Nell Quickly.

Pistol vented a deal of wind. In truth he roared and bellowed like Anger in some holiday play and swore he would make two men of Nym and serve up his entrails in a pie. But Pistol is a dog who barks loudest when chained, and Nym knew this well and leaned against the wheel of the cart and picked his teeth and smiled sweetly whilst this false Achilles raged and stamped.

At length, Pistol broke free of the valiant Hostess Quickly and poked me violently in the ribs, demanding that I stand up and get me hence, whereupon I groaned most piteously though truly I would fain have put out his eyes and fed them to the sparrows.

My tactics were well conceived, however, for good Nell Quickly clambered into the cart, threw her fleshy arms about my neck and said that I was a poor lambkin and much wronged and dribbled tears into my beard, and turned wrathfully on Pistol and declared that she would rather plight her troth with the Devil himself as marry such a misbegotten knave as he.

In such wise was I welcomed back into the bosom of the Boar's head.

At Calais

On the Eve of Saint Cyprian.
(Wednesday 25th September 1415)

Hal has taken Harfleur.

Truth to tell, he took it on Sunday last and was long enough about it too for the siege commenced a good six weeks ago. The news is that he has lost a good many of his men through battle and the flux, and will garrison the town strongly before retiring to winter in England.

With ten thousand men he should have reduced such a piddling nook as Harfleur in a weekend, yea, and heard vespers in the town church on Sunday night. Six weeks! And with cannon too!

Now it is said by many that cannon are blasphemous instruments and the Devil's work for they imitate God's thunder and kill from afar without regard for age, rank or sex. For myself, I see only flattery in imitation and have yet to hear of a flight of arrows that could distinguish young from old or man from woman. It is all one. Hal has a cannon called *The King's Daughter* and surely she is a brawny lass with a spiteful tongue for she is two bow-lengths long and can throw a stone of five hundredweight.

And still it took that fragrant ninny a month and a half to discomfit a few dozen Frenchmen. And what does the jobbernowl do then but forbid his men to sack Harfleur? All that for nothing! He never did have the stomach for the taking of a purse.

I have forgotten myself. The ways of war do not sit well with a pilgrim's cloth. I shall return to my scriptural meditations and continue my narrative from where I left off last Monday night.

I returned to the Boar's Head shortly before the old year's end—on or about Saint Cuthbert's Day.[15] I lay unconscious for a few hours and then recovered swiftly, although not so swiftly as to excite suspicion. Just after Lady Day, I received a visitation from the good Doctor Monks to whom I slipped three florins on condition he prescribed wine as a restorative. He duly told Mistress Quickly that I was very sick and like to die and that only the beneficial effects of best Bordeaux wine might reverse my decline.

If Pistol had still been resident at the Boar's Head my stratagem might not have been so easy of execution, but my good Dame Partlet was tearful at my condition and a pitcher of Guyenne and a paper of cinnamon were placed next my bed that same morning.

I readily returned to my old routine. A week saw me rally mightily and return to the inglenook. A night's sprightly dancing at Easter saw me back in bed. A further week saw me in the inglenook again and the day after May Day saw me bedridden once more. At Whitsuntide I drank so deeply while dicing with Nym and Bardolph that I should have had to spend a week in bed anyway.

I continued thus as the days lengthened into summer and, though my hostess Quickly demurred from time to time, saying that my sickness was costing her a king's ransom in wine and provender and that she doubted that entertaining whores was a treatment found in Galen, I had a merry time withal and had no mad moments with magistrates and was in every expectation of being summoned to Westminster to claim my just rewards when, as it will with annual regularity, August came round.

Now Bardolph, Nym and Pistol, having been reluctant to hazard their fortune in helping Hal put down the Scots or, indeed, the Lollards the year before, saw much profit in trailing the pike across France. Thus they put themselves under the Duke of Clarence: Bardolph and Pistol as ancients and Nym as a corporal. Truth to tell, I was much put out of countenance at their resolve: they all three being abject cowards and I, the one true heart, counterfeiting sickness and unable to make myself their captain.

As a brother-in-arms, that muddy rascal Pistol was once more tolerated at the Boar's Head and, within a few hours of his re-admission, had advanced from shamefaced contrition to bombastic familiarity. Never in my life have I witnessed such egregious hypocrisy. He entirely forgot his mistreatment of me, his poking me in the ribs and his spluttered insults, and called me his good Jack, his noble, valorous Horatio, *clarum et venerabile nomen gentibus*[16] and suchlike fustian fiddle-faddle.

The only way you may commonly dissuade Pistol from such effusiveness is either to rattle his brains with a cudgel or prick his guts with your sword, the both of which I have done many a time and oft. Yet how could I, mortal sick and like to die, do thus? Besides, such martial vigour, though momentarily displayed, would impose a fortnight's rest at least and I had designs on going to Bartholomew Fair. And so I suffered.

Having advanced thus far, Pistol entrenched and secured his position. From my outpost in the inglenook I observed him cozening and fawning right and left till he had made allies of them all. God's Blood, he even let Bardolph win at dice and Bardolph may well be the worst dice-player as ever touched ivory.

I knew his strategy from its inception. Before three days had passed, the victory was his.

Unknown to all but me, he had been besieging Hostess Quickly and, on the Sunday night, she lowered her colours. It was the second drinking-bout of the day, not counting by-drinkings, when Pistol roared out for silence and lifted her atop a table. There she solemnly declared before all the company that though Corporal Nym, who had paid her court in Pistol's absence, was a man of good heart—with which I agree—he was too fond of thieving and drinking and dic-ing and was like to squander what profit they make. She had, she said, sorely misjudged Pistol and taken him for an egregious rogue, aye and an ill-tempered, and had been wrong to deny him her hand even though he had been inverte-brate with Sir John, which he surely did out of fear that Sir John would do her mischief and not out of base spite or cruelty; and besides, he was of sound body and belike had many years before him if he did not get himself killed in the wars, which the Good Lord and Heavenly Saints preserve him from.

To this, all save Nym and me said "amen". Nym did not because he was choked with choler; I did not for I knew that, were Pintpot Quickly thrice wid-owed, she would yet be more fortunate than in spending her remaining years with such an abject, base slave as Pistol.

Now, were Nell Quickly possessed of the beauty of Andromeda, the wit of Aristophanes, the genial intelligence of Aristotle and the clarity of thought of Archimides, and if she possessed more taverns than there are bogs in Ireland and more groats than there are blebs on a leper's backside, I *still* would not marry her. The bare fact that she is devoid of one atom of these qualities counts for naught in my argument—it is simply that marriage is a poor price to pay for anything! I would rather put my head through a hangman's noose and cry "pull away".

Had I been Nell, I should have chosen Nym for a spouse, for such a mar-riage may well have been the reformation of him. In truth, Bardolph would have made her a better husband yet, but his face is his misfortune and he never had luck with women except he paid dearly first.

The betrothal thus reaffirmed, the company fell to toasting the couple, which, since all drinkings were at Mistress Quickly's cost, they did copiously and often. Nym would not drink at all but left the Boar's Head in murderous mood and I never saw him again till the hour of my death. For myself, I toasted with all the rest for I am no King Canute to order back the tides of ill-fortune. I knew well that, once married, Pistol would banish me from his court with little ado, and thus I thought it meet to reduce his dowry. If I did not empty a hogshead of wine that night I am a collared eel.

Pistol and Nell married on the morrow, the banns having already been called before my return from Gloucestershire. The priest was persuaded to marry them in haste since Pistol was shortly to depart for Southampton, there to embark for France, and Hostess Quickly had given him a firkin of Bordeaux wine to distribute amongst the poor.

When I awoke the thing was accomplished.

I awoke feeling grievous sick. Now in my long life I have been wondrous free of sickness. Others have sickened and died about me, kith and kin, and yet, as a stout oak flourishes long after lesser trees have fallen and rotted, my own life has lengthened as theirs were cut short. I do remember one other occasion when I was as sick as I was that day - and that resulted from the collision of a few pints of Malmsey and a gallon of oysters one Michaelmas. But on the afternoon of Nell Quickly's wedding I was well and truly prostrate. I lay on my back for I know not how long. My skin felt cold and yet there was a heavy dew upon it as if I had lain in a summer meadow. When I opened my eyes a little, the roof-beams turned like a miller's wheel and my guts heaved mightily, and thus I swiftly closed my lids again. My head resounded like Hephæstus' anvil, my tongue was swollen and my joints ached. Nevertheless, I thought that, given a decent space of time, I might recover and so I lay immobile.

I felt the better for it. The church bells rang sexte[17] and I heard Nym and Bardolph talking in the street below. I opened my eyes once more and I fancied that the roof-beam turned a little less. I stirred myself and called out, but none heard me. Finally, I pulled my cudgel from my belt, for I was yet fully dressed, and struck the floor with it until, at length, a boy appeared at the door—one of those gawking bean-sticks who loll about the taproom and spend all day over a half-pint of pudding-ale. I bade him enter, which he did and stood cap in hand beside the bed.

It was a purgatory of time before I could speak to him for my tongue seemed altogether the wrong size for my mouth. From outside I heard Pistol's windy bellow gusting about, which, with Nell Quickly's piping prattle, made me think of some spring gale buffeting the ancient timbers of the Boar's Head. I heard Nym's voice raised in anger.

I motioned the boy to bend his ear towards me and, when he had eventually done so, I whispered that if he would go down and tell Mistress Quickly of my infirmity I should find him some useful employ in my service. I added that I wished to be undressed and put to bed and that it would take more than a willow-switch of a lad such as he to accomplish that. He seemed content with this promise of advancement and left forthwith.

Truth to tell, I had no need of a servant and least of all a boy who is likely to forget what you tell him, skive off when he can, and eat and drink enough for a brace of pikemen. There are those—Edward Poins among them—who would not keep a servant were he *not* a boy, and dark-eyed too. Yet, though I am loaded with the wickednesses of seventy years, I cannot count the lewd sin of Sodom among them.

He took his time, that boy. Outside some manner of violent dispute was afoot between Pistol, Nym and Quickly. I heard the braggart Pistol shout that I and Doll Tearsheet should be put out of the tavern and surely he must have been overcome with either choler or wine for Doll decamped to Southwark nigh on two years ago and has not been heard of since. He also called me her espouse and yet, though I loved her well, yea and often, we never plighted troth.

At length there was a hurly-burly on the stair and the boy rushed into the room, closely followed by Mistress Quickly, her husband, Bardolph and Nym.

I must have looked a piteous sight for Nell threw herself about my neck and blubbered into my beard and told me not to die for, in faith, I should surely be restored to the King's favour and be a great lord and rich, and that, between whiles, I might rest at my ease in the Boar's Head, God bless me, till my humours be altered for the better. On hearing this, Nym's eyes also began to water and Pistol shuffled from foot to foot and mumbled into his beard. Bardolph's face went from damson to mulberry and he started to blubber too.

Seeing this, I began to feel much better. In faith, it sprang into my mind that my over-drinking might finally have done me more good than harm for being truly sick saved me the effort of counterfeiting.

They all took a hand at undressing me and heaving me under the coverlet, at which I groaned through very real discomfort. Pistol propped my head against the bolster while his good wife tucked the sheets about my chin till I was swaddled like a new-born babe. Then all five sat about my bed till evening and tempted me with meats and wine and milk and honey and chided me for refusing them and told me I should do this, that or the other, to all of which advice I gave no answer for I could still barely speak above a whisper. When one is sick, visitors are a tiresome thing for, being whole themselves, they are always full of good counsel.

Towards evening I must have fallen asleep for when I awoke the room was lit by a single candle that guttered in the draught and dripped tallow in great buttresses. The roof-beams had ceased their spin but the candle flame cast flickering shadows on the walls, which disturbed me somewhat. Little by little I became conscious of an obscene snorting beside the bed. It sounded much like a sow in farrow but turned out to be Bardolph dozing in a chair.

Sleep had done me much good for the pain had retired from my head and joints and my tongue felt more as a tongue should and less like a dormant ferret. It was as I lay thus that I began to conjecture about my future.

I knew Pistol well enough to know that my return to health would be but the prologue to my ejection—whether my good Dame Partlet willed it or not. And what would I do then? Stay in London? If I stayed in London I would have to turn thief or coney-catcher[18] or perhaps pander in order to earn my crust, thus destroying any hope of entering Harry's favour. Moreover, there were creditors—good Christians all, though some of them Hebrew—who had refrained from plaguing me on account of my grievous sickness. They would certainly not delay once I was well again. Returning to Gloucestershire was out of the question, for any beggar will tell you that it is better to be poor in the city than in Gloucestershire.

True, I would gain a brief breathing-space while Pistol was away at the wars and it might be that he would not return from them. Yet, knowing Pistol, I could be certain that if it were humanly possible to avoid a pike-thrust or a cannonball he would accomplish it and that, being appointed sutler,[19] he would come back with coin.

It was then that I was struck by one of those swift-flying bolts of inspiration that has always marked me from the common herd. Here follows the substance of it. It was thus. If Pistol could return rich then why not I? For there is much money to be made in a war if you do not get yourself killed.

I turned this thought over in my head as Bardolph snored and snorted beside me. Hal's army was already gathering at Southampton and Pistol, Bardolph and Nym would join it on the morrow. Now a dying man could not, in all conscience, leap from his bed and brandish the martial sword. Perhaps I could have passed it off as a miracle. In Spain or Italy such a thing is commonplace, but your Englishman is of a less credulous turn of mind and your Londoner less credulous yet, and your Eastcheap ale-swiller is of such a level of credulity as would make a Pope of a Lollard. Besides that, there was another reason: Harry had forbidden me to come within ten miles of his person.

Now Hal was not at all strict in his enforcement of this ban. The Boar's Head was, when all is said and done, no more than a mile or two from Westminster. Yet, were I to turn up at Southampton, begging a captaincy, I would like as not to find myself back in the Fleet before you could say "clap me in irons and brush me buttocks with a besom".

Yet there is as much coin to be made from following an army as fighting in it. I might even meet up with some fleeing Frenchman, take him captive, hold him to ransom and restore myself to favour into the bargain. More modestly, perhaps, I might requisition livestock and sell it to the troops. And there again, conquered towns must be garrisoned and I, a soldier of no little renown, would certainly acquire my captaincy if I presented myself to the commander. A little time after Hal's army had left.

My ideas were various, sometimes in conflict and sometimes in harmony. One thing stood out, however. That the prospect of adventure in France, and eventual profit thereby, pleased me greatly. From there it was but a short step to how it might be realised.

I began my strategy by grunting softly. Through one half-closed eye, I surveyed Bardolph to gauge the effect. There was none.

I grunted louder. Louder still. Bardolph, doubtless thinking me some lovesick pig, smiled sweetly and smacked his lips before redoubling his snoring with a passion. I changed my grunt to a piteous groan, soft at first and then louder. Bardolph, perhaps in the first throes of porcine ecstasy, spluttered a little and nodded his head.

I had had enough of this dialogue. I withdrew one foot from the coverlet and kicked him soundly. By the time I had replaced it and closed my eyes, Bardolph had given a start and began to cough. He opened his eyes. I opened mine and regarded him from under heavy lids.

"Bardolph," said I, in a hollow voice, "I fear I am dying. Bring hither Nell Quickly that I may make my peace with her."

Bardolph's eyes grew round. Two moons in one. He gave a whimper and scampered from the room. I heard him banging on Hostess Quickly's door. I heard Pistol growling at him. This was a wedding-night they would not forget. Before you could say *requiescat in pace*, they were all about my bed. Pistol was bleary-eyed and foul-breathed; Bardolph clutched his cap and whimpered. Nell Quickly was already tearful and wringing her hands.

I played my part better than any whoreson actor, I can tell you. And with less swagger too. In a weak voice I commended them to each other's care and adjured Bardolph to leave off drinking and amend his life, which he said he would do, the lying rascal. I even summoned up a pathetic sally of wit—fancying I saw a flea on Bardolph's nose and likening it to a soul roasting in hell-fire, whereupon the men made a great show of laughing. Nell Quickly redoubled her tears.

Since it has always been my intention to die as I have lived, I asked for a cup of wine, which was brought me and I sipped a little of it. More I could not manage. I then solemnly repented of my evil life and said that women were devils incarnate—present company excepted—and that the female race had been the death of me, upon which all agreed, the hypocritical malt-worms.

I then slipped softly out of life. I fumbled a little with the sheets and fancied that the embroidery on the coverlet were real flowers and played with them and sang a snatch of "hey-diddle-diddle" and smiled upon my fingers' ends and babbled so inanely about the summer's fields in Gloucestershire that had I not been dying they would have thought me ripe for the madhouse.

By this time all were crying such tears as would have floated the *Trinity*.[20] I thought of crying out *Eli, Eli, lama sabachthani* but, on reflection, considered it a little too Biblical and, besides, the closest that any of them had got to Hebrew were the moneylenders in Paul's Churchyard. So I contented myself with wailing "God" three or four times and then asked Nell to put more covers on my feet. I closed my eyes.

Now there was much truth to my shivering for, although it was August, the night was cold and windy and there was an intolerable draught blowing through the shutters. I felt Nell Quickly touch my feet. Then my knees and thighs and chest and, of a sudden, she took to wailing that I was gone and in Arthur's bosom and suchlike fiddle-faddle and embraced my body most uncomfortably till Pistol and Bardolph dragged her away and helped her through the door and locked it behind them.

I was dead.

It felt wondrous good to be dead. In truth it was the best I had felt all day. I lay awhile enjoying the silence till finally the candle glimmered out and the room was in darkness. Distantly, I could hear Nell Quickly's sobbing and Pistol's low growl.

I felt a twinge of sorrow for Nell Quickly. Certainly as much sorrow as anyone can muster for a simpleton.

I pulled myself up, threw back the coverlet and quietly put my feet on the floor. The boards creaked a little but I comforted myself with the thought that few people expect the dead to rise again and even fewer that they will pace about the room. Besides, the night was gusty and everything in the Boar's Head creaked that was not liquid.

I moved to the window and fumbled with the catch. I opened the shutters wide and looked down into the dark street. It was a long drop for any man.

One leg over.

Two legs over.

A good stout heave and I landed heavily in the kennel.

At Calais

On Wednesday last, I wrote for such a time that I all but missed supper again. It was roast beef, of which I am uncommon fond.

I have read what I wrote then and I see that I have been far too ready to relish my iniquitous past. There misses the correct note of remorse and repentance. God's wounds, I even called Nell Quickly a simpleton, which she surely is but there is no need to set it down in writing. Today, I shall attempt to adopt a more seemly tone.

Rumour has it that Hal is not to withdraw to England for the winter but will move on Paris and occupy it, thus forcing that mad beggar Charles[21] to cede him the crown. I doubt not that the French will protest strongly at this disregard for the closed season but when there is a throne at stake you cannot afford to worry about the niceties of modern warfare.

Be that as it may, Rumour is a false mistress who seldom bestows the favours she promises. There again, what is in every man's mouth is not spoken without cause. We shall see. In the meantime, I shall wait on events in Calais, and continue my confessions.

I had jumped from the upper window of the Boar's Head and landed in the kennel.

Now, it is an unfortunate man who puts his foot in a London kennel and that outside the Boar's Head was fouler than most, it having received the divers results of a week's drinkings. Add to which, I was clad in my shift and bruised and winded to boot. Lo, to what a pass had my debauchery led me! There was I, near naked, shivering, penniless and friendless, with my shift soaked and smelling foul. And yet I was in good spirits: triumphing in my infamous conduct and with my eye firmly set on future gain. Beside me lay a broken broomstick. I grasped it, levered myself to my feet and hobbled away.

The thought of what turmoil my disappearance would provoke amused me greatly, and I had not gone further than the corner of the lane, where Eastcheap debouches into Fish Street Hill, than I had to sit down on a mounting-block for I could no longer control my mirth. Nell Quickly, bless her, was sure to think me spirited away by the Devil for I had died unconfessed. Bardolph, ever of a superstitious turn of mind, would surely agree with her. Nym and Pistol might think what they liked but the word would soon be around Eastcheap that Jack Falstaff had been carried off by Satan and a pack of cacodemons to roast in eternal hell-fire. If it were ever so, I would make a tender morsel.

In truth, I could have used a little hell-fire then. The squally wind and my wet shift, not to mention my bare feet, had me shivering like a dog. My first action, therefore, would have to be the procurement of some dry clothes.

Now it is no easy matter to find clothes on Fish Street Hill in the middle of the night. Nor in the day, for that matter, especially when you have no coin. Thus, grasping my broomstick, I stumped off down the hill in the direction of the river.

The street was as deserted as if a pestilence were upon us. A party of the Watch crossed over into Pudding Lane and I hid from them in a doorway but else was there not a soul abroad.

I entered onto London Bridge and groped my way along until I came to the far gatehouse with its diadem of heads—the Earl of Cambridge's among them.[22] One day, in a happier time, some enterprising Lord Mayor will have a stand of torches set the length of London Bridge for the lofty houses that straddle it obscure the moonlight, when there is any, and the place is a very paradise for footpads. You must feel your way along it like a blind man in a coal shed, never knowing when you will feel a knife in your ribs or the kiss of a cudgel upon your pate. Still, as I believe the poet Juvenal had it, *cantabit vacuus coram latrone viator*[23] and I reached the end of the bridge without mishap.

The gate was closed—as I had much expected—and so I settled myself to wait until it opened. *Ergo*, I found a sheltered nook behind a woodpile and sat myself down.

I was gazing absently on the dark churchyard of Saint Mary Ovaries and the huddled dwellings of Southwark beyond, and was busying my mind with divers plans for the procurement of clothes, when Fortune once more smiled upon me.

A shadow issued from the bridge and approached the gate. As moonlight fell upon the figure, I recognised a pilgrim's hat and gown.

Now your pilgrim's apparel is befittingly modest and simple, but it is wondrous warm. Indeed it has to be for your pious traveller spends many a night in the open and his hat must be his roof and his cloak his walls.

The good pilgrim was doomed to the same frustration as myself. He approached the gates, rattled them as if vibration alone would replace the key and then stood back and stared at them as though praying for them to open. God had smiled on me but, alas, not on him. He had his back to me. We were alone together.

Dame Fortune, cruel maid, helps men of good courage. I crept up behind him and blipped him with my broomstick.

Now I thought I had blipped him with some delicacy and nicety. It was one of those blips that hold back a little, that do not so much as break the skin and would not raise a bump bigger than a sparrow's egg. The poor man fell as if poleaxed.

I dragged his body behind the woodpile, stripped him and donned his clothes. He was not young but was sturdily built, and, though his hose pinched a little, his houppeland,[24] shoes and hat fitted me passably well and his heavy cloak hid any shortcomings. He bore with him a stout staff, a well-thumbed missal, a bowl of becoming humility and a well-stocked purse—all of which suited me well. Within a short space of time, I was the very picture of a pilgrim.

As for the careless traveller, I must confess that my first impulse was to introduce him to some fellow jetsam in the Thames, but I am not a cruel or callous man and Christian Charity prevailed. I tore my old shift into rags, bound him and gagged him, and left him behind the woodpile for later discovery.

Swaddled in my warm cloak, I sat down beside the gate and continued my vigil. By the time dawn began to colour the gusty heavens, there was a fairish crowd of us gathered there, including several fellow pilgrims. At length the bells of London rang for matins and along came a yawning gatekeeper who let us out.

Now, as I have said many a time before, eight yards of uneven ground are twenty leagues afoot for me and the distance between London and the Channel ports is as far away as the edge of the world. I set my sights, therefore, on Gravesend—that being the nearest port from which I might embark for France—and I trusted that my good Dame Fortune would put a horse in my way before I had walked a bow-shot further.

In the meantime, I maintained a steady enough pace along the Kent Road until finally the scattered hovels of Southwark were lost from view and the summer's sun was well set forth on its day's journey.

I was by no means alone: the road was busy with carts and people on horseback and peasants driving sheep and cows and all of this, together with the gusty wind, raised great clouds of dust which stung my eyes and parched my throat. I was also plagued with great rumblings and cramps in my belly for I had hardly eaten for nigh on two days and had not thought to breakfast in Southwark. Indeed, Southwark is not a place where many folk would think to breakfast. And moreover, in spite of the wind, the day was warm and I began to sweat. And as I sweated, my hide began to itch owing to the tightness of my garments.

At length, I could stand it no longer and sat down on a milestone and took off my hat and cloak and mopped my brow.

The former tenant of my clothes had clearly been a pilgrim of no little standing for my hat bore divers leaden badges, which I now had leisure to examine. There was the arrow of Saint Edmund, the archbishop of Saint Thomas of Canterbury and various other ornaments that I could not properly identify for, in truth, the comings and goings of religious zealotry have received little of my attention over the last seventy years. I would gladly have removed them for they made the hat uncommon heavy, yet then I would have looked less the pilgrim.

Yet, all is vanity in this godless world. There is many a base beggar who counterfeits a pilgrim for gain. An ape is still an ape though it wears a badge of gold, and a hundred leaden souvenirs do not make a pilgrim. Yea, you may walk from Eastcheap to Bishopsgate and purchase as many.

But I did not doubt their authenticity for the man had money in his purse—to the sum, as I remember, of eight pounds and three florins. He was likely some merchant or landowner atoning for his avarice. He had surely atoned for it now.

I sat by the roadside till midday. The sun grew hot and, little by little, the wind lessened. Soon there was only the slightest of breezes stirring the treetops. As afternoon drew on, there were fewer travellers upon the road and for much of the time I was quite alone in the awful silence of the countryside.

By now, my earlier good humour had somewhat dissipated and the thought of having to walk to Gravesend engendered an excess of blackest melancholy. I had almost decided to abandon my plans and hie me back to London when a four-wheeled cart laden with barrels and drawn by two great oxen drew up beside me.

The driver was a thickset man clad in a dowlas tunic with brown leggings. In truth there was little extraordinary in that for, in my long life, it has been my experience that any man below the rank of apprentice-tapster does tend to wear a dowlas tunic and brown leggings. He was eating an apple that he seemed bent on finishing before he addressed me, for he spent an unconscionable length of time silently eyeing me up and down while he champed and smacked his lips. His oxen munched in much the same rhythm and together the three of them made me feel like some poor starveling begging scraps in a tavern.

At length, the fellow tossed his apple-core into the road and wiped his mouth with the back of his hand.

"Cant'bury?" he said.

"Canterbury? Aye, and further," said I.

He nodded towards the cart and I climbed in beside him. Once I was safely installed, he flicked a hazel switch at the oxen and we began to rumble on towards the coast.

The carter offered me an apple from a small sack which he had beside him and I accepted it with some show of grace. Now, as a rule, I am not over-fond of apples, which is a foodstuff best fit for horses, yet I had eaten nothing all day and was consumed by a ravenous hunger. Soon the apple was devoured and I begged another one, which I ate just as quickly.

Observing my sorry plight, the driver reached into his sack and brought forth a loaf of bread which he broke in two. Had any of my old companions seen me thus they would have wet their breeches laughing. Jack Falstaff dining on bread and apples?

Yet the belly has no ears and I fell to as if tasting the best meats at a banquet fit for royalty. Then, when I was finished and my hunger was assuaged, I cast a longing glance back to the barrels with which the cart was laden.

Though of bovine appearance, the carter was yet blessed with a quick wit for he swiftly caught my meaning.

"Salted beef," said he. "For the port of Sandwich."

But he had a leathern bottle of small beer which he gave me to drink and I managed to choke down a few mouthfuls.

At Calais

On Michaelmas Day.
(Sunday 29th September 1415)

I do fear my appetite got the better of me on Friday last. I was—as I see—writing of my great hunger on the Kent Road and it was that which did it. I was obliged to descend to the taproom and order up a dish of cold roasted rabbits which, together with a pint or two of wine, left me in a humour ill-suited to quiet meditation.

Today, being a Sunday and rainy, I have time enough to write at some length. I shall not, therefore, waste it in idle gossip but continue my narrative, the sooner to conclude it.

The name of my deliverer on the Kent Road was Thomas Clarell of Saint Albans who had been entrusted by his worthy neighbour William Attwood, a butcher of that city, with the delivery of a shipment of salted beef to a ships' provisioners in Sandwich. This Clarell was a quiet-spoken man and a sober, and yet he was of a friendly and trusting nature, though taciturn of phrase. As is the case with most quiet-spoken, taciturn fellows, we had not gone many miles before he had told me of his wife, Mary, with whom he had been ten years married, poor soul, and of his two daughters—Kate and Alison, if I remember rightly.

He showed much interest in my pilgrimage. In truth, this was something I had considered but little. Clarell pointed to my hat and declared that I must be bound for foreign parts, for the only shrine that lay between London and the sea was Canterbury and I had already visited that. I was a trifle put out of countenance at this for, as I have written, of the leaden badges on my hat I recognised but two. Clarell, however, read my hat as if it were a rosary: the shrines of the Blessed Lady at Walsingham, Saint Edward at Westminster, Saint Edmund at Bury, Saint Cuthbert at Durham, Saint Etheldreda at Ely, Saint William at York and divers others that I can no longer bring to mind. God's Blood! If I had known what a pious gadabout that pilgrim was I would have robbed someone profaner.

Yet Clarell was full of admiration and questioned me about my present destination. Now I could not, in all reason, remove my hat and try to find some foreign shrine that was not represented there. Instead, I decided to trust to Good Fortune and declared that I was bound for the tomb of Saint James at Compostella, which is always a safe option in such circumstances.

"Ah!" said Clarell, nodding as he bit into another apple. "Compo Stella, eh?"

"Even so," I answered, thinking quickly. "I intend to take ship at Gravesend, whence I shall sail for Madrid."

"Ah!" replied Clarell, chewing mightily and spitting out a pip. "Madrid, eh?"

Divining that "Madrid" meant about as much to Clarell as the words "Pythagoras" or "cerebellum", I offered an explanation.

"Madrid," I said, "is a great port and the capital city of that land."

"Ah!" exclaimed Clarell. "What land?"

I could now see that this was in danger of developing into one of those conversations that you wish had never commenced. In terms of futility and eventual over-complexity I can only liken it to discussing the transmigration of the soul with Nell Quickly's grandmother, a kindly and passably honest dame who made her granddaughter appear a very Ararat of intellect.

"Spain," said I.

"Ah!" said Clarell. "You cannot sail for Spain, good sir."

"Can I not?" said I, supposing he thought Spain might be somewhere in the Midlands. Near Coventry, for example.

"Nay, good sir." said Clarell. "Not from Gravesend at any rate. For every ship in Gravesend has been pressed into the King's service to carry his great army to France. Come with me to Sandwich, if you will. There you may find a foreign boat as will take you thither."

I was grateful for this information for Gravesend is, as its name implies, the final resting place of human society. Add to which, Clarell's company was endurable and undemanding and thus I accepted his offer and introduced myself as John Faulkner, a noted landowner from Tewkesbury in Gloucestershire.

Now the Kent Road is broad and firm and runs straight and true from London, through Canterbury, to Dover. It was built by Julius Caesar and is called Watling Street after the street of the same name in London, which it resembles not at all. You may travel from Dover to Chester by way of Westminster and Saint Albans and never leave this road although, in faith, I know not why a man of sound mind should wish to go to Chester, for it is a cold and draughty place forever threatened by marauding Welsh and scoured by rain from January to December. The town of Chester is famed for its play of the Deluge or Great Flood.

Thus, since the road was good and straight and the weather clement, we made exceedingly good time. Your ox is not a sprightly beast but it shambles along steadily and gains in constancy what it lacks in celerity. Moreover, Clarell was bent on reaching Sandwich as quickly as he might, the sooner to return to his family. By late afternoon, we had reached Dartford. Here we stopped awhile and gave fodder to the oxen and refreshed ourselves in an alehouse.

The ale-wife served us salted herring, cold pig's trotters and bread, on which I gorged myself till the last vestige of hunger was driven from my frame. To drink we had halfpenny ale and bragget, of which Clarell took little and I took much. I would have preferred to have slept the night at Dartford but Clarell would journey on till nightfall and so I paid the reckoning and, to protect us from the chill of evening, I invested three groats in a cask of malmsey wine and a pewter cup, which I had from the tavern at the sign of the bull. This cask I had tapped and placed between us in the cart, that we might each help ourselves whenever we wished. Thus provided for, we set out once again.

Now this Thomas Clarell was, as I have written, a man of sober appetites. He was much amazed that a pilgrim with many a long league before him should squander three groats on a cask of malmsey. So is it always with your honest labourers: they toil from dawn to dusk, heaping farthing upon farthing, groat upon groat, that they might have two pigs in place of one or a bushel of grain in place of a peck or a fine brood mare in place of a broken-down jade, and in the meantime suffering all manner of miseries and privations—starving in winter and sweating in summer—and to what end? They die. So do we all. Are there pockets in a shroud? Does Styx's ferryman ask more than an obolus? Once dead, their life-savings are taken in taxes or squandered by ungrateful children and their good name, so carefully nurtured over the years, is buried with them. For myself, when I have a groat, I spend it. The pleasures of this world are transitory, which means that they must be oft repeated lest they be forgotten. Would God have provided wine if he meant us not to drink it? If coupling be solely for the begetting of children, why is there such pleasure in it? If frugal eating be blessed, then surely kings and bishops must be damned for I never yet saw one eat frugally if he were not compelled to it.

To ignore such pleasures is to scorn the Omnipotent, for a gift refused is a common insult to the giver.

I discussed the same unto Clarell and the Devil within me wrought his mischief well. Such reasoning, issuing from the mouth of a venerable pilgrim, a respected landowner and a magistrate, had quick enough effect. Clarell took the pewter cup from me, filled it with malmsey, quaffed it down greedily and smacked his lips. Thus did grey iniquity once more sow corruption. And yet I think the soil on which it fell was uncommon fertile that it took root so readily.

By the time the vespers bells had rung, Clarell was in a merry mood, the pewter cup having made a score or so of pilgrimages to the shrine of Saint Malmsey. As is true of many a travelling man, he had a large store of tales—some valorous, some jocular and most lewd. At times, he became so immersed in their recounting that the oxen wandered to and fro across the road and cropped the grass that bordered it. It was thus that we covered the three or so leagues from Dartford to Strood in almost as many hours, by which time the cask of malmsey rang hollow when knocked.

Now the village of Strood does not boast a tavern worth the visiting and so we drew rein before an ale-stake[25] and refreshed ourselves with a pint or two of pudding-ale, which despite its thickness drove away the cloying aftertaste of malmsey. We endured some difficulties in finding our way back to the cart but perseverance carried the day and we covered the league to Rochester before we were fully aware of having left Strood.

Rochester has one of the best inns on the Pilgrim's Way, though I cannot remember its name. It was there we exchanged our empty cask of malmsey for a full cask of Aunis wine. Clarell puked over an ostler; the ostler struck Clarell on the nose; I struck the ostler on the pate and we continued on our way. Truth to say, we continued back in the direction of Strood but, recognising an ale-stake at which we had refrained from stopping, we turned about and shambled back into Rochester again.

At Calais

On Saint Melorius' Day
(Tuesday 1st October 1415)

Of the pens I bought a fortnight ago, all but two have split. This morning I went to the merchant of whom I had them at his shop in the Rue du Bon Edouard, thrust the damaged quills under his nose and told him that he was a base tyke to treat an honest pilgrim thus, and that, were he not to make immediate restitution, I would box his ears, flatten his snout and lead him before the Deputy Lieutenant, who would have him whipped through the streets of Calais with his split feathers round his neck.

I have always prided myself on my skill at dealing with tradesmen. I do possess some delicacy in such matters and so I should for one does not become a boon companion of the King for lack of diplomatic nicety. Thus have I now a score of finest goose-quills and a sharp knife with which to trim them. With the right approach, you may always have more profit from a dishonest merchant than from an honest one.

On Sunday I wrote of how we—that is to say, Thomas Clarell and I—travelled as far as Rochester. In truth, when we entered that city for the second time it was already becoming dark—Phoebus clearly being as in need of a bed as we were. For my part, I would gladly have put up at the inn where I struck the ostler but then I would have had to pay for Clarell too, for he had but little coin about him, and so we drove a short distance out of the town and made our encampment a stone's throw from the road.

Now not very far from Rochester lies a place called Gad's Hill, which is notorious for the rogues and thieves that frequent it. Woe betide the traveller who makes camp near that spot for, if he wake again at all, it will be sanz purse, sanz shoes or sanz virtue, and belike all three. Thus we settled ourselves no more than a bow-shot from the city walls.

Since neither of us were willing to confront the business of lighting a fire, we helped ourselves to two or three draughts of Aunis, uncoupled the oxen and curled up beneath the cart, swaddled in our cloaks. The worthy Clarell commended me as a fine fellow and said that one day's journey in my company was worth a score of others but, before I could reply in like manner, he was asleep.

On the morrow, we began our journey late. The sun was well risen when I awoke to the sound of carts rumbling along the road. Clarell was snoring loudly and I had not a little difficulty in waking him. Eventually, we broke camp in silence and indeed there was not a word exchanged between us till we reached Chatham where we bespoke breakfast—salted herring, cold pigeon, pease soup, cheese and halfpenny ale. I felt much improved for that and so too did Clarell for the colour returned to his cheeks, and his eyes, which had hitherto been of a somewhat Bardolphian hue, were restored to something like their customary brightness.

By so much were our spirits elevated that, as we left Chatham, we even attempted communication. Clarell succeeded in commenting on the pleasantness of the day, which was no more and no less pleasant than the day before. I, for my part, ventured that there were a good many folk abroad whilst the Kent Road was emptier than ever I saw it. Our mutual standing thus re-established, we relapsed into silence till we reached the town of Sittingbourne.

At Sittingbourne there is an inn named the Red Lion in honour of John of Gaunt, Hal's grandfather. There are many inns named thus, which I find passing strange for John of Gaunt was a man of the utmost seriousness and sobriety. God's wounds, you might have extracted more wit and merriment from a block of Aberdeen granite.

It was I who suggested that we refresh ourselves at this hostelry, for the weather was warm, the road dusty and our ill humour not entirely exorcized. Clarell gave vent to a summary protest yet the relentless jolting of our cart had quite unsettled his bowels and he was in much need of a specific. I therefore bespoke two jugs of hypocras and we settled ourselves on a bench without the door, there to take our ease in the sunshine.

Now your hypocras is blessed with wondrous restorative properties and by a jug and a half we had somewhat recovered our good spirits. We were joined by an ostler who brought with him his cup of pudding-ale and sat beside us and then by a carter who was bound for London, charged with stone. The carter, as I remember, was called Hugh. I have forgotten the ostler's name.

Clarell introduced me as His Worship John Faulkner of Tewkesbury, a mighty landowner and magistrate, at which both carter and ostler were so impressed that they must drink my health. I therefore bespoke another four jugs of hypocras.

Your ostlers are a breed apart. By consorting so much with horses they end up eating and drinking like them, and it would not surprise me if they were not shut up in a stall and rubbed down at the end of each day's work.

Be that as it may, this ostler had a prodigious thirst and before Clarell and I had finished the first quarter of our second jug, he had quaffed off his entirely.

Hugh the carter quickly followed him and thus it behoved us to drink up lest we be thought unmannerly. Out of good fellowship, for indeed the hypocras had somewhat oiled my generosity, I offered the company another jug. This was accepted.

At length, we resumed our journey in the very blithest of spirits, once we had accomplished the hazardous business of seating ourselves in the cart. We were assisted in no small measure by the efforts of the ostler and Hugh the carter, and this with many a good wish for the road ahead. The ostler also entreated Clarell to remember him to his good wife and daughters, and myself to the excellent people of Tewkesbury. Hugh the carter said rather less, and, indeed, looked surpassing pale.

At Calais

On the third day of October, being a Thursday.

I had meant this book to be a daily record of my confessions and yet I observe that it waxes grievously short on confession. In truth, since I began it, I have dealt little with my wrongdoings here in Calais and much with the catalogue of mischievousness that brought me hither. This is because my life here is quite blameless. Though it is busy, and abustle with soldiery, Calais is nonetheless a small town and there is little to divert mind and instincts. Since the place was captured by the third Edward, the populace has lived in perpetual anxiety lest the French host fall upon them and drive them into the sea. Though their defences are stout and well-manned, the *Calaisiens* live insecure lives and a feeling of impermanence pervades the town. It is as if their baggage was always packed in readiness.

Their spirits were elevated when Harfleur fell, for perhaps this marked the beginning of the reconquest of Normandy, Picardy and Artois. Since then, however, Hal has sat scratching his breech and counting his losses, and common opinion has it that he will decamp to England. If it be so, the French will waste no time in retaking Harfleur and avenging themselves on Calais. The present rumour—or at least the last that I heard—is that they have amassed an army of one hundred thousand men,[26] captained by the very flower of chivalry: the Constable of France, the Marshal Boucicaut, the Dukes of Orléans, Bourbon, Bar and Alençon, and the counts of Eu, Richemont, Nevers, Vaudemont, Blamont, Salines, Grandpré, Roussy, Marle, Dampmartin and Fauquembergh. All in all, enough to make any *Calaisien* soil his chain-mail.

Add to this the certain knowledge that the Lieutenant of Calais, Lord Bardolph—who is no relation—is to stay with the King's army instead of returning to defend the town and I am forced to consider that it is high time Calais and I parted company. Since leaving London, I have squandered much time and money that would have been better spent in furthering my journey to Compostella and Jerusalem. God's wounds, I passed a month in Sandwich and I defy anyone to spend as much time in that dismal place.

I shall, therefore, hasten my confessions to a conclusion.

Despite quitting Sittingbourne in temulent state, Tom Clarell and I managed to journey as far as Canterbury. That night, Clarell once more slept beneath his cart but I, having drunk less than the night before, walked to the pilgrim's hostelry without the west gate of that city and passed a far more uncomfortable night on a palliasse in a long dormitory with a hundred other pilgrims who snored, scratched, groaned, tossed, turned and vented wind till cock-crow. I was stung like a tench into the bargain.

The following day, being a Friday and the day of Holy Innocents last and thus of ill omen,[27] we spent in Canterbury. For want of aught better to do, we visited the shrine of Saint Thomas, which I had never seen before though it was not difficult to counterfeit familiarity for Clarell's sake.

Now this Saint Thomas, or Thomas à Beckett as he is better known, was a man of lowly antecedents who yet rose to defy a king. Since we English have scant respect for kings—except when we make war upon the foreigner—he is an uncommon popular saint. For every four or five men or women who pilgrimage to Canterbury to be relieved of some affliction, there is at least one who journeys thither as an act of spite against the monarchy.

The cathedral at Canterbury is easily found for it dominates the city like a great ship among a flotilla of longboats. Unfortunately, in order to reach the shrine of Saint Thomas you must stand in line for many an hour, and indeed on this day there was a file of pilgrims running almost as far as the great door.

It must be some measure of Saint Thomas's efficacy that a pilgrim does not leave the shrine more diseased than when he came. I never saw a more beggarly congregation of halt and distempered in my life, unless it was without the royal palace at Christmastide. Tom Clarell and I shuffled forward for a good two hours and damnable unpleasant it was too. The day was hot and the stink of our fellow pilgrims soon reached such an apogee of fetor as would have caused Asmodeus himself to hold his nose and retch.

Yet, despite the long line of people, the shrine itself was worth its wait in gold. As I bowed my head before it, I could not but reflect that the prophets of yore—your mad, mud-caked Isaiahs and Ezekiels so beloved of Holy Writ— would have chided the pious of today for abasing themselves before such gilded luxury. You may keep your orb and sceptre, the Crown of Saint Edward and your other paltry royal gewgaws. Give me a score of stout-hearted knaves— such as will not flinch from defiling hallowed ground—and let me steal into the cathedral beneath cloak of darkness and make away with the tomb of Saint Thomas. It is certain I would have more use for it than he, for Thomas is long past caring. And what is more, if an honest thief such as I does not do it, you can be sure that some misbegotten king will.

I found the shrine of Saint Thomas a wondrous uplifting experience.

On the next day, Tom Clarell and I completed our journey to Sandwich and we took leave of each other with many an expression of regret. I shall not dwell overmuch on my stay in that town for there is little worth relating. Apart from a gaggle of fishing-boats the port was deserted, all larger vessels having been impressed into Hal's service to ferry his army to France.

I took a bed at the sign of the Bell and shared its damp and draughty upper room with a motley assortment of mariners, travellers and ne'er-do-wells. As to finding a boat, it was a task that I pursued with my customary lack of diligence—some days loitering upon the quayside, some days loitering abed. Several boats came and went though I did not go with them. Towards Saint Giles' Day there were gales that kept the fishing-boats in port and myself in the taproom. These winds blew hard for the best part of a week, by which time the fishermen were feeling the prick of poverty and I the backwash of Burgundy.

It was a few days after the storms abated that a Dutch vessel put into port, the *Op den Goder Vaert* by name and captained by a certain Mijnheer Janszoon. She was a stout boat and a yare[28] and carried a cargo of salted herring. I fell in with Janszoon in the taproom of the Bell and we took an instant liking to each other for he was built like his ship—wide of beam and deep of draught. He disdained wine and would drink only ale and that in prodigious quantity. If his ship had taken on such liquor, it would have foundered before it crossed the bar.

Janszoon told me, in passable mariner's English, that he was bound for his home port of Harlingen by way of Calais, where he would sell more herring, and Antwerp, where he would take on cloth for the Baltic trade. For one gold noble, he would take me to France. As this was but twice the normal rate and he a Dutchman, I thought it uncommon generous.

At length, after half a day and half a hogshead, we settled on three shillings payable in advance.

On the eleventh day of September, being a Wednesday, the *Op den Goder Vaert* set sail on the morning tide. Besides myself and Captain Janszoon, there were five crew, four other passengers and two horses. As provisions for this long and perilous voyage I took with me a cask of malmsey, two cold capons, a cooked rabbit, two loaves of bread and a pigeon pie. Salted herring there were in plenty.

The wind was brisk from the west and, before long, the sea began to plunge and toss like an unbridled colt. Now I am a landsman born and bred and the sea holds no more attraction for me than does the Fleet Ditch. Yea, the furthest I had ever travelled by boat was but from Eastcheap to Charing Cross, and there are wondrous few tempests on the Thames. Yet, for all that, I found nothing fearful in the sea's distemper. The wind blew the waves and the waves rolled up and down and the ship rolled up and down with the waves. There was nothing to it save base mechanics. As to drowning, it is but a form of death like any other and, I dare say, less painful and troublesome than most. In exemplification, the crew of the *Op den Goder Vaert* comported themselves as if the ocean were as calm and still as a mill-pond, though they did make great show of bellowing in that prolonged gargle that serves your Dutchman for a tongue.

My fellow passengers were stricken with abject terror. I watched as their countenances changed hue from pink to white and thence to green. For the most part, they alternated between offering muttered prayers to Jehovah on high and noisy libations to Neptune below, which afforded me great entertainment. I wrapped myself in my pilgrim's cloak and sat with my back braced against the mainmast in company with my cask and swore that, if I were to drown, it were better to do it in malmsey than in rank sea-water.

Your malmsey is a wondrous specific for your seasickness and is much to be recommended.

At length, the good Captain Janszoon tired of his men stumbling over prostrate bodies or being buffeted about as his passengers scrambled to the gunwales, and ordered all but myself below. He then joined me at the foot of the mainmast and there I introduced him to the pleasures of malmsey wine, a beverage which, it appears, is little appreciated in the Low Countries. I must say he took to it with tolerable enthusiasm.

It took us three days to make Calais. Once the malmsey was exhausted, Janszoon broached a cask of hoppe-hoppenbier, which I had never before tasted for it is considered poisonous in England. If that is truly so then I would gladly dine on a gallon of hemlock for I found it much to my taste. Cask followed cask. Had that not been so, I dare say we would have reached port sooner for all the crew joined us when their various duties allowed and, before many hours had elapsed, I believe they could not have told a backstay from a yard-arm, let alone sail the ship.

In all of these three days, I went below but twice for there it stank of vomit and salted herring and, in its darkness and loathsomeness and creaks and groans and mumbled prayers and cries for deliverance, it was closer to the pit of Hell than I would ever care to venture.

In short, after the first few hours of our voyage, I never saw my fellow passengers again till Holy Cross Day when we were fast moored to Calais dock.

They crawled forth from the bowels of the *Op de Goder Vaert* like pale spirits new released from Purgatory.

The horses were not seasick as far as I marked.

At Calais

On Saint Faith's Eve
(Saturday 5th October 1415)

My confessions seem much given over to vanity and boastfulness. Shamed as I am to admit it, I believe this to be a just reflection of my character: as a man is, so is his talk.

I was adjured by the King himself to amend my life and I am resolved to do it. (The King, by the by, lingers yet in Harfleur and seems somewhat disinclined to face the mighty French host, for which I cannot entirely blame him. Sadly, he seems equally disinclined to go home, which I would certainly do.)

Such a reformation of my life can only be accomplished by carrying out the pilgrimage on which I have embarked. If I stay much longer in Calais, I shall fall back into my old ways and bring further dishonour upon the name of Falstaff. If that be possible.

All life is a pilgrimage of sorts and Man is but a vagabond—*homo viator*—bound from the womb to the tomb, from dust to dust. Thus, if I may wend my way from Jack Falstaff, the Duke of Norfolk's page-boy, to Sir John Falstaff, Knight, and from childish innocence to my present lewdnesses, so may I also journey further.

And thus, on Monday next, being the seventh day of October and the Eve of Saint Oswald, I shall go forth from Calais. Exactly where I shall go forth to is another matter. Compostella, perhaps? The Holy Sepulchre in Jerusalem? At any rate, Paris lies between here and anywhere and so that city shall be my first goal. Divine Providence will supply my final destination.

As I sit here in quiet contemplation, it occurs to me that, though I may be all too well known to others, I am but a stranger to myself. In truth, I abandoned the Boar's Head with thoughts of gain uppermost in my mind. And had I blipped a wool merchant with my broomstick, I might well be selling cloth in Antwerp. Instead I chose a pilgrim—or rather the pilgrim chose himself—and so a pilgrim I have become. And yet, perhaps, this is most fitting for though I count humility among my most treasured virtues, it is not one that has seen much exercise in recent years and its cultivation may allow me to see clearer within myself. Perhaps I shall never reach my destination. Not every man arrives at Corinth.

This afternoon I bought a horse. I lack exactitude: it is a mare. She cost me nine shillings and I have christened her Mistress Quickly since she is small, fat and slow. In truth, I had little to choose from, for Calais is ill-provided with horseflesh and what little there is, is dear. I should have much preferred a stallion for it sits ill with me to be ill-seated and Mistress Quickly, though strong enough to bear a gentlewoman to matins, supports my bulk badly.

I have also bought a bastard-sword[29] of German fabrication, which I have named Gut Cutter, and a short dagger of Italian provenance which shall remain anonymous—in the true tradition of furtive little blades. I shall admit that these weapons may be considered excessive for a pilgrim but I shall be an Englishman travelling through hostile territory along roads that are dangerous enough in peacetime.

I have taken two further precautions. Firstly there is the matter of my name, which is far too English-sounding and thus, in honour of the good Captain Janszoon, I shall counterfeit the Dutchman. Henceforth I shall be Jan van Staf, a wool merchant of Antwerp. To lend further verisimilitude, I have been practising a Hollander's speech, which involves a great deal of gargling and spitting. My fellow guests at this inn have regarded me with no little consternation.

I doubt not that my disguise will prove impenetrable. Your Frenchman scarcely speaks his own language, let alone Dutch.

Secondly. What was secondly? I have forgot.

Secondly, I have paid the reckoning at *Le Père Abailard*, which was not excessive, even considering the fleas, and changed the remainder of my money into French coin. I got for it eighteen *livres tournois* of which I had the hostess of *Le Père Abailard* sew six into the hem of my cloak. Your *livre tournois*, by the by, is worth roughly six shillings and is divided into twenty *sous* and each *sou* into twelve *denier*. Your *denier* is thus of very little worth.

This will be my last entry before I quit Calais.

I commend my life to Our Lord Jesus Christ and the Blessed Virgin and my fortunes to Saint Christopher. May they protect me from the dangers of the road and speed me home in safety.

At Saint Omer

This night I am sleeping at a small inn, or *auberge,* within the walls of the town of Saint Omer. This inn bears the curious name of *Le Glaive Cassé* or, to put it in plain English, The Broken Sword. Exactly how the sword came to be broken, or why anyone should see fit to name an inn after it, are questions that the innkeeper has so far refused to disclose—either because he does not know or simply because he is the surliest rascal who ever drew breath. It was only with the greatest reluctance that he deigned to show me to the upper room and his sole comment on its appointments, which are meagre to say the least, was that I would find naught better in Saint Omer, and that the other landlords disliked foreigners even more than he.

It is a fact that the French word for foreigner and stranger are one and the same and it makes no difference whether you come from the next village or an entirely different country—you are a foreigner and that is that. Most Frenchmen are thus strangers to each other and when they venture abroad had best be on their guard for they are fair game for any trick or fancy.

I cannot write for long this evening for I am much fatigued and my joints ache as though I were rheumatic. I have ridden ten leagues today, which is the furthest I have gone a-horseback in two years and the slowest I have covered such a distance in my life. Mistress Quickly's name is not matched by her celerity. To her, a trot is a gallop and cannot be sustained for more than half a league, whereupon she reverts to a sedate walk. You may curse her all you will and take a stick to her rump if you have a mind, but it makes no difference.

I found all this most vexing for the country between Calais and Saint Omer is as deserted and melancholy as if The Death were still upon us. Houses large and small are abandoned, gardens overgrown, fields untended. Fruit rots unpicked upon the trees. The few inhabited villages I passed through were squalid, miserable places and I had no wish to stop in them. What disaster can have so emptied the land of people? Perhaps they have fled in fear of an English advance. Perhaps their closeness to Calais filled their hearts with dread. Whatever the reason, it was a sorry landscape I journeyed through today and sorrier still under the unabating rain.

I left Calais at daybreak and shared the road with a company of merchants from the Rhineland. They were bound for home but seemed in no hurry to get there. On reaching the village of Ardres, which lies no more than three or four leagues from Calais, they decided that they had gone far enough for one day and would stop at the inn there. In truth, it seemed as comfortable a place as I have seen today and was provided with fine ale which the landlord called *godale*—doubtless an attempt to say "good ale". By so much are the French indebted to us.

I accompanied them as far as the third drinking and then took my leave.

The road to Saint Omer is straight and well-founded but in a grievous state of disrepair. I have heard that it was once one of the great roads of France. For myself, I doubt that France ever had any great roads—at least none that could compare with Watling Street. This one was covered with beaten earth laid over wooden faggots, which I had ample opportunity to view as it lay open in so many places. The beaten earth had turned to mud and there were holes you could have hidden an army in and still had room for the camp-followers. In some places the street had slipped away entirely and taken refuge in the ditch.

I was told in Calais that this road was taken by the third Edward when he travelled to Rheims sixty-odd years ago, and even then it was in such a grievous state that he took five hundred servants with him to flatten it with shovels and mallets.

I reached Saint Omer as dusk was drawing in and stopped at the first hostelry I saw, which happened to be the *Glaive Cassé*. Under such a leaden sky, Saint Omer looks gloomy and woebegone. I shall not tarry here but set forth at first light.

I have bought a leg of mutton in the shambles here. It cost me three *sous* and I have asked the host of *Le Glaive Cassé* to have it roasted for me—though whether he will or not is another matter. That, together with a few jugs of good wine, should sufficiently restore my vitality.

The stub of candle by which I write is guttering and my eyes begin to prick. I shall continue this daybook tomorrow night.

Still no news of Hal. Harfleur must be a merry town that he is so loath to leave it. To me it looks like a boiling pot out of which he would be well advised to jump before the French light a blaze beneath it.[30]

At Frouge (Fruges)

On Saint Oswald's Day
(Tuesday 8th October 1415)

I am scratching still. *Le Glaive Cassé* was likely broken in an attempt to slay the divers animals that inhabit the inn's beds. A pack of fox hounds has fewer fleas than crawled over me last night.

When I was ten years old and yet in Thomas Mowbray's service, I went swimming in the River Lea with Sampson Stockfish and Will Fletcher. Swimming, I write, but indeed I could not swim, only splashed in the water whilst my two companions, who were several years older than I, raced each other to the far bank and back. When they tired of this, they sought out such other diversions as the River Lea could afford—one of which, as I remember, was ducking me under the water and another of which was throwing me into the deepest part of the river and dragging me out by the hair when I began to turn blue. At length, I tired of these diversions and bloodied Will Fletcher's nose to underline my point. At which, he and Sampson Stockfish seized me by the arms and legs and tossed me naked into a bed of nettles. I was stung all over and cried all afternoon.

And even then I was not quite so stung as in *Le Glaive Cassé* last night! If this had been in England, I would have refused to pay the reckoning. Sadly, I am in France and an Englishman to boot. It behoves me not to draw such attention upon myself.

Today I had enough of what the French call *un grand chemin*. I decided to progress to Paris by way of Doullens and Amiens on a road that they call simply *une voie* but which is in a decidedly better state of repair than its more prestigious cousin. As night fell, I decided to break my journey in this village of Frouge. Since Frouge comprises no more than five or six houses clustered around the church, I enquired of a red-faced housewife where I might find lodging for the night. She directed me here, to the priest's house.

Père Mathieu, or Father Matthew as I shall call him, is a shock-haired giant of a fellow who looks as if he wrestles several rounds with Satan every morning before breakfast and holds him in a headlock while he eats it. I confronted this Holy Hercules on his threshold and begged that a poor pilgrim be vouchsafed bed and board.

He was a little loath. In truth, he acted for all the world as if my request were an imposition. By the by, however, the novelty of my company won him over and he accepted me into his house. Over an excellent dinner of roasted pork, thrushes, chicken in pastry, pears and walnuts, he told me that since the English soldiery were poised to ravage the land and companies of renegade soldiers and mercenaries were profiting from this disquiet to plunder and pillage where they wished, even the priesthood had become wary of extending the hand of Christian Charity to unfamiliar faces. Indeed, on the subject of the English he was most vociferous and injurious and grew very red in the face and struck the board with such violence that our trenchers leapt into the air and wine slopped out of the jug. He asked me if I did not find the English the most greedy, gluttonous and ungodly race of barbarians ever to infest the world, to which I had little choice but to agree. To lend credibility to my agreement, I punctuated it frequently with *Chott zye ferflookt*[31]—a colourful Dutch blasphemy which I had of the good Captain Janszoon. In fact, together with the two words "ya" and "nay", it is the only Dutch I have.

I need not have been so scrupulous in my dissembling. When supper was finished, Father Matthew took up the Bible and, after brushing away the scraps of food and slops of wine before him, laid it reverently on the table, opened it at nowhere in particular and began to read in a loud voice.

Now such has been the iniquity of my latter years that study of the Scriptures has not been among my daily pursuits. And yet, for all that, I had as good a Christian upbringing as any other child and was taught my catechism as soon as I could utter speech. *Ergo,* I quickly recognised the passage to be from the book of Samuel—the bit about the daughters of Israel being clothed in scarlet and David and Jonathan being "lovely and pleasant in their lives". It therefore came as no small surprise to me to perceive that the Good Book was open at the First Epistle of Saint Paul to the Thessalonians.

I waited to hear if the extended quotation from the book of Samuel was but the prologue to some arcane commentary on Saint Paul's epistle but it was not. The second chapter of Samuel wound its tedious way to a conclusion and Father Matthew snapped the book shut with an expression of deep satisfaction.

"How true. How very true," said I. "Indisputable, in faith."

For the life of me I could not see a single truth therein and least of all any relevance to our present situation, unless Father Matthew was considering an imitation of David's relationship with Jonathan, which, on the whole, I rather doubted. Be that as it may, my comment, such as it was, appeared to satisfy him for he quaffed off what remained of his wine in a single gulp, pulled his chair nearer the fire and, without any further word, fell asleep.

Thus I was at least certain that Father Matthew read no Latin and it was a plausible supposition that he could not read at all. I therefore continue with my daybook in comfort and security as this good but ignorant cleric dozes opposite me.

Today dawned cloudy but dry. Before quitting Saint Omer, I searched out a saddler and bought a capacious cowhide saddle-bag that easily takes my bowl, missal, daybook, ink-pot and pens, and leaves room aplenty for provisions. I also bought a leathern bottle that I had filled with Guyenne wine. I wish now that I had also bought a new saddle, for the one I had in Calais is hard and narrow and has given me more sores than a Tilbury harlot.

I was on the road again before the tierce chimes.[32] Before I had ridden very far, the clouds above me began to disperse and the busy sun broke through to bathe the countryside in its fresh morning light. The terrain, which around Saint Omer had been much of a flatness, became increasingly hilly but Mistress Quickly, though disdaining to progress above a lazy shamble, seems no stranger to hills and takes them in her stride.

By midday I had crossed the River Aah.[33] To tell the truth, I am not certain that the river is so called but on passing the time of day with a toothless crone who was washing rags at the ford, I took the opportunity of asking her the name of the river which is, or seemed to be, the Aah. Now whether this was a mispronunciation which owed itself to the good wife's singular lack of teeth or some local nickname arising from the exclamations of luckless travellers who fall therein, I know not. I think the latter explanation may be the correct one for the ford was narrow and slippery and the water rushed over it at great speed. Few rivers in France seem blessed with bridges.

The country that I passed through today was more prosperous than that of yesterday and yet it was emptier of people than anywhere else. For most of the time there was not a soul visible from horizon to horizon nor any sign of human habitation. I did see one or two processions crossing distant meadows, priests and parishioners alike clad in black. With the hale and pious grouped at the head of the column and the infirm and reluctant lagging behind, they looked much like giant tadpoles struggling through a mess of pondweed. I passed one such army on the road. Being good, devout Christians all, they glared at me without exception—even the shrunken little priest who led them. One old man limped along bearing a great wooden box which belike contained the relics of some saint or other. If there are as many saints as there are bones purporting to come from them, there must be barely sufficient sinners to go round.

Tomorrow is the Feast of Saint Denis who is the patron of the French. Perhaps this is why they all looked so miserable.

In the early afternoon, I came across a group of boys who had tied a cockerel to a stick and were stoning it to death. When I was a lad I amused myself in just the same way, but it is a shameful waste of a good fowl for they would certainly have left it to rot by the wayside when they had done. With this in mind, I bellowed at them to desist—this with as terrible and angry a face as I could muster—whereupon they stopped immediately, and began to stone me instead. As luck would have it, one of these missiles struck Mistress Quickly upon the rump, causing her to break into the closest thing to a canter that I have experienced since I bought her. She did not slacken her pace for another league or two, which added greatly to our progress.

Such encounters were exceptional. I saw but three other travellers abroad this day and they were all going towards Saint Omer. In all my long life I have not met with such awful emptiness and silence. Unless in the plague years, when folk dared not venture out. For most of this day I could well have been a second Adam, yet it is well for humankind that I am not for there was no Eve that I could see and to reach my ribs would take an eternity of slicing.

Judging by his grunts, Father Matthew is awakening. Though I am quite sure that he cannot tell English from Hebrew, it were as well that I put my daybook aside for he has read to me in Latin and it would offend him if he thought I understood.

At Villez Boccage

Today being Friday, I am constrained to rest. Thus I am staying at the only inn in this village of Villez Boccage. Above its door it bears the arms of Charles d'Albret, Constable of France, and has been renamed *Le Connétable* in his honour, although the villagers who frequent its taproom still refer to it as *Le Pis d'Or* or Golden Udder, which was its previous name.[34] I find this a rare comment on the worth of Charles d'Albret.

By the by, it seems that Hal has at long last quitted Harfleur and has embarked on a magnificent *chevauchée*[35] in the manner of the Black Prince, though I also hear that he has been prudent enough to head straight for Calais by way of the coast. He will thus avoid battle with the French who, led by a Golden Udder or not, would certainly discomfit him. All the same, I am sure he looks pretty enough galloping along in his armour and that he will greatly impress the cowherds and orchardmen he meets along the way.

The Golden Udder is not a clean hostelry. I must share my bed with a blacksmith from Doullens who is journeying to Amiens to bring back his son who has run off with a serving wench. Now your smiths are commonly well-acquainted with fleas and lice and all manner of vermin, yet even he refuses to doff his clothes in bed and complains that it contains a greater multitude of beasts than the royal menagerie.

Last night I slept at the village of Fréyent. Such curious circumstances attended my staying there that I shall recount the episode in detail, the better to meditate thereon. My hand pains me greatly—as well it should—and this exercise of writing will be penance enough.

On Wednesday morn, I took my leave of the good Father Matthew and quitted the village of Frouge. The weather was clement, save for the odd shower of rain, and Mistress Quickly and I made tolerable progress. By a little after midday, we had passed through the uninteresting town of Saint Pol sur Ternoise and looked well set to reach Doullens before evening.

We were hardly a league from Saint Pol when the road dipped down into a shallow dale, at the bottom of which ran a brook spanned by a narrow wooden bridge. To my amazement, there was a considerable knot of people gathered on either bank, all of them staring at a single motionless figure who stood in the middle of the bridge with arms outstretched. So intent was their interest that few of them even took the trouble to acknowledge my approach.

I drew rein before the bridge and stared with the rest of them. For the life of me I could not see how so much inaction could engender so much interest, unless it be that the figure on the bridge was of such singular appearance. I judged it to be a man though, God knows, it could as easily have been a woman for he faced the opposing bank, was clad only in a sackcloth shift and had matted yellow hair that reached halfway down his back. It was only the hairiness of his arms and legs, which were no more than skin and bone, that gave any indication of his sex. In general appearance, he compared unfavourably with one of those scarecrows that farmers set in fields.

The crowd sat and stared. I sat and stared. The man on the bridge stood and, presumably, stared too. Mistress Quickly, whose attentiveness is not of the best, began to crop the grass at the roadside.

Now in my full life I have seen several things that have excited the interest of the populace, but all—executions, floggings, sermons and fires, *et cetera*—have had something of the spectacular about them. I have never yet seen a crowd gather to watch an oak tree grow or a housewife clean her front step. Thus, when a few minutes had passed with no promise of excitement, I began to grow impatient and would cross the bridge and continue my journey. That I did not immediately spur Mistress Quickly forward owed itself to two reasons. Firstly, I was still plagued by a certain curiosity that this excess of motionlessness might yet be the prologue to some notable action that would be worth the wait. Secondly, the fellow was blocking the bridge and I could not get past anyway. And so I was patient.

By the time a Thames-full of water had passed before me without any notable action being undertaken, my curiosity and my patience were at an end. Thus I cleared my throat noisily, which caused several of the peasants to look round but had no visible effect on the man on the bridge.

"Well met, messire!" I called out.

Still nothing.

"If you would be good enough to step aside and let me pass, I shall proceed on my journey!" I shouted.

I might as well have addressed a garden gate. Finally, I urged Mistress Quickly forwards and onto the bridge itself and yet still there was no movement from the man.

Now had he and I been the only two present, I should have run him down with no further ado for I confess to being singularly un-Job-like when it comes to matters of patience. However, surrounded as I was by people who were clearly, for reasons best known to themselves, in awe of this fellow, I had little choice but to draw rein again.

I continued to shout at him for a goodly time. Having rapidly exhausted the possibilities of French invective, I threw caution to the winds and turned to English—letting fly such a volley of abuse as a kennel-sweeper's doxy would have coloured at. This, however, only drew angry murmurings from the crowd.

The bridge was as assuredly blocked as though a platoon of infantry was occupying it. I had no choice. Shaking and seething with rage, I turned Mistress Quickly from the bridge, trotted her a little way along the bank and spurred her into the brook. We quickly reached the far bank and scrambled up it. I was soaked to my thighs and my missal, though happily not my daybook too, was ruined by the water.

I admit that my missal was no great loss as I never read it anyway, but it was well copied and bound in vellum and worth a groat or two if I had had occasion to sell it. Therefore, before continuing on my way, I turned about in the saddle and called out to the man on the bridge, calling him a stockfish and a bull's pizzle and a whoreson tailor's yard and much else besides. All of which was merely waves breaking on a cliff, for the fellow did not so much as blink in my direction. God's wounds, I believe he even smiled!

It was no more than an hour later when it began to rain most heavily. As I was already half-soaked and had no desire to be full-soaked, I took refuge under an oak tree, which being of great stature and yet well-leafed kept off much of the downpour. This shower did not last long but, being comfortably seated beneath the tree, I decided to dine before continuing. I had all but finished the cold capon I bought in Saint Pol when I heard soft footsteps approaching along the road.

This solitary traveller turned out to be none other than the hairy, sack-clothed rogue who had blocked my passage at the bridge. No sooner had he passed than I heaved myself into the saddle, threw away the carcass of my capon, and set off in pursuit.

To tell the truth, the pursuit did not last long for he had not gone more than a few yards on the road before I overtook him. I was about to swing my pilgrim's staff at his head when, of a sudden, he turned about, bowed low before me and then straightened up and made the sign of the cross.

I fear he could have defended himself no better had he wielded bastard-sword and poignard. His dignity and humility disarmed me before I could strike.

"God give you good afternoon, messire," said he.

"And you, sir," said I, put out of countenance.

"My name," said he, "is Denys. I would be glad of your fellowship on this lonely road."

"I too," said I. "My name is Jan van Staf and I am come from Antwerp town as a pilgrim bound for the Holy Land."

"Well met, Jan van Staf," said he.

And with that we set off together, Denys walking as swiftly on his two legs as I did on my four. My anger was now abated and curiosity had once more taken its place for I wished to know with what manner of man I was in company. Thus did I enquire of him his destination.

"Everywhere and nowhere," he answered, helpfully. "Where the Lord takes me, there do I go."

"You are a vagabond then," said I.

"Not so," said he. "For a vagabond has no purpose in his wanderings."

"And what is your purpose then?" I asked.

"To explain Holy Writ," said he. "And teach the word of God to men."

"Then you are a holy man?" said I.

"Even so," said he.

In truth, he was an exceedingly filthy holy man. When I was a boy, I found birds' nests that were less tangled than his hair and from where I sat on Mistress Quickly's back, I could plainly see the lice crawling upon his skin, which appeared to trouble him not one jot for in all the time we were together I never saw him scratch once. It is clear to me now that he regarded their presence as a mortification, for later in the day he confessed that he suffered badly from the corns but found consolation in the knowledge that their every twinge and prick was yet another sinner consigned to the fiery abyss of Hell. He also showed me where, beneath the rough sackcloth, he had the name of Jesus scratched across his heart, which script he kept bright and shining through frequent rubbing that the mingled blood and pus should be the illumination thereof.

At length, I expressed some curiosity as to Denys's rare performance at the bridge. My words seemed to take him by surprise, and he looked askance at me as if to assure himself that I was merely a fat man on a horse and not some naughty sprite intent on distracting him from his devotions through the asking of inane and superfluous questions.

"Messire!" said he. "The river and the bridge together did make the Holy Sign of the Cross. Holier still that the river was made by God and the bridge by man."

For the life of me I could not see why that should make it any holier, but I was loath to confess my ignorance in the matter and so I attempted a different tack.

"And how long did you stand thereon?" I asked.

"I know not," said he. "An hour? A day? A week?"

Of a sudden, I hoped very much that there were no further bridges on our way, else would my pilgrimage be long indeed.

This Denys was much given to divine revelation. It would come upon him at almost every bend in the road and, in particular, at crossroads where he would suddenly halt, throw wide his arms in just such an attitude as when I first set eyes on him and spend several minutes, or longer, in silent and blissful meditation. Although this did not delay our progress excessively, it did make conversation difficult.

I was anxious to know the manner of Denys's life and what had caused him to follow so painful and tedious a path but he seemed correspondingly reluctant to tell me. By and by, however, I learned that he had once been seneschal to the Duke of Anjou and a man of some influence and power until the Blessed Virgin came to him and told him to renounce the vanities of the world and go abroad to preach God's Holy Word.

Now, it is a thing that one does not readily own to in writing but, since this daybook is, after all, a sort of confessional, I must record that I am not a great believer in visions—particularly when they concern the Blessed Virgin who seems to be forever appearing unexpectedly and telling people to do this or that. From what I recall of the Scriptures, the Mother of Jesus is mentioned but little after the miracle of His birth and it surprises me greatly that she has been so busy since.

Denys had his own version of Holy Writ which was a rare amalgam of Latin tags, various Biblical quotations, proverbs, parables and pure invention. Thus one of the many sermons that he inflicted on me during our time together began with the words *Radix omnium malorum cupiditas est*. He delivered these words with great deliberation and then looked askance at me once more as though I, and not Greed, were the true root of all evil.

I expected some sort of adjuration—that I mend my ways, *per exemplum*—but, to my relief, the tag was a prologue to the history of the prodigal son. I write "history" instead of "parable" for history it was: Denys appeared to be privy to details of the Prodigal's life that the Bible sees fit to ignore. His account was of great length—largely owing to exhaustive interpolation—and described in prurient detail the riotous living by which the Prodigal wasted his substance and the particular routes that he took in his wanderings, including where he slept, what he ate and the precise sums of his tavern reckonings. Perhaps Denys procured this additional information from the Blessed Virgin herself.

The history of the Prodigal brought us almost to Fréyent and, when it was at last concluded, Denys recited the Psalter until we reached the outskirts.

Now in this village of Fréyent there is a large market-place before the church and in this market-place stands a cross. The market itself was abustle despite the lateness of the day, but Denys had eyes only for the cross at the centre of the crowd. Breaking off the Psalter in the midst of the sixteenth psalm, he mounted the steps of the cross, threw wide his arms once again and waited silently with eyes closed until the peasants, merchants and curious gathered about him. I never saw a man cursed with so much patience. Between Denys and the Holy Rood behind him there was not such difference as an owl would have blinked at.

Once there was a score or so of yokels at his feet, Denys began to preach. Not in the reasonably quiet voice with which he had regaled me upon the road but in a resounding bellow that would have shaken his simple-minded listeners to their shoes had they actually possessed any. God's wounds, he impressed even me although it must be said that the substance of his sermon was much the same as I had heard earlier: the vanities of man and the wrath of the Lord and things of that ilk. I listened until thirst got the better of me and then sought out an alehouse. It was not difficult to find for Fréyent is a grievous small place.

As in all small villages, the presence of a stranger causes much stir. I had progressed no further than my second jug of *godale*, or *grambille* as it is known there, when I was asked, with great civility, whence I came and what my business was in Fréyent. I answered with my usual story and added that I had come thither in the company of Denys the Holy Man. This turned out to be a name known to all and, by my association with him, my company was much sought after. Nobody seemed at all curious as to why a companion of Denys was quaffing in an alehouse while Denys himself lived on weeds and water, and a third jug of *grambille* was put before me and then a fourth, by which time my wit and fancy were fired to lend the history of Denys as much colour as he himself had bestowed on the Prodigal Son.

My story filled all with wonder but this was little achievement for they were simple rustics all and would have wondered at the description of a ploughshare if it were dressed in pretty language. By the by, however, the novelty of hearing Denys himself prevailed over my history of him and they left the alehouse severally, leaving me with only the ale-wife for company.

So I bespoke another jug of *grambille* and settled myself against the wall. The ale-wife lit her rush lights, it being almost vespers, and seated herself in the far corner of the room where she stared fixedly at one of the trembling flames and set to chewing her gums. That troublesome demon Common Sense whispered to me that I should find lodgings for the night yet, in truth, the ale had made me feel so comfortable that I heeded him not. From outside, the rantings of Denys came to me fitfully upon the wind.

At length, however, I finished my jug, pulled myself to my feet, paid the ale-wife her due and went forth in search of Mistress Quickly whom I had quite forgotten was tethered without the door. Thinking to find her fodder and stabling, I led her back into the market-place. It was there that a truly wondrous sight met my eyes.

The place was ablaze with light, given off by a score or more of torches. Denys stood yet on the steps of the market cross in terrible illumination, bawling his lungs out and flailing his arms wildly. Around him, nigh on the entire populace of Fréyent was assembled, silent, immobile and open-mouthed—for all the world as if turned to stone.

The one true miracle I ever saw Denys perform was to discourse on the same subject for five hours without appearing to repeat himself, which prodigious feat was accomplished in Fréyent that night. As I watched, I quite pitied the miserable population of that village, for Denys was making it clear beyond any misunderstanding that it was exclusively their vanity and their corruption that was responsible for all the sins of mankind, from the days of Adam onwards.

I listened for a while longer and then led Mistress Quickly from the market-place and out onto the Doullens road where, after an intolerably long and tedious walk, I came upon a wayside hostelry. There a crone bit each of the three *denier* I proffered her before showing me to the stable-yard where, there being no ostler, I must unsaddle and feed Mistress Quickly myself. I declined to take a bed at the inn for it was the meanest I ever set eyes on, and I would rather have slept naked in a haystack than provide yet another feeding-trough for lice. So it was that I turned my steps back towards the village.

In the market-place the crowd had undergone a transformation. If I believed in Pythagorean transmigration, which I do not, I might have thought that the bodies of the citizens of Fréyent had been possessed by wolves. Their former silence and immobility were gone. Now they screamed and bellowed and danced with very rage and frustration and the more they screamed and bellowed the more violent grew Denys's condemnation of them. Having worked his way up from Adam by way of the Pharaohs, the Fall of Troy, Belshazzar's Feast and countless other *exempla* of God's just wrath upon the vain and corrupt— the most part of which I had fortunately missed—Denys was now ascribing the rapacious behaviour of Hal in Normandy to the unfortunate Fréyentais. God's judgement on their sins, he said, was that the English host, led by the most foul and extremely demonic *Henri d'Angleterre*, would fall upon them with fire and the sword, slaughtering and mutilating the men, violating the women and carrying off the children. Wrong-headed as it was, this statement brought renewed shrieks and bellows of mortification and rage. When he went on to say that their savings would be confiscated, their crops despoiled and their houses burned, the resulting distress of the multitude beggars description.

Now Fréyent is a small, thriving village of no consequence where such performances come once in a lifetime if they come at all. In London there is hardly a day goes by that you do not hear some poxy, lice-ridden vagabond exhorting the ignorant and foolish to part with what little they have to save themselves from this or that. Most Londoners regard this as mere gratis entertainment and would no more part with their wealth on account of some vile-smelling holy madman than they would sit down in the kennel and gobble up someone else's dinner. But in Fréyent, Denys ploughed virgin earth and reaped a rich harvest for his efforts.

It came as no surprise to me when he exhorted his congregation to bring forth their tawdry ornaments of silver, copper and brass, their necklaces, rings and bangles, their fine clothes, playing cards and dice, and build of them a bonfire that these objects of luxury and vice be consumed in cleansing flame. Nor was I surprised when a good half of the crowd instantly rushed to their houses in search of such luxury and vice. I was moderately surprised when they returned with laden arms and I perceived that such luxuries and vices actually existed in Fréyent. Once they had piled these objects into a pyre and Denys had seized a torch and gleefully set fire to them, I was far more surprised to see the Fréyentais return in search of more luxury and vice to contribute to the conflagration.

Indeed, the poor peasants of Fréyent—nay, I cannot put "poor"—the surprisingly wealthy peasants of Fréyent seemed marvellously pleased with this work and danced about the blaze as if it were Midsummer's Eve. I saw a heavy silver necklace thrust into the flames, followed by fox-fur and sable, a copper cup, a handful of rings, a handsome doublet, a carved chest of plate and even a book.

The above was written this morning. Not the book—I mean this entry written on Saint Wilfred's Eve at the village of Villez Boccage. It is now afternoon. About two o' the clock, I think. I have just dined on salted hake, it being a Friday. I do not like fish. The hake has given me the wind most grievous.

Now no one stirred from the market-place at Fréyent till the flames of that most expensive of bonfires had quite died down and there was naught left of the riches of that village save glowing embers. As the blaze waned, so too did the enthusiasm of the crowd. There were one or two, as I noticed, who regarded the ashes with some regret and I even heard someone close by whisper that the most foul and extremely demonic *Henri d'Angleterre* could not have despoiled the village any worse than they had done themselves.

When all was silent, Denys led the villagers in a final prayer, during which I noticed yet more of them looking distinctly woebegone despite having just been saved from the Wrath of God, or at least his instrument. When Denys was done and had thoroughly blessed his now quite miserable congregation, the market-place swiftly emptied.

I approached the cross on the steps of which Denys was sitting.

"A fine night's work," said I.

"Aye," he answered, with great satisfaction.

Further conversation was thwarted by the arrival of the village priest. He introduced himself as Père Guillaume, or Father William, and he was as mealy-mouthed and fawning as any priest I have seen. Worm-like though he was, he offered us hospitality, which was some relief to me for it had begun to rain.

We were vouchsafed a satisfactory meal of roasted pork and a chicken baked in pastry though only Father William and I partook. Denys dined on raw turnip and water, which he ate with many a grimace of disgust.

Father William clearly held Denys in some esteem for he addressed his every remark to him and ignored me completely. Now commonly I should have been much put out by such insolence and yet I was not for it obviated any troublesome questions about the nature of the town of Antwerp or the problems of being an itinerant wool merchant and I have not, as a rule, had happy commerce with priests in any case. Add to which the stench emitted by Denys's person was not entirely masked by the odour of Father William's abode and I was saved the predicament of sitting next to him and thus enduring the mortification of his mephitic breath.

Be that as it may, I was effectively prevented from the enjoyment of my food. Not by the ecclesiastical prattle but by the memory of the wanton destruction I had witnessed. I doubt greatly that I was the sole person bemoaning the great loss of that Wednesday evening, and yet belike it was a salutary experience for the people of Fréyent for it is said that the fool, when he has taken hurt, becomes wise. Being wise enough already, I was thrown into the blackest melancholy.

It was as I was picking at my chicken bones and trying to console myself with the foolish maxim that there is little good in crying over spilt milk that a thought occurred to me. It was as foolish as the maxim, but at that time it seemed the very wisest of revelations. I know I have just written that I am wise enough already but no man since Adam has been wise at all hours.

I had been thinking of the heavy silver necklace I had seen cast into the fire. In search of some solace, I asked myself what use I would have had for it anyway. I could not have worn it for fear of being thought an effeminate Edward Poins popinjay and I knew no fine lady to whom I could have offered it. The only value it might have had would have been its weight in raw silver. It was then it came to me. Though the fire had certainly destroyed what cunning design and workmanship the ornament possessed, it could hardly have done more than melt the silver. Somewhere among the ashes of the bonfire, lay a rough ingot and who knew what besides.

I determined that once mad Denys and the cozening priest were asleep, I would slip from the house and recover what remained.

It was not long before Father William retired to his room and not much longer before Denys was snoring and snuffling, a suitably mortifying distance from the fire. When all was quiet, I stole forth and made my way to the market-place.

It was deserted, as I had expected it to be. In front of the village cross lay a grey stain, no longer smoking now for the rain had extinguished it. I knelt in the mud and began to stir the sodden embers with a stick. It was a deal of time before I encountered anything solid, but finally my perseverance was rewarded. I touched something heavy. Scraping away the ashes, I encountered a mass of fused metal but it had no light to it and was certainly some of the plate.

There is not a witch stirs her cauldron with the devotion with which I stirred those embers. My cloak grew sodden and heavy, and the wetness of the mud was travelling up my hose. In faith, I was on the point of giving up my search and returning to the comfort of Father William's fire when my stick overturned a piece of bright, glinting metal. It was the necklace.

Now thus far I had been loath to venture into the remains of the fire for, by then, it was a morass of grey mud and it is bad enough to be wet-through without being filthy into the bargain. So I attempted to knock the necklace towards me. Unfortunately it was stuck fast in the debris. I bored my stick under it in an effort to prise the whoreson thing loose, which merely succeeded in pushing it further away. The only course of action was to wade into the embers and pick it up. Thus, confident that the rain had squeezed out every last drop of heat, I pushed myself to my feet and plodded forwards.

Now I shall admit to being a man of some girth. Not fat, mark you! Of a comfortable plumpness. It was then, as on many an occasion, that this protective girth saved me from grievous harm.

To pick up the silver, I must bend over. This I did with too much violence, causing me to pitch forwards. Instinctively, I put out my right hand to catch myself and therein lies the only reason why I am able to write at all this day. It brushed...nay, it did more than brush...it lay contiguous with the necklace. At first I heard the slightest sizzle, as of fat beginning to fry in a pot, and then burst upon me a very volcano of pain the like of which I have not felt in many a year. I thought I had thrust my hand into molten lead and to say I withdrew it with the utmost celerity is like saying apples grow on trees. Yea, the last time I moved so swiftly was while executing a strategic retreat at the battle of Gaultree Forest.

I thrust my hand into the wet mud, which eased my suffering somewhat, but as I sit here in The Golden Udder it throbs even now. Truth to say, I forgot all notion of salvaging the necklace. It would have been simple work with the aid of the stick but by then my interests lay elsewhere.

I returned immediately to Father William's house but was in too much pain to sleep and left before dawn. I trudged to the hostelry where I had left Mistress Quickly and proceeded on my pilgrimage without further ado. Also without breakfast.

I am now branded with a perpetual memento of my greed as surely as any felon. Perhaps this shows the true holiness of Mad Denys, whom I have much maligned, in that he prevented me from profiting from the loss of others. No, that is nonsense. Mad Denys was asleep and, had he not built his bonfire of the vanities in the first place, I would not have roasted the skin off my hand. I have also caught a cold.

This is so much melancholic introspection. I forget that I have profited thereby. I arrived at this village of Villez Boccage half a day earlier than I would have done and the recounting of my adventure has occupied fully this Wilfred's Eve, which is the day of Holy Innocents last. And a fish day to boot.

On the road to Paris

It is midday. I am sheltering from the rain under a narrow wooden bridge. I have been here for a good hour now and judging by the leaden heaviness of the heavens I shall still be here a day hence. God's wounds, I have not seen such rain as this in twenty years. It would make Noah's Flood seem a mere dripping nose. I am soaked to the skin again. I shall catch a worse ague on account of this and belike die. I, who have been the friend of kings, the terror of furious rebels and magistrates! That I should perish through a drop or two of rain! And French rain at that! To think that I have survived princes, pox and pestilence to succumb to a surfeit of water!

My hand pains me yet. Were I in London now, I would hie me to the good Doctor Monks, or send a boy. Though Doctor Monks is, beyond all reasonable doubt, the quintessence of quackery, he has some wondrous salves that can take away the pain of a cut or a burn or a boil as quickly as a hangman can lop off an ear. Yet there is little profit in wishful thinking. I am not in London—I am sheltering under a leaky bridge by a swollen stream on the wind-blasted plains of France.

And as if these discomforts are not enough, I have not eaten since leaving the Golden Udder early this morning and my leathern bottle, which I had filled with wine, is now empty.

What naughty demon possessed me to embark on this miserable journey, forsaking my native land? I might be taking my ease in some tavern now where the only distance between me and a jug of wine would be the time it took to bespeak it. I could be gorging myself on roasted mutton with Doll Tearsheet frolicsome on my lap. No, Doll is gone to Southwark.

In faith, this is a fool's pilgrimage and I shall inscribe the cover of my daybook thus so that whenever I open it in future, my folly will be before my eyes. I shall journey no further. I shall break my pilgrim's staff and cast it away. What need have I of a peasant's weapon when I have Gut Cutter at my side? My bowl I shall abandon here. As for my pilgrim's hat—it will keep the rain and wind at bay as well as any other but I shall cut off its leaden badges. A rogue of my girth has little need of ballast.

If it were not for...[36]

At Breteuil

On Saint Wilfred's Day.
(Saturday 12th October 1415)

Breteuil is little bigger than Villez Boccage but is provided with a handsome inn, *Le Chat Basillant* by name, which means The Yawning Cat. The proprietor of this somnolent feline is a certain Jean who is a short, talkative man and a merry. He made me welcome and insisted that I gave him my wet apparel, which is now drying before the fire. Moreover, he sent out for a leg of mutton and had it roasted and served to me together with a large jug of Aunis wine. I now sit in the upper room, swathed in a warm cloak, with another jug of Aunis close to hand.

Breteuil squats on a junction of roads and thus is busy and prosperous despite its diminutive size. It is here that the road from Amiens divides in twain, one branch going to Beauvais and the other to Clermont.

Amiens, by the by, is a wealthy city with a lofty cathedral that dwarfs all around it. I stopped there shortly after leaving Villez Boccage and replenished my leathern bottle, but I did not linger, preferring to reach Paris as soon as I may.

Paris, according to my host, lies a mere twenty leagues hence. Three days' travel at the most.

I do repent of what I wrote this morning. The Good Lord had put trials in my way and I failed Him most miserably. Hereafter, I shall attempt to comport myself as a pilgrim should.

I have not seen a wench worth the tumbling since leaving England, which is a grievous disappointment. In England, there is a notion that your French lass is unsurpassed for her beauty and lightness, to which I can only reply that your beautiful French lasses must be of such uncommon lightness that they have floated away entirely and are offering their favours to the saints in Heaven.

I am mistaken. I did see one saucy-looking wench in Saint Omer, of all places, but when I smiled on her and winked my eye, she made as though she had not seen me and gave off such an air of coldness as would have frozen the dew on a midsummer morn. So much for lightness. If a lusty wench can pass Jack Falstaff by without her fires quickening then Beldame Virtue has swept all before her and bawdy-houses will be nunneries hereafter. As this is clearly not the case, I can say that in this country beauty and wantonness do not go hand in hand.

Yet, for all that, your Frenchman is a fortunate rogue for he has wines of the finest. They lack the cloying sweetness of your English wine, which is shipped by way of Bristol, but possess a pleasing dryness that excites the appetite wonderfully. From Saintonge and Aunis come sharp, bright, ruby breakfast-wines that sparkle and scintillate upon the tongue and clear the mind of dull waking humours. From the Duchy of Burgundy come proud, stately wines that have the mellowness of hautboys. And on a draughty autumn evening, no wine can compare with those of Guyenne for they warm and quicken the blood when the body's lusts are cold and give wings to Wit and Fancy that they may fly free and nimbly. Those who know not the virtues of wine are ignorant of life itself for nothing else can liberate the intellect from its diurnal shackles.

I fear that my intellect may have been a little too liberated this evening. I shall go down to the taproom to see if my clothes are dry.

On the road to Paris between Breteuil and Clermont

On the thirteenth day of October, being a Sunday.

I have fallen in with most delightful company and, for once, such as befits my rank. Presently, I am travelling with one Count Guillermo, together with his family and retinue, which is of great number. This count hails from the great city of Alexandria in Egypt, of which he was the sometime ruler, and his history is most sad and lachrymatory.

I overtook this party some two leagues south of Breteuil. This is no tribute to improvement in Mistress Quickly's celerity but to slowness in Count Guillermo's progress—as is common for a great lord with many retainers.

Truth to say, I did not at first recognize the Count to be a man of any substance at all, nor did I perceive the chattering throng about him—which included many wild children running hither and thither between the carts—to be his advisors, ministers and the families thereof. They were all of them most shabbily attired and dirty. There was not a child possessed of footwear and though their carts were gaily painted, which was surely in an effort to lend a cheerful countenance to their misfortunes, they had clearly seen much service and were in the dotage of such conveyances.

Indeed, such was the rowdiness of this company—for they were all shouting at each other in a foreign tongue—that I was disinclined to join them on the road and spurred Mistress Quickly to a slight trot, the sooner to pass them. As I was overtaking the fellow riding alone at their head, he saluted me and complimented me on my fine horse.

Now though I had considered Mistress Quickly to be many things since quitting Calais, a fine horse was not one of them. Doubtless aware of the compliment bestowed upon her, she had moderated her slight trot to her customary sedate amble and fallen in alongside the count's proud stallion. I still could not judge her as being particularly fine and even the word "horse" seemed a somewhat excessive estimation. This evaluation obviously did her great disservice and is little to my credit for your counts, as a rule, are very expert when it comes to horseflesh.

"I thank you for your compliment, messire," said I, with greater courtesy than the fellow's appearance merited.

"It is no compliment," said he. "I have not seen the like of your mare in all my years in France."

This I readily believed.

"What is your name and provenance?" he asked.

"Jan van Staf," said I, guardedly. "From Antwerp town in the Low Countries."

"I am honoured to meet you, Jan van Staf," said he. "Our wanderings have been many since we left our native land but Antwerp I have never seen, though I believe its people to be honest, yea, and industrious too."

Your nobility devote much effort to the cultivation of pretty manners and are forever fond of using them.

I enquired his name and when he told me that he was a count I was much surprised and not a little confused in view of his ruffianly aspect.

"I know," said he, casting a sorrowful glance upon his ragged followers, "that I have not the appearance of a count, but I assure you that I am one nonetheless. You see yonder fellow? He in the cart behind us with the white beard and the patch over one eye? My chief minister, Antonio! A man of great wisdom and nobility! It grieves me now to see him thus!'

I could see how it might, and begged him to relate his sad history, for my curiosity was now great.

"In Egypt," he began, "I was a great lord with many men at my command and lands that stretched from the Mediterranean Sea to the deserts of Arabia. My lands were fertile and my people prosperous and happy. We knew no drought nor flood and I was accounted by far the richest of the Sultan's vassals."

"The Sultan?" I asked.

"Of Baghdad. To whom I paid tribute. It was therein lay my doom for my pride became too great and I disdained his lordship. And he dared do naught against me."

He cast yet another melancholy look towards his lumbering retinue.

"My pride did not stop there," he continued. "It was of such magnitude that I thought my shaming of the Sultan of little account and declared to my people that the Pope in Rome was but a mere pretender and that none but their own temporal lord—me—should be their Holy Father. I claimed to interpret Holy Writ better than any pope or prelate."

"For shame," said I, shaking my head sadly.

"The news of my apostasy spread to Rome where the Pope was sorely angered. He dispatched a mighty army to Egypt and lay siege to my castle. At length, hunger and thirst did their work and so, clad in sackcloth with ashes rubbed into my hair, I surrendered my body, my castle and my people to the Pope's army."

"I feared the Pope would have my life for, as I have said, his anger was great. Yet, in his divine mercy, he spared me and my people. He decreed that we be expelled from Egypt to wander the world for seven years."

"How do you live from one day to the next?" I asked

"We trust to Christian charity," answered Guillermo. "And we trade a little in horses, which is permitted. I don't suppose you'd like to sell me yours?"

"Not really," said I, regarding my fine horse with a new affection.

Guillermo shrugged his shoulders.

"We were one thousand in number," said he. "But through disease and privations we are shrunk to the pitiful few you see here now. Our seven-year wandering is long passed. When we begged the Pope to let us return to our native land, he refused, saying that we were not yet truly contrite. In mitigation, he ordained that any bishop or abbot we meet along the way should pay us the sum of ten *livres* to relieve our deprivation and that other pilgrims and travellers should give us alms according to their station and means."

He cast a wistful look upon my purse at which I could not prevent the hot tears from rolling down my cheeks. I fumbled therein and brought forth three *sous*. With the true nobility of one ashamed to accept alms, he pushed my outstretched hand away but when I pressed him further he pocketed the coin and blessed me for my generosity.

He offered once more to purchase Mistress Quickly but I refused again for my pity does not extend to walking. He did not seem in the least put out of countenance but drew rein and, when all behind had also stopped, presented me to the Countess Maria, to his two sons Rodolfo and Iago, and to his daughter Isabella who is a most comely wench with a great mane of jet-black hair and fire in her eyes.

Throughout the afternoon Count Guillermo entertained me with stories of his travels, which have been extensive, as one might expect. If I remember correctly, they have journeyed through the Holy Land, through Cappadocia, Thrace, Dacia, Russia, Bohemia, Illyria, Helvetia and Germany. His tales were recounted with wit and modesty—as befits a gentleman—and thus I accepted from his lips accounts of such passing strangeness that if I had heard them from others I would have thought them mere invention.

It is now evening and I write this by the light of a rush lamp in the tent belonging to the Count himself. He and his family are busy preparing for a great feast that they are holding in my honour.

I have had my fortune told. It was the Count Guillermo's comely daughter Isabella who is the mistress of this art. I paid her six *sous* for the service for she told me that if the palm of her hand is not crossed with silver, the fortune-telling has no worth. She told me that I shall be going on a long journey, and that I shall find what I am seeking, whatever it is. She also told me that I would have a long life and die a rich man.

A servant of the count has just announced that supper is served. I shall continue my narrative on the morrow.

At Saint Just en Tel (Saint Juste en Thelle)

On the fourteenth day of October, being a Monday.

A black pox on all Egyptians! I have been robbed of my horse and my purse. I have been gulled like some thin-faced village simpleton. Guillermo is a whoreson rascally knave and his family and retainers cozeners all!

I have walked afoot to this village of Saint Just. Two league afoot! Afoot! I shall be damned before I walk a foot further!

The Devil and all his minions take that whoreson coxcomb! May he be racked till his joints start! May he die in agonies and roast in eternal fire! A count? I have known beggars with more sores than Lazarus have greater nobility about them! If Guillermo be a count then I am the Emperor Charlemagne!

It is not so much the loss of my horse that I bemoan—Mistress Quickly being the slowest, most broken-winded jade that ever I saw—and only slightly more the loss of money, for I yet have six *livres* sewn into the hem of my cloak, it is the shame of being brought low by such transparent cozenage and robbed like any caterpillar merchant. It is enough to make you forswear wine and betake you to a monastery.

But meditation is a good remedy and, now that I write them down, I see that these complaints and lamentations are not worth a flea. *Factum stultus cognoscit.*[37]

At the conclusion of my last entry in this daybook, I put aside my pen and ink and joined the company of Egyptians for their feast. They had built a great fire and a whole sheep was turning over it, which set me to thinking about whence the animal had come, for I had seen no livestock of any kind about the encampment. Not so much as a chicken, let alone a sheep. Finally I decided that Guillermo must have visited a neighbouring bishop and taken the animal in lieu of the customary ten *livres*. Whatever its origin, the meat gave off a most delicious odour.

I was seated in the place of honour next to that filthy pox-sore Guillermo, who feigned hospitality as well as he could. Marry, he feigned it well enough to deceive me though, in extenuation, I had been alone and friendless for many a day and was sorely in need of laughter and pleasant conversation.

Guillermo served me himself and gave me of the tastiest morsels and took care that my cup was never empty—which, given his assiduity in the task, might normally have aroused my suspicions.

The feast lasted a good two hours and when it was done there was music, for two of the company played the tabor and rebec. With this came singing and dancing and much drinking. Thieves though they be, the Egyptians do know how to make merry.

Strange to relate, among this people it is only the men who sing and the women who dance, which was a source of some regret for the men have loud voices and the songs much resemble the caterwauling of a bagpipe, and the women dance with such sinuous lewdness that I would have much liked to have got up with them. Isabella in particular danced with such hot lasciviousness that Salome herself, had she seen her, would have dressed herself in dowlas and sold fish at Billingsgate.

My last recollection of that evening is sitting with Isabella cradled in my arms, my face warmed by wine and firelight, whilst about me whirled a multitude of dancing shapes, for all the world like falling leaves on a windy autumn day. I also recall the music howling and screeching in my ears. I recall getting to my feet, for what reason I cannot say, and then the spheres of Heaven tumbled down upon me and struck me to the earth.

It was daylight when I awoke. My body was cold and stiff and the great bell of Saint Paul's was striking matins in my head. The remains of the fire still smouldered beside me but of the Egyptians there was not a sign.

It was a long time before I could recover my wits but when I had done so and remembered, in part, the doings of last night, I perceived that Mistress Quickly was no longer grazing where I had left her and soon after that I found that my purse had been cut. My saddle-bag had also been opened and its contents cast upon the ground but nothing had been taken. I was also surprised to find myself yet in possession of my sword and dagger and the other appurtenances of my journey. This puzzled me greatly for most of my accoutrements were worth a groat or two and an able felon, possessed of wit and refinement, would have slit my throat as well as my purse-strings and made off with the lot. It grieves me that I was not only gulled most shamefully, but by amateurs to boot.

At Saint Just, whither I have walked, there is an inn called *Au Renard de Tel* or, in honest language, the Fox of Tel. The innkeeper is a morose and melancholy man by the name of Thomas. Nonetheless, he made much of my arrival and showed me the upper room, which seems moderately free of vermin and of which I am the sole occupant. At my behest, Thomas has sent out for a capon and a piece of pork.

I must find a horse, or at the very least a carter who will transport me to Paris. From this point of view, Saint Just is not promising, for apart from *Au*

Renard de Tel there is only a church and a dozen or so hovels. However, my trials of the last two days have left me weary and dispirited and it would do me well to rest here a while that the balance of my humours be restored and my vitality replenished.

A pox on all Egyptians.

At Saint Just en Tel

On a Tuesday, being the fifteenth day of October.

Host Thomas' wife, Mathilde, is as good a cook as I ever knew. This night I ate roasted goose, a dish of roasted quail, a dish of eels and half a cauldron of pease soup, all of which was prepared in so goodly a manner that a Lord Chamberlain could not have found fault. Moreover, Goodwife Mathilde is of such a merry, bustling disposition that, were her dishes to fail in some particular, the pleasure of her company would more than make up for it.

I have often noted that when it comes to relations between the sexes, those of antithetical humour tend to attract each other. It is as if Dame Nature recognizes the shortcomings of one and seeks to remedy them with the strengths of the other—so creating a harmonious whole. Thus, is Hostess Mathilde as sanguine as her spouse is melancholic.

It is certain that Host Thomas would not be quite so melancholic were he not beset with a multitude of problems, the greatest of which is *Au Renard de Tel* itself.

The inn is not a large one but it is clean and welcoming and provided with the finest food and drink of the region. In spite of that, few people take the trouble to stop here, the reason being the inn's position, or rather the position of the village of Saint Just in which it lies. Travellers coming from the south, east and west will stay at Clermont, and those from the north at Saint Just en Chaussée, whence they can proceed to Clermont in half a day or less. I must confess that I would not have stayed here myself had I not been constrained to do so for lack of a horse.

That *Au Renard de Tel* has survived thus far is thanks to a handful of customers who stay here regularly and to others who are unable to find a bed elsewhere. Naturally Thomas serves wine and ale to the villagers and neighbouring peasants but his taproom provides him only with his crust and a meagre one it is at that.

Thomas told me of his predicament over supper and I was moved to sympathy. I straightway offered to take wine with him, whereupon he removed my wine from the board and replaced it with something more to his liking.

"This is good wine," he explained with great sadness.

"What was the other?" I asked, with some puzzlement.

"That was good wine too," he replied.

Good it certainly was, but it only turned his melancholy into the blackest despair. After my unfortunate experience at the hands of Guillermo, I was on my guard against charitable outbursts of sympathy, but it seems that the older I become the softer grows my heart. Now that I have reached the age of three-score and something even the most banal tale can move me to tears.

I urged Host Thomas to put aside his melancholy for sadness brings scant profit to anyone except poets, and then precious little. I told him roundly that if his inn was ill-provided with guests then he must find a way of bringing them there.

At this, Thomas gave me one of those looks that landlords cultivate with some nicety and reserve for those customers who offer to pay their reckonings on Tuesday week when the boat carrying their cargo of rare spices from Cathay, presently battling through a storm in the Bay of Biscay, docks at Southampton. Fortunately for him, however, I was not to be so easily dissuaded from giving him the benefit of my vast experience of life.

"To bring folk hither," said I, "and I mean such folk as will pay you handsomely for the fine services you offer, is a matter of no great difficulty."

"How so?" said he. "Why would anyone want to come to Saint Just? There is naught here save an inn and a church, and France is well-provided with both."

"If there is naught of interest here, then you must furnish it," said I. "God's wounds, man, I have seen folk undertake a journey of ten leagues just to see a pig with five legs or a bull-calf that gives milk or some such freak of nature. Yea, and pay to see it too."

For a brief moment Thomas seemed hopeful but then melancholy clouded his face once more.

"There are no freaks of nature in Saint Just," he mumbled. "There's the smith's son. He is an idiot. But I can think of nothing further."

"No, that will not do," said I, scratching my beard. "Idiots there are in plenty."

"Perhaps," said Thomas, "we may buy a freak elsewhere and pass it off as our own."

"No," said I. "That will not do either. Any man who possesses a good, profitable freak will sell it dearly if he sells it at all. Furthermore, it will take an unconscionable long time to find aught worthy of the trouble for you'll need more than an old crone with face-whiskers to bring the curious to Saint Just."

I had never thought I would miss the company of Mad Denys but I will admit that he can fill a market-place quicker than any vagabond preacher I have seen, and he would have been a fine addition to the population of Saint Just if he could be persuaded to stay here. Yet it is the nature of vagabond Holy Men not to stay anywhere and so, with regret, I abandoned this idea.

Yet it was then that Divine Inspiration came to my aid. This I write for who but the Lord Omnipotent could have put the thought of Canterbury in my mind? Before my eyes floated a golden vision of a great crowd of pilgrims waiting in line before the extremely valuable tomb of Saint Thomas.

The expression on my countenance must have seemed surpassing strange, for Thomas, who was in the act of morosely quaffing his cup of wine, halted and looked upon me with concern.

"What's the matter, Messire van Staf?" said he. "Are you not well?"

"A miracle!" I exclaimed.

Thomas looked about him and, finding no miracle, returned his attention to me.

"Of what miracle do you speak?" he asked.

"I speak of a miracle that is to come," said I. "A miracle of which the children of women will speak for generations. A miracle that will bring fame and fortune to the village of Saint Just."

"Fortune?" said Thomas.

"Even so," said I.

It was clear he thought me one of Mad Denys' persuasion, but as I outlined my stratagem he was swiftly disabused of this and at length, when I was done, he confessed that he liked the plan well and that we should put it to execution tomorrow night.

As with all great plans, it possesses the utmost simplicity.

Tomorrow, on waking, Thomas will complain of great pains in his foot. Why his foot? Because the pain will be such that he will not be able to walk without limping heavily and all will mark the gravity of his affliction. As the day progresses, so will the pain increase till, there being no physick in Saint Just, he will be obliged to call on the services of Father Luc, who is the priest here. I have already seen Father Luc and if he can so much as write his own name that would be a miracle in itself. Being slow of wit, he will ascribe the pain to diabolical intervention and I will eat my daybook if that be not so. That being the case, Thomas will attend vespers in the village church, which ordinarily he is unable to do for his labours do not permit it. During the service he will make great show of piety, imploring the Lord to rid him of his malevolent curse.

During this time I shall dress myself in raiment borrowed from Hostess Mathilde over which I shall drape a clean linen sheet, taking care to cover my hair and beard. This done, I shall secret myself in the bushes without the door of the church and await the end of vespers.

Though it is yet twilight when vespers begins, the night is as black as coal when it ends. As the folk issue forth from church, I shall step out of the bushes and Thomas, on seeing me, will cry out "It is the Holy Virgin!" and fall to his knees—followed, I doubt not, by the other parishioners. He will then utter a great cry and roll upon the ground, allowing me to profit from this diversion by letting fall the sheet, thus rendering me invisible. I shall then withdraw behind the bushes and, having safely stowed the sheet within my houppeland, return to the inn. Thomas will meanwhile recover from his fit and find that his foot has been miraculously cured. So much so that he will dance and skip with delight.

For complete success, the stratagem depends on the night being as dark as I imagine it will be, for only then will Mistress Mathilde's black houppeland render me invisible. There may well be some parishioners who possess more wit than their fellows and who will suspect the evidence of their eyes but I am confident that the enthusiasm of their neighbours will dispel or at least discredit their reservations. At any rate, whatever they believe, it will take a brave man to cast doubts on a miracle. Moreover, as there will be no obvious profit for Thomas is his dissembling, I cannot imagine anyone taking issue with him.

It is true that both Thomas and Mathilde expressed some qualms about my counterfeiting the Blessed Virgin—believing it to be blasphemous or somesuch nonsense—but I pointed out that your cunning artists think nothing of fashioning her likeness out of wood or stone and I shall merely be doing the same in flesh.

I shall now retire to my bed for this promises to be such a jest as I have not known since Hal's time, and I am impatient to begin it.

At Senlis

On Saint Etheldreda's Day.
(Thursday 17th October 1415)

I am now only ten leagues from Paris and once more provided with a horse. For this, I have Thomas to thank, for it was he who procured it and provided me with wine for my journey and three *livres*.

In faith, I am much fatigued and I shall go to bed soon, though it be not yet vespers.

I am staying at a hostelry on the banks of the River Nonette. It is a small inn and I must share a bed with a merchant of Compiègne, but truth to tell I think that I would even sleep soundly in the taproom of the Boar's Head on Twelfth Night, so tired am I.

I arrived here about midday, having ridden through most of the night. My journey, therefore, was a difficult one until dawn for the road between Saint Just and Clermont is in an execrable state of disrepair and my new horse was unaccustomed to bearing one of my greatness. Add to which, I twice fell asleep in the saddle. Once, I awoke to find myself going nowhere at all and the second time to find the stupid horse cantering cheerfully back to Saint Just. This latter was not a fact that quickly made itself apparent for I was unfamiliar with the road, the night was moonless and I knew not how long I had been asleep. I even began to praise my mount for showing a turn of speed that Mistress Quickly could not have achieved downhill with a following wind. It was only when we stopped to negotiate a great oak that had fallen across the highway that I recollected having done likewise in the opposite direction. By that time we were only a league or so from Saint Just where my reappearance would have been both unexpected and unpleasant.

I shall not grace my new horse with a name. There was never a house brick possessed of so little wit. I shall sell it as soon as I reach Paris.

My apparition of the Virgin Mary was a resounding success, though the final result of my labours was less to my liking.

At first, all went according to plan. Thomas's limp was most grievous to behold and the entire population of Saint Just—about twenty-five souls—was thrown into great consternation. Father Luc, though possessed of the sort of native suspiciousness that is all too common among your French peasantry, duly declared Thomas's painful affliction to be the Devil's work and prescribed essence of prayer and tincture of self-denial as the surest remedies. My appearance at the door of the church was of such gentle majesty that were I to renounce pilgriming I could make a comfortable living on the miracle-play circuit. I cannot say the same of Thomas. Though effective enough, his performance was grossly overdone. He bawled out "It is the Holy Virgin!" at such intemperate volume that if the Mother of Jesus had truly been present she would have betaken herself back to Heaven with great speed and given up this business of visions for good.

On returning to *Au Renard de Tel*, I hastily changed back into my own clothes and descended to the taproom just in time to meet the miraculously cured Thomas and his cohort of wonder-struck yokels. Mistress Mathilde and I, being the sole members of the company not to have witnessed the miracle, were treated to a detailed description of the events and thus it behoved us to receive the news with proper expressions of wonder and awe. I believe we both accomplished this well—with much opening of mouths, widening of eyes and exclamations such as *Déa!* and *Vechy merveilles!*

Now it is well known that fame engenders rivalry. The story that Thomas related in the taproom of *Au Renard de Tel*, though undoubtedly miraculous, was a plain tale plainly told. However, no sooner had he reached the point at which the Blessed Virgin made her remarkable entrance than the platoon of halfwits who crowded about him must add their groatsworth. It was not enough that Christ's Mother was clad in shimmering white—a great tribute to Mathilde's laundering—but now She also glowed with a heavenly radiance. Was there not, said one worthy, the sound of celestial trumpets? Were they all so senseless, added another with some indignation, that they had not smelled the sweet fragrance that emanated from Her person? Another swore blind that She had smiled upon them all and uttered the words "Peace be with you" in tones of unsurpassed beauty. A stunted little rascal with a hare lip who proved to be the village smith—he of the idiot son—shouted out that She had ascended into heaven on a fiery cloud and that he would box the ears of any who said different.

All of this afforded me much amusement. In fact, I would gladly have burst out laughing but to have done so would have been most imprudent for so transported were they that any display of mirth would have gone badly for me. Be that as it may, I did have to bite my tongue when it came to the miraculous healing of Thomas's foot. It seemed that the good Virgin had not only exorcized my host's pedal demon but had also cured the miller's toothache, the cobbler's warts, the ditcher's nosebleeds and a husbandman's backache. For good measure, She had also mended the blacksmith's hare lip and, though it was still there for all to see, nobody was sufficiently foolhardy to gainsay it.

It was only the priest who remained aloof from all of this.

Now many is the time I have sat in some tavern or other, enjoying good fellowship and conversing over a jug of wine, and the talk has turned to...masonry, *per exemplum*. In faith, I cannot recall ever talking about masonry but I know full well that, if I had and there had been a mason present, he would have been quick to add his words to ours. Even Bardolph, who mistakenly prided himself on his fine singing voice, never hesitated to offer an opinion—and even, God help us, a demonstration—if music was the subject of discussion. In view of this, you would have thought that Father Luc might have had a deal to say on the subject of miracles—especially when one had just taken place in his own churchyard. You would have thought that at least some trace of excitement might have troubled his pinched features.

Not so. He hung back from the throng and listened to their din in silence. When asked to confirm this or that, he would smile and nod as though he were enduring the prattle of children and bore the look of one who is turning events over and over in his mind. At one point I caught him staring at me through narrowed eyes, though at the time I thought little of it.

That such a man should presume to lead his flock to Heaven and yet scorn the evidence before him! And many, I am sure, are the tedious sermons he has given on the falseness of Goodman Thomas who denied the truth of our Lord's resurrection. By so much are your priests hypocrites!

It was later, when I had retired to bed and was sleeping the sleep of the just, that I was awoken by Host Thomas who was shaking me rudely.

Now as a rule I am not in the best of humours when awoken thus and, I must confess, I berated Thomas severely. However, at length the reason for his anxiety became manifest.

It seems good Father Luc had just quitted *Au Renard de Tel* and before taking his leave of Thomas had told him that, in his opinion, I was not what I appeared and that ill-fortune would attend my continued stay in Saint Just. Moreover, he had said that before taking the cloth he had travelled widely and visited the Low Countries and that I sounded less like a Dutchman than any he had met. I seemed—so he said—more like an Englishman, both in my speech and in my mode of dress. I might, therefore, be a spy in the pay of *Henri d'Angleterre*.

Exactly what an English spy might usefully accomplish in such a toe-end of the world as Saint Just en Tel, Father Luc did not see fit to divulge. Nevertheless, he did say that on the morrow he would hie him to Clermont and request a magistrate to have me arrested.

Now though Thomas had no great love for the English—excepting perhaps as potential customers—he was yet reluctant to show ingratitude to one who had helped him.

"I shall help you flee, Messire van Staf," said he, with the utmost sadness.

"Then I shall be in your debt," said I.

"Not so," said he, unhappily. "For this day am I in yours."

I needed a horse and Thomas got me one. When I was comfortably saddled, it came to me that Thomas might be prevailed upon to further subsidise my pilgrimage. I therefore demanded money of him.

It grieves me to have to write that he seemed a little disinclined to accede to this demand and so I reminded him that if I were taken by the magistrate and his men, I would surely be put to the question and, being a man advanced in years, the answer I might give could well include my counterfeiting of the Virgin Mary. Thomas produced two *livres*. When I added that he would then be tried for the sins of blasphemy and sacrilege, he produced a third, together with a leg of cold pork and wine for my bottle.

A pox on all your tradesmen! For them, the giving of a *denier* is like the squandering of the king's exchequer.

Yet I was content with this transaction and, after commending myself to Thomas's good wife and wishing him a long life and much profit thereby, I cantered off down the street and out of Saint Just en Tel.

I shall now betake me to my bed for I can no longer see clearly and am grievous fatigued.

At Paris

On a Sunday, being the twentieth day of October.

I have been here in Paris since yesterday evening, having ridden in a single day from Senlis where I stayed on Friday last. I am lodged in the Rue Saint Bon at the sign of the *Coq Hardi*, which means Brave Cock.

Now your French set great store by their cocks. Marry, for them your cock is like unto your *fleur de lys*, so much is it the emblem of their nation. For myself, I cannot see why a cock should be braver than any other beast, and your lion or your ramping leopard, or belike even your African elephant, are certainly more endowed with valour than your farmyard chicken. Notwithstanding, your Frenchman, when he becomes excited—which, as far as I can see, happens many times a day—is wont to shout out "Cocorico!" in imitation of this fowl.

However much your Frenchman esteems the bravery of his cock, he is happily not averse to killing and eating it.

The *Coq Hardi* is a small hostelry and yet clean. It is held by a certain Gilles who has a lean, pale, rat-like face with eyes of the blackness of coals.

Gilles has little time for his guests for it is quite clear that he likes not at all their constant interference in his affairs. On asking my name and whence I came, he did me the courtesy of fixing me with a stony stare, and when I gave him my customary answer he merely grunted impatiently and shouted to his wife to show me to the upper room. Since then he has shouted a great deal—most of all at his wife who screeches back at him like a cat hanged by the tail—and, albeit to a lesser extent, at his guests, if he must call them to table or to pay their reckonings. As this is France, his guests shout back at him in like wise, which makes the Brave Cock the noisiest hostelry that ever I slept in—the Boar's Head not excepted.

The upper room has four beds in which seven people are now sleeping—counting myself among them. However, by paying double, I have secured my own bed and an arras that I can pull closed to give me some small privacy. I like not this business of paying double, yet I am a man of some comfortable girth and the beds are narrow and I would risk smothering a bedfellow if I turned over too violently. Add to which, a gentleman should be ready to pay double if he must—more's the pity.

I was much impressed when I first set eyes on Paris yesterday. I had mounted to the top of a low hill near the village of Mont Martyr and there lay the city beneath me, swathed in autumn mists, with the two lofty towers of its great cathedral thrusting upwards through the murk. The River Seine, on which it lies, is a mighty flood, almost as wide as the Thames, and when it nears the cathedral, it splits in twain, creating an island on which much of the city is built. From such a distance Paris resembles an immense ship ploughing through the swift waters under twin sails and towing behind it a smaller craft—that being a lesser and deserted island called the Isle of Saint Lewis. I counted no less than five bridges spanning the river.

I entered the town through a massive gate and was struck dumb with amazement—or would have been had I been speaking—at the loftiness of the houses that surrounded me. On the street leading from this gate to the centre of the city, which is called Saint Martin's Lane, there was a house with *seven* floors, each built separately upon that below. I counted them one by one. This is all very fine and, like as not, will inspire awe in all but the most phlegmatic of dispositions, and yet I could not help wondering what manner of fool might wish to live upon the seventh floor. For myself, if upper rooms could be had upon the ground floor, I would be well pleased.

As I neared the river, and thus the middle of the town, I was further amazed by the bustle and noise, which is such that would put London to shame. In faith, every day in Paris is a very Bartholomew's Fair. There is such a din of horses and carts, babies bawling, children screaming, bells ringing and dogs barking, not to mention the various bellowings of hawkers and street-criers, that you must shout doubly loud if you are to be heard at all. As all Parisians are constrained to do so—and indeed would do so were they constrained or not—the resulting row more resembles Babel than any sane man could imagine.

I pity the poor peasant who ventures hither. If he is not immediately rendered deaf by the uproar, he will surely lose his way before he has come a bowshot through the gates and then, being lost, it will be no easy matter to procure directions, for Paris is awash with foreigners of all nations and you may walk through certain lanes without hearing a word of French. In all my years in London, I never saw so many folk of divers lands in one place: Turks, Moors, Ethiopians, Italians, Greeks, Spaniards, Germans, and even those of Tartary and Ind.

This morning I sold my horse. I got a *livre* for him and was glad of it for I have seen week-old haddock with more spirit and intelligence than that creature possessed.

With my *livre* in my purse, I repaired to a stew[38] in Saint Denis's Lane and spent eight *denier* on a bath and another two on the hire of a towel. Feeling much refreshed thereby, I then spent another eighteen *denier* on a whore.

This whore was Marie by name. When I took my leave of her, she said that I might return whenever I wished and that, were all the men in Paris blessed with my skill and vigour, gentlewomen too would turn whore and maidenheads be as rare as Colchester pearls. Her words were something to that effect anyway. I do not remember Colchester actually coming into it.

I have just eaten a fine supper at the *Coq Hardi*. And so it should have been after the deal of shouting and squabbling that went into its making. First I had turnip soup, then a pastry, then a dish of fish that Gilles grimaced at and called *gardon*, then roasted capon, then another pastry, then a dish of thrushes, then a roasted leg of mutton and finally, to end the meal, another pastry. I drank wine from Poitou, which is a melancholy red of hue though it dried out the turnip soup wonderfully.

I think I may well stay in Paris for several months before proceeding to the shrine of Saint James, or the Holy Land. Belike there is much money to be made in such a city and the open road is grim enough without adding poverty to its hardships.

I see that my cup is empty. I shall descend to the taproom to replenish it.

At Paris

On a Tuesday, being the twenty-second day of October.

Today has brought momentous happenings that will assure my future in this town. More of that anon for I have other matters to report.

You cannot go anywhere in Paris without hearing talk of *les Anglois* and *Henri d'Angleterre*. In faith, it sometimes seems that Hal is held in greater respect here than is Charles of France, for the Parisians talk of their own king with open contempt and any news of the movement of the English host is greeted with the greatest interest.

Hal's army is sadly depleted through sickness and hunger, and yet he has made swift progress for all that. Towards the end of last week, he passed by Amiens and on Saturday he crossed the River Somme, having been prevented from doing so for several days. Indeed, he was constrained to follow the river almost to its source and has thus extended his journey to Calais by several leagues.

The latest news is but a day old and I cannot vouch for its surety for I had it of a *talemelier*, or baker, who was taking his ease in the *Coq Hardi* and your bakers are at best a race of rumourmongers and are not to be believed sober let alone drunk. The intelligence is thus: The Dukes of Orléans and Bourbon have sent heralds to Hal telling him that their lordships are resolved to do battle with him before he reaches Calais. This bodes ill. With his army whole and in good order, Hal could thrash the French were they to outnumber him fifty to one. In fact, if I were there at his side to counsel him on tactics and stiffen his courage, there is not an army in the world could overmaster him. It is just like your kings to banish those who can help them most.

As I see it, Hal has but one advantage and that lies in the stupidity of his foe. The French yet think that being full of fire and dash is the way to win battles and they shun the longbow as a peasant's weapon. Now Harry Hotspur was fuller of fire and dash than any boy you could imagine, and much good did it do him.

I wrote at the beginning of this day's entry that there have been momentous happenings afoot and so, indeed, there have been.

This morning I awoke in an ill humour. The source of this distemperature was a certain tapster, Guillaume by name, who cornered me in the taproom when I descended thither yesterday night and forced me to drink the healths of the Duke of Burgundy and sundry others, including—if I remember right—

ourselves. This I was constrained to do copiously for it is Guillaume's opinion that a health should be drunk with no less than a gill and no more than a quart. Thus, being men of brave mettle, we drank quarts and remained thus for many a long hour and waxed right merry. Between healths, Guillaume regaled me with the history of his family, which, unsurprisingly, is of Burgundian provenance and, like the centipede, has many members.

It was my fortune to be rescued from this sorry predicament by the unexpected arrival of my Host Gilles who—he and his good wife having had their sleep disturbed by our carousing—was of a somewhat choleric humour and cuffed Guillaume soundly around the pate whilst loosing upon him such a stream of unintelligible invective as would have taken a cloister-full of monks ten years to decipher. As he did not so much as acknowledge my presence in the taproom, I left that place as hurriedly as I might, sought out my bed and fell fast asleep.

Therein lies the explanation for my ill humour.

Thus, this morning, after having breakfasted lightly on bread, salted herring, *coloppes*[39], cheese and ale, I ventured forth with an unpleasant queasiness of the bowels and a numbing pain in my head.

Now when you are thus afflicted, the narrow and bustling streets of Paris are not the best places to frequent. Being a man of some slight physical abundance and one who generally prefers to saunter rather than scurry, I was often jostled and rudely pushed aside, which did my bowels no good at all. The incessant clamour did little better for my head.

Within the space of no more than an hour, I had developed an ardent dislike of Parisians and since then I must confess that a certain amount of this disaffection has remained with me. Your Parisian is grievously uncouth towards his fellow citizens, but his most unmannerly behaviour is reserved for strangers, to whom he displays the greatest arrogance imaginable. This appears to stem from a belief that all that is best in this world is not only to be found within the walls of Paris but actually originates therein. Thus when I introduce myself as Jan van Staf and say that I am come from Antwerp town, this news is greeted with the utmost indifference. Indeed, such is their singular incuriosity that if I claimed to be a second cousin to the Man In The Moon and had arrived here by way of Samarkand my interlocutor would doubtless pick his nose and complain about the price of bacon.

Also your Parisian stinks most abominably. Now I have yet to meet a Frenchman who did not stink somewhat but it takes a true Parisian to refine this art to the point it has now attained. It is as if he has profited from this most cosmopolitan of cities by taking all the various and lesser stinks from other countries and distilled from them a quintessence of fetor with which he anoints himself daily. Those who do not stink *au nature*, blend their malodour with sundry perfumes that the combination thereof may lend them some distinction. In such a wise does your Parisian show his mastery over we lesser men.

Your Parisian is most particular in the manner of his dress. In faith, I have not seen so many popinjays since the second Richard's day. It must be said that the women do attire themselves with adequate modesty but the young men favour fashions that bode ill for their manliness. They array themselves in tight-fitting surcoats that end just above the codpiece, the size and shape of this outward projection being further accentuated by their hose, which cling to the legs like snow to a mountaintop. And the colours! None is eschewed. When I was a young man, which is not so very long ago, green was thought to signify an overly amorous disposition and its wearer risked being laughed to scorn on its account. A rogue who clothed himself in yellow did so to advertise his bellicosity and must possess both strength and martial skills, for all his fellows would gladly see just how bellicose he was prepared to be.

Yet it was not so much the noise or the stinks or the sight of such parti-coloured coxcombs that turned my distemper to ire. It was the reckonings.

I had not been jostled so very far from the door of the Brave Cock when, on a sudden, I was overtaken by a most grievous thirst. I therefore entered in at a tavern and bespoke two cups of wine. Now your cup is a wondrous implement for it can be as small or as big as the landlord wishes. If he likes not your company or desires to close his doors and repair to bed, you can be sure that a cup will be the size of a child's thimble. If you are favoured, or the landlord, God help him, is an honest man, it will hold a pint or more. I therefore thought myself more than favoured when the two cups set before me were the size of episcopal chalices and as, with much happiness, I contemplated a good half-hogshead of wine I wondered greatly that the landlord should be so honest and generous with a mere stranger.

Now I have not space nor energy enough to rant about the quality of this wine. Suffice to say, I have poured better liquor over a salmagundy and two draughts sent me scurrying to the jakes. Nonetheless, thinking that this beverage might be usual in your Parisian tavern, I quaffed it to the lees and demanded my reckoning quickly in case the landlord might feel yet more generous. He demanded ten *denier* of me! Elsewhere in France you may purchase five cups for that price! If I had wanted five cups, I would have bespoken five cups! Nor did it help my humour to see other drinkers sitting before common-sized goblets whilst I, mooncalf that I was, was outfaced by two mighty vessels the size of milk-buckets.

"Ten *denier* seems a high price to pay for two cups of wine," said I to the landlord in a low growl.

"They are big cups, messire," said he evenly.

"And yet I did not order *big* cups," said I.

"Ah, but you did not order *small* ones, messire," said he.

To this logic I could make little answer. Had I been in Eastcheap I would have boxed the rogue's ears and jammed one of his cups on his head but I had no wish to explain myself to a French magistrate and risk being hanged as a spy for my trouble and so I contented myself by slamming ten *denier* down upon the board and giving the landlord such a glare as would have made a basilisk retire to the country and take up knitting.

And yet this landlord was no more roguish than the rest of them. I visited several taverns this morning and all their proprietors played similar tricks.

At length my wanderings brought me onto the island on which the cathedral sits—which island is called the Isle of the City. The cathedral is called The Church of Our Lady of Paris, and I doubt not that the Parisians believe that the Mother of Our Lord was born thereabouts and that Her Son was crucified on the Buttes of Mont Martyr by a troop of Roman soldiers from Boulogne.

Before this great house extends a wide, open place which I now know to be called the *Parvis* of Our Lady. I stood on this parvis and regarded the cathedral with baleful eye. But it is surely an awesome spectacle for its two towers reach up to the clouds above and it has three great doors around which saints and martyrs and a vision of the Last Judgement are cunningly worked in stone, and I was much moved in spite of my ill humour.

The parvis was abustle with folk entering and leaving the cathedral and attempting to sell various tawdry wares. Your Parisians are forever hastening to do this or that but with very little visible result. Witnessing such confusion once more set me to bemoaning the costliness of Paris and I wondered greatly as to whence a poor pilgrim might derive some honest money to compensate for his expenditure.

Occupied as I was with these and other thoughts, I found that the throng had carried me within the doors of the cathedral without my really knowing it. A service was in progress but the voice of the cleric, whom I could not see, was all but lost in an echoing cacophony of shouting, singing and chattering.

Now, to my shame, I cannot say that my three-score years and ten have brought me within the doors of many churches and cathedrals. But, drawing on what little experience I have, I can say that, when empty they are silent, and when full, they are the noisiest places in creation. It is little wonder to me that prayers to the saints are so seldom answered for I doubt very much that they are even heard.

In this respect, the Church of Our Lady of Paris is the worst I have seen. If you had told me it was Manningtree Fair with buttresses I would have believed it. There were even men and women selling cakes and wine therein—and doing good trade too.

I sauntered about and looked upon the coloured glass and gazed up and down the graceful columns, and then fatigue and boredom got the better of me and I bought a cup of wine for four *denier* and sat me down at the base of a pillar to drink it.

It was as I thus refreshed myself that I heard a sobbing. There was a young girl crouching next to me whom I had not noticed before. She had long, black hair straggling down her back and was clad in a woollen shift that was tied about her waist with hempen rope. As I am not one to let maidenhood weep unconsoled, I shook off my ill humour and laid my hand upon her shoulder, at which she started and looked upon me with fearful eye. I bestowed a kindly smile upon her.

I judged her to be about seventeen or eighteen and, in faith, on this subject I am none the wiser yet for she has no idea how old she is herself. A peasant girl, to be sure, but blessed with a fineness of feature rare in those of her condition. Wild eyes of softest umber. Pale skin as smooth as vellum.

It was I who broke the silence.

"What ails you, lass?" I asked. "Can an old man be of some comfort?"

She sniffed a little and wiped her nose upon her sleeve and then cast herself into a garbled narrative of the events that had led her to her present misery.

Truth to tell, so garbled was it that I understood but few of the details, yet the main points I comprehended easily enough, for indeed her history is an old one.

Her name is Jeanne and she is eldest daughter to a poor villein called Mathieu. Her family live out a squalid and miserable life on the estate of a Robert de Ligny, a vassal of the Duke of Bar. This Robert has a son, Thomas by name, who, being a lusty country lad and heir to his father's lands, deemed it meet to increase the yield thereof by casting his seed far and wide. Having seen in the comely Jeanne a pasture worth the dibbling in, he ploughed and harrowed her well and, in truth, she proved most fertile. At length, harvest tide came round and Jeanne was delivered of a baby boy. But Thomas is a poor husbandman who declines to reap what he sows, preferring to give his harvest to an old serf of the village. Unwilling to ally herself thus to villainous decrepitude or to become a further burden on her hard-pressed family, Jeanne anointed her child with salt and honey, wrapped it in clean linen, bestowed on it a farewell kiss and stole from her father's house by dead of night. Having walked barefoot to Paris, she looked for work but found none and thought herself destined for the town's end to beg her life away.

I was much touched by her story. Lord, Lord, how easy it is for base lechery to corrupt the innocent!

I determined to give her such assistance as lay in my power for it is through works of Christian Charity that even the blackest sinner may receive redemption. I therefore took her by the hand and raised her to her feet. I could see that young Thomas had not broadcast his seed so very indiscriminately for she was straight and firm of limb with ample breasts and sinuous hips.

Although I could well see that her first necessity was nourishment, I must confess here that I had scant inclination to sit at table with one who most resembled a dispossessed shepherdess, and a passing filthy one at that. I took her to a seamstress where I bought for her a *cotehardie*[40] of pale blue stuff and had her wash her face and hands and had the seamstress comb her hair. This accomplished, Jeanne looked as comely a lass as ever broke hearts and attracted many an admiring glance as we wended our way back to the *Coq Hardi*.

On the way, we stopped to buy divers foodstuffs, which set poor Jeanne all agog with anticipation, and, when we reached the Brave Cock, I instructed Host Gilles to have them cooked and served. I expected some ado from him about the lateness of the hour—it being almost nones—but, to my surprise, there was none. Nay, he acceded most readily and lavished much attention on us, and upon Jeanne in particular, and served us himself with sweetmeats and wine until his good wife began to rail at him, at which he disappeared into the taproom.

We dined on capon, pastries, salted venison, roasted beef and cheese, with wine of Guyenne. It was clear that Jeanne had never eaten or drunk so well. Truth to say, her manners were not the prettiest for there was much smacking of chops and dropping of crumbs here and there and she largely disdained the use of the knife, preferring to rip and rend with her fingers.

Our dinner done, I bespoke another jug of Guyenne wine and we took our ease before the fire. Drawing closer to me, Jeanne declared that she had never dreamt that there was such fine food extant and that at home she was rarely allowed wine at all.

That she had had so little commerce with wine occasioned me some wonder for she quaffed it off as if she was elder daughter to a brace of tapsters. In the meantime, she sustained an unremitting flow of chatter, which I took to be a detailed account of her journey to Paris though it could just as well have been a commentary on the Third Punic War for all I understood of it.

It was as she babbled thus that Jeanne began to wax amorous. Now, as a rule, you need not serve me with a declaration indited thrice by a clerk-at-law before I know that womenfolk have designs upon me. Yet, when Jeanne rested her head upon my shoulder and traced patterns with her fingers up and down my arm, I thought but little of it. It was only when she began to nuzzle my ear that I could plot the true course of her intentions, which were made clear beyond doubt when she set her hand in a very particular place and gently squeezed what she found there.

Old as I may be, my sinews need little stiffening and I do not shrink from a hard encounter. I stood full fairly and led Jeanne upstairs where she showed me her gratitude in a woman's tender wise.

It is when the body's lusts are sated that the spirit may fly free and roam about at will. Thus, as I lay beside my sweetheart, that natural inventiveness and ingenuity that set Jack Falstaff aside from the common roll of men swiftly contrived a solution to the major problem besetting poor Jeanne and myself.

The said problem could be distilled to a single essence: coin.

Now your common artisan, possessed of a skill or trade coveted by others, rarely lacks a florin or two. He may travel from Land's End to John O' Groats and always find someone in need of his services. Jeanne is unlettered and ill-bred, yet she does have one indisputable talent that can be turned to our advantage, for in the commerce that we had lately concluded she had displayed surprising skills and natural aptitude. Furthermore, she seemed to have derived the greatest satisfaction from her labours, which is a rare thing in even the most dedicated of craftsmen. Thus did I propose that henceforth she do for profit what she had just done for pleasure.

For all her beauty, which none but the blind could deny, Jeanne is a trifle slow of wit. It was some time before the full import of my words broke upon her.

"You mean whoring?" she said, eyeing me mischievously.

She then lay staring at the opposing wall and biting her fingernails.

"And I shall be well paid for this?" said she, regarding her finger-ends.

"Very well paid," said I. "That which young Thomas de Ligny sampled *gratis* will henceforth be dearly purchased."

At this Jeanne gave a long sigh and put her hand in mine.

"It is a sin," said she. "A mortal sin and I shall pay for it when I die."

"But many men will pay for it before that," said I. "And have you forgot the blessed Mary Magdalene, well-beloved of Our Lord? The Kingdom of Heaven was not denied to *her*! Yet those who squander their God-given talents are damned for all eternity."

She needed little more convincing, although she did express doubts regarding a sufficiency of clients. I told her to have no fears on that account for I would charge myself with finding her work in plenty. Not only that, I should also entrust myself with the protection of all monies so earned, to keep them safe from the depredations of dishonest customers.

Though I may be called immodest for setting it down here, I must state in all fairness to myself that I was as good as my word for, as I sit here writing in a calmer corner of the taproom, Jeanne is entertaining a wine-merchant of Poitou and my purse is five *sous* the heavier. After supper I shall find her further clients if I be not too fatigued. For the moment, the merchant of Poitou has been with her for two pages of my daybook and that, I think, is quite enough.

My ill humour of this morning is now quite dissipated. I may yet leave France a rich man. God's wounds, if I become rich, I may never leave France at all. *Ubi bene, ibi patria.*[41] Marry and amen.

At Paris

On Saint Crispin's Eve.
(Thursday 24th October 1415)

My purse waxes fatter *sed surgit amari aliquid*.[42] Since Tuesday last, Jeanne has earned four *livres* and two *sous*, being her fee for services rendered to ten gentlemen. As I write, she is busy with an eleventh. Four *livres* and two *sous* is six hundred *denier*, which is as much as your common labourer earns in a half-year. If I were a woman, I would have done this long ago for in what other trade may you make such a fortune without so much as leaving your bed?

Yet there's the rub indeed. I am the one who runs hither and thither, searching out new customers, arguing terms and conditions, cavilling on every *denier* and fawning worse than a pampered lap-dog. I am the one who must guard the money with the heavy cares that brings. God forfend that I should judge my partner at less than her value but if to lie abed and foin[43] from dawn to midnight be work then may God heap all the labours of Hercules on me.

I stagger to bed at I know not what o'clock, bated and unfleshed. Yet, when I then claim of her my due—being no less than she bestows upon any man who labours less than I—she says that she is too much fatigued or that she is smitten with a headache, and I am constrained to lie by her side like a stuffed bolster while she snores the night away. And when, come morning, I lay hold of her and would enjoy her, she pushes me from her saying it were a pity to waste her vital energies in providing *gratis* what other men must pay for.

Thus is my generosity rewarded! My own words tossed carelessly back at me!

I have neither the stomach nor the force to write for long this night. I have bespoken another pint of Aunis wine and I shall drink it in peace.

At Paris

On the twenty-sixth day of October, being a Saturday.

> O glorious day! O righteous victory!
> *Hal has thrashed the Frankish king.*
> *Loud sing cuckoo!*
> *The Duke of Bar is dead, ha ha!*
> *And the Golden Udder too!*

Stout-hearted Harry! Brave lads! Saint Crispin's Day has seen such a battle as men will speak of a hundred years hence. Nay, a thousand! Not since Thermopylae, when young Alexander[44] pushed back the Persian hordes,[45] has such a feat of arms been seen! After marching clear across the country, and in foul weather too, he gave battle to the proudest knights of France, together with their host of a hundred and fifty thousand men-at-arms[46] and brought them low upon the field of Azincourt.

It is said here that the English arrows obscured the sun and turned day into night and that at their first volley ten thousand men perished beneath their points. Would I had been there! It would have been rare sport.

Yet Destiny ordained that I be here in Paris town and it is a foolish man who rails against Destiny. In faith, I was not needed—there's the truth on it. It is when the battle is hard fought and victory stands doubtful, when the enemy's pikes are nudging your belly and the earth reeks of your comrades' blood, when you are outflanked and outnumbered, your energy spent and your sword hacked in splinters—it is then that you cry out for Jack Falstaff! What need is there of me when you can pick off fourscore French knights as easily as rabbits on Hampstead Heath?

Were I in London now, I should be drinking Harry's health and were he to have such health as I would drink, he would not so much as sneeze for the rest of his life. There'll be merry times in Eastcheap this night, I'll be bound. Alone as I am in Paris, I can but rejoice on paper.

I had thought the Parisians greatly disaffected but they have greeted Hals's success with gloom and despair. I have witnessed men and women weeping in the streets and the churches are so full of folk you would think the pestilence was upon us. Those who do not openly lament or implore God's mercy and forgiveness seem numbed with shock and go about their work as if bereft of wits. It little behoves me to throw up my pilgrim's hat and lose myself in revelry.

Shall I ever return to Eastcheap? If Pistol has survived this encounter—and like as not he has for a more egregious coward never took to his heels—then belike the answer is no for he will be sure to amplify his exploits till, to hear him boast, Agamemnon, Ajax and Achilles, if smelted together, would not comprise even half his own mettle. I could not brook that. As for Nym and Bardolph, if they are safe it is by dint of hiding in the baggage train and if they are not it is because they have danced for the hangman. Their necks were ever of a thickness.

Enough. There is a young rogue above who is too eager in his foinings. I must ascend and demand further payment.

At Paris

On Hallowmas Eve.
(Thursday 31st October 1415)

It is All Hallow's Eve. This day has seen many a foul deed wrought by the legions of pixies and hobgoblins who roam about at will but few of such demonic intent as that committed by my sometime host Gilles and his beldame. God's blood! Had the wickedest hag in Hell galloped down the Rue Saint Bon on her pitch-black stallion, she could not have done worse.

We have been evicted.

It happened this morning when we descended for breakfast.

I thought Host Gilles was of a surlier mien than usual and as he served us I could see his wife peering round the door of the kitchen. I smiled and waved to her, at which she vanished instantly. Yet so innocent was I of her intent that I paid this no heed and fell to eating, for sleep had given me a grievous appetite. It was only when the meal was finished and I had bespoken another jug of wine and Gilles had brought it to me as if he would fain have kept it in the barrel that I marked that something was amiss. Not being one to waste time in idle dalliance, I asked him what the matter was.

Now you would have thought that I had asked him to sign a pact with the Devil himself and send a copy to the Almighty, for he drew back as if bitten and I think he would have withdrawn to the kitchen there and then had not his wife called out his name in a tone that brooked no disregard. I cannot recall ever seeing such abject pusillanimity. It is no wonder the French were discomfited at Azincourt. Give your Frenchman some small authority and he becomes a very tyrant, but set his wife at his heels and he scurries away like a dormouse from a Roman legion.

It was thus at the prompting of his good wife that Gilles delivered himself of a lengthy monologue, which, he being too much the coward to look me in the eye, he addressed to the jug of wine. To tell the truth, his speech was so beset with hesitations and equivocations that I would not waste good ink in setting it down here but the nub of it appeared to be that since its arrival in the Bold Cock, together with its paramour, the jug had besmirched the reputation of the hostelry and word was around the neighbourhood that the inn had turned leaping-house. It was thus, said he, with regret that he must demand that the aforesaid jug and the paramour of the aforesaid jug quit his establishment forthwith.

Having delivered himself of this, Host Gilles regarded the jug most earnestly and I noted that his ears—which enclose his rodent features like great parentheses—turned a becoming shade of pink. The jug, being a jug, said nothing.

Yet silence, though it is every freeman's right, is no particular defence, and so I leapt to fill the breach. I also leapt at Gilles but the table came between us and I sprawled across it in a most unlawyerly manner, so causing the unfortunate and knavishly maligned jug to hop to safety on the floor where, being a container of a somewhat delicate constitution, it broke.

I was now full of ire. I bellowed at our host with such magnitude that his liver mounted to his face while his ears turned the colour of beetroot. I called him a whoreson rogue and much else besides, some of which was quite extempore and not found in the common canon of curses, be it English or French. Finally, having exhausted empty epithets, I turned to particulars and told him roundly that the Devil—and here I looked pointedly at his wife who yet skulked at the kitchen door—had put evil thoughts in his mind.

"If an honest, virtuous woman of spotless reputation cannot entertain a few gentleman friends in privacy without idle tongues accusing her of whoring then honour and decency are become rare commodities indeed," I growled. "And the world a very haven of iniquity!"

This he seemed to accept for he nodded profusely though I dare say that he understood not a word. By this time, his good wife had sortied from the kitchen and stood behind her spouse with arms folded and a look upon her visage that boded ill for any attempt at re-establishing myself in the Bold Cock. I saw that it behoved me to accept defeat with a good grace.

"My good Host Gilles," I said, in a righteous tone. "It grieves me greatly to hear that your fine inn has turned bawdy-house. You are an honest fellow and a true and therefore I know that you will understand that my lady wife and I can no longer reside beneath your roof lest our good reputations be compromised."

At this, Gilles' wife gave such a snort that brought to mind one of Justice Shallow's sows. It is curious how such irrelevancies come upon one.

And so I paid our reckoning, which was surprisingly modest, and Jeanne and I gathered our few belongings from our room and took our leave of Host Gilles and his wife. All might then have ended amicably had I not, in parting, observed to Gilles that if he truly wished to run a leaping-house he had best set a dish of prunes in the window. This caused his wife to let out a screech followed by a torrent of low French. She also attempted to strike me but this without success for Jeanne—who had hitherto played no great part in our eviction—grasped her by the arms. They began to wrestle. This was most excellent sport and I would gladly have watched them grapple for the rest of the morning and perhaps have made a small wager to boot, yet Gilles, forever fearful for the good reputation of his tavern, which seemed now beyond redemption, did not wish to see his wife a-brawling in the street and stepped between them, fetching Jeanne a sound slap across the chops.

Now to strike a woman is a most cowardly thing for they are the weaker sex and cannot return the blow in equal measure. I therefore returned it on her behalf.

Once Gilles had picked himself up, he leapt at me furiously and let fly such a murderous blow that, had it ever connected with my chin, might well have accomplished what rebel pike and hangman's knot have so far failed to do. Happily, like most Frenchmen, he is small of stature and unused to buffetings of this sort. For myself, I am of an Englishman's height and of two or three Englishmen's girth and have seen more buffetings than a billy goat. The sum of these qualities was that Gilles' clumsy attempt at beheading me did not so much as tickle my beard.

A further advantage of having two or three Englishmen beneath one's belt lies in what you might call the "circumferential variability" that mere breathing allows. In this particular, with Gilles in intimate proximity to my navel, it took no more than a short, violent exhalation to propel him a lance's length into the kennel. For a few perilous moments he teetered wildly on the brink, his feet slipping and sliding in the slime, and then, with the lumpish inevitability of a log falling off a cart, he sploshed backwards into the ooze and offal.

This brought much laughter from the onlookers.

Perceiving his plight, Gilles's wife left off her wrestling and ran to assist her husband, yet the fight had quite gone out of him and he made no attempt to rise. Instead, he began bawling for the Watch and thus, discretion being the better part of valour, Jeanne and I pushed our way through the crowd and quitted the Rue Saint Bon.

It did not take us long to find new lodgings. In the short course of her dealings, Jeanne had discovered that most of her fellow tradeswomen are lodged in or about the Rue Saint Denis, which is to Paris what Cock's Lane is to London. I do not find that this said very much for the patron saint of France.

We duly found a private upstairs room at the sign of the *Flanchet d'Or* which the landlord was willing to let to us for the sum of four *sous* a day and no questions asked. According to Jeanne, a *flanchet* is a piece of beef cut from the lower belly of the beast. As this house is situated between the butchers' shops in the Rue de la Boucherie, or Shambles, and bearing in mind the other dominant profession of this neighbourhood, the name *Flanchet d'Or* couples both trades quite prettily.

Our room is clean enough and comfortable but the *Flanchet d'Or* has two disadvantages. Firstly there is the pervading stench of rotting meat. Yet you must expect this if you live in a shambles and what better *memento mori* can there be than to awaken every day to the stink of corrupting flesh? Secondly, despite its name, the *Flanchet d'Or* provides no food other than turnip soup, the odour of which vies with that of the rotting meat to curious effect. Naturally, this also means that, unless you are a great lover of turnip soup—which I am not—you must take all your meals in a tavern ordinary.

I note with sadness and contrition that my earlier intention of writing in this book every day has lapsed somewhat. Henceforth I shall discipline myself to do so.

At Paris

On Hallowmas Day.
(Friday 1st November 1415)

I have been drinking with some French this afternoon. Now the Lord knows, I do not commonly write down the histories of my drinkings and by-drinkings for, if I did, each day would take ten quires of paper, yet there is some value in giving an account of this afternoon's revelry if only to further illuminate the foolish ways of man.

In short, there is a moral to be drawn from this narrative. At the moment, I cannot think what it is. It may come to me anon.

It is my custom to eat my dinner late—at the hour of sexte or thereabouts. This I do because I rise late and breakfast late and since I do not wish to incur accusations of gluttony by starting the next repast straight after the first, I prefer to leave a decent interval of one or two hours in between.

Now in Paris it is only your commonalty who dine so late, whilst your nobility eat at about the fourth hour of the day,[47] directly after Mass. For all that I care not a fig for Mass, I do confess that it would better befit my station to dine at the earlier hour yet I am obliged to oversee Jeanne's business and the cares that that brings ensure that I do not retire to my bed until late. Once there, there is little for me to do but sleep. Such is my reward for my industry.

Thus today, at my usual hour, I repaired to a tavern ordinary in the Rue Saint Denis where, it being a Friday, I bespoke soup, boiled salted cod, a dish of pease and a pastry.

The ordinary was full of folk and I shared the board with seven others—idlers all, as I saw at a glance. I only learned the name of one of them—he being called Toussaint. As this is the day of All Saints, he made much noise about it being his name-day as though he expected some sort of culinary reward for this coincidence. He was attired with the utmost extravagance—like some peacock second son to a chamberlain—though he bore himself like a haberdasher and this in spite of the air of condescension with which he addressed those around him.

Next to him sat a rat-catcher who said little throughout, being more intent on stuffing as much food into his face as his cheeks would allow. It was no pretty sight. To his right was a pudding-faced ruffian who said even less for he spent most of the afternoon asleep with his cheek on his trencher.

Against him, at the end of the table sat a rogue of the greatest choler who stoked himself with wine and said naught but he shouted it. He reminded me of Pistol.

Then there was a pinch-faced little man in a liripipe hat whose speech, though considerably quieter, was scornful and sneering. He might have provided good sport for the rat-catcher if he could have multiplied himself by fifty.

Penultimate lounged as lascivious a whore as ever stole forth from Southwark.

Now I have had some small commerce with whores over the years and I have come to learn that most of them ply their trade because they can do naught else in life—or at least naught that brings such profit by so small an outlay. There are poor whores and rich whores—the richer tending to frequent the palace of Westminster—but the greater part of them have one thing in common: they are making a virtue of a necessity. Just as a shopkeeper will smile and fawn on you though he knows you not at all and, with open face, will declare that you and the hat or cloak you consider buying are made for each other though both garments were clearly made for someone else, so a whore will sell her body with enthusiasm and, if she knows her trade, will counterfeit the act of love with greater abandon than any housewife. But there you have it! All is counterfeit. Peer round her bedroom door an hour after you have left her and you will find her counterfeiting with someone else.

Not so the whore in this ordinary. I have seen physics with less sense of vocation. Come to that, *most* physics have less sense of vocation. She might well have been comely twenty years ago: her visage, worn into an unwelcoming sharpness, was yet fine of structure, her hips were well rounded and her breasts high, firm and disturbingly exposed. She had a smile for every man in the tavern and more than a smile for those who erred within her reach. Beneath the board, her bare feet made such pleasant and frequent contact with the legs of her fellow diners that I soon began to wonder just how many feet she had.

With all this in mind, I was greatly puzzled as to why she should reserve the greater part of her favours for the one eating-companion I have not yet mentioned. He was a beggarly rascal, clad in threadbare rags who had bespoken a dish of beans and a cup of pudding-ale and ate his beans as though they were stuffed peahen and quaffed his pudding-ale as if it were finest Malmsey. Judging by the glint in his eye, he enjoyed the whore's caresses as much as she enjoyed bestowing them but whenever she would whisper in his ear, belike to make some timely assignation, he would pull back and address himself to his legumes with the air of a man who has been asked to invest in transporting six ounces of gold-dust across the Irish Sea in an extremely rusty colander.

Each of the seven seemed to know the other well.

I had no commerce with them until the meal was done, whereupon Messire Toussaint, the putative haberdasher, invited me to join them in a cup of wine. Had I not been sitting at the same board, I doubt that this would have happened. Nor would it have happened had Messire Toussaint not been present, for, despite his proud and disdainful air, he was by far the most sociable of the group.

I introduced myself to the company.

"From Antwerp?" said Messire All Saints. "A fine town!"

"In truth!" bellowed Messire Choler. "A fine town! Blessed with goodly people!"

"I did not know you had been to Antwerp," said Messire All Saints to Messire Choler.

"I haven't," glowered Messire Choler. "Have you?"

"No," said Messire All Saints.

Having delivered themselves of this doubtful compliment, they promptly lost interest in me, which, as I have written before, is the way of most Parisians. Yet when my cup was empty, they refilled it quickly enough and, for an hour or two, their company was undemanding for they would only smile and nod at me, at which I smiled and nodded back, and once in a while one of them would say "Do you not agree, messire?", to which I would reply "Yea, verily!", or "What say you, messire?", to which I would reply "I believe that my opinion is fully congruent with your own." In truth I was not entirely sure about the word "congruent" and may have said "confluent" or possibly "fundament", but as they paid so little attention to my response anyway the question is superfluous.

After an hour or so, my interest in following the banalities of their discourse began to wane. The wine was good, it was raining without, and I had little inclination to walk back to the *Flanchet d'Or* where Jeanne would be fully occupied for most of the afternoon. Thus I fell into a pleasant reverie.

I was awoken by the words "Saint Just en Tel".

Now to tell the truth, I had been allowing the French language to waft about me like so much discordant music, but this arrangement of syllables instantly impressed itself upon my mind. I stuck both forefingers in my ears and gave them a goodly waggle to make sure the way was clear. The words "Saint Just en Tel" were repeated.

Perhaps there was more than one Saint Just en Tel. There is more than one Stratford. Yet my doubts were dispelled when I heard Father Luc mentioned in a tone of great respect and immediately I gave Messire Choler my full attention for it was he who was bellowing.

Saint Just en Tel, he announced, had been a village of no great importance—nothing more than a few hovels, a church and a small inn. Then, a mere two weeks ago, a miraculous visitation had taken place. The Blessed Virgin Mary and a host of angels and archangels had appeared to the villagers as they were quitting the church. The Virgin had spoken and said that France would suffer a grievous defeat at the hands of the bloodthirsty English but, through prayer and fasting, the country would ultimately be delivered out of the hands of *Henri d'Angleterre*. With that, she blessed the assembled villagers and ascended into Heaven on a fiery cloud whilst the host of angels, archangels, cherubim and seraphim sang psalms and scattered rose-petals, one of which, floating to the earth beside the church door, took root and, before the astonished eyes of these simple village folk, a rose-tree sprang up and blossomed. Not only that. The village innkeeper, who had been lame from birth, was miraculously cured as were others of divers afflictions. Since then, pilgrims had come from far away to worship at that church and even the Bishop of Beauvais had come to pray with the village priest, who was now an archdeacon. Lepers had been cured by rubbing their sores with leaves and petals from the rose-tree and no sooner was one plucked than another grew in its stead. In like wise, the blind had had their sight restored and the deaf their hearing.

Messire Choler delivered this information in a hushed voice, or at least as hushed as he could manage. The others, with the exceptions of the pudding-faced man who was snoring peacefully and the rat-catcher who would not be distracted from his second or third dish of eels, listened to him in silence with gaping mouths and wondering eyes.

I was glad that Host Thomas's foot had been cured. Had I known that he had suffered such an affliction from birth it might have saved us the trouble of counterfeiting it. On the other hand, it did not surprise me at all that Father Luc, who had cast such doubts on the veracity of the miracle and had chased me out of Saint Just, had successfully profited from the occasion by becoming an archdeacon and the praying-companion of a bishop.

I began to laugh. As I thought it wiser to keep my mouth closed, my laugh sounded more like a cough. Messire All Saints bestowed a concerned look upon me and patted me gently on the back, at which, despite anything I could do to prevent it, my laughter sprang forth—I threw back my head and roared.

The company transferred their gazes from Messire Choler to me. Even the rat-catcher glanced up from his dish of eels. Messire Choler himself grew red in the face.

"Why are you laughing, messire?" he roared. "Are you Heathen Turk?"

"I am laughing," I spluttered helplessly, "because I have not heard such tom-foolery since Twelfth Night last!"

"How so?" thundered Messire Choler.

"I shall tell you how, messire," said I, "if it please you."

Having composed myself a little, I related to them the true history of the Miracle At Saint Just En Tel, which I recounted in all particulars saving the reasons for my hurried departure thence. As my history unfolded, I could not help but mark that my revelations were greeted with something akin to amused disbelief. When I arrived at the conclusion of my tale, there was profound silence. Profound, that is, save for the slurping and chewing of the rat-catcher and the pleasing snores of the pudding-faced man. I looked about me with innocent eye. Six pairs of impenetrable eyes looked back.

My gaze lighted on Messire Choler whose face had now paled, comparatively speaking. I feared that he was about to do me injury.

"A *jest*!" he shouted. "A goodly pleasantry!"

And, breaking out in mirth, he slapped the board with such violence that the remains of the eels jumped a good six inches. The rat-catcher scowled at him and the pudding-faced man was jolted awake.

"A jest!" squeaked the scornful rodent at the end of the table.

"A Flemish jest!" cackled the ragged old man.

And with that, all seven of them began to laugh. Messire Choler roared heartily; the haberdasher tittered behind his hand; the rat in the liripipe hat snickered dryly; the whore squealed and gurgled whilst rubbing the thigh of the ragged old man who, not to be outdone, was cackling like a farmyard goose. The rat-catcher, who appeared not to have listened, managed a chuckle, and even the pudding-faced man chortled stupidly, although he clearly had no idea why.

My few protestations that the history was indeed true and not told in jest were greeted with even greater hilarity.

"They know a good pleasantry, these Flemish!" exclaimed the rat in the liripipe hat, between snickers.

"It's the way he tells it!" gurgled the whore.

"I know one worth three of that!" bawled Messire Choler. "Hearken here!"

And, with that, he embarked on the exceedingly lengthy story of a miller and his two daughters, which involved many an obscene gesticulation and must have been of a subtlety beyond compare for I understood not a jot of it.

Its conclusion was followed by much low sniggering and, sadly, was merely the prologue to a miscellany of jests and quips—some passably witty, most not—which occupied the remainder of the afternoon.

I have oftimes wondered that persons in want of wit should strive so hard to show it. I have also noted that wine in plenty will supply merriment when none is merited and so, my cup being never empty, I greeted the ensuing sallies of dullness with much laughter, which made the assembled company think me a fine fellow. Indeed, it was often said, during those long intervals that want of invention provides for the dull, that if all citizens of Antwerp shared my good humour, then that city must be a merry place indeed.

An hour or so ago I wrote that there was a moral to be drawn from this narrative though then I knew not what it was. Truth to say, I am none the wiser now.

It is right enough that I counterfeited the Blessed Virgin at Saint Just en Tel. But what of the miracles?

Host Thomas was not cured of his lameness for there was none to cure; of that I am certain. Likewise the fat bacons who crowded into *Au Renard de Tel* and claimed to be delivered from this or that were clear victims of their own gullibility and naught else. But what of those who came after?

Might I not have created a true shrine where true miracles are wrought? And if this be so, what of the other shrines? What of brave Thomas Beckett at Canterbury? Or the Blessed Virgin at Walsingham? What of Saint James at Compostella? Are they all the inventions of credulous minds?

If the Bishop of Beauvais took the trouble to pray in Saint Just, then there must be more there than rumour suggests, for the furthest I ever saw a bishop travel was square by square and obliquely.

Enough! This is dangerous ground for a man of my years. If one sip of wine be bitter to the taste, must the whole hogshead be thrown away? There is only one moral to be drawn and it is *oculis magis habenda fides quam auribus.*[48]

The wine I drank this afternoon must be adulterate for my head pains me greatly. I shall ascend to our chamber. Perhaps Jeanne will soothe it, though that I doubt.

At Paris

It is the hour before supper.

This afternoon I was about to enter in at a tavern in the Rue du Bourg l'Abbé—this being for the purpose of solicitation—when I met, going in, a raggedy rustic going out. Truth to say, he was going out headfirst and with some considerable celerity, and he struck me a glancing blow in the belly before he embraced the earth. Thus, for a moment, I thought I was attacked and drew my sword and would have spitted the rogue upon it had not my attention been diverted on that instant by the appearance of a second man, tall of stature and heavy of build, who, emerging from the tavern, delivered a mighty kick to the fellow on the ground and spat upon him and called him a son of a whore before turning about and re-entering the inn.

I divined that the second man was the proprietor of the tavern and that the fellow on the ground was an unwelcome customer and thus, since I have no great love of tavern-keepers who are, by and large, as mean-spirited a race of mongrels as ever drew breath, I sheathed my blade and went to the aid of the mishandled wretch.

He proved to be a certain Guillaume, William, a serf from Touraine.

Now it is little to the credit of your French kings that they continue to hold a sizeable proportion of their subjects in bondage. True, there are villeins extant in England too but they are precious few when taken against the general population, and it is mostly your churchmen who keep to this practice of serfdom, for they have much need of sweated labour and are always pleading poverty. In faith, I have seen good Nym of Eastcheap put his hand in his own purse more often than any cleric I have met, and to say that is to say much.

It is indeed a great evil to bind a man to the soil and profit from the labour of his back. If I remember Holy Scripture rightly, the Lord Jehovah was forever allowing his underlings, including humankind, the freedom of choosing their own path. Admittedly, they usually chose the wrong one and were condignly punished. But, God's wounds! Even Lucifer himself chose his own destiny. The Lord God said unto him: "Lucifer, you may sit on my right hand and enjoy everlasting bliss or become the Prince of Darkness and of the World, Lord of the Flies and Enemy of Mankind, commonly known as Satan. As such, you will reside in Hell and consign sinners to everlasting perdition. What do you say to that?" Lucifer thought about it and decided that he would rather be his own master than sit on a cold slab for all eternity, which choice did God reward by giving him a great deal of hair, a tail, a pair of horns and cloven hooves.

Now if Lucifer himself was vouchsafed such choice, why is it denied to your honest yeoman? Here in France, if your serf be discontented with his lot and quits the demesne on which he works, his meagre strip of land and all his possessions are forfeit! This is great foolishness, for your commonalty will bear the yoke only as long as it sits comfortably upon their shoulders but once it begins to raise sores they will throw it off and that with great violence, as happened in England a mere five and twenty years ago. There was then much damage to life and property and the rule of law. Let those who will keep serfs beware: it is but to fashion a rod for your own back and there's the long and short of it.

This William was not so much a rod as a bent twig. He was tired and dirty and famished nigh to death. In truth, the dogs of the street looked better nourished.

So, I was moved and took pity on him. I brought him to a nearby ordinary and gave him meat to eat and ale to drink and, when he had done and his great hunger was satisfied, I bade him tell me his history.

This William has a daughter, Evote by name, who, tiring of the mundane village life and fearing that she might be married off by the lord against her will, ran away to Paris. Thus far is the story a familiar one. As such tales customarily run, the lord in question would then levy a fine on William, Evote would be given up as a bad lot of whom he was well rid, and no more would be said about the matter. But this lord, the Seigneur de Montrichard, is a greedy and covetous rogue who told William that, if his daughter was not found within a year and a day, all his goods and chattels would be forfeit. He little expected that William would try to seek out Evote for this would mean neglecting his husbandry, resulting in penury and starvation for his family, but William was blessed with two lusty sons to work his smallholding, and thus he took his meagre savings and set out for Paris town.

Since then, three months have passed and poor William has heard no news of Evote and fears that she may be dead or gone to some other place—he knows not where. Even Southwark may not be without the bounds of possibility.

Having come to the end of his sorry tale, William gave way to despair and collapsed on the board, blubbering considerably and pulling his hair, as folk will when they are sorely vexed. At that point I realised that Providence had brought us together and, laying my hand upon his shoulder, I told him to be of good cheer for perhaps I had seen a way out of his dilemma.

"How can that be?" said he. "Have you news of my Evote, good sir?"

"Nay, man!" said I, in answer. "That I have not, though I would it were so. You must resign yourself, good William. Paris is awash with young lasses such as yours and full of rogues who will claim to know her in return for such small coin as you have about you. Have you coin, good William?"

"Aye, messire," said he. "A whole *livre*."

"A *livre*!" said I, with some amazement. "How did you come by such a sum?"

"By honest means," said he, a trifle defensively. "By the sweat of my brow."

"You must have sweated more than somewhat," said I. "If you have a *livre* about you, why in the name of heaven are you starving?"

"I thought I might need it to purchase my Evote's freedom, messire," said he. "From a pander or some such rascal."

"You must give up all hope of finding your daughter, let alone purchasing her freedom," said I, gravely. "But there may yet be a way of preserving your land and chattels."

"Oh?" said William, in a tone of mixed brightness and despair.

"Listen well," said I. "I have told you that Paris is awash with maids of your Evote's age and it is true enough. And what is it, I ask you, that marks them apart? Naught! One may be slightly more comely that the other..."

"My Evote is not comely!" William interjected, with a new cheerfulness.

"Few are," said I. "And so much the better. If I know your lords of the manor—and, I may say, I have known more than a few—they will not cavil on the brightness of an eye or the shapeliness of a hip. They have little interest in anything more than sturdiness of limb and fruitfulness of womb and there's an end on it. Provide them with a healthy wench of about the same age as your Evote and they will not quibble about her pedigree. Find another girl to return to Touraine with you and the Seigneur of Montrichard will be none the sadder."

"And where, in the name of the Blessed Virgin and all the saints, could I find a wench who will give up her freedom for a life of bondage in a strange village?" said William, with scornful eye.

"It is not an easy task, I grant you," said I. "But I can accomplish it."

"You can?" said he.

"Aye," said I. "For a *livre*."

And so I told him of Jeanne, saying that she herself was the runaway daughter of a villein and that she regretted bitterly having come to the city and desired above all else to return to the bucolic delights of serfdom. At this, William's joy knew no bounds and he fell on my neck and blubbered his gratitude, which I would rather he had not done for he stank worse than a score of middens.

Before we parted company, I told William to bring himself and his *livre* to the Parvis of Notre Dame at the hour of vespers, at which place and time I should deliver the wench up to him.

I am greatly satisfied with this arrangement. This night will see me a *livre* richer and, perhaps, else besides.

At Melun

On Saint Leonard's Eve.
(Tuesday 5th November 1415)

The *Cerf du Saint Hubert* is a fine inn. I have not slept in the like since first I quitted the Boar's Head. As I am, once again, a gentleman of no small means, I have decided to stay in a manner befitting me and so the landlord has installed me in a private room overlooking the forest. It is calm and tranquil. The upper room at the Boar's Head gave onto Eastcheap on one side and the graveyard of Saint Michael's on the other, and I know not which was the noisier of the two.

At the *Cerf du Saint Hubert* there is no necessity to provide the cook with meat and the food is good and plentiful. For supper I ate soup, boiled mutton, a dish of thrushes, a leg of venison, a roasted pullet and a pastry, and drank a fine, sweet wine that my host calls *vin cuit*.

I have been counting my money and find that I have five *livres* and eight *sous*, which calculation includes the *livre* I had of William for providing him with a daughter and the two *livres* I spent on a horse this morning.

The horse in question is a chestnut mare of disputable age that I bought of a merchant in Charenton. I shall not go to the trouble of christening her for she bears my weight badly and I shall sell her as soon as I may.

Thus far, my pilgrimage is proving a more uplifting and rewarding experience than I had dared hope for. In the space of a mere two weeks I have rendered aid to many unfortunates and given one of them such spiritual and moral guidance as will last her a lifetime.

Truth to say, Jeanne did not greet the news of my philanthropy with any great enthusiasm. In faith, she looked upon me with a somewhat outraged countenance and said that if I thought she was going to return to serfdom in the company of some filthy and loathsome old man simply that I might gain a few *deniers* then I had best think again. And that I had best look for another bedfellow too for of her I would have naught.

I was tempted to reply that naught of naught were little indeed but I thought better of it and carefully explained, in terms within her comprehension, that she had only to depart from Paris with poor William that night and, once in the obscurity of the countryside, give him the slip and return. A little walking was small investment for the getting of a *livre* and belike much less fatiguing than her usual method.

This stratagem was purely in her own interests. Had I not deprived her of my company by quitting Paris whilst she accompanied poor William, she would have doubtless descended further along that dizzy gradient of degradation that leads to the black abyss of Hell. Furthermore, I took with me the money that she earned in such lewd wise and thus amply demonstrated to her the vanity of her profession. Now that she sees that no profit ever accrues from harlotry, she will belike comport herself in a more seemly and modest fashion, such as befits a wench of her years.

As for poor William, he is now parted from *livre* and daughter and this will grieve him mightily. Yet he cannot claim that I did not furnish what I promised and, if he is possessed of some modicum of wit and intelligence, he must see that I have done him a great service. After all, he would have attempted to gull his lord and master—which would have had grave consequences—and I have successfully prevented this deception. Secondly, now that he has been so careless as to mislay two daughters, belike he will be more careful with the third.

Though I be erring perilously close to the sin of pride, I believe that I may honestly write that I have acted in a true spirit of Christian Charity. Were Jeanne and William here now, I am sure they would bless me for it.

It was no easy matter to leave Paris by night, ill-shod and un-horsed as I was. I paid a waterman to row me to Charenton and that dearly too for he was not enamoured of the expedition, claiming that at that hour no one in Charenton would wish to journey back to Paris and that he had been on the point of retiring for the night and his good wife would rail at him for being late abed. Truth to tell, I could not blame him for it took us many a long hour against the flood, which was swift and powerful, particularly as we neared our destination where the rivers Seine and Marne interfuse.

No sooner had we reached land than it began to drizzle most abominably. It was too late to procure a room for the night but I found a stable left open and I crept inside and slept soundly and dryly enough on a bed of straw.

The *Cerf du Saint Hubert*, which, by the by, means Saint Hubert's Hart, suits me wonderfully well and I may stay here for some time. I do not think I shall return to Paris—not for a few weeks at any rate—for I would risk encountering Jeanne there and her excess of gratitude would discountenance me greatly.

Perhaps the forest without my window is the same in which Saint Hubert was hunting when he saw a hart with a crucifix between its antlers. This was a strange thing to see indeed and a curious. His vision was probably no more than the result of a violent collision between the beast and some unhappy friar yet good Hubert was made Bishop of Liège on its account and thus, I suppose, his hart was in the right place.

At Montereau

On the eighth day of November, being a Friday.

A filthy black pox on all Italians! There cannot be a more whoreson cozening, double-tongued race on the face of God's earth! Unless it be the Egyptians.

I have been robbed.

It happened on Wednesday last, which was Saint Leonard's Day.

A party of ten Italian soldiery arrived at the *Cerf du Saint Hubert*. They bore all the marks of hard travel and were so much fatigued that no sooner had they been shown the larger upper room than four of them took straightway to their beds. The remaining six descended to the taproom where they bespoke meat and drink and fell to eating as though they had seen no provender since Michaelmas last.

Now I had spent the afternoon of that day sitting before the fire and stimulating my intellect by frequent applications of fine wine. Much good did it do me. Nevertheless, I lacked company and, having perceived that one of the Italians had some French, I approached him and made myself known to him.

This man was their captain and bore the name of Enrico, as more than a few Italians do. He came from Genoa, whence he had led his party of crossbowmen to fight for whosoever would pay them, his fellow countrymen being not averse to fighting but reluctant to pay for it.

Had he not identified himself as their captain, I would never have believed it, for his raiment was every bit as ragged and filthy as that of the others and his countenance radiated all the wit and intelligence of a Hereford cow. He addressed me constantly as *dottore*—which I took to mean "doctor". Although I did my best to disabuse him, saying that the closest I had come to a university was the jakes at Westminster Hall, he persisted in this form of address throughout our conversation. I can only conclude that your common Italian is so bereft of wit that anyone with more intelligence than a housefly must be a doctor at law. This raises great doubts about the ability of the Pope.

At first Enrico regarded me with some suspicion but I bespoke wine and cinnamon and he then seemed willing enough to talk as much as his limited French would allow. Little by little, I reconstructed his history and this was no simple task for he used many words of Italian, Spanish and German, which are languages that I do not comprehend. For all that, his tale was of great interest to me for he had lately fought in the great battle at Azincourt, where Hal had triumphed against the French.

However, try as I might, I could not persuade Enrico to talk about the battle. He only muttered the word "massacro" and stared across the taproom with black, empty eyes.

The most that he would say was that he and his men had been constrained to abandon their weapons and accoutrements. As they marched southwards Enrico was able to buy a horse from a farmer but his men had scarcely coin enough to provide themselves with food and lodging: they had not been paid for their services and now will never be so, for their commander Charles of Orléans was slaughtered in the battle.[49]

Though I was jubilant at Hal's victory, I could not display it. Instead, I bespoke more wine for him and for those of his men who were not sleeping. We drank deep and toasted those who had followed in death's dance.

It was then that Enrico brought forth dice from his purse and asked me whether I would hazard my fortune in a game.

Now I am no stranger to dice. God's wounds, if I possessed all the ivory I have rolled between my fingers there would not be a prince of Africk richer than I. However, I was greatly mistaken on the question of Enrico's wit. I had thought his ability to speak all languages somewhat and none of them well to be a mark of his excess of dullness and not, as I now know, a measure of his wide experience and cunning. I accepted his challenge readily and we fell to gaming.

It would not greatly surprise me if a forefather of Enrico was that self-same Roman soldier who diced with his fellows at the foot of the Holy Rood and possessed himself of our Lord's raiment, for in all my years I never saw dice fall so much to the advantage of the caster.

Now had I been in Eastcheap, I would have drawn my dagger, tickled Enrico's chin with it, disembowelled his dice and exposed his cozenage for all to see. Yet surrounded as I was by six battle-hardened soldiers who would have sliced me into carbonadoes and served me up with garlic and stewed onions, I was constrained to surrender my money with a good grace and continue the game, lest I be thought insolent. In short, if they had simply cut my purse, it would have saved us all a lot of time and trouble.

It was only the fatigue of my adversary that saved me from complete ruin but by the time he yawned and scratched his codpiece and confessed himself too tired to persist in his thievery, he had won four *livres* of me. Thus it was that when he and his men had retired upstairs and I had taken stock of my situation, I perceived that the *Cerf du Saint Hubert* and I must part company.

And so I am now sitting in the upper room of a wayside hostelry without the town of Montereau. Being a Friday, the day of Holy Innocents last, I am compelled to remain here till the morrow, which I would prefer not to do for this inn is called the *Poule d'Eau* or Water Hen and is every bit as aquatic as its name suggests. It overhangs the river in a most alarming manner and its rooms are dank and draughty as a consequence. I shall catch a rheum and belike die.

Tomorrow I shall resume my pilgrimage. May Dame Fortune aid me in it.

At Auxerre

On Martinmas.
(Monday 11th November 1415)

If I have been lax in keeping my daybook these three days past, it is only because I have been too occupied with the saving of lives.

This is indeed an occupation that well befits a knight and pilgrim and, though I would certainly have done the same had those lives belonged to common beggars or simple yeomen, I may say that I have gained no little profit from my valour. Thus does Fortune aid men of good courage, even if kings do not.

This night I am sleeping at a fine inn called the *Auberge du Cheval Noir*, or Black Horse Inn, in this town of Auxerre, being the gateway to the Duchy of Burgundy. I may eat and drink my fill and need not concern myself with the reckoning, for I am the guest of Jehan de Bazois whose life I have saved, together with that of Edmond, his intendant. Jehan de Bazois is a great landowner and a man of much influence at the court of Duke John of Burgundy, whom men call *Jean sanz Peur* on account of his being fearless, and of whom he has his lands.

I hope that at some future time I may be introduced to Duke John. Aside from any profit that might accrue from such a meeting, I am curious to know whether this great nobleman is quite as fearless as is claimed. If so, I feel sorry for him for to be without fear is a damnable affliction. Harry Hotspur was without fear—as devoid of that quality as he was of those of base intelligence, intelligibility, and common sense. The people of Northumberland greatly esteemed his wit and would laugh heartily at his jests, yet on the one or two occasions when our paths crossed—before he espoused rebellion—I found him slightly less interesting than a carrot and that without being edible. I can only think that the Northumbrians were either easily amused or wise enough to laugh at anything he said, witty or not.

Both Jehan and Edmond are of an age, that is to say about three-score and five years, but there all similitude ends for the master is small and thin whilst the servant is tall and inclined to fatness. Were it not for their raiment, you would think that the servant was the master. Also Jehan has the garrulity of a fishwife whilst Edmond utters no more than ten words a day and that *in extremis*. In faith, I believe that if he found himself about to utter an eleventh word he would immediately stop his mouth, however perilous the situation.

For all that, they are united in their gratitude, as well they may be.

I shall record the history of this incident in detail for it will be much talked about in times to come.

On Saturday last I quitted Montereau at break of day, thinking to put many leagues behind me before I rested for the night. My direction was southwards for there lies the country of Spain and the shrine of Saint James.

Now it had already become clear that if I did not purchase a new horse soon, my journey to Compostella would take a pitifully long time. In faith, it was entirely possible that I would reach that city a few months after Judgement Day and be able to make the acquaintance of Saint James personally.

Now my good Mistress Quickly—she of the four legs—was surely no Pegasus of the highways. Yet, for all that, she could maintain a steady pace and I even knew her to canter upon occasion—when struck by a stone or afrighted by some loud noise or other untoward event. Not so the chestnut mare.

The chestnut mare appeared to have an aversion to linear progress of any sort, much preferring to stand still and eat what came to hand. Once this was exhausted, she would then move herself towards a fresh supply and I soon perceived that riding would be a question of convincing her that there was naught eatable in the immediate vicinity and that the best nourishment lay at our destination.

Unfortunately, it is no easy matter to convince a dumb beast of anything. Though I whispered and often shouted in her ear that there would be oats aplenty in Sens and enough water to fill her already distended belly to capacity, she always favoured immediate gratification over promises of future abundance. Any patch of grass that took her fancy merited a pause and she would refuse to amble off until it was as close cropped as a friar's pate.

At first, naturally enough, I essayed all those subtle tactics commonly employed by horsemen: spurring, kicking and thrashing. The only resort that brought concrete results was dismounting and leading her afoot, which rather defeated the purpose of having a horse in the first place.

Thus I had no option but to wait on her until she had eaten her fill and then guide her as rapidly as possible to a fresh supply of fodder. This accomplished, I would then sit patiently in the saddle till she was sated. If anyone passed us by, I would feign a disinterested air and pretend to be admiring the view.

On the day we quitted Montereau the weather was wet and windy and there was little view to be seen anywhere, and there you have as complete a recipe for misery as could be devised by a regiment of master cooks.

By the time we finally arrived at Sens in the early evening, I was soaked to the skin and shivering. I determined to sell the chestnut mare there and then but could find no one that would give me a *livre* for her. As a fresh mount could not be secured for less than two *livres*, I resigned myself to another long day of dampness, fatigue and tribulation and hied me to bed.

It was on the next day that my fortune changed. The chestnut mare quitted Sens at a rapid trot in search of fresh grass and, having found it, wandered off the road for a second breakfast. It was a pattern that continued till mid-morning, when the chestnut mare halted a mere stone's throw from a small village and I, preferring to take my ease at an ale-stake while she ate, dismounted and tugged her reluctant carcass towards the dwellings before us. We had barely reached the first house when there, approaching us, was the very mirror of ourselves.

In truth, the man was both younger and thinner than myself and the horse was a massive black stallion that seemed somewhat disinclined to be led like a common milch-cow. The chestnut mare, who had lately taken to walking with her head drooped as though she had lost something and was looking for it, raised her eyes and regarded this midnight beast with an expression usually reserved only for an exceptionally succulent blade of grass. The black stallion pranced, whinnied and rolled his eyes in a cavalier fashion. The fellow who led him, who was clad in a leathern jerkin and brown leggings, hung onto the bridle and cursed his animal roundly.

"God give you good morrow," said I.

"Well met," said the fellow, still struggling.

"You have a fine horse, messire," said I.

"Fine? Aye! But the very devil!" said he, struggling yet.

"A beast of spirit!" said I.

"Whoreson evil spirit!" he replied. "If I had a good brood mare such as yourn, I would sell him in a trice. He is naught but trouble. A pestilence on the beast!"

Truth to tell, I had never regarded my mount as a "good brood mare". I began to look upon her in a fresh light.

"Aye," said I. "There's quality there. She will bring forth rare offspring."

Which, as I saw it, was not far from the truth.

The stallion, as if to confirm this appraisal, renewed his bucking and prancing and seemed greatly anxious to be better acquainted with the chestnut mare.

In my long and, I may say, close association with royalty and nobility, I have seen the best horseflesh that England has to offer, and Europe and Araby come to that. Rarely had I beheld a creature of such awesome magnificence.

"I might be prevailed upon to part with her," I continued, bestowing a look of pride upon my droop-headed nag.

"What say you?" said the fellow, struggling mightily.

"I will sell her to you, if it please you," said I.

"Yon mare?" said the fellow. "I have no coin. I cannot buy her."

"You have no need of coin," said I. "I will take your horse in exchange."

The fellow gave me a startled look.

"He be the very devil," he warned. "More trouble than his worth."

"Good sir," said I, "I am the master of any horse. He will do my bidding."

And thus the bargain was quickly struck. The stallion, whom I have named Pistol, was formally introduced to the chestnut mare and had a merry time with her as stallions will. For her part, the chestnut mare seemed curiously unmoved by the whole affair and quietly set to cropping the grass once it was accomplished.

When the horses were done, the fellow in the leathern jerkin held my stallion whilst I, by dint of much struggling and not a little cursing, put my saddle on him.

"He be the very devil," repeated the fellow, in a voice laden with foreboding.

Yet in truth he did not seem so. Though mounting him was an onerous task, we set off at a merry trot. I was much pleased with my trade and could not comprehend why the fellow in the leathern jerkin should have exchanged so fine an animal for a broken-winded nag. In faith, he seemed a most manageable beast and pleasingly high-spirited. Owing to this harmless braggadocio, I decided to name him Pistol.

We trotted briskly for about two leagues until we reached a long, descending gradient bordered by dense forest. It was a most gloomy place and an inauspicious, for such spots are the common haunt of robbers and outlaws. It seemed as if something of this sinister atmosphere imparted itself to Pistol for his ears twitched nervously and he broke into a canter, snorting mighty plumes of vapour.

Of a sudden there was a flash of black and white and a chatter of panic.

Now it is said by many that your magpie is a bird of ill omen when it appears singly and, indeed, there is some truth to this belief for few creatures can have presaged such fateful events as this one.

Pistol bucked and plunged, neighing loudly. I heaved at his reins and dug my spurs into his flanks in an effort to control him. This, I now know, was the worst thing I could have done for Pistol is a horse who can be managed only with kindness and gentleness. He leapt forward as if fired from some great cannon. Abandoning the reins, I threw my arms about his neck and to this swift action alone do I credit my deliverance. I never knew a horse gallop faster. We thundered down the lane at a furious pace, I hurling abuse in Pistol's ear as if mere words alone could have had any effect.

The hill down which we sped ended in a sharp bend. Such was our celerity that, for the life of me, I could not see how Pistol would be able to turn, and I was sure that we would plunge off the road and into the trees and undergrowth.

This vegetation came rapidly nearer. I shut my eyes and muttered some sort of prayer to the Lord on high. Exactly what it was, I have forgotten, yet I can vouch for its efficacy for, with a sudden sideways lurch, Pistol swerved violently round the bend.

Perceiving that the immediate danger was passed or, at least, that no catastrophe had befallen us, I opened my eyes only to see four men sword-dancing in the middle of the road a dozen yards in front of us, which distance took no more than a few blinkings of an eye for Pistol to cover. I recall four startled faces looking up and then we were upon them.

Pistol smashed directly into one of the dancers, which collision halted him sharply and caused him to plunge, thereby working great mischief upon the person of this dancer, and then rear up. My backside slid out of the saddle and momentarily I hung suspended from Pistol's neck before flying through the air and landing very heavily on a second dancer whom I bore to the earth.

It was a goodly while before I could pick myself up for my flight had quite winded me. I was a trifle bruised but my limbs seemed sound and I could clearly thank the dancer on whom I had landed for breaking my fall. Sadly, the fellow in question was in little state to receive my thanks for he lay spread-eagled and unconscious. His breath rasped in his throat and there was a trickle of bright blood flowing from one corner of his mouth.

The two surviving dancers—the one who had first collided with Pistol appearing to be quite dead—were transfixed with amazement. I was on the point of apologising for having so rudely interrupted their festivities, not to mention having seriously injured one of their party and killed another, when these two threw themselves upon me, not with murder in their hearts, as I first thought, but with every expression of joy and gratitude.

It is curious how first impressions can betray one. Until that moment, I had been convinced that I had interrupted an impromptu celebration, belike brought on by a spontaneous excess of joy on the part of these four men. In fact two of them, Jehan and Edmond as I now know them, were struggling for their very lives against the murderous intent of two brigands. It was only my daring intervention that had prevented them from being most heinously done to death.

Jehan and Edmond congratulated me with such ardour and profusion that modesty forbids I should set down the details of their gratitude. Suffice to say that I endured their flattery for a decent space of time before slitting the injured robber's throat.

Though this may well appear to be a low thing to have done, had we attempted to move him he would have died in any case and if we had eventually succeeded in bringing him alive to the nearest magistrate he would have been promptly hanged.

While this was going on, Pistol had located Jehan and Edmond's horses, that had wandered a short way down the road, and was making himself intimate with Edmond's mare. Doubtless I have her to thank that he was not halfway to Spain.

And thus, having thrown the bodies of the two brigands into the ditch, we mounted our steeds and rode on together.

There is a lot to be said for Edmond's taciturnity. Having established that he was beholden to me, he relapsed into what I now know to be a customary silence. Would that Jehan had done the same. There never was such a chewet. As we rode, he chattered incessantly about how grateful he was to be saved from robbery and certain murder; about my daring leap from the saddle, which had settled the second robber; about the present war with England and how it had made travelling so very difficult and perilous; about how he hated going to Paris but then needs must for there was an important contract to be negotiated for the sale of wine that had risen in value on account of the war; about how the wet September weather had meant a bad grape-crop; about how I spoke such good French but then, of course, Flemings always do; about his wife, his daughter, his two sons, his lands, his servants and, most of all and in exhaustive detail, his pigs.

For myself, I was almost as silent as Edmond for it was as much as I could do to inject half a dozen words into this ceaseless flow of prattle. He has continued in like vein ever since and I wonder that he can yet find subjects to blather about and I no longer wonder that Edmond chooses to say naught at all.

Last night we slept in Joigny. To be exact, Jehan slept. I slept but little. As to Edmond, I do not know whether he slept or not for he occupied the servants' quarters.

There was a twofold reason for my lack of slumber. Firstly Jehan is even more fond of garlic than your ordinary Frenchman. Secondly he snores, which action propels the said garlicky effluvium about the room most noisily. As I had to share a bed with him it was many a long hour before I lay in the arms of

Morpheus, and then only by dint of stuffing my ears and nose with tallow. God be praised that here, in Auxerre, I have a bed to myself.

In Joigny I confessed to being an Englishman. I must admit that this was not a step that I took lightly for here in France it is a difficult matter to know where sympathies lie, and in certain company merely to state a preference for roast beef is like as not to see you hanging from the nearest tree. Yet Jehan had shown constant contempt for the twin houses of Valois and Armagnac and, given that any man here is generally a supporter of one or the other, it seemed safe to declare myself for neither. Add to which he had shown great admiration for *Henri d'Angleterre*—a feat that even I find hard to emulate.

On my confessing my true provenance, Jehan was, at first, somewhat put out of countenance for I had hitherto lent much colour to my history of Jan van Staf, describing in detail the winding lanes of Antwerp and offering a few useful pointers as to the best leaping-houses in that city. However, once he had accepted the fact of my being an Englishman of noble blood, Jehan showed himself more than delighted. Truth to say, I was quite relieved that I no longer had to continue in my role of the swag-bellied Hollander—so relieved, in faith, that I told him of the great and close friendship between Hal and myself and also about my heroic slaying of Harry Percy and capture of Colville of the Dale.

Unfortunately this confession created more problems than it resolved for I had then to explain my presence in France and that in such a way as would justify my extreme distance from the main body of the English army without appearing to be a spy. It is my experience that there is no such thing as a good or benevolent spy.

I was, I said, a secret ambassador plenipotentiary to the court of Pope Benedict in Avignon and felt very pleased therewith for the idea was improvised on the spur of the moment and yet appeared to win Jehan's sympathies entirely. In faith, it went quite against the grain for me for, as anyone knows, there is but one Pope and he sleeps in Rome.[50]

Be that as it may, Jehan was greatly impressed and asked me if I did not hold many lands of the King of England. To this I answered that I was not to be numbered amongst the great landlords of the realm, being possessed of little more than the counties of Sussex and Hampshire, as well as some minor properties in the city of London. I also added that, if my mission to Avignon was successful, I could expect to be rewarded with the Duchy of Cornwall and a few smaller interests beside. For safety's sake, I also said that my task was one of extreme delicacy and, though it was in no way prejudicial to the interests of Burgundy—on which they had my word of honour—I would esteem Jehan's discretion greatly. To this aduration he acceded with many an earnest oath and nod.

I was well pleased with this subterfuge for, as I have written, it was devised *extempore*. My clandestine mission also accounted for my lack of retinue, without which great lords such as I seldom travel.

Thus today I was not only accorded the gratitude I merited as the saviour of Jehan—and Edmond too—but also the respect and deference due to one of noble blood. So it is that I share a bed with this great lord of Burgundy. Moreover, he has insisted that I stay as his house-guest before proceeding with my embassy.

With a show of some reluctance, I have consented.

At Corbigny

Tomorrow we shall arrive at Jehan's manor-house at Saint Germain en Bazois, from which demesne his family takes its name. I am in great expectation of our arrival there for Jehan has told me much of it—especially of his piggery and daughter.

Truth to say, I do not look forward to viewing his piggery with any great enthusiasm. In general, your pig is a beast that leaves me powerfully unmoved, unless it be roasted and set on a platter, and, in particular, I have heard enough of Jehan's piggery, its disposition, population and accoutrements, as to render any visit superfluous. His daughter is a different matter.

Jehan began speaking of her yesterday, following a period of prolonged and therefore uncharacteristic silence. It was as we three rode from Auxerre to Clamecy—in which village we slept that night—and both Edmond and myself had been luxuriating in this unexpected tranquillity that, of a sudden, Jehan cleared his throat noisily and, with many an "ahem", embarked on a ponderous diatribe against the base state to which womankind had fallen.

Now I had been riding along quite peacefully, settled in abstract contemplation of Pistol's ears, when this tirade fell upon me. I could see in it about as much relevance to our current occupation as the price of cockles in Constantinople but two days in Jehan's company had already taught me that sheer pointlessness is a quality he values most highly. In truth, I had not remarked that the state of womankind was any baser than it had ever been and, as far as I am concerned, were it to plummet a further hundred leagues into the abyss of iniquity, it would yet be a mountaintop higher than that of men.

Yet I listened patiently to his discourse with many a "Go to" and "Well now" and nodded my head sagaciously when I felt that he was making a point of slightly more weight than the others.

The substance of Jehan's complaint was that womankind had become faithless, frivolous, unfilial and unfinished, brazen of tongue and bearing, given to the giddiest of caprices and ignorant, and—when not ignorant—negligent of her duties. The ideal of womanhood, said he, was exemplified by your Roman matron and it was a great pity that girls were not taught the Latin tongue, else would they be able to read of these proud, sober, modest dames for themselves and model their comportment thereon.

Now from what I recall of my own study of the Roman Authorities, desultory as it was, sober and modest dames were fairly thin on the ground in the days of the Caesars and most of the women I encountered in the dusty volumes of Thomas Mowbray's library seemed much given to poisonings, stabbings, suicides, lewdnesses and wantonnesses, and those who were not so occupied tended to die both young and horribly. Belike I read the wrong Authorities.

For Jehan, there are only two women in the world who properly reflected these otherwise lost virtues: the one being his good wife and the other being his daughter. Of his wife, he has said but little and I therefore feel that in her case you must add the extra virtues of brevity and taciturnity. Brief in that she is seldom spoken of and taciturn since, with such a chattering jay for a spouse, she can be no other.

The daughter is called Agnes and it seems that there is not a woman extant who combines beauty, wisdom, accomplishment and virtue to such perfect and pleasing result. Not only is her beauty without peer, but her modesty would make Lucrece a very harlot by comparison. Her grace would shame the delicate and youthful Hebe; her wisdom is that of a second and fairer Solomon. To descend to prosaic particulars, she is versed in every domestic and artistic accomplishment. She knows at what season and in what wise her father's lands be cultivated. She knows what payments are due his servants and sees to it that they correctly perform their divers duties. She knows all aspects of the making of woollen cloth, from the shearing to the loom. She knows the law as it applies to estates and seigneuries. She knows the management of arms and can shoot a crossbow and wield the short sword and quarterstaff. She also sings and plays prettily upon the rebec.

Now though I have never myself sired progeny—or at least none that I know of—I have kept company with enough fathers and mothers to know that they are wont to vaunt the qualities of their offspring from time to time. My good Mistress Quickly of Eastcheap, *per exemplum*, was forever lauding the accomplishments of her daughter Kate. It made little difference to her that Kate died of the dropsy five and twenty years ago—in faith it merely gave her the opportunity to speculate on what wondrous deeds Kate might have performed had she not exchanged the serving of pudding-ale in the Boar's Head for the quaffing of nectar in Paradise. However, such was Jehan's extraordinary eloquence on the subject of Agnes's merits that my curiosity was well and truly whetted. In faith, it occurred to me that had such a paragon of virtue and accomplishment been present at Saint Just en Tel, there would have been little need for my counterfeiting the Blessed Virgin.

Jehan's eulogy lasted a good many leagues and terminated, after a deal of digression, in his bemoaning the lack of a fitting suitor—for it seems that, despite her manifold endowments, Agnes is yet unwed. There was not, said he, in the whole of Burgundy a man who had displayed the necessary qualities for such a match—not excepting the courtiers at Dijon. The fellow who married her, he said, would be happy indeed and go without want for the rest of his life for he would gain the very pattern of a comely and dutiful wife, and a large dowry besides.

Now were I a Burgundian, I might have felt inclined to offer myself as her suitor, for being without want for the rest of your life is not a proposition to be dismissed out of hand. Yet even the commonest habits of your Burgundian are alien to my nature. God's wounds, on listening to his master's disquisition, Edmond's behaviour was startling to behold. He greeted every revelation of Agnes's beauty and skills with loud coughs, tuggings of his beard and rollings of his eyes. In England, a simple nod is considered an adequate sign of agreement. I cannot consider spending my autumn years expectorating my accord and contorting my face like some whoreson actor.

There was then a lengthy silence. The only sounds were of birds twittering in the trees and the steady "clop clop" of our mounts.

"My Agnes!" bellowed Jehan, with a sudden vigour that startled Pistol, "Is no less than the Three Graces inhabiting one body!"

Pistol pranced a little and then quietened himself. Edmond coughed his concurrence in a manner so violent that I feared he would fall from the saddle.

At Saint Germain en Bazois

On Saint Machutus' Eve.
(Thursday 14th November 1415)

I now know the reason for Edmond's coughing. If Agnes is truly the embodiment of the Three Graces, it is because she is as fat as all three put together.

In my three-score and ten years I have seen many women to whom the gift of beauty has been denied but seldom one to whom it has been denied quite so thoroughly as the daughter of Jehan de Bazois. And mark my words well: a woman does not have to possess all the attributes of Helen to be comely, but at least one or two do not come amiss.

It would not amaze me to learn that Agnes was wet-nursed by one of her father's sows, for she more resembles an inflated pig's bladder than any living thing I have seen. If you laid her on her side, you would be hard put to tell top from bottom. Perhaps this further explains why she has survived six and twenty years a virgin.

I tell a lie. There is some slight difference between north and south. Sitting atop this fleshy sphere is a smaller globe of dough-like aspect which, in its turn, is surmounted by a rich mane of black hair. It is commonly called a head.

As I sit here writing, I find that I cannot adequately describe her features. In faith, they are difficult to discern, foundering as they are in a sea of spotty fat. Her most salient point is her nose, which is truly Bardolphian in both form and hue. If a woman's face be her fortune then poor Agnes is doomed to penury.

Yet I reserve her worst quality till last. It is her voice. In repose—that is to say, at those moments of the day given over to tranquil and leisurely discourse—it seldom rises above a mild screech, but only let the conversation wax more animated or, worse yet, incur her vexation, and it mounts by rapid degrees to an ear-splitting shriek.

The rest of Jehan's family are unremarkable enough. His wife bears the name Thiphaine, being born on Epiphany. As her name suggests, she is of a somewhat pious turn of mind and spends much time at her devotions. She is thus correspondingly meek and melancholic and any violent disturbance is wont to send her to her rosary. As her daughter is Agnes, the click of beads is heard frequently.

Jehan has two sons, Esprit and Jean-Baptiste by name. Of these two, the elder is the former. He has twenty-seven summers and is betrothed to the daughter of a neighbouring seigneur. The younger, Jean-Baptiste, is but seventeen years old and has the furious and mercurial temperament of his age.

Once I had been made known to them, I was greeted with much warmth and gratitude for the saving of Jehan's life, and with all the deference due my rank. The men bowed low before me and then must rush to help Agnes to her feet for she had attempted to curtsey. I was offered bread and salt and a cup of warmed hypocras, and then a bath was drawn for me, which I accepted gratefully for I had not bathed since quitting Paris and was beginning to stink somewhat.

Suitably cleansed, perfumed and refreshed, I was then invited to accompany my host on an inspection of his house and grounds whilst Agnes and Thiphaine directed the servants in the preparation of our supper.

Jehan's house is large and well-founded. It is built of hewn chalk, the walls thereof being almost a full yard thick. Below, there is a great hall with a gallery and a chimney, and above are three rooms of equal size. In addition, there are two smaller chambers at ground level of which the larger has been allotted to me, and it is therein that I now write.

To the right of the hall there is an adjoining cow-byre with a hay-loft above it, and to the left of the hall there is the chapel, kitchen and scullery.

It is many a year since I was last in a great house that boasted its own chapel. There are many who consider this to be the height of luxury and convenience for you may pray at any hour you will—day or night. Admittedly, it is a luxury and convenience that *I* could do well without but here in Saint Germain en Bazois it is almost a necessity for it keeps Thiphaine away for most of the day. She appears to have a depressing effect on everybody.

The roof of Jehan's house is most skilfully tiled and Jehan tells me that in the bitterest weather, when wind and rain buffet it from dawn to dawn, not so much as a drop passes through.

Without, and near to the house, stands a great barn in which there is a wine-press operated by an ingenious screw, and many casks of wine. Not far away, there is a cave dug into the chalky earth where more wine is stored till it is needed. The ranks of hogsheads are wondrous to behold.

Besides all this, there is a dovecote, a hen-house and the celebrated piggery, which I heard and smelled though I did not see it for it was growing dark and the distance was too far to walk. Instead, Jehan escorted me back to the barn where he gave me a taste of his wine, which was fine indeed and bore some resemblance to blackberries.

It must have been clear to him that I had not been greatly impressed with the qualities of his daughter for, instead of praising her without reservation, he began to bemoan the fact that not even the promise of a large dowry had succeeded in getting her off his hands. Now I am not such an old fool that I cannot perceive insinuation when I hear it. It is clear to me by now that Jehan thinks me a fat trout to be caught by tickling. For myself, I thought then as I think now: if the dowry were as great as Hal's treasury, it would take considerably more before I allied myself to such a travesty as Agnes.

For all that, I enquired as to how much the dowry was. Upon this, Jehan gave a grunt of satisfaction and, with an air of pride, told me that it was no less than one hundred *écus d'or*.[51]

This is indeed a large sum, which I would gladly have. Yet the fact of the matter is that whilst a hundred *écus d'or* would be most welcome, Agnes would most certainly not be. Moreover, it is sure that Jehan thinks he has more to gain from this transaction than I, for I am a step or two further than middle age and, should I fail to produce offspring, Jehan's family will inherit all lands and property belonging to myself. When I die, that is.

Thus, though Jehan looked upon me with anxious eye, I did not pursue the matter and, with he both disappointed and yet hopeful, we went in to supper.

Now the supper well befitted an honoured guest. I ate frumenty[52], leek potage, a dish of pullets, a roast leg of one of Jehan's more unfortunate pigs, a dish of trotters, a dish of pigeons and pigs' ears in jelly. I also drank rather more than a little of new wine from Jehan's vines.

Unfortunately, I made a mistake common amongst foreigners. I praised the wine. To a Frenchman, and especially to a Burgundian, this is an invitation to embark on a lengthy—and in Jehan's case lengthier—dissertation on the finer points, and many of the baser ones, of viticulture.

Fond as I am of wine, and I may say that few of my race are fonder than I, I confess to having scant interest in its elaboration. It is the same for everything. Though I love beef dearly, my enjoyment of this meat is not enhanced by knowing the name of the poor beast from whence it issued or whether the animal had a preference for clover or bog-buttercups. If I sit down to a plate of fishes, which, by God's wounds, I am constrained to do as often as three times a week, it little mitigates my ordeal to know that those members of the finny tribe were gathered on the Dogger Bank on Ash Wednesday by a Suffolk man with a squint. All this is pure superfluousness. If the wine be good then I drink it. If it is not, I don't. There is all the viticulture I need.

But I had to play the guest and so I listened to this drivelling dotard for well-nigh an hour with all the customary go-tos and well-nows thrown in for good measure. My concentration was not aided by young Jean-Baptiste who sat glaring at me throughout the meal and toyed with a bone-handled dagger as though he would have liked to cut out my kidneys and grill them for breakfast.

When this was done—by "this" I mean Jehan's discourse and not Jean-Baptiste's cutting out my kidneys—Esprit began to display his wit.

I pray to God that he has exhausted it this evening for if he has not mealtimes will be parlous trying in Saint Germain. Not since I sat in the tavern ordinary in the Rue Saint Denis and listened to the distilled dullness of Messire Choler and his six friends have I met with such a quintessence of banality. The truly disturbing feature of his sallies was that the entire family behaved as if they were the very nonpareil of drollery, especially Jehan who cackled till the tears coursed down his cheeks and Agnes who shrieked worse than a hot oven full of tomcats. Yet worse was to come.

By now Jehan was in merry mood and, doubtless to further display the accomplishments of his beloved daughter, he called on her to play the rebec.

Now the rebec, played at its best, is not an instrument that I regard highly, for I am inclined to the belief that the best thing to be stroked with a bow is an arrow and as far as sawing is concerned, I would rather spend a month in a shipyard than an evening listening to the rebec. For all that, I have heard some passably good players in my time who have contrived to make the instrument sound reasonably unlike the squeaking of a dry axle. Agnes is not to be numbered amongst this company.

To heap on further injury, she began to sing.

The song, I think, was a lament about Launcelot and Guinevere. At least I assume it was a lament for she sang it most lamentably.

In truth, as I now reflect upon it, it does surprise me that so much time and trouble, not to say expense, is devoted to the fashioning of complicated and ingenious instruments of torture when Agnes has two naturally-given devices at her disposal that could reduce the most hardened and intransigent felon, traitor or heretic to a gibbering wretch in less than an evening.

When she had finally wailed and screeched her way to a conclusion, we all applauded her—her family being so effusive that she blushed most hideously. May God preserve us all for now she will surely sing again.

I was spared further ordeals by Jehan who confessed himself much fatigued and hied him to bed. Thus did the assembly break up and we all retired to our various rooms. I too am quite fatigued and so I shall end my daybook for this day.

May God and the Holy Mother guard my sleep and render Agnes voiceless.

At Saint Germain en Bazois

On Saint Hugh's Day.
(Sunday 17th November 1415)

Heavy rain has confined me to the house these three days past. This is a mixed blessing. On the one hand I have yet been spared a visit to Jehan's piggery and on the other I have perforce been close to his family, and to Agnes in particular.

Whether on her own initiative or at Jehan's behest, Agnes has taken to following me about. No sooner am I seated before the fire with a jug of wine to hand than she appears by my side as if conjured. It amazes me that one of her bulk can move so nimbly and so silently. This morning the mere leaving of my chamber was enough to call up her massy apparition. I had not taken more than two steps into the hall, and these most tentative ones with much glancing to right and left, when, of a sudden, there was a piercing shriek that well-nigh shocked me out of my hose.

I had lingered too long in glancing to my right and Agnes had materialised on my left.

"God give you good day, messire Falstaff!" she screeched.

"Er...good morrow, lady," I answered, with a sigh.

"You have rested well?" she squealed.

"Till now," I replied, under my breath. "Like the dead, lady. Like the dead."

And it is in such a circumstance as this that one even envies the dead.

Thereafter she dogged my footsteps all day. Yesterday, I was able to escape her from time to time by repairing to the jakes, claiming a flux. However, this stratagem has little to recommend it for the jakes is a cold and draughty place and the stink is most foul. And even then she lingered around the door and I was obliged to give an occasional groan or expression of relief to convince her that I was not dead or asleep.

This afternoon I contrived to elude her for a short while when she was called away by her mother and I took advantage of this by creeping out to the barn where I sampled a jug or two of Jehan's wine. Yet I received such a soaking between house and barn that I dared not linger long for fear of catching an ague and so I returned to dry myself before the fire, whereupon I was intercepted again.

This Agnes is indeed a rare creature. In my time, I have met murderers who could sing or dance most prettily, thieves who could recount a witty tale and whores beautiful beyond compare. In faith, I cannot recall meeting anyone who was totally devoid of all finer quality till now. Disregarding her voice—which is no small feat in itself—the substance of her conversation is such that a farmyard duck would find tiresome. When she is not discoursing thus, she smiles upon me in a manner that I find most distressing.

And it is not that I have not tried to find some small merit in her—something, however paltry, that might make her company tolerable. On reflection, as I sit here in my chamber beside a guttering candle, I believe that I *have* discovered one minuscule iota of endowment. Here follows the manner of its finding.

This evening, when we had done with eating, Agnes was once more prevailed upon to sing—as indeed she was yesternight and the night before that. When she had finished and we had applauded her efforts, Jehan excused himself saying that he had to examine the household accounts with Esprit. He then turned to Jean-Baptiste—who had been hunting all day in spite of the foul weather—and spoke to him peremptorily, saying that he looked much fatigued and should withdraw forthwith. Jean-Baptiste glared at me and declared that he was not fatigued in the least, at which his father fetched him a cuff about the ear and told him that he was surely more fatigued than he felt.

Now as Thiphaine had withdrawn already to busy herself with her post-prandial devotions, this would have left Agnes and me alone, for which I had little relish. Moreover, I was rather nettled that Jehan's stratagem had been carried out with such lack of finesse. To my knowledge, he has spent most of the day "examining the household accounts" and, as long as this foul weather holds, he will doubtless do the same tomorrow. The said accounts must be of a complexity that beggars the imagination that they need quite so much examining.

I therefore spoke up and said, with many a yawn, that I too was much fatigued and would retire also, at which Agnes looked extremely crestfallen and Jean-Baptiste brightened a little, or at least as much as he is capable. For his part, Jehan was much discountenanced but recovered with surprising agility, saying that it was a pity to retire so early for he had ordered Edmond to bring me a jug of his finest wine, together with a platter of olives and goat's cheese.

Now as a guest, one has certain obligations and, further to that, I esteemed that a jug of most excellent wine was sufficient payment for another hour of Agnes's company and so I acceded with many a bow and took my seat again. The wine and meats were brought and Agnes and me were left alone.

We sat a while in silence. I smiled at Agnes and Agnes smiled at me. This was reason enough to desist from smiling and so I poured myself a cup of wine and tasted it. It was indeed excellent and most strong.

"Shall I sing for you, messire?" asked Agnes at last, in a soft caterwaul.

"Nay, good lady. Nay," said I. "Even true perfection can cloy through repetition."

"Shall I play for you upon my rebec?" she pursued.

This being the lesser of the two evils, I gave my assent. It also circumvented the painful duty of making conversation.

I must confess that her playing seemed rather more expert than before but perhaps that was merely my perception of it, for by this time I was somewhat inclined to temulence and might well have found tunefulness in a choir of jackdaws had they been then present.

Whether it was an effect of the music or the wine or the flickering firelight or an amalgam of all three I cannot say, but it did seem to me then that even Agnes had some slight charm to recommend her. It is said that in the darkness all cats are grey and I have been without a woman for nigh on two weeks. As Agnes's more than generous form was silhouetted in the firelight to some advantage, it crossed my mind that even her doubtful favours might be worth the seeking.

I write that the notion crossed my mind but thank God it did not tarry there. Common sense asserted itself, for I reasoned that it was unwise to risk Jean-Baptiste's bone-handled dagger in my ribs when a few *deniers* might purchase a merry frolic in the hay with some lusty country lass. I confess here that I did have a sudden lustful vision of Jeanne's buxom body, for which I do most solemnly repent.

Agnes's music wound its way to a doleful conclusion. I sighed. Agnes smiled. I sighed again.

At this point there occurred to me one of those inconsequential irrelevancies that are wont to come upon one in moments of quiet reverie. In the halflight, I fancied that Agnes's face reminded me of Jeanne's buttocks with Bardolph's nose peeping out from between them. The closer I looked, the more it seemed so. I could not conceal a smile. At this, Agnes smiled too and Jeanne's buttocks creased most curiously, upon which I burst out laughing. I laugh yet as I write this.

Agnes too began to laugh and Jeanne's buttocks jiggled up and down, at which I laughed the more.

We were both still laughing as I took my leave of all three of them and sought out my chamber.

Perhaps it may be worth my while marrying Agnes after all. Though my days and nights may be dull, my evenings will never be miserable.

At Saint Germain en Bazois

On Saint Edmund's Day.
(Wednesday 20th November 1415)

I have spent the last three days riding about Jehan's demesne, the rain having ceased to pour and the wind to blow. Sometimes I have been accompanied by my host and sometimes by Esprit, but most often I have ridden alone.

Besides satisfying my curiosity as to the nature and extent of these lands, my jaunts have served the twofold purpose of exercising Pistol—who little likes the confines of a stable—and of absenting myself from Agnes, who continues to pester me.

I have not, I fear, been able to further resist inspecting Jehan's piggery, which task was accomplished yesterday. For the life of me I cannot see the attraction of these beasts for they do naught but grunt and wallow and they stink worse than a gaggle of Parisians.

For all that, I am mightily impressed with Jehan's demesne. His lands are extensive and well-managed and I dare say that in spring and summer you may not find a prettier place in all the world. It would be a pity not to have some claim upon such property.

And yet, if I marry Agnes, she will doubtless wish to accompany me to England. If we return thither, she will quickly discover that I do not own the counties of Sussex and Hampshire and have as much expectation of gaining the Duchy of Cornwall as Jehan's pigs have of learning the rebec. This is, in faith, a thorny problem.

But Fortune's wheel has many turns. I have lost Hal's favour once and so it should be a simple matter to lose it again. I would not be the first ambassador to return home and find his lands confiscated. Agnes has no English and would readily accept my tale of ruin and rejection.

There again, if I return bewifed and befortuned, Hal may well see in this a true reformation and restore me to favour. I could then sell Sussex and Hampshire, which would excite little curiosity for I am an old man to manage such great estates.

Yet what if Harry should die before I return? What then?

This room has grown cold, for I am shivering. I shall retire to bed.

No. Come what may, I shall marry her.

At Saint Germain en Bazois

On Saint Cecilia's Day.
(Friday 22nd November 1415)

Following my resolve of Wednesday last, I have attempted to improve my standing with Mistress Agnes. This requires no little fortitude. Still, I can console myself on two counts: firstly, as I grow older I shall surely grow deafer and therefore Agnes's voice will be reduced to something approaching normal volume; secondly, as she cannot possibly get any fatter, she must either get thinner or stay the same. My situation can only improve.

A further consolation lies in the deteriorating relations between the houses of Armagnac and Burgundy, of which Jehan often speaks when he strays from more porcine issues. To the Burgundians, control of the French throne by the Armagnac faction is a far greater evil than the rampages of Hal and his men in the north. Jehan himself can see no other outcome than a grand alliance between England and Burgundy with the object of destroying the Armagnacs once and for all and setting Hal on the throne of a slightly diminished France.

This being so, and Jehan being a man of advanced years, it is certain that Esprit and Jean-Baptiste will be expected to represent the de Bazois family on the field of battle. To me, Esprit looks ripe to get himself killed for if he knows one end of a pike from the other then I am a soused gurnet. As to Jean-Baptiste, though he may well put his bone-handled dagger to good use against the Armagnac, he is cursed with a most choleric temperament and his excess of spleen will surely see him spitted in some tavern brawl.

We live in evil times and it is the destiny of the young to die young. Many are the pitfalls on life's pilgrimage: famine, pestilence, hunting accidents, *et cetera*. The countryside abounds with rogues who will think nothing of slitting a throat for a groat—a pretty way for the heir to a fortune to die.

Though it grieves me to consider how such flowers of chivalry be cut in their springtime, it is the way of the world and there is naught to be gained by bemoaning it. *Pallida mors aequo pulsat pede pauperum tabernas regumque turres.*[53] Marry and amen!

Yet it is an ill wind that blows no man to good. If Jehan and Thiphaine be left heirless then I at least, old as I am, will still remain to guard their fortune and tend their lands. For as much as I dislike such matters of duty, yet would I do them this service.

I shall end this entry here for today is a fish day and I feel unwell.

At Saint Germain en Bazois

On Saint Clement's Day.
(Saturday 23rd November 1415)

Alea iacta est![54] Indeed it was cast in the herb-garden this very afternoon.

I had almost despaired of getting Jehan on his own today, but finally I intercepted him returning from the piggery and I invited him to stroll with me. In truth, I had some difficulty in restraining my impatience for he insisted on delivering himself of a lengthy encomium, extolling the virtues of one of his pigs, Clothilde by name, who is in farrow. It therefore took some time before I was able to broach the subject.

Adopting as disinterested a mien as I could muster, I asked Jehan if, in the absence of a fitting suitor from Burgundy, he might not be prepared to marry Agnes to a foreigner.

I fear my enquiry sorely discountenanced him for he stopped abruptly and gave me a sharp look and coughed and spat on a thyme bush.

"A foreigner?" said he. "Well, now. A foreigner, say you!"

"So say I," said I.

"I might," said he. "I might indeed if a worthy one came forward."

For a moment I thought that this was to be the sum of his reply.

"But not an Italian," said he, having reflected a little. "For your Italians are villains. Rogues. Cozening rogues. And much given to lewdnesses."

Thinking back to Captain Enrico, I could only nod my head in agreement.

"It is the same with your Spaniards," added Jehan, "for they are of the same stock."

"And I cannot abide your Germans," he continued, after a further pause. "They are a proud and haughty race. Moreover they lose their lands like a crone loses teeth for they are forever fighting between themselves. To be a German count is as commonplace as having ears."

I told him that I had heard as much myself, which was not the truth.

"Your Swiss are dangerous for they are by too much fond of liberties. And, mark you, they are hypocrites to a man for, desiring peace at home, they make war abroad and sell their swords to whoever will pay them."

I told him that this was most true though, for the life of me, I know not whether it be true or not for, in faith, I have never met a Swiss and know nothing of that country. In fact I was beginning to think that Jehan had embarked on yet another weighty dissertation that was to take in the entire male population of the world, not excluding the inhabitants of Lapland and Ind.

"Your Frenchman is faithless," said he, "and too loving of pleasure. I would no more marry my daughter to a Frenchman than ally her to the devil himself. Yea, by the Mass! And we shall shortly make most furious war upon them and then where would my little flower be, or I for that matter, with an enemy in the family?"

I attempted to think of Agnes as a little flower but the undertaking was too great for me.

"No, it must be a Burgundian," said he, adamantly.

And then he looked upon me with hooded eye.

"Or an Englishman."

"An Englishman, say you?" said I, with feigned surprise.

"Even so," said he. "Your Englishman and your Burgundian are—how shall I say?—of a kind, so to speak. They are somewhat, if I may say so without offence, somewhat like your pig. Modest. Fearless. Truthful. Faithful. Honest. Moderate."

I did my best to look like the very embodiment of these virtues whilst, at the same time, appearing as un-piglike as possible. In truth, I have never heard of an honest pig but, on the other hand, I have never heard of a pig being hanged for theft either, so there may be some truth there. I cannot recall hearing a pig boast or lie, but then I have never had much commerce with pigs at all.

"I am sure, messire Jehan," said I, "that you will have little difficulty in finding a young man possessed of these qualities."

"A young man?" said he, aghast. "What a plague have I to do with a young man? No, no, no! Young men are cursed, messire John. Cursed! Hot-blooded. Capricious. My own son...look at him! Say if you will that he is not as choleric a young fool as ever drew breath."

I could not but agree.

"No, messire John," said he. "My Agnes is a delicate creature. She is like yon ivy plant that must cling to a wall of solid foundation."

"An old wall?" said I.

"One that has withstood the tests of time," said he.

"Of ripening years then," said I.

"Even so," said he.

Now I would never have thought of comparing Agnes to an ivy plant but, now that I reflect on it, the simile is most apt. She is nondescript, covers a large area, and is most adept at creeping.

So then I said: "Such a man as myself, perhaps?"

And Jehan said: "I could think of none better."

And he smiled at me.

Then I confessed that since my arrival at Saint Germain I had been much amazed at Agnes's attributes, which, if anything, was an understatement. At this, Jehan embarked on the self-same catalogue of her virtues that I have now heard at least a score of times. On this occasion he ended his recitation by saying that she had been examined and declared fit for child-bearing, which was not a virtue I wished to contemplate at any length.

Now I have never been one for equivocation and so I came swiftly to the point.

"You say that you will offer a dowry of one hundred *écus*," said I.

"Even so," said he, glowing with pride and satisfaction.

"I think you put too small a value on such a rare and costly prize," said I.

"You do?" said he, a trifle anxious that he has run a long and exhausting race only to stumble before the finish.

"The journey to my English estates will be a long one," said I. "Aye and an arduous. Though I myself, travelling simply as I do without a great fortune in my purse—given the secrecy and hazardous nature of my mission—will gladly endure discomfort and laugh at the perils of the way, I shall not suffer my young wife—she being, as you say, of great delicacy—to thus experience such hardships."

"Indeed not," said he. "In faith, I had not thought on that."

"Just so," said I.

"Indeed," said he, scratching his beard.

"Pray tell me what you consider a more fitting dowry," he adds. "Bearing in mind the exigencies of your journey."

"Two hundred?" said I.

"A hundred and fifty?" said he.

"Done," said I.

It must be said that, bargaining apart, Jehan was more than a little overjoyed. He straightway called for Edmond and bade him serve us young wine and cakes, which we duly consumed in the barn and therewith sealed our understanding. Jehan then hurried off to tell his family the good news, leaving me alone with my wine and my somewhat mixed feelings.

The betrothal will be held five days from now on the feast of Saint Simon and Saint Jude. I was told the customary form over supper. The banns must be called on three Sundays, each consecutive upon the other, and thus the wedding day has been set for the feast of Saint Thomas the Apostle.

It is true that under normal circumstances an Advent wedding would not be permitted by Holy Church but Jehan has already dispatched a messenger to the papal court at Avignon to obtain a dispensation and he has every confidence that this will be granted, for Benedict is most anxious to curry favour with the Burgundians. Jehan did do me the courtesy of asking me whether I objected to the assent of the Avignon Pope but I told him nay for, indeed, Avignon is considerably nearer than Rome and the word of one pope is as good as that of another as far as I am concerned. I asked Jehan if he did not fear that the Pope might refuse him, but at this he laughed out loud, saying that as *vassus vassorum* to the Duke of Burgundy he might ask as he liked and that the Pope would do as he was bidden, if he knew what was good for him.

There is one happy custom observed here. Agnes and I shall only be vouchsafed each other's company in the daytime and not more than three times a week at that. On hearing this, I feigned mortification and was much assisted in this by Agnes herself who threw her arms about me and hugged me to her bosom, thereby all but suffocating me, and by Jean-Baptiste who glared at me with such vehemence that if I had been an egg I would have been boiled on the spot.

Jehan was in a merry mood at supper, full of plans and promises. For her part, Thiphaine seems quietly satisfied, as well she might for when her daughter quits Saint Germain she will henceforth enjoy an atmosphere better suited to pious contemplation.

I asked Thiphaine if the betrothal pleased her, to which she replied that she was very happy though she would have preferred it had her daughter not been constrained to go abroad and had the marriage not been celebrated in Advent, but this being God's will, she dared not gainsay it. She also added, in tones of considerable pride—which she would do well to guard herself against for it is a mortal sin—that Agnes is a virgin and that I must be gentle with her. To this I made answer that I had never doubted her virginity for one instant, at which remark all save Jean-Baptiste seemed mightily pleased. Agnes blushed deeply and her nose lit up like a lantern, Bardolph fashion.

In truth, Agnes was remarkably silent this evening, which was a blessing, but made up for it by smiling a great deal. Once we are married, I shall impress upon her the inadvisability of doing this, for radiance does not in the least become her. I also hope that she will not regard our betrothal as a licence for lewd behaviour for at one point this evening, as her father was holding forth on the great alliance of two mighty houses and nonsense of that nature, she placed her hand upon my thigh. In faith, I was grievously put out of countenance. I gently removed the offending member and squeezed it and gave Agnes such a look as

I hoped might be interpreted as one of frustrated longing. Yet, in truth, I do not think I could have been more shocked had the cold capon upon my trencher arisen and curtsied to me.

Esprit rounded off what was, on the whole, a satisfactory supper by toasting Agnes and myself several times. He might have done better had he wished us a lot more and toasted a lot less for before very long he showed himself to be most mightily drunk. This being the case and Esprit being Esprit, he launched into a lengthy anecdote about some exploit of John the Fearless. I confess that I quickly became lost, partly because of a proliferation of names—which are doubtless familiar enough to your Burgundians but unknown to me—and partly as a result of Esprit's thick dialect. For all that, I contrived to laugh at the correct moment, adding my jovial guffaw to Jehan's suppressed titter and the hysterical shrieks of Agnes. Thiphaine did not laugh and shot a look of sourest reprehension at her son. From that I concluded that I might have enjoyed the jest well enough if only I had understood it.

Jean-Baptiste did not laugh. He did not laugh or smile or speak throughout the entire evening. He merely picked at his food with his bone-handled dagger and glared at me.

At Saint Germain en Bazois

On Saint Catherine's Day.
(Monday 25th November 1415)

I commence to wax uneasy over Jean-Baptiste's glaring. In general I care not a whit for glowerers and glarers for they dissemble not—in fact, there is more honesty in their antagonism than in many a smile. But when these same glowerers and glarers begin to fawn and flatter, it behoves you to look well to your defences for there is danger afoot.

Such has come to pass with Jean-Baptiste.

This morning I was leaving the great hall, in which I had breakfasted on hastelets[55], bread, sheeps' feet and wine, and was proceeding in the direction of the barn with a paper of cinnamon begged of the cook, when I happened to pass by the door of the larder. Now fond as I am of all those things with which the good Lord provides us as a means of sustenance, it is not my habit to linger without larder doors. As a rule, I do not linger without any door. I either pass it or I enter.

What arrested my attention on this occasion were whispered, or should I say hissed words that issued from within. The words in question were: *ce chien d'un Falstaff*. Whispered or not, they were undoubtedly spoken by Jean-Baptiste.

Jean-Baptiste's words were soon followed by his person. He saw me as he came through the door for, indeed, I was standing just outside it, and assumed a strangely lopsided smile. He bade me good morrow. I answered him civilly. He then said it was a great pity that we had had so little conversation thus far and he begged my pardon and hoped that I had not mistaken his shyness for hostility. This amounted to a single sentence of roughly thirty to forty syllables, which constituted at least tenfold the number he had so far bestowed upon me. By way of answer, I regarded him evenly and said that I believed I had not mistaken anything for anything.

At this he smiled the more and said that he regretted that his father's business must take him away immediately but that, if it pleased me, he would be glad of my company for a day's hunting on the morrow.

Now from what I have seen and heard since my arrival here, Jean-Baptiste has considerably less interest in his father's affairs than does the good and extremely pregnant sow, Clothilde. In faith, it is most likely that Clothilde, being a potential supper-dish on her master's table, has much more interest in his business than her master's son. Be that as it may, I answered Jean-Baptiste that his invitation pleased me well.

He then left me. I tarried a while without the larder door for I knew full well that the words *ce chien d'un Falstaff* could hardly have been addressed to a leg of ham or an exceptionally intelligent cheese. Sure enough, the door was carefully opened and Edmond appeared. Yet he betrayed no agitation on seeing me. He gave a little bow and mumbled *messire* in a deferential tone and went about his duties.

It would surprise me greatly if Edmond were plotting my demise for he has naught to gain by it and, if Agnes fails to quit Saint Germain, much to lose.

For all that, my spirit was troubled, and when my spirit is troubled I drink. This I proceeded to do and eventually fell asleep in the barn and thereby missed dinner. Fortunately, I was finally awoken by a maidservant come to fetch wine and was thus spared the double penance of missing supper too.

At supper, Jean-Baptiste reassumed his hostile taciturnity. I shall now attempt to sleep and keep anxiety at bay for it does little profit to any man. *Timor mortis morte pejor.*[56]

We shall see what tomorrow brings.

At Saint Germain en Bazois

On the eve of Saint Simon and Saint Jude.
(Wednesday 27th November 1415)

Today has brought Jean-Baptiste a broken leg. Here follows the manner of its breaking.

It was at about the hour of prime[57] when we set forth to our hunting and, truth to tell, I would have much liked to have found some excuse for not going. In the first place, the hour of prime is one I would as soon miss from my daily round, for having had the misfortune to see the sun rise on many occasions in the past and having been singularly unimpressed by it, I have scant interest in repeating the experience. Secondly, I had every reason for believing that Jean-Baptiste's intentions for that day were less than benevolent, and I am not writing here of his slaughter of divers woodland creatures for the supper-table.

Yet it would have been most discourteous to have thus refused the son of my host. After all, he is my future brother-in-law, be he fifty years my junior or not.

My trepidation was not lessened when Jean-Baptiste greeted me with crossbows in his arms.

Now for some reason I had assumed that we would go hawking and that any accident that Jean-Baptiste had planned for me would somehow entail the business of riding a horse. Thus I had entertained the notion that, being a passable horseman, I might be able to evade his murderous intent and come home safely, having discharged my obligations as a guest.

It is rather less easy to avoid a crossbow accident. Your hawk cannot kill anything much bigger than a rabbit, but your crossbow is a powerful instrument of war. When cocked, it is sensitive to the touch and will loose its bolt without much urging. On being loosed, this bolt will fly straight and true for many a yard and will surely find its mark, especially when it is aimed.

As I took my bow from Jean-Baptiste, which I did with many a pleasant smile, I had a disturbing vision of William the Conqueror who was dispatched with just such a weapon by a traitorous subject while hunting in the Forest of Windsor.[58] I therefore decided it was best to lag behind Jean-Baptiste as much as I could and allow him the least opportunity to test his weapon on good English flesh.

It was a dull day and before we had ridden a few furlongs it began to rain. With that, any slight enthusiasm I might have summoned up for this expedition vanished forthwith. Ahead of me, Jean-Baptiste crouched sullenly in his saddle, cradling his crossbow with every sign of affection. In truth, it was only Pistol who appeared to be deriving any pleasure from this foolhardiness for he has an unhealthy fondness for the open air, whatever the weather.

Having traversed a broad expanse of open heathland, we came to a steep, heavily wooded hillside that dips down to the valley below where flows the River Aron. At this point, Jean-Baptiste bawled out that here was a fine place for boar and deer and, without troubling himself to ask my opinion on the matter, spurred his horse on and plunged into the forest with much hallooing and brandishing of his crossbow. If, indeed, there are any boar and deer in that wood they must be exceeding deaf ones.

I had little choice but to follow. In faith, I had thought myself relatively safe in the open for I had kept Jean-Baptiste well in view. The forest was a different matter.

I contrived to keep my young companion ahead of me. This was no easy task, for the way waxed ever steeper and the ground, consisting of a sort of chalky clay, was anything but firm. No horse is so well shod that it never slips and, together with Pistol's damnable exuberance, this meant that I was in constant peril of either falling from the saddle or, even worse, overtaking Jean-Baptiste. I was exceeding loath to do this for my back presents a better target than most, but finally I saw my future brother-in-law disappear into the thickets to my right and, being unable to halt my steed's mad career, I was ahead of him.

At last the trees stopped abruptly and Pistol, pleased to be free of such hindrances, lunged swiftly forwards. It was only with the greatest effort that I was able to rein him in and God blind me if it were not most fortunate that I did so! No more than a lance's length from where we stopped the ground itself disappeared from view.

I dismounted somewhat cautiously, walked a little nearer to the precipice and peered over. Far below me a flock of crows wheeled and cawed and, far below them, the Aron seethed and tumbled furiously.

Now ten years ago I would never have done so foolish a thing as to turn my back on an enemy. But age has blunted my wits and by so much was I relieved at having cheated death in one direction that I ignored it in the other.

Dame Fortune is a curious creature. She bestows her favours in defiance of all logic. Of a sudden, I heard a cracking of undergrowth behind me and I glanced round to see the cause. What happened next happened so swiftly that I must reflect a little before I record it.

No more than twenty yards distant, Jean-Baptiste was rushing towards me with his bone-handled dagger naked and glinting in the November light. His face was twisted with what might have been rage but was certainly passion of a sort. Perceiving that I had noticed him, he let out a blood-curdling shout, which was doubtless intended to render me stiff with fright and thus an easier target.

Fortunately for me, and unfortunately for Jean-Baptiste, my goodly horse lay somewhat between the two of us though, at that precise point, slightly to one side—allowing my attacker free passage.

Now had it not been for Jean-Baptiste's blood-curdling shout—a typically unnecessary example of Burgundian histrionics—his passage would have remained free and, doubtless, I would have eventually accompanied his bone-handled dagger to a brief encounter with a flock of crows and a yet briefer enjoyment of the River Aron.

Now Pistol is, by and large, a sweet-tempered beast if, at times, a little inclined to high spirits. However, he is not to be startled with impunity, as I and two scoundrels on the road to Auxerre know to our cost. Jolted by Jean-Baptiste's cry, he snorted and moved suddenly to his left. The said manoeuvre effectively blocked Jean-Baptiste's charge and brought him up against Pistol's rump. Being thus affronted and howling with rage and frustration, Jean-Baptiste fetched Pistol's rump a stinging blow.

This was not wise.

Pistol's hind legs lashed out with such force and celerity as deceived the eye. However, they succeeded in catching Jean-Baptiste neatly in the midriff, causing him to let out an audible "Ooof!" before he arced gracefully backwards to fetch up against a tree-trunk with a noise that I felt at the bottom of my stomach. The bone-handled knife flicked high in the air and vanished over the cliff, alone.

I drew my sword and assumed a defensive guard.

Jean-Baptiste was very quiet. At first I thought he was dead, for which I was not entirely sorry, and I was settling myself to thinking of how I might best explain this to his father without incurring his animosity and thereby jeopardizing my marriage when I perceived his chest rising and falling in a manner normally associated with life.

I approached him and slapped his chops a little and, by and by, he recovered his senses. He was bleeding from the head, where it had fetched up against the tree, and his right leg was bent in a most uncommon fashion.

"Why, in the name of all that is holy, did you attempt to slay me?" said I, for want of anything better to say.

"You are a dirty Englishman," he muttered bloodily.

Now I shall willingly confess to being an Englishman for it is a mere statement of essential nature and only to my credit. As to being dirty, that is a different matter. No man who washes his face and hands every day and takes a bath at least once a month, when he is able, can justifiably be called dirty. Besides, a Burgundian calling anyone dirty is like the pot calling the kettle black.

"Since when has my being an Englishman been a reason for murder?" I asked, being genuinely curious.

"Since you desired marriage with my sister," said Jean-Baptiste, reasonably enough.

As I gazed down on the lad, I could not help but admire him. It is no small achievement to be defiant when you have a cracked pate, a broken leg and belike the odd fractured rib to boot. I had been in half a mind to stab him a little and cast his corpse where he would doubtless have cast mine, yet now I thought better of it. He was only a boy after all and it is not commonly considered seemly or courteous to murder your host's son, be he the second son or not. And so I helped him to his able foot and lifted him over the saddle of his horse, which action occasioned him great discomfort and no little pain. This gave me some small satisfaction and dispelled any further notions of revenge. I remounted Pistol and led Jean-Baptiste back through the forest towards his father's house.

In point of fact, it was rather a long time before we reached Saint Germain for no sooner had we quitted the wood than it began to rain again most heavily and, not wishing to catch my death of an ague, I sought shelter beneath a pine tree. Sadly it was not quite broad enough to accommodate Jean-Baptiste and his horse and I was not prepared to add to my soaking by hauling him out of the saddle. Yet when the rain had slackened, I perceived that he was still alive, though exceedingly wet and cold.

It pleases me to relate that I am now considered the saviour of both father and son for, to save Jean-Baptiste's honour, I have generously concocted a history of a hunting accident in which only my quick thinking and prompt action preserved the young rogue from death. Jean-Baptiste has had little option but to corroborate my tale though he did so with many a wince and grimace. His father now deems him an ungrateful wretch.

Perhaps Jean-Baptiste will die. Who knows? The ways of God do truly pass all comprehension. If he lives, it may be that we will come to an understanding.

I have seen to it that Pistol receives an extra ration of oats.

At Saint Germain en Bazois

On the feast of Saint Simon and Saint Jude.
(Thursday 28th November 1415)

I have never been betrothed before. It is a queer feeling.

The ceremony took place in the hall after supper at about the hour of compline.

There were few guests, for which Jehan made great apology, saying that there had not been time to summon all he would have liked. Most notable among the few that were there were Tristan de Corbigny who is a neighbouring seigneur, his daughter Constance who is betrothed to Esprit, and the Archdeacon—or *Archidiacre* as they will have it here—who is Jacques by name. There was also the village priest, Father Simon.

The supper was a fine thing and consisted of no less than three *mets*. First there was frumenty followed by a cabbage soup strong on garlic, then a boar's head, then beef cooked in wine, then roasted suckling pigs and a pastry. The second *mets* was a light soup flavoured with almonds, then roasted partridges, then fowl boiled in wine, then roasted leg of pork, then a dish of trout, then tarts, then roasted rabbits and a pastry. The third *mets* was a custard, then a roasted kid, then sweet beignets and a pastry. For those of us who had yet some space to fill, there were dishes of walnuts, olives and cheese. All of this accompanied by flagons of wine.

Being a largish feast and this being Burgundy, there was much rushing about of servants and yelping of dogs and clattering of bowls, not to mention a deal of cursing and shouting. I have not seen or heard the like since I quitted the Boar's Head.

Nothing pleases like variety and, truth to say, I have somewhat tired of the company of Jehan and his family. Thus did I welcome the addition of guests, whosoever they might be.

The least companionable of those present was Father Simon who, judging by his air, seemed to have been here greatly against his wishes for he looked about him like an alderman who has fallen in with beggars. As is so often the case with priests, he is a thin man and has ever a grimace upon his countenance, as though he were weaned on vinegar.

Father Simon was, as might be imagined, exceedingly dainty with his food: breaking his bread into seven pieces and drinking his wine in five draughts, and of these the fifth twice in memory of the mixed blood and water that flowed from our Blessed Saviour's side. Happily, he excused himself early in the evening when Esprit broke into a rousing and exceptionally ribald rendition of *Deu vouse save, Dame Emme!* For this service I can almost forgive Esprit his other transgressions.

Now Archdeacon Jakes was more the sort of churchman I prefer: a goodly stout man and a merry. Though he is, I think, a little too inclined to prolixity, he yet matched me cup for cup and guffawed most convincingly at the repetitious sallies of Esprit's damp wit.

And so we come to Tristan de Corbigny. Sieur Tristan is an aged knight of some three-score and five years—white of hair and deaf of ear. In faith, he is the noisiest silent man I ever came across: silent because he lives in silence and noisy because, believing everyone else to be as deaf as he, he bellows like a Dutch bo'sun.

Fortunately, I was seated at one end of the board and Tristan de Corbigny at the other with Jehan at his elbow and was thus spared the painful pleasure of conversing with him.

Now Tristan's daughter Constance is a girl of some sixteen summers, and every one of them bedecked with flowers and radiant with sunshine. In truth, it is a great pity that I did not save *her* father's life for those qualities that mark out my dear Agnes from the common roll of women—her fatness, her stupidity and her strident voice— are pleasantly lacking in Constance and, conversely, the finer points of Constance—her slim, voluptuous body, lascivious eye and ready wit—are either entirely absent from my Agnes or buried so deep within her fleshy walls as to defy detection.

The de Bazois family were reduced in number owing to the indisposition of Jean-Baptiste, who took his food in his chamber. Jehan looked especially pleased with himself all evening, as befits a man who is about to add Hampshire, Sussex and the Duchy of Cornwall to his family acquisitions. Thiphaine was pale and tearful as a dutiful mother should be; Agnes was flushed with pride, passion and wine, and Esprit behaved himself worse than any of the inmates of his father's piggery.

Esprit's table-manners, though adequate in principle, always deteriorate in due proportion to his state of drunkenness. After half a dozen cups, he will bite his bread instead of breaking it, chew with both sides of his mouth, laugh and talk with his mouth full, disdain to wipe his lips before drinking... God's wounds, I could write a page on his inebriate boorishness and still not cover the half of it!

The greater part of the conversation during supper was either agricultural or political in nature, and as I find agriculture somewhat less interesting than an algebraic translation of Saint Paul's Second Epistle to the Thessalonians and politics passably interesting when it concerns England but otherwise not at all, and as most of this was blasted to and fro between Jehan and Tristan de Corbigny at a volume that beggars description, it is small wonder that I spoke both seldom and little. However, one of the few occasions when I did feel moved to participate was when Archdeacon Jakes set to recounting the strange and marvellous happenings that had befallen a small village in Picardy, Saint Just en Tel by name.

It seems that the Blessed Virgin Mary had appeared to a group of poor shepherds with the Infant Jesus cradled in Her arms. Immediately a one-legged shepherd—which disability must have made the business of shepherding uncommon difficult—had had his missing appendage restored to him. The village blacksmith had been cured of a hare lip. Before ascending to heaven on a fiery chariot drawn by massed regiments of angels, archangels, cherubim and seraphim with the odd saint blowing a trump for good measure, She had unleashed a thunderbolt, which, striking the ground before the church, had cleft the earth in twain. A mighty oak tree had instantly sprung up which since had wrought miraculous cures on all those halt and distempered persons who had touched it.

This news was greeted with much open-mouthed wonderment. Unfortunately, my own mouth was closed in the act of containing a copious draught of Burgundy, which had remained there as I listened to this tale unfold. More unfortunately still, the laughter that convulsed heavenwards from my belly met this copious draught and, finding no issue around it, propelled it forwards, thus showering poor Thiphaine with a fine, vinous spray, with which she was not best pleased. I was effusive in my apologies and she accepted them gracefully and with the sort of expression of long suffering that commonly plagues the pious. By the time I resumed my seat, agriculture and politics were re-established in favour.

It was at about this time, as I remember, that we were joined by three musicians.

I am sometimes of the opinion that your musicians are a curse upon the world. Wherever you look in the Histories, there is hardly a foul deed that has not been accompanied by music of some sort—be it only humming. Take John the Baptist *per exemplum*. John would not have lost his head if Salome had not danced, and Salome would not have danced if her musicians had not played. *Ergo*, John the Baptist was beheaded on account of a handful of tuneless ne'er-do-wells. Take your Emperor Caligula. Or was it Nero? It could have been Marcus Aurelius. I forget. Your emperors are much of a muchness in any case. Whoever it was considered that naught but burning the city of Rome was sufficient accompaniment for his wondrous attempts at melody. God be thanked that Harry Percy merely whistled.

Were it not bad enough to be so suddenly hemmed in by musicians, they began to play upon the bagpipes—and that with every appearance of gleeful enthusiasm.

Now disliking the rebec as I do—and that most heartily—I reserve the greater part of my disrelish for the bagpipe. Why any sane man would wish to blow into the internal organs of a goat in order to approximate the noise of screeching cats is a question that would dumbfound the most agile of philosophers. The practice might be considered excusable if the pipes were an easy or pleasant instrument to play but they are not. I myself tried to coax a few notes from them one Michaelmas and succeeded only in imitating the sound of Bardolph's bowels after a dish of cabbage. Furthermore, I made the error of sucking instead of blowing and thereby received a lungful of malodorous vapour. I suspect the piper had neglected to empty the goat's belly before making an instrument of it.

In France this engine of ordeal is called the *muse*. I cannot conceive of a greater misnomer for, if of divine inspiration at all—which I much doubt—it is surely no work of Terpsichore or Polyhymnia. Primeval Chaos would be a safer bet.

In short, your bagpipe is belike good enough for your wild Celt but it is no instrument for civilised man.

However, this caterwauling caused Constance to spring to her feet and she insisted that I join her in a dance. Truth to say, she asked Esprit first but by this time her betrothed had some difficulty in balancing on his legs. I therefore determined to show these Burgundians how an Englishman could cut a caper and I think I show no immodesty in writing that I danced surpassing well. Certainly Constance seemed to agree for she smiled and laughed and winked at me with her lascivious eye.

Sadly, this innocent familiarity did not go unnoticed by Agnes.

Now Agnes had been drinking deep in honour of the occasion. She did not spring gracefully to her feet as Constance had done but rather rolled upwards and then swayed from side to side like a barrel coming to rest. Her jealousy, or her sudden elevation, had rendered her pale and this much improved her looks.

I did not deem it politic to excite Agnes's anger at this our betrothal feast, and so I forsook Constance and led my sweetheart from the table. We began to dance.

Round and round we went. Round and round. For all the world, like the earth and moon. To grant this comparison verisimilitude, Agnes's face waxed from pale to shining white. Round and round we went.

After orbiting me for several minutes, my moon began to wobble on her axis and finally she quitted her allotted sphere and careered wildly across the firmament to the very edge of the universe where, hanging her head out the window, she produced the most musical sounds heard all evening.

In truth, by this time, the entire company was quite drunk. Saving, that is, Thiphaine and myself—Father Simon having already made good his escape. Agnes, now rid of her excess of wine, staggered back to the table and resumed her seat. No sooner had she done so than Jehan thumped the board mightily and roared out:

"Edmond!"

"My Lord?" said Edmond quietly, from a distance of about three inches from his master's left ear.

"Oh, so there you are," said Jehan. "Bring hither the villagers, that they may witnesh the betrothal and know it to be true."

Edmond bowed and swiftly performed his duty. Soon there was a silent group of tenants and serfs gathered within the door, all of them doubtless wishing they were safely at home in bed. I caught one or two of them gazing longingly at the table and jealously at the dogs munching happily beneath it. Jean-Baptiste, glaring magnificently, was carried in on a litter.

Jehan bade Agnes and me arise and this we did.

"Djohn," said Jehan, swaying dangerously and offering me a cup of wine that got emptier by the instant, "take thish cup and give it to my daughter, that she may pledge the binding lawsh of cononuble...of connubialishmy...of marriage."

I rescued the cup and proffered it to a rather pallid Agnes, though by that time there remained precious little wine therein.

"Take this cup and drink to the binding laws of marriage," said I, smiling sweetly.

Agnes drank of the cup and was promptly sick again—this time over Jean-Baptiste. Poor boy. He is attended by ill-fortune.

Thus was our betrothal consummated. The villagers were dismissed and shuffled through the door with every air of not knowing why they had been there in the first place. Jean-Baptiste, growling with ire, was wiped off and carried back to his chamber; Jehan slumped gratefully into his chair, and the revelry recommenced.

Despite being in full agreement with each other, Esprit and the Archdeacon contrived to enjoy a most noisy dispute about the madness of the King of France. It started noisily and ended in great tumult with Esprit pounding the board with his fist and bawling out that the good cleric was an egregious bastard, whereupon Jehan fetched his son a resounding box upon the ear. Quite rightly too. For all I know, the archdeacon may well be a bastard but that is no reason for Esprit to put his father out of countenance at table.

Agnes and Thiphaine soon gave way to fatigue. Thiphaine arose graciously, cast a reproving glance at her elder son, and bade the company good night. I think I was the only one who noticed her departure. Agnes, having already collapsed in her trencher, was carried to her chamber by Edmond and two lusty manservants.

By this time, the pipers, whose attempts at music had gone largely unheeded, had long since abandoned their bagpipes and, after loitering awkwardly behind the table in the hope of being asked to play again, now withdrew, muttering and grumbling to each other. The evening suddenly began to promise more than I had expected.

In due course, Tristan de Corbigny, who had vainly attempted to follow the noisy dispute between Esprit and the Archdeacon and had since delivered himself of a brief but exceedingly loud monologue on the price of pepper—to the common mystification of all—departed also. Sadly he took Constance with him.

Thus the evening was left to Jehan, the Archdeacon, Esprit and myself.

By this time, Esprit appeared to have developed some manner of visual impediment. As each spoke in his turn, he would regard us with the sort of gaze commonly employed by mariners when surveying some distant object seen fleetingly through the ocean mists. He continued to shout even though Tristan de Corbigny was no longer with us, and this especially loudly when discussion turned once again to the Armagnacs. Finally, he terminated a largely incoherent denunciation by swearing, at the top of his voice, that he would forsake the changing of his linen till he had met their host in combat.

Such is the impetuousness of youth. *Dulce bellum inexpertis.*[59] In faith, his oath sounded a good deal more heroic than it actually was for it is no great sacrifice for a Burgundian to forsake clean linen.

It now came to that hour of the evening when each of the company was expected to deliver himself of some virulently stated opinion. As is common, the substance of such an opinion is of very little account—it is the manner of its statement that matters.

The Archdeacon inveighed against poor Pope Gregory in Rome. This till he had finally exhausted his lexicon of fitting epithets, whereupon he lapsed into an indignant silence and frowned at the rest of us as if we were personally responsible for this evil schism in the most holy Catholic Church.

It was I who rescued us from this silence by stating roundly that Hal was sure to launch a fresh offensive in the spring and would put paid to the houses of Valois and Armagnac once and for all. I added diplomatically that John the Fearless would doubtless be king of a much-enlarged Burgundy by the end of next year.

My declaration met with much favour, as I had much expected it would. Jehan attempted to rise to his feet but thought better of it and, from a seated position, proposed a toast to *Henri d'Angleterre*. This toast was echoed around the board and finally punctuated by a dull thud as Esprit collapsed in a dead faint—an event that went entirely disregarded by his father who, entering upon a vehement discourse on the hardships of pig-rearing, gave further emphasis to the more stirring passages by repeatedly jabbing his son's head with his forefinger.

Together with most of Jehan's family and friends, I knew better than to attempt to dislodge him from this subject. The Archdeacon did vainly assay to steer the conversation back to a slightly less agricultural topic but it remained firmly rooted in the pig-sty. Finally he renounced his efforts and, after a good show of yawning, retired to bed—so causing the company to break up. Jehan dragged Esprit from his seat and hauled him to his chamber whilst continuing to shout his porcine observations across the hall to me. I remained at the table for some short time, revelling in the silence.

I have had a bellyful of pigs.

At Saint Germain en Bazois

On the first day of December, being a Sunday.

Three days have passed since last I wrote in this my daybook. Truth to say, I do not approach it sanguinely. It is a simple thing to recount the events that befall me upon the highway but much less simple to describe my commonplace, diurnal activities, let alone my nocturnal ones.

Cold weather with much rain. There, I ask you! It will be small comfort in the years to come to know that the first day of December in the third year of the reign of King Henry was cold and rainy.

Archdeacon Jakes, who had been expected to stay here for some few days, has been packed off home in disgrace. He was caught *in flagrante delicto* with a maidservant in the hay-loft. Had they been found by anyone except Thiphaine, no more would have been said about the matter but Jehan's good and exceedingly pious wife was greatly discountenanced that such immorality should take place beneath her roof and demanded the instant dismissal of the lusty cleric. Exactly what Thiphaine was doing in the hay-loft, I am at a loss to say.

I was at church this morning. This does not represent a startling change in my attitude to religion but a recognition of the realities associated with marrying Agnes, for the banns must be called and I must be present to hear them.

In truth, I did not hear a single thing. It comes as something of a disappointment to me to find that after so many years of avoiding churches I might just as well have saved myself the trouble, for with slightly fewer crosses and slightly more hogsheads they would make admirable taverns. Certainly they are no less noisy.

Nobody save I seemed the least put out by the uproar of the congregation and certainly not Agnes and Esprit who bawled at each other throughout the service and seemed largely indifferent to the words of God. Father Simon, bless him, did his level best to communicate these words to his congregation but his disdainful shouting only added to the row.

Given that the function of banns—as I understand them—is to assure yourself that you are not marrying your sister and assure everyone else that you do not have a wife for every day of the week and two for Sundays, then I might have as many wives as King David and every one of them my mother for all the populace of Saint Germain would know. If there ever was a more superfluous exercise, I should like to know of it.

There is a picture of Saint Christopher on the wall of the church, most cunningly wrought. I shall go and look upon it before I continue my pilgrimage. It will bring me good fortune on my way.

The bell of the church is called Augustine though whether it be named after Augustine of Hippo or Augustine of Canterbury or some other Augustine entirely, I know not.

The sermon given by Father Simon was mercifully short and pleasantly inaudible. It is a pity that Mad Denys was not there to see it for he, more than most, could use a lesson in brevity.

Agnes now eats her supper in her room. This is a most refreshing novelty but one that will sadly end once we are married. From now to our wedding, I shall see her only on Wednesdays, Fridays and Sundays. As two of these days are meatless, I have begun to associate my future wife with fish. Hake, to be precise.

At Saint Germain en Bazois

On Saint Nicholas' Day.
(Friday 6th December 1415)

It has rained fish in the Monts du Forez. This is true. I had the news of Jehan who had it of Edmond who had it of the miller's wife.

I am at a loss to say how this piscine downpour came about but, bearing in mind my entry of Sunday last, I can only construe it as a blessing on my nuptials. After all, it is not even as if the few inhabitants of the Monts du Forez have any particular need of fish for it seems they are well-enough fed and want for naught—or at least for little more than anyone else. For myself, if the Lord On High saw fit to relieve my destitution by raining haddock on me, it would be enough to turn me apostate on the spot.

I may well have written this before—and I shall be damned for a fool if I am going to read through all this fiddle-faddle to find out—but I am not overfond of your fish. I was compelled to eat it today, it being a Friday and I being neither too old nor too sick nor too pregnant to merit dispensation. When I consider that I have been devoutly constrained to eat fish twice a week for the past three-score and ten years—week in, week out, cod, herring, gurnet, dace, hake, luce, trout, eels and God knows what else—it surprises me greatly that there yet remains one of this finny race extant. Let alone enough to rain on the Monts du Forez.

Fish, in faith, is all that I am not: cold, thin, silent, pale and phlegmatic. We English are not known for our phlegm, excepting that villain Pistol who is much given to expectoration. Perhaps Pistol's habit of spitting owes itself to a surfeit of fish for, though he is by no means a pious man, he has a great liking for eels and consumes many of them. Marry, now that I reflect thereon, he also smells of fish. So too does his wife, the sometime Mistress Quickly. Yet she was ever a curious amalgam.

Indeed, Nature produces many such amalgams. Your mariners tell of a fish that flies through the air, having wings like a bird. And what be your great leviathans of the deep but mere elephants with fins?

Enough. This daybook is a place for solemn meditation and not for the frivolous arguments of science.

Yesterday afternoon, I was visited by a tailor who rode all the way from Autun just to measure me for my wedding gown. I would just as soon do without one but Jehan insists on all due ceremony and who am I to gainsay my father-in-law?

The tailor was a small man who danced about me for a most unconscionable time before he had my measurements, and twittered and squeaked like a demented bat. You would have thought he had never seen a man of ducal proportions. Your provincials are all alike.

This morning, Jehan's messenger returned from Avignon with a most imposing document indited in Latin, this being the papal dispensation for marrying in Advent. It seems that the messenger was kept waiting for two days before he was granted access to the papal court and this has angered Jehan greatly. Still, we may now marry *in facie ecclesiae* and before Christmas too. This gives me some solace for I feared having to spend Christmastide in the company of my in-laws.

At Saint Germain en Bazois

The day after Saint Lucy's Day.
(Saturday 14th December 1415)

Today was of such villainous dullness that I disdain to describe it.

Yesterday, by contrast, saw one of those mystical conjunctions of forces, celestial and human in origin, that shapes the destinies of men. Firstly, it was Saint Lucy's Day and thus the shortest day of the year. Secondly, it was a Friday and the thirteenth day of the month and thus unlucky of aspect. Thirdly, it was a fish day. Fourthly, it was one of those days on which I am permitted Agnes's company.

I thus decided to take a long ride for, with the sun entering the sign of the goat, I would not trust myself to spend an hour alone with my betrothed, lest animal passion drive her to unbridled carnality.

I wrote that such conjunctions are apt to shape the destinies of men. Truth to say, yesterday's conjunction did precious little to shape mine, either for good or ill. In fact, were it not that my other days are so entirely lacking in interest, I would not take the trouble to record yesterday at all.

As with many a Saint Lucy's Day, the sky was dark and overcast and there was a bitter wind blowing. It was the first time I had ridden Pistol since the day of my hunting expedition with Jean-Baptiste and despite the inclemency of the weather he was as happy as I to escape the confines of Saint Germain and sortie into the open country.

We might well have ridden all day had not Dame Fortune cast an alehouse in our path.

It is a foolish man who defies Dame Fortune—especially with the sun entering the sign of the goat—and thus, with some reluctance, I yielded my neck to her yoke and dismounted.

I call it an alehouse though house it was not. In truth, it was a dismal place of wattle and daub. The thatch had not been repaired in many a summer and seemed bent on rejoining its living brethren upon the ground.

I call it an alehouse though ale there was not. But there was some new wine that was clear and sparkling, and there was *vin de couvent* which was most foul. However, in the middle of the room there was a cheery fire upon which a cauldron of cabbage and garlic soup boiled and bubbled. There also seemed to be an absence of fish.

And so I dined on soup and from somewhere there appeared a dish of cold pig's trotters and I washed it all down with a flagon or two of new wine. This took the chill from my bones and restored my good humour, which I had somewhat mislaid during my journey thither. I invited the ale-wife, or wine-wife, if you will, to join me in a cup, together with the only other patron of the place. This latter was Raymond by name and he was an ostler by trade.

In truth, both ale-wife and ostler were much flattered that the future son-in-law of Seigneur Jehan de Bazois should thus honour them and laughed heartily at all my jests, of which, I fear, they understood but few.

Raymond, though clearly he had felt the pinch of poverty and belike was feeling it yet, was a merry soul and offered to show me a game of cards, which they play often in this part of the world and which is called *Taroc*. I confess that, though we played this game three times, I understood little more of it the third time than I did the first. The result of this was that Raymond won thirteen *denier* of me, which he did with many professions of apology, each of which was greeted with the ale-wife's cackles. I knew that I was being gulled when we were no more than halfway into the first game, but I was being gulled with the greatest nicety and charm and the few *denier* that it cost me were worth the entertainment.

I passed what remained of the afternoon before the fire. I have drunk in better places and I have drunk in worse but, for all that, I much preferred the honest fellowship of Raymond and the ale-wife to the tedium of Jehan's house. Moreover, the weather without being cold and windy, I was in no haste to return to Saint Germain.

Thus it was that when I finally rode into the precincts of Jehan's manor, darkness was already falling and I was in a merry mood and slightly unsteady in the saddle. Jehan met me at the door and told me that the household had been much concerned at my lengthy absence and that Agnes herself had passed much of the day in tears. As Agnes's face does not suffer lamentation gladly, I observed to Jehan that it was indeed most fortunate that I had not been there to see it. He seemed vexed at this remark.

Supper was boiled salted hake, which the Burgundians call *merlu*. I gave it several appellations as it lay steaming on my trencher, of which appellations *merlu* was not one. Marry, it is fortunate that the de Bazois family have no English, else would my marriage prospects have ended there and then.

Over the hake I regaled the family with the history of Pope Joan[60] on which I lavished all the colour and detail which that tragic story merits. I was much surprised that no one had ever heard of Pope Joan but such was the case. Towards the end of my account, Thiphaine grew even paler than usual and felt it necessary to excuse herself, which, in my opinion, bore out all I have said about the hake. It was a great pity that she missed the conclusion of my history for the others followed it with much interest and amazement and then laughed out loud when I had concluded it. This strikes me as surpassing strange for there is little of the comic about the story of Pope Joan.

It grieves me to confess that I fell asleep at table. Though this spared me another helping of the hake, it has done little to improve my standing here. It seems that Jehan, Edmond and Esprit carried me to my chamber.

At Saint Germain en Bazois

On the sixteenth day of December, being a Monday.

It is snowing hard and the ground is already ankle-deep in the filthy stuff. It is also grievous cold.

There are but two places in Jehan's house where you may escape death through the frostbite: one is the kitchen—where I contrive to spend as much time as possible—and the other is before the fire in the great hall, where you are obliged to exchange pleasantries with Jehan, Esprit and whosoever should assault you with them. Thus it is only that I seek quiet and solitude that I find myself seated in my chamber and only that I am shrouded in my pilgrim's cloak and the thick bed-quilt that I am not already an icicle in human form. I do not think I shall be able to write for very long.

The house is all of a-bustle with preparations for the wedding but, despite the many rushings hither and thither and the shoutings and cursings and the protracted disputes, very little seems to have been accomplished so far. I tell a lie: yesterday the tailor brought my wedding gown from Autun. It fits me well, as indeed it should after such a deal of measurings.

Since our betrothal, I have kept company with Agnes no more than a dozen times and for all the conversation we have had it might as well have been once. This could be thought a considerable improvement yet, unfortunately, her verbal communication has been replaced by more physical intimacies. She is becoming increasingly amorous: like a wide-bellied pot that has simmered for six and twenty years and is finally in danger of boiling over. That I am largely spared the Calvary of her shouting is certainly some small comfort, yet her sugared phrases and spaniel fawnings are such that I am hard put to know which is worse.

The last time we met was on the Sunday just gone. When dinner was finished and those others present had departed to go about their afternoon's business, Agnes nestled up to me and tickled my beard and said, "I shall give my lord many fine children."

For a few happy instants I entertained the fallacy that she meant some other lord but, sadly, she meant me. I know not whence she will procure said children but it is certain that I shall play no part in it.

I doubt not that she is greatly flattered to be marrying a handsome English lord in the prime of his life, but I would she did not show it so.

159

Damn me if I shall go through with this! Had I not tarried in this whoreson place, I could have been in Jerusalem before now. Or Compostella. Hal would laugh me to scorn if he saw me, and rightly so. A hundred and fifty *écus d'or*! God blind me if I have not done less for more.

A black pox on this writing! My finger-ends wax numb.

At Saint Germain en Bazois

On Saint Thomas's Eve.
(Friday 20th December 1415)

The snow has given way to rain. If it is not one thing then it is another!

The rain has transformed the land around Saint Germain into a miry morass in which the oxen sink fetlock-high. And yet it has not prevented the arrival of Jehan's sister and brother-in-law from Dijon.

This sister, Marie, is every bit as citified as Jehan is rustic. She regards everything concerning the manor of Saint Germain with unconcealed distaste. She insisted on being carried bodily from her ox-cart to the threshold, which required the services of no less than four sturdy manservants for—though it defies belief—she is yet fatter than Agnes. In spite of this, any mention of pigs causes her to shudder with revulsion. In faith, were it not for a common laziness of eye, you might say that she and her brother resemble each other not at all.

Her husband Geoffrey—or Geoffroi, if you will—is a notary. That is all the description that is needful.

Thiphaine and Jehan greeted these two with all the formality and deference that one would normally accord an archbishop, though they stopped short of the kissing of rings. Honeyed wine and bread and salt were offered them, at which Marie grimaced with disgust and forced down a little of each with the greatest show of difficulty.

I was presented to them as Milord Jean de Falstaff, friend, confidant and emissary of His Majesty King Henry of England, with which they both seemed much impressed. As well they might. There followed a good deal of bowing and curtseying and kissing of hands. My famous exploit on the road to Auxerre was recounted in full, as was my saving the life of Jehan's younger, though apparently not least beloved son.

It grieves me that my valour is better esteemed by these foreigners than by my own countrymen. Out of selfless service to my nation and loyalty to my sovereign, I vanquished two of the most furious rebels as ever took up arms against their lawful king. And what thanks did I get? A banneretcy! God's blood, even sailors get that!

Geoffrey and Marie have been allotted Esprit's chamber; Esprit has been allotted Jean-Baptiste's chamber; Jean-Baptiste has been consigned to a corner of the hall. Poor boy. If I were attended by his misfortune, I should kill myself. And belike fail in that too.

Thus we were seven at supper, Agnes being allowed to break with tradition and eat with us in honour of our guests. It was an even more tiresome affair than usual. Geoffrey on his law-suits provides a limited diversion from Jehan on his pigs but there all advantage ends. Marry, so long-winded is he that, if I were a magistrate, I should hang all his clients, whether plaintiff or defendant.

Marie was all fawning attentions, as I had half-expected. To be treated as a peer of the realm is flattering at first but, by degrees, it becomes uncommon irksome. Perhaps ennoblement has its disadvantages if you become a butt for such conceited lickspittles.

I wonder greatly that Marie is fatter yet than Agnes. Is there some element peculiar to Burgundy that so engenders rotundity in women? Now a man, a fat man I mean, or one inclined to roundness, is no more than Nature's advertisement of virility. This is well known. We eat and drink more copiously than others because we have a greater frame to fill and the nutriments thus stored are, when occasion demands, transmuted to valour, wit and fecundity. If indeed, as learned men say, there is perfection in a circle, then is it not palpably true that the closer we resemble that form, the nearer we ourselves approach perfection? This is true of all men.

It is not true of women. I have never known female obesity be coupled to valour, wit or jollity. In faith, of the women I have known who could justly be termed fat, I cannot name one who was content to be so. They all yearned after a slim waist and a shapely leg and, waxing ever more melancholy over these absences, ate and drank the more, thereby only increasing their bulk and likewise their misfortune. I have yet to meet a man who behaves thus.

Agnes sang. Alas. She will know no dearth of companionship if we arrive together in London, for she has merely to open wide her mouth to meet all the jackdaws and starlings for miles around. She sang four songs and all of them sounded much alike. The first, as I recall, was called *Lamento de Tristan et Rota*. Poor Tristan and Rota! To be star-crossed lovers is bad enough without having Agnes sing about you.

Naturally it was to be expected that everyone would applaud loudly, which proved to be so. Geoffrey even shouted *Bis! Encore!*

Thankfully Agnes declined an encore, complaining of a sore throat—which I did not doubt in the slightest—and took her seat beside me, her face a glowing beacon of pride, embarrassment and exertion.

Now according to my experience of life which, extending as it does over three-score and ten years, is both full and varied, you may have as much difficulty in preventing a confirmed singer from singing as you will have in keeping a confirmed whistler from whistling, a confirmed stammerer from stammering, or a confirmed nose-picker from gouging his nostrils. This being the case, and as I may look forward to being regaled with Agnes's voice for my remaining years, I have been considering how best to turn her talent to advantage. It has not been an easy task but, by dint of much conjecture and cunning reasoning, I have arrived at a possible solution. What better way can there be of hastening the departure of unwelcome or lagging guests than to unleash upon them the unparalleled discord of Agnes's windpipe? Pistol for one—the ancient, not the horse—is oftimes guilty of outstaying his welcome and is, moreover, uncommon fond of music. With any luck, he will never return.

The party broke up at about the twelfth hour and this with much nudging and winking from Geoffrey and Esprit concerning the proximity of my wedding night.

If the salted hake had not made me sick enough already, these remarks would surely have accomplished it.

At Saint Germain en Bazois

On Saint Thomas' Night.
(Saturday 21st December 1415)

It is finished. Lady Agnes Falstaff—or *de* Falstaff, if you will—lies abed. I have lain awake beside her for many a long hour but now it is time to take up pen, book and candle and exorcize my demons.

What a day this has been! And what a night!

The day dawned blowing a blizzard from the north-east. At once Saint Germain became a pismire's nest of activity. I was awoken by Edmond and, clad in my shift and heavy cloak, I breakfasted on day-old bread, wine, cold pork, sheeps' feet and a fowl baked in pastry. I then withdrew to the jakes to prepare myself for my day's ordeal and also to escape the noise and commotion. Sad to say, the blizzard without causing draughts within, I was compelled to abandon my haven and steer my caravel through the rough currents of the hall to the calm waters of my chamber.

Here Edmond had set out my wedding gown upon the *perche-manteaux* and I dressed myself at my leisure for—I doubt not—the last time.

The gown is made of red woollen stuff embroidered with thread of gold and with it I wore crimson hose, a heavy black cloak trimmed with sable and, to top it all, a chaperon hood of cherry-red velvet. I think I may write with no great immodesty that I cut an imposing figure. And so I should for it cost me enough.

I then fortified myself with two cups of hypocras and a third for good measure and set myself to demonstrate in what wise an Englishman might meet his fate. And so I ventured into the hall and there met Jehan and Geoffrey who were conversing volubly amidst a gaggle of guests and servants.

Having admired my raiment and complimented me on my commanding mien, they accompanied me to the fireplace where we each downed a flagon of wine in honour of the day, thus warming ourselves both inside and out.

We were on the point of sending for a second flagon when there was a great ado on the gallery above. With a dignity that defies emulation, Agnes bounced down the stairs like an over-inflated pig's-bladder, closely pursued by Thiphaine, Marie and divers other ladies and servants.

My betrothed was clad in shimmering white: a houppeland of silk stuff about her body and a cloak of velvet trimmed with ermine over her shoulders. Her head was covered by a gauzy veil that entirely masked her countenance.

Aside for the fact that this rather increased her resemblance to a pig's-bladder, I considered it an entirely happy addition.

It is a most wise custom in this part of the world that the veil is not lifted till the marriage be accomplished. In England we have a similar observance: that the groom shall not set eyes on the bride until they arrive in the church. It is quite clear to me that both traditions are devised to prevent the man from coming to his senses and fleeing with all speed. Marry, if I had caught the merest suspicion of what lay beneath Agnes's veil, it is quite likely that by now I would be halfway to either Calais, Jerusalem or the ecclesiastical court in Dijon.

Doubtless similarly gulled, Jehan rushed up to his daughter and kissed her on what was approximately her face before taking her by the arm and leading her to me. I did what was expected: gave her a low bow, kissed her lardy hand and gazed on her with what I believe to have been a finely blended compound of respect and adoration.

"My lord, will you take wine with me?" she squeaks.

I readily assented, being much in need of further bracing.

Now I know not for what reason, but Agnes too drank more than deeply. This have I noted much of late—since, in fact, the night of our betrothal. Marry, I should say that she seems as fond of good, red Burgundy as a pig is of acorns. Which simile is all the more apt given the gruntings and smacking of lips and squeals of pleasure that punctuate her drinkings. In faith, I begin to wonder whether that Bardolphian illumination of her face is not maintained by liquor.

All told, however, she made a pleasing contrast with Thiphaine who was so small and thin and tearful.

Unfortunately, we were soon joined by Esprit and Jean-Baptiste of the late bone-handled knife; the former nudging and winking in a manner that does not become untried youth to sagacity, and the latter supported on a pair of crutches. These conveniently spared him the trouble of bowing.

There were roughly two-score guests of whom I knew only the Archdeacon—lately forgiven his transgressions in the hay-loft—Tristan de Corbigny and his daughter Constance. Of the others, I can call only a few to mind though this belike owes itself to the indulgences of later.

Agnes and I sat and drank and welcomed guests till the bell Augustine rang the eighth hour, upon which Edmond announced, with uncharacteristic loudness, that the hour had struck. It was just as well he did for no one else heeded it.

And so cloaks were donned and all sallied forth into the teeth of the blizzard. The cortège wended churchwards. A sorrier procession of miserable wretches there never was. Agnes and I rode at their head followed by Jehan and Thiphaine and a shivering, grumbling line of dark-cloaked well-wishers. Bringing up the rear was Jean-Baptiste, frozen and glowering in the back of an ox-cart. Poor lad.

It is at such times that the unnaturalness of moderation and temperance is most clearly manifest and shines forth for all to see, though few choose to look thereon. Having no goodly girth upon them, the starvelings behind fared most miserably. Though adequately fat, Marie of Dijon had gagged down no more than a thimbleful of Jehan's rustic wine and was as wretched as the rest. However, my bride and I felt little of the intemperate weather, as we had been just as intemperate ourselves. From time to time, when the snow gusted against us with more than usual violence, we refortified ourselves from a leathern bottle of pimento that Agnes had cunningly concealed about her massy person.

Thus did we progress along the lane towards the village not as a joyful company bedecked with flowers and laughing and jesting together but rather as a straggling troop of hunched, silent riders. As we rode through the village, a handful of surly peasants stood ankle-deep in snow and cheered us half-heartedly.

At the church we were greeted by Father Simon and there in the porch, surrounded by a glum, shivering company of family and guests, Agnes de Bazois and I exchanged our *paroles de présent*. There was no singing. Indeed we had little need of singing for there was accompaniment enough in the form of stamping feet, chattering teeth, the stifled sobs of Thiphaine and the occasional hiccup of Agnes.

I stood on the right and she on the left. I said, "*Ego do corpus meum.*" She said, "*Recipio.*" She said, "*Ego do corpus meum*" and I said, "*Recipio.*" Father Simon spread his stole over us, which must rank as as great an act of self-denying charity as has been seen since Saint Martin hacked his cloak about, for it is sure he had greater need of it than we.

I gave Agnes a gold ring that I had of a corpse on Shrewsbury field. May it bring her better fortune that it did its first possessor.

It was then, to the manifest relief of all present, that we entered the church to hear the wedding mass. This consisted of holding a lighted candle till the tallow dripped on our hands and then eating a scanty meal of thin wafer biscuit and watery wine. It is little wonder that your clerics are such a sallow, scrawny tribe.

I then lifted Agnes's veil—by now besmirched with wine stains—and kissed her for the first time. She returned this with extraordinary passion, much to my dismay and to the embarrassment of Father Simon who grunted and coughed till she was done.

I am at a loss to account for Agnes's excess of passion and can only hope that its potential extent is not a reflection of her physical girth. My kiss had been fittingly perfunctory—a mere matter of compunction and naught else. Marry, no woman of Agnes's age has kept my company unkissed for as long as she.

Herein lies a great irony. If, say six months ago, some Sibylline buffoon had told me I would marry within the half-year, I would have laughed him to scorn. And if he added that my bride would remain untouched and inviolate till the wedding night, I would have said his wits had turned and he was for the open heath to feed on worms and roots. And yet it has come to pass for the evidence lies abed as I pen these words.

On regaining my father-in-law's house, we were greeted by the servants who brought us cups of *chandel*, a drink of warmed wine. This was most welcome, for Agnes's flask of pimento had been emptied shortly after we left the church and the cold had begun to penetrate even my fleshy exterior. Many healths were drunk before we sat down to supper.

It is worth recording the details of our fare, for the supper was worth the mass if naught else was.

Premier Mets
Frumenty and venison
Leek potage
Boars' heads
Roast ox
A dish of capons
A fricassee of rabbits
Roast pig
A pastry

Second Mets
Pease soup
Roast pig
A dish of roasted pigeons, snipe and ducks
Two large luce set about with smaller fishes
Hens boiled in wine
A *pain perdu*
A pastry

Troisième Mets

An almond custard
A dish of collared pig
Roast pig
A veal pie
A dish of thrushes
A dish of eels
A jelly
Sweet beignets
A pastry

I did not eat the pastries. Too much pastry makes you costive. This is well known.

All of the above was served with the finest wines that Jehan could provide. I shall be sorry to take leave of his wine-cellar. In truth, it is the only thing at Saint Germain I *shall* be sorry to leave. The wines of Burgundy are as fresh and crisp as young apples. Here they often add wine to the gravy, which much improves the flavour of the meats. They mistakenly call this concoction *sause*.

Sad to say, during dinner we were regaled by the self-same three musicians who bagpiped their way through the betrothal feast. I fear that three weeks have not moderated my opinion of this parliament of screech-owls. Everyone else seemed to delight in it but as they also appear to esteem greatly the singing of my good wife, I can only assume that to be born Burgundian is to be born tone-deaf.

On a happy note, Agnes refrained from singing in spite of numerous requests to do so. In faith, she had consumed so much food and wine that anything approaching a song would have found egress from her body uncommon difficult. To say she ate with a goodly relish is to say but little. She brayed like a confined ass at the slightest indication of wit, and squeezed my hand and thigh at every opportunity.

At length came the hour to retire. This was advertised by Agnes who had, for a long time, abstracted herself from the surrounding chatter and now began to yawn prodigiously whilst stroking my leg with her pudgy hand in a most unpleasant manner. Of a sudden she leaned over and whispered loudly: "Go, my cabbage! Your wife will await you in bed."

Now I have been called many things in my life: a dove, a flower, a petal, a lambkin, a roaring lion and even—by that ungrateful whelp Hal—a bombard of wine. And that is to name but a few. I have never before been called a cabbage. As a term of endearment, it only serves to demonstrate the essential poverty of your French language, which can find no better symbol of affection than some lumpish brassica.

Upon saying this, however, Agnes rose and tottered up the stairs. Her departure engendered divers ribald remarks from all sides. The musicians squeezed their bagpipes suggestively.

Now normally I am little discountenanced by such comments for, in truth, I have even uttered similar ones myself, yet I am not accustomed to being the butt of them and I could scarcely conceal my contempt for such low insinuation. Had not my cheeks been flushed with wine, I should have fairly blushed. And yet the ladies present indulged themselves in quite as much base vulgarity as the menfolk. Only Thiphaine and Father Simon remained aloof.

After a decent interval, during which I had to brook these ribaldries with smiles and nods and chuckles to this side and that, I arose and mounted the stairs, followed by the priest, the musicians, the dogs, and the rest of the company. In her chamber, now become *our* chamber, Agnes was sitting up in bed clad in a night-shift and cap and looked much like a great pudding steaming in its linen.

In a vain attempt to introduce some measure of decorum into the proceedings, I betook me behind an arras in order to strip to my shift and yet propriety there was none for many a mad wag—and notably that young villain, my father-in-law—saw fit to peer at me and they even pulled the arras away as I was removing my hose. My patience being at an end, I bellowed at them to desist but I fear my roarings served only to redouble their laughter. It was a laughter, moreover, in which my own wife's asinine braying was well to the fore.

Add to all this the barking of the dogs and the infernal squalling of bagpipes and you have the closest representation of a Scotch leaping-house it were possible to find south of the Border.

At last I was seated next to my wife and Father Simon proceeds to the blessing of the bed or *benedictio thalami* as it is properly called. Being much used to bawdy-house din, he performed this service inaudibly and with all due reverence though, to my thinking, he was a little too lavish with the holy water. When the Father, Son and Holy Ghosting was done, this good ecclesiastic betook himself from our bridal chamber with great solemnity, nose in the air as if he had been blessing the jakes.

We were then congratulated by all present, which seemed excessive to me for sitting upright in a bed is no great feat. Jehan bent over and squeezed Agnes's cheek between finger and thumb whilst winking slyly at me; Thiphaine threw herself on the quilt and burst into a fresh broadside of tears and had to be brought away by her husband; the Archdeacon smiled upon all, vacantly, benignly and more than a trifle drunkenly; Geoffrey and Esprit, supporting each other unsteadily, shouted unintelligible comments in broad Burgundian, the meaning of which needed little guessing at. The only two well-wishers who did not appear to be overcome with hilarity were Marie and Jean-Baptiste. Marie regarded the proceedings with distaste, the greater part of which she reserved for her husband. Jean-Baptiste grimaced at me briefly before hobbling out of the room.

Yet finally the shouting and skirling of pipes retreated down the stairs and we were left alone.

Agnes gave as mighty a yawn as has not been seen since Goodman Jonah was eaten by the fish, and smiled upon me sweetly.

There we lay: two great cocoons, each the other's dupe. Agnes closed her eyes and, still smiling, heaved herself towards me, placing her head upon my chest and a heavy hand upon my leg. I knew then that the hour of reckoning was nigh.

Now I had not given much thought to what might eventually take place when we were finally abed together. This is not entirely surprising for you do not go about your daily business with your thoughts fixed on what you will say to the magistrate if you are arraigned, how you will conduct yourself if you are grievous sick, or in what wise you will behave towards the priest when he comes to give you extreme unction. You trust that, when the time comes, you will somehow know what to do and leave it at that.

Now that the time *had* come, I confess that I did not know what to do at all. I stared at the rafters for a goodly time and counted the cobwebs in the corners of our chamber and I believe that I entertained some vague hope that the Archangel Gabriel would suddenly appear, declare that Agnes was to be the next Virgin Mary, and save me the trouble of impregnating her myself.

Yet there was no intervention, divine or otherwise. Thus I reached over and attempted to caress the folds of fat on Agnes's back.

It was at this juncture, as we lay there so positioned and I was deliberating on how the necessary union might be best and least painfully obtained, that I was startled from my theorising by a pig-like snorting. At first I thought that one of Jehan's sows must have escaped and had, in some manner unknown, effected entry into our chamber.

I attempted to rise but was prevented from so doing by the weight of my spouse and was on the point of letting fly a cannonade of good English invective, to the effect that the fat turnip should move over, when I perceived that the grunting and snorting came not from one of Legion's brethren rooting behind the arras, but from my own good wife, snoring.

Now Bardolph, who spends much time sleeping when he is not thieving or drinking, snores with a noise like the last trump. Pistol, when primed with a few pots of wine, can honk and splutter like a leaky bellows. My Mistress Quickly whistles most tunefully in her sleep. But never, never in my years—not even when I shared a bed with Agnes's father—had I met with such a blaring, snorting, wheezing cacophony as that which now issued from my spouse's throat.

As I write this, in the furthest corner of our chamber, wrapped in my heavy cloak and with the first greyness of dawn touching the snow, she is snoring yet. I have nipped her nose; I have put my hand over her mouth; I have rolled her from one side of the bed to the other. God's wounds, I have only stopped short of suffocating her entirely! She neither wakes nor desists.

Thus, as with many a bridegroom on his wedding night, I have slept but little. Though I have been prevented from performing my conjugal duty, I fear that this is an unpleasantness deferred.

I have written enough this night. I shall descend to the kitchen and procure a jug of wine.

At Saint Germain en Bazois

Natale Domini.
(Wednesday 25th December 1415)

It is Christmas Day afternoon.

I expected the celebration of Our Lord's birth to be a miserable affair; I did not expect it to be quite as miserable as it has been. The entire household is possessed with the illest of ill humours, which owes itself to the excessive merrymaking that followed my wedding.

I can well understand that everyone was much pleased with Agnes's being at last married and likely to quit Saint Germain soon thereafter, yet to recommence the festivities on the morning after our nuptuals and continue them unabated till the early hours of Monday morning seemed somewhat disproportionate to an event of even this magnitude. The condition resulting from this revelry was little improved by the further excesses of last night, which they call here the *réveillon*.

Agnes is in the worst state of all for I have encouraged her in her drinkings these past nights in order to further postpone our consummation. Although she has needed scant encouragement, I blush to retell this stratagem. That I, Sir John Falstaff, knight banneret, slayer of the mad dog Hotspur, capturer of that valorous and most naughty rebel Sir John Colville of the Dale should be reduced and abased by a mere virgin wench of six and twenty summers! Tell it not in Gath: publish it not in the streets of Askalon!

On the morning after our wedding night, two things came to pass that confirmed me in this policy.

On returning to our chamber with a pint of wine and a paper of sugar, I found Agnes awake. To my perplexity—though doubtless owing to her inebriation of the previous evening—she seemed unable to recall either the benediction of the bed or anything that may or may not have happened subsequent to it. Now I have never been one to let a good opportunity flit by and found it an easy matter to convince her that the marital act had not only been performed but had been performed with all due satisfaction to both parties.

"Did I give you pleasure, my lord?" she asked eagerly.

"Aye lass," said I. "You acquitted yourself like a true professional."

She seemed a trifle nettled by this compliment though I am at a loss to understand why. Your women are strange creatures.

The second incident came to pass after a good many plashy kisses when my good wife arose from our bed and removed her night-shift in order to dress for the day.

Now in my time I have seen a good many shiftless women. Marry, when I was but a pip to the apple I now am, I often saw my own sister unclothed—God rest her soul—and, since then, many is the wench that I have seen in the state of nakedness. Yet never had I set eyes on such a corruption of the female form as I did that morning.

Chin met neck met breasts met belly met thighs in a very pyramid of corpulence.

Myself, I am of a somewhat portly build. God's wounds, I have even been, unjustly, reviled as fat. If that be true—and one must occasionally defer to the judgement of others on such matters—then it is a robust, healthy fatness as becomes a man of mark. It is a manly fatness bred of beef and ale. The wit and valour I possess need an ample dwelling.

Yet there is no such extenuation for Agnes. Her roundness is no vessel for wit, accomplishment or virtue. It is but a pulpy poultice—vapid and pastry-like.

Thus was any trace of passion driven from me.

For herself, Agnes is as hot as any hedge-sparrow and it is as much as I can do to prevent her from ravishing me whenever we are alone, which we are as seldom as I can contrive. During the day, I pretend to be exhausted from our energetic dalliances of the preceding evening. These dalliances she does not remember, as well she may not. At supper, I ply her with prodigious quantities of wine and, when she is on the point of prostration, I take her in my arms and escort her to our chamber. No sooner have I undressed her and heaved her into bed than she is asleep.

For these amorous attentions, the de Bazois family account me a lusty knave who will furnish them with many a fine child. Thiphaine even regards my apparent eagerness with something approaching disapproval. There is no pleasing some people.

For herself, I fear that Agnes waxes more than a little perplexed over love-making that she does not recall and for pleasures for which she has only my word as evidence. My stratagem is frail and I must invent another.

There yet remains the question of Agnes's snoring, which is both loud and persistent. With much ingenuity, I have devised an engine that renders this more endurable. Under the bed, I have secreted a small bowl of bread-dough and by stuffing a small quantity of this mixture into each ear I now sleep tolerably well.

At Saint Germain en Bazois

On Saint John's Day.
(Friday 27th December 1415)

I must be done with this. Yesternight Agnes insisted on drinking in moderation. I therefore remained at table until all the family had retired, in the hope that fatigue alone might get the better of her. I fear it got the better of me instead.

I was only able to escape her embraces by complaining of the earache, which was not entirely untrue. I thus adopted a doleful countenance and, with great show of regret and frustration, said to her that I have suffered thus since childhood as a result of falling from my father's horse. Sadly, this engendered great solicitude on her part.

"May I see the wound, my husband?" she asked.

"Nay! Marry, it is naught," said I, pulling away from her.

"But you must let me see," she said," for I am your wife and must share your sufferings."

"Very well then," said I, seeing no harm in it. "Examine me all you like. But you will see naught for the wound lies beneath the skin."

And so she peered into my ear, holding a candle aloft, the better to see.

"There is something lodged therein," said she, with the quiet deliberation of a physick.

"Wax, belike," said I. "Your ears are uncommon full of wax."

And before I could prevent her, she had inserted her finger and pulled something out.

"It is not wax," said she, rolling it between her fingers. "If I did not know better, I would say it was bread-dough."

It behoved me to think swiftly.

"Aye, my lass," said I, feigning admiration. "It is the only way my affliction may be cured. By stuffing my ears with bread-dough. And avoiding needless exertion."

At this she raised an eyebrow and declared that it was indeed passing strange that a knight of my greatness could be incapacitated by so small an injury and, indeed, that *any* injury could be cured by an application of yeasted flour and water.

"It is an old English remedy," said I. "Very old."

And with that I groaned and rolled my eyes in such a pathetic manner that she was moved to pity and called me a poor cabbage and stroked my forehead and clasped me to her bosom.

We repaired to bed. I limped up the stairs most grievously.

"It is perhaps our doings of these six nights past that have caused your ear to hurt so," said Agnes, as we stripped. "Fill your ears with bread-dough and rest tranquilly."

With no outward show of relief, I did as I was bidden. At least, as far as the bread-dough was concerned. As soon as I was sure Agnes was asleep, I crept downstairs and borrowed some wine and sugar from the kitchen.

This cannot endure! God's death, when I take her with me to England, I will have to spend a fortune on her wine and a second fortune on bread-dough. No, I fear that Agnes and I must part.

This is only right and proper. It little behoves a man of my advanced years to live in sin with a wench two-score years his junior. Our dispensation to marry in Advent came from that holy imposter in Avignon! A true pope would never have countenanced such sacrilege. And, what is more, our marriage is as yet unconsummated.

No, Agnes is my paramour and my keeping her will entangle us both in a web of lies and deceits. It were better to be quit of each other entirely. As with all women of easy virtue, she pollutes the souls of honest men.

Tomorrow, therefore, I shall go to her pander of a father and procure of him my dowry and say to him that I must accomplish my mission to Avignon. I shall then return to Eastcheap and have no more of France till Hal overmasters it.

A hundred and fifty *écus d'or* is a goodly sum of money. A man might set himself up very well on less.

At Saint Germain en Bazois

On Holy Innocents Day.
(Saturday 28th December 1415)

I shall quit Saint Germain on the morrow, but not alone as I had hoped.

This morning I confronted Jehan directly after he had performed his devotions, trusting to find him in a pious frame of mind. I had thought long and hard about the manner of approaching him and had decided to counterfeit the aspect of a magistrate, for I have had much occasion to observe them in the past and can play the part well if I must. I cannot believe there is a great difference between your magistrate and your royal emissary.

Now it is the way of your magistrate to declaim ponderously, as though he were serving up each word on a silver salver and presenting it for the scrutiny of all. Thus it was with much solemnity that I declared to Jehan that I had dallied too long in Burgundy and that, delightful as his company had been and loath as I was to be parted from my young wife, my duty to my King must take priority. I added—perhaps a little too hastily—that I would carry out my embassy as quickly as possible, the sooner to reclaim my beloved Agnes and escort her to my castle in England.

The mention of my castle seemed to strike the correct note with Jehan, though he made a brave attempt to imitate dejection at the loss of his daughter.

There then came the question of the one hundred and fifty *écus d'or*, which posed something of a dilemma. Representing Agnes's dowry, this money was mine by right, though Jehan had seen fit to hold it in safe-keeping since the day of our wedding. To have asked for all of it immediately before my departure for Avignon would certainly have suggested that I had no intention of returning and thus, with some regret, I determined to content myself with half and considered that seventy-five *écus d'or* was a small price to pay for never having to set eyes on Agnes again.

In truth, Jehan seemed reluctant to part with any of it but he had to acknowledge the importance of my making a fine show at the papal court, and also that the money was mine when all was said and done.

As it turns out, I shall have all of it, thanks to a happy accident that befell me this afternoon.

Wrapped in my heavy cloak, I was reclining in the barn in quiet contemplation of a jug of wine and congratulating myself on having escaped Agnes for the best part of the morning. This would be at about the seventh hour.[61] Despite the coldness of the weather, I had left the barn door slightly ajar in order to shed a little light upon my meditations and to afford me advanced warning should Agnes come rooting after me. From where I lay, I had a clear, though not particularly interesting view of the cow-byre, above which is the hay-loft where the good Archdeacon Jakes had been so rudely surprised.

It was just as I was on the point of rising to my feet in order to refill my cup that a movement caught my eye. A pair of brown, comely legs appeared at the top of the ladder leading from hay-loft to courtyard and were closely followed by the ample curves of the self-same maidservant—Marie by name—who had so lately compromised the Archdeacon. Although I thought but little of this, I continued to gaze on her, for Marie—and particularly those aspects of Marie that were then presented to view—is certainly the only feature of Saint Germain that merits such close scrutiny.

At the bottom of the ladder, she halted and looked about her, though naturally she did not notice me. At this point, I was sorely tempted to call her into the barn to pour me a cup of wine but it is well that I refrained for, having looked about her, she called softly to someone in the hay-loft above. No sooner had she done so than a figure clad in a black houppeland descended to the cobbles below.

Now Jehan suffers from the gout, which renders his walking both difficult and painful. For all that, he descended the ladder nimbly enough. He appeared to be in a state of great agitation for he glanced anxiously about him as though he expected the Armagnac host to arrive at any minute. Without a word, he took a few coins from his purse, pressed them hurriedly into Marie's hand and made off in the direction of the piggery. Marie smiled to herself, straightened her bodice and tripped away in the opposite direction, chinking the coins.

After a late and scarcely digestible dinner of eels and day-old bread, it being a Saturday, I offered to accompany Jehan to his piggery. This offer he accepted readily for there is naught Jehan likes more than to show off his pigs.

As we trudged pigwards through the mire, I embarked on a lengthy disquisition on the nature of Sin, for which the even lengthier disquisitions of Denys the Mad furnished much of the argument.

I explained to Jehan that the enormity of Sin should be considered in relation to seven points of view. Jehan attempted to look as interested as anyone can be when they are listening to a lecture on theology while wading calf-deep in mud.

"Let us take, *per exemplum*, adultery," said I, in my best magistrate's voice.

Jehan sniffed loudly and continued to plod.

"By all means," said he.

"First of all," said I, "one must look at adultery through the eyes of God. Did He not, in His infinite wisdom, make His seventh commandment—which commandment is doubly important for having such a holy number -Thou shalt not commit adultery?"

Jehan appeared to think hard for a moment.

"So it appears," said he, sniffing loudly again.

"God the Father is unequivocal on this matter," I continued. "Now, in second place we must view adultery through the eyes of the sinner. Let us take *per exemplum* a man of mature age. Is it not so that a Sin excusable when committed in the fire of youth becomes abhorrent when allied to the gravity of years? For youth falls easily victim to base animal instincts, whilst your mature man, shrugging aside morality and Holy Writ, wallows in his depravity with open eye."

"Indeed so," murmured Jehan, with his eyes fixed abstractly on the distant piggery.

"Thirdly," said I, "one must consider matter."

"Must one?" said Jehan.

"Indeed one must," said I, in my most stentorian and Pistol-like voice. "Enough to say that the organs of generation were granted us for the begetting of children in holy wedlock. And not for idle dalliance in the *hay*!"

At the mention of hay, Jehan started visibly but otherwise continued through the mud with admirable composure.

"Fourthly consider circumstances," said I. "And in this must we contemplate extenuation for it is very true that the man of riper years, burdened with an ageing spouse, may find some solace in the lustiness of youth. Especially if his spouse is of an over-pious nature."

I watched Jehan carefully from the corner of my eye. He appeared to blanch a little.

"Fifthly let us consider intention. This is quite plain. The intention of adultery is mere carnal gratification and is thus to be reviled. Sixthly...!"

"We have a sixthly then?" asked Jehan, in a weary voice.

"Indeed we have a sixthly," I answered patiently. "I told you the enormity of sin should be looked at from *seven* points of view, thus we have a sixthly. Sixthly is the nature of the sin. Adultery is particularly pernicious for it betrays the sacred trust of marriage. If the woman in question be unmarried, it engenders the foulest wantonnesses; if she be married, it makes a double crime. By adultery, even the humblest *serving-girl* may fall as low as Lucifer."

It pleased me to see that Jehan's face had now taken on a definite pallor. He quickened his pace, doubtless the sooner to reach the piggery and end my uncomfortable monologue.

"Finally!"

I bellowed the word with such force that Jehan flinched.

"Finally, we come to the seventh point: the consequences. Let us not dwell on the pains and terrors of eternal damnation. Let us ignore the grim horrors of the Pit where souls are racked with endless torments: pinched with hot irons, disembowelled with blunted knives, flayed with sharpened stones...let us not speak of such things. Rather let us think of the earthly Consequences: honour defiled, chastity betrayed, ruin, corruption...death!"

Jehan jumped and staggered a little and his beard twitched convulsively.

"And the shame!" said I. "For few things go undiscovered, believe you me! The most venial slip from grace will be revealed in time. And then imagine, if you will, the shock to a pious wife, if she were to hear of it."

My face became as solemn as Solomon's.

"Even," I added, in a low voice, "were it nothing more than a quick tumble with a maidservant in a hay-loft."

Jehan nearly fell on his face. I caught him by the elbow and supported him whilst he regained his balance.

"Whoa there!" said I. "It is uncommon slippery underfoot, do you not think so?"

"Indeed," said Jehan, feebly. "Uncommon."

There was a long silence.

"I hope you found my disquisition edifying," said I, innocently.

"Most edifying," said Jehan, his face as pale as a clout. "I have been thinking, John. This journey to Avignon...are you sure you are well enough provided? Financially, I mean."

"Half of my dowry should be sufficient for most needs," said I. "I am a man of modest tastes, Father. Extravagant shows of luxury sit ill with me."

I sighed loudly.

"And yet, it is the way of the world that folk judge you by your outward aspect. I only hope that His Holiness will understand that I cannot progress through a hostile country bedecked with costly silks and dragging behind me a full retinue of servants. I hope that he will recognise in me a true emissary of the English King."

179

"Let us leave nothing to chance," said Jehan, with a bitter smile. "You must take with you the full amount of your dowry. One can never be too sure with this Pope."

And thus did I procure the full amount owing me. Truth to say, I was much impressed with my own eloquence. In faith, I have yet to meet the priest that could lay hands on so much gold with so short a sermon.

I shall confess to being a trifle extortionate in the matter and it is true that it little befits one who has had as much commerce with whores as I to censure the peccadillos of Jehan, but at need we let the Devil help us and there's an end on it.

However, by the time we eventually reached the piggery Jehan had quite regained his composure: sufficiently, in fact, to berate the swineherd for some minor sin of omission. I lingered with him for a little while and expressed some complimentary opinions on his favourite boar before returning to the house alone to break the news of my departure to Agnes.

She received this intelligence little better than I expected and cried and wailed like a Hebrew fishwife, beslubbering my garments and tearing her hair in a manner most alarming. Your Burgundian, being no better than your French in these matters, is a creature of fire and air and is easily excited to passion. Your Englishman rarely shows more passion than is passion's due. I was thus less moved by her pother as I am by a dish of salted cod and yet I felt it politic to soothe her. And so I stroked her damp, dishevelled hair and kissed her spongy cheek and whispered in her ear that I would soon return and be hers for all eternity. If I do I am a stewed prune.

I wrote at the beginning of this entry that I am not to leave alone. This unforeseen amendment to my plans was told me at supper when, over yet another plate of collared eels, Jehan formally announced my departure, which everyone present knew of anyway, placed before me a small casket containing one hundred and fifty *écus d'or*, at which I feigned surprise, and finally declared that he himself, together with Esprit and Edmond, would accompany me as far as Saint Etienne.

To this I made loud protestations, saying that the way was difficult and the weather foul and that they would surely miss the Twelfth Night festivities.

"Nonsense," replied Jehan, with a peremptoriness that I had not heard before. "The road to Saint Etienne is most perilous for the solitary traveller. Especially for one with a hundred and fifty *écus d'or*."

Agnes also said she wished to come. To my relief, and with my permission, her father forbade her.

Now this unexpected company has compelled me to modify my plans. I had intended to ride in the direction of Avignon only as far as the village of Decize, which lies no more than eight or nine leagues hence. At Decize I would then have turned about and followed the course of the River Loire in the direction of Paris. Now I am constrained to detour as far as Saint Etienne and may God and the Saints preserve me if Jehan should further alter his plans and accompany me to Avignon itself. God's wounds, he may even insist on accompanying me into the papal court!

This comes of precipitating such a venture on Holy Innocents Day.

It is clear that Jehan means to keep me to my word and assure himself that I am indeed bound for Avignon and will return thence to Saint Germain. Well, I shall find some way of ridding myself of these dangerous protectors or my name is not Jack Falstaff.

It grows late. I shall to bed, there, for the last time, to curl up in the lee of my snoring, wine-soaked sow.

At Bourbon-Lancy

On Saint Silvester's Eve.
(Monday 30th December 1415)

We are lodging at the *Bouc qui saulte* or the He-Goat Which Jumps, as it means when done into English.

I am at a loss to explain such an obscure and curious name and the enquiries I have made as to its origin have met only with shrugs. The general opinion of both landlord and patrons would seem to be that it is as good a name as any. Perhaps it is a reference to some achievement of arms, just as in England we call some inns The Sun after Richard the Lionheart, The White Hart after his unfortunate namesake of Pomfret[62] or The Red Lion after John of Gaunt. I have never yet seen the shield of a great lord emblazoned with a jumping billy goat but I dare say it may be so—your French are full of strange fancies.

In confirmation of this, Jehan and Esprit are, as I write, immersing their bodies in salt water in the belief that this is good for the bile. Your French and Burgundians are forever prattling on about bile and the liver that contains it, as though that particular organ is possessed of some special mystic power denied to all others. *Per exemplum*, they never suffer from an over-indulgence in wine but have a "crisis of the liver", which engenders pains of the head, limbs and throat, a sensation that their mouths are compounded of sackcloth, a general paleness of countenance and a desire to vomit at any mention of the word "herring".

In any event, as this town of Bourbon-Lancy is, it seems, famed for its salt water, Jehan and Esprit could not leave without soaking their livers therein. Fools had never less wit in a year. Your sea, which is so broad in extent that it reaches even to the end of the world, is full of salt water. This I know full well for I have tasted it myself on many an occasion. You may soak yourself in it to your heart's content and pay naught for the privilege and yet, for all that, I have met with many a bilious mariner. Yea, in truth, it would be easier to count your mariners who are *not* afflicted by the bile. And what is more, if any of Jehan's kin merited such physick it is Jean-Baptiste of the Broken Leg, who possesses more bile than all of them put together. Yesterday he would not so much as do me the courtesy of bidding me farewell and I saw him spit out of the window as Pistol bore me from the courtyard.

On the other hand, Agnes and Thiphaine cried enough salt tears to supply the baths of Bourbon-Lancy for a year. I fear that Agnes loved me dearly, which causes me some regret at having used her so. Yet have I done her a service by quitting her so speedily for I should only have brought her misfortune and misery and if she pines a little it can do her naught but good.

The last time we travelled together, Jehan chattered unceasingly about this and that and principally about his daughter and his pigs. Now that he knows me to be acquainted with his daughter's qualities, his discourse almost entirely concerns his pigs. No longer having competition from another quarter, Jehan has given free rein to his porcine panegyric. By the time we had reached Decize, I not only knew their various names but also their lineages, which are confused, their habits, which are mostly unsavoury, their personalities, which are singularly anthropomorphous, and their offspring which are many and, thus far, happily innominate. I am also so well-versed in their husbandry that I could discuss the same with any swineherd without loss of countenance.

The only relief from this prolonged treatise on swine-rearing was the occasional sally of Esprit's sodden wit.

To one such as I, who prides himself on the agility, forgetiveness and pertinence of his wit, Esprit's pedestrian irrelevancies produce little beyond an inward groan. I shall record one such instance of his inanity as a cautionary *exemplum*.

Apropos of nothing at all, he suddenly shouts out:

"Once there was a buxom wench who must visit her uncle in the next town!"

At the mention of "buxom wench" Jehan had already begun to cackle. You would have thought that buxom wenches had brought him enough trouble already.

There was a short hiatus as Esprit attempted to recall what followed.

"As she walks along the lane, along comes a rascal on a grey mare. 'Good morrow,' said he. 'Good morrow, fair maid. Whither are you going?' 'To yonder town,' said she. 'To see my uncle.'"

At the word "uncle", Jehan cackled the more. It is lucky for all of us that it was not the maid's grandfather, else would he have been stricken with apoplexy.

"'Then jump on the back of my grey mare,' said the lad, 'and I shall take you there.' So up she jumps. After they have gone several leagues, they come to a crossroads. One road goes to the east and the other road goes to the west, through a BIG DARK WOOD. At the crossroads sits an old man. 'Tell me, old man,' said the lad. 'Whither leads the road that goes through yonder BIG DARK

WOOD?' The old man looks at the young rascal on the grey mare and he looks at the buxom lass behind him. 'Straightway to the altar, lad,' said he!"

At this, Jehan laughed so loud he was like to wet himself. Even Edmond gave way to a throaty chuckle. Not wishing to be discourteous, I also chuckled a little but it grieves me to think that Jehan and Esprit think me wanting in wit, which they surely do.

Why, in the name of all that's holy, do young, lusty lads always ride grey mares? What has the colour and sex of his steed to do with it? Why are fair maids always buxom? Why do roads always go north, south, east or west? Why was the old man sitting at the crossroads? Was he so confused as to his geographical position that he decided to go nowhere at all? Why are woods always big and dark?

But thereafter, Jehan continued to repeat "straightway to the altar" with much rubbing of his eyes and slapping of his knee.

As if all this were not enough, the wind was bitterly cold, the road that flanked the River Aron was deep in mud and even my brave and faithful Pistol, who had begun the journey in merry mood, was soon reduced to plodding like a broken-spirited cart-horse.

We reached Decize shortly before nightfall. It is a miserable town which huddles between the rivers Aron and Loire and is surrounded by water-meadows and marshland.

We passed the night at the house of Gilbert, a friend of Jehan, though I am sure we would have been more comfortable at the inn for the three of us shared a bed in a chamber that was home to more draughts than the taproom at the Boar's Head. I marked Jehan's prevailing stench of garlic less than I did on the road to Saint Germain but I feel that time has done nothing to moderate his snoring, which I now accept as a family trait.

We also ate scantily, for Gilbert had not expected our arrival: salt-beef, soup and bread. But Gilbert's steward saw to it that our cups were never empty and, owing to his living near the river, our host had a goodly stock of news and gossip.

It seems that the parliament at Westminster has granted Hal a subsidy on wool for life. This is, in truth, a signal honour. I do not believe I have ever heard of the like. Perhaps now that he has wool enough, he will be less cold-hearted.

Another piece of news, which might have sorely affected my supposed mission to Avignon, concerned the Emperor Sigismund. Rumour has it that this interfering old fool has persuaded the Spanish kingdoms to abandon the anti-pope in Avignon and transfer their allegiances to Pope Gregory. This renders my embassy yet more inexplicable for not only does Hal support Gregory too but, as far as I know, he also wishes to curry favour with Sigismund. I received this news gravely, as befits an emissary, though happily I was saved discussion of the matter.

We arose at cock-crow this morning and were abroad at first light. A red murrain on travelling! No sooner have you lowered yourself onto your bed than you must lever yourself up again.

We journeyed a good ten leagues today and if I be not most grievously worn down by it I am an anchovy. We plodded along the banks of the Loire with an icy wind at our backs and only the crows for company since none but fools and husbands would venture forth on such a day. We reached this town of Bourbon-Lancy by mid-afternoon and then what happens? These egregious blockheads must slope off to the salt-water baths before supper! As if they have not seen enough water today!

I hear Jehan's voice below. With any luck, he has caught an ague.

At Furze (Feurs)

On Saint Edward's Eve.
(Saturday 4th January 1416)

Today being a Saturday, and thus ill-omened,[63] we do not venture forth. In faith, I am reluctant to tempt Providence in any way lest Jehan should decide to escort me to Avignon.

Furze is the capital town of the Forez, or so I am told. It lies, like most other towns and villages on our route, on the banks of the River Loire. On the other side of the river a flat plain extends to the Monts du Forez, where it rained fish. These are the loftiest mountains I have ever beheld.

Furze owes its importance to its position on a crossroads formed by the highways that join Clermont to Lyon and Roanne to Saint Etienne. By virtue of this fact, it is exceeding bustling. As I write, Jehan, Esprit and Edmond, all muffled against the wind, are exploring the market which, it is said, is well worth the visit. Were it a very Bartholomew's Fair, it would not tempt me out in such weather. Besides, I have little interest in food save when it is cooked and set before me. Thus I have elected to remain behind and write my daybook over a pint or two of wine.

This inn, by the by, is called *Le Chat Boiteux*, or The Crippled Cat, and there is a plaster statue of a three-legged feline above the door. The landlord, a certain Master Guillaume, tells me that in his grandfather's day the inn was called simply *Le Chat*, until a local ruffian decided that the statue made too tempting a target and shied a stone at it, whereupon it became *Le Chat Boiteux*. I doubt not that at some future time it will be called *Le Chat Sanz Pattes*, *Le Chat Sanz Teste* and finally *Le Chat Disparu*.

Thus does my enforced journey wend southwards. Since quitting Bourbon-Lancy we have passed by Digoin—where they make pots, having naught better to do—Marcigny, a miserable clump of flea-ridden hovels, and Roanne, which is a largish town situated prettily between the mountains of Madeleine and Beaujolais.

I shall waste little paper on the details of our journey. The only story of any interest concerns an accident that befell Edmond yesterday when, having dozed off in the saddle, he slipped from his horse and cracked his pate on a rock. Though he bled generously he was not rendered senseless and the incident provoked much laughter, though not, I fear, from Edmond himself who remounted his horse rubbing his pate and proceeded to grumble and curse for a good half-league thereafter. This too engendered great mirth for generally Edmond is of a taciturn cast and would make a Carthusian seem a very gossip by comparison. It is said that he who is silent about all things is troubled by naught. If this be true, Edmond must have a wonderfully unvexed mind.

There are a brace of saucy, dark-eyed maidens of Mistress Tearsheet's persuasion lodged at this inn. Now were I unencumbered by my in-laws, and yet monied as I am, I dare say I might not stray from the Crippled Cat till puss's other limbs were knocked off.

I had best cease writing. A man has just seated himself opposite me and is showing more than usual interest in my daybook.

It is now night. I sit by my bed, cold as it is in this upper room, and write by candlelight.

Dame Fortune has smiled upon me. Tomorrow I am rid of Jehan and his pigs, his buffoon of a son, and his surly intendant.

The man who seated himself opposite me and obliged me to stop writing this afternoon is one Thierry de Royat, a merchant of Clermont, who is bound for Marseille by way of Lyon, at which town he will take boat and sail down the River Rhône.

When I told him my destination was Avignon, he was amazed that I should travel by way of Saint Etienne and said I might accompany him over the Lyonnais Mountains and take boat together. To this I readily agreed though, in truth, I have no intention of going further south than Lyon. I shall take a boat upstream along the Saône as far as the town of Chalon and thence travel a-horseback to Paris and Calais.

Thierry de Royat dresses in a manner more befitting a nobleman than a merchant. His only companions are his secretary and a boy, neither of whom I have yet seen. Indeed, it is a great wonder that he has succeeded in travelling safely this far for if I was given to thieving—which, as God is my witness, I am not—I should have cut his purse and his throat along with it before he had gone a league from home.

Thierry buys and sells spices and he is pursued by a fragrance of cinnamon and ginger. This I find most agreeable. Marry, he is the first Frenchman I have met who does not stink.

In my discourse with Thierry, I have reverted to my alias of Jan van Staf. Fortunately, he is as ignorant of Dutch as he seems to be of English. For myself, I have little difficulty in counterfeiting the Hollander for my hair is white, my eye blue and my belly as comfortably swollen as though I have seen a lifetime of hoppe-hoppenbier and cheese. By dint of much coughing and spluttering I can also imitate your Low German as well as may be necessary.

I have told Thierry that I am enquiring into the possibility of furnishing wool to the papal court, though exactly what interest the Avignon pope could have in Dutch wool I fail to imagine. It is my good fortune that Thierry's knowledge of the wool-trade is on a par with his proficiency in languages, else would I be on all accounts discomfited.

Thus, as soon as Jehan and Esprit returned from market, I acquainted them with my change of plan, saying that it was no longer needful to escort me further for I had found safe company for the journey and they might return to Saint Germain in the knowledge that my life and monies were not at risk.

I had expected much protestation and had counter-arguments on hand should they have been needed yet, on the contrary, they seemed greatly pleased by this intelligence and Edmond even managed the thinnest of thin smiles.

"I have bought a fine piglet at market," declared Jehan, proudly. "I had thought to leave him here at this inn and collect him on our return journey but, now that you are in safe hands, I may convey him straightway home."

I shot a glance under the table but could see no piglet there. I would not have put it past Jehan to have invited it to supper.

"He is in the stables," explained Jehan, correctly divining my suspicions. "The ostler has made him a bed of dry straw."

I can conceive of no person other than Jehan who would be ready to ride for five days through difficult terrain in the foulest of weather with a pig stuffed inside his cloak. And to abandon his son-in-law for a mere juvenile porker? Are ties of family and friendship become of such little consequence? God's blood, this is no world for righteous men!

The supper that the pig missed consisted of salt-beef boiled in wine with olives. I liked it well and consumed three bowlfuls. It was only then that Jehan demonstrated any concern at parting from me by rather cursorily drinking my health and wishing me Godspeed. Then, after conferring with Esprit in a hushed tone, he rose from the board and the two of them disappeared upstairs with the two dark-eyed wenches I had espied earlier.

How can a man of my years find salvation in the midst of such black iniquity? Were I heathen Turk, I should yet have greater chance of God's grace than in the company of such pious, Christian rascals.

Enough. I am well rid of Jehan and I have his money, so there's an end on it.

At Lyon

On the feast of Epiphany.
(Monday 6th January 1416)

I arrived here this afternoon at about the hour of nones.[64]

Lyon is a fine town built sturdily between the confluence of the rivers Saône and Rhône which together form a mighty flood pouring to the south. Its northern limit is bounded by a great wall and a moat. It is also heavily garrisoned with French soldiery yet this more out of fear of the Savoyards to the east than of the English or Burgundians to their rear.

According to that abject coward Thierry de Royat, Lyon is famed for its cooking. Now, on hearing this, my first impulse was to dismiss the claim as yet one more *exemplum* of your French braggadocio, for your French are forever vapouring about the quality of their cooking, which I find markedly inferior to English fare. For all their vauntings, your French nobility eat no better than your English and oftimes worse. Your French peasant is so poor that he is sometimes reduced to eating oysters, frogs and snails and suchlike.

In short, I expected little for all Thierry's talk, and my opinion seemed to be confirmed when, on asking the landlord of this inn what he had to offer me—the inn, by the by, being called the *Au Père Burchard*, or Father Burchard's Place—I was told that there was only sausage, pig's trotters, crayfish, capon and salad, which seemed most meagre.

Having resigned myself to a fast-day upon compulsion, and today being a Monday at that, I was amazed to find the sausage light and subtle of flavour, the pigs' trotters small and grilled to a delicate perfection, the crayfish served in their own gravy, and the capon studded with those aromatic toadstools that the French call *truffes*. I was also vouchsafed a slice of spicy cake called *galette*, which is fashioned especially for this day of Epiphany. The whole was served with young red wine from the mountains of Beaujolais.

In all truth, it was as fine a repast as I have ever eaten, for all its simplicity. After finishing it, I could not resist unlacing my doublet and dozing before the fire and this in spite of garrulous soldiery dicing at a nearby table.

The journey from Furze has been long and arduous. Thierry de Royat's secretary was as miserable a drip-nose as I ever met and the boy... well, he was a boy. Braver than most, perhaps, but a boy all the same.

We had not long quitted Furze before the ground began to rise steeply. The highway was little more than a track, uneven and strewn with stones, which twisted about abominably as it mounted the hillside. Moreover it was raining steadily, which it continued to do all day. Having breakfasted lightly, we had not slipped and slithered more than a brace of leagues before we were all chilled to the marrow. The wind increasing its force as we ascended further added to our discomfort and rendered conversation well-nigh impossible. I dare say that in spring and summer it is a pleasant enough journey but I would rather pass a night lashed to Tyburn gibbet than spend an hour on that road in winter.

At midday—or what I judged to be midday for the sun had the good sense not to show itself in such weather—we dined on dried sausage and bread and a pint or two of wine. Thus fortified, we continued our climb until we reached the summit, when the road descended to the village of Saint Foy, which we gained in the late afternoon. Since breakfast I do not think we had exchanged more than a dozen words.

Saint Foy was not so much a village as an expectoration of hovels surrounding an overgrown church. Nonetheless, being situated on a trading-route of some importance, it boasted an inn, which appeared to be nameless and deserves to remain so. It was hosted by the most villainous cut-throat I have set eyes on since quitting Eastcheap. And when I call a man a cut-throat it may safely be assumed that he is one.

In Eastcheap I would doubtless have befriended the knave for, in general, there is usually something to be gained if you are the friend of a felon and much to be lost if you are not. Yet, as a foreign traveller and a prosperous merchant—for such I appear to be—any claim of friendship I had made would have received short shrift. It therefore behoved me to look to my guard.

Thus, since a show of anxiety tends to engender unwelcome interest, I attempted to make light of my bulging saddle-bag. Yet it is difficult to disguise the chink of coin however much you cry "ahem". Had I been alone, it is certain I would not have survived the night but the villain dared not murder three men and a boy, for such deeds are wont to give an inn a bad reputation.

For all that, as we ate and drank and talked, I never let the saddle-bag out of my sight and, when I had to void my bladder, I did not stray from the patch of light cast by the open door and continued my conversation unabated.

Now whether out of sheer nervousness or to compensate for a day's silent travelling, Thierry chattered away worse than any starling. His principal subject was his own amorous adventures, which he recounted in vivid and exhausting detail.

I have oftimes noted that it is men who have done little in their lives who are quickest to advertise their slight achievements, whilst those of us whose lives are swollen with triumph and disaster feel small need to prate and swagger. It is the way of the world that these same hollow blusterers are accounted men of mark whilst the true hero's modesty betrays his good opinion. That rascally ancient Pistol is one such unscarred braggart. He is forever roaring out his vanities and capering about, point in hand, thrusting here and there and showing off guards and wards that would not discourage a sickly milliner.

Where was he at Shrewsbury field? Where was he at Gaultree Forest?

I know full well where he was. At Shrewsbury he was gallantly defending the King's rear from the taproom of the Black Bull in Preston Gubbals. At Gaultree Forest he passed a pleasant and distinctly undangerous day wandering about the baggage carts looking for the battle. Yet weak-minded fools judge him a Trojan, a very Hector! Nell Quickly ups and marries him, tickle-brained pox-box that she is. I, the true vanquisher of Harry Percy and John Colville, am banished to France for my modesty.

So was it with this Thierry de Royat. Solomon himself had not so swiven. There is not a depravity written of in Petronius or Boccace that this Frenchman had not bettered. In all of Christendom, and divers heathen lands beside, there was no sparrow so lecherous or bull so brimming with potency. Not a songbird could charm with its music as he could with his silver tongue. If he were not the most egregious liar then there is not a maidenhead intact between here and Shropshire.

I am not such a fool as would attempt the topping of these extravagant fancies and so I held my peace, save for the odd chuckle or expression of wonderment. For all that Thierry knew, I might have been blessed with all the lustiness of the Grand Turk. Certainly he expressed little interest in aught I might have had to say. At one point he did venture, "And in Amsterdam, you have many light wenches, eh?", to which I made answer, "Yea, and in Rotterdam too."

In such a wise did we pass the evening. In truth, I was in scant hurry to go to bed: not so much for fear of being murdered in it or of having to share it with this satyr of Clermont, as of the divers livestock it contained. I scratch yet as I write this.

This morning we quitted the inn at Saint Foy in something approaching high spirits, which had little to do with the weather—that being every bit as bad as the day before—but much to do with putting such a disagreeable place behind us. Our good humour was somewhat moderated as we wound further down the valley.

The road led through a defile along the bank of the River Brevenne and, owing to a large number of fallen rocks and the thick woods that struggled up the hillside, we were obliged to ride one behind the other, Thierry leading the way and I guarding the rear with the boy at my back for good measure.

I never in my life saw so gloomy a place. On either side of us the mountains lost themselves in a coverlet of grey cloud that poured forth its charge of rain in a ceaseless stream. Beside us, the River Brevenne rushed and tumbled amidst great heaps of moss-laden rock and ground its muddy waters against the bankside with such a mighty roar that we could not communicate with one another without shouting. Even the stones themselves seemed to exhale dampness. As we crept deeper into the valley, it grew so dark that, had I not known full well that it was morning, I would have said it was dusk and that night would soon be upon us.

Night came swiftly to one of our number.

We had passed a great rock which, sprouting from the earth, thrust aside our rude highway. Of a sudden, there was a most hideous screaming and shouting and six men leapt out of the woods before and behind us. They were clad in buckram and all wore masks around their faces.

Before I knew what had come to pass, the snivel-nosed secretary had been felled by a blow from a billhook and struck the earth at Pistol's feet. A bloodier sight I have not seen since Gaultree Forest for his head was well-nigh severed from his body.

Thierry de Royat, being the true hero, straightway spurred on his nag, brushed aside the rogues before him, ducking a wild sword-swipe as he passed, and was out of sight before you could say Jack Rugby, leaving the boy and I to fend for ourselves as best we could.

It is at such times that wit, erudition and philosophy will avail you naught. We were outnumbered three to one and would most likely perish. Considering that I would rather be poor, naked and alive than poor, naked and dead, you might have thought that a few well-chosen words, to the effect that our opponents might have what they wished if they spared our lives, would have saved us all a deal of trouble. However, what with the roaring of the river, the screams and curses of our attackers and the neighs and whinnyings of our horses as they pranced and wheeled within the narrow confines of the path, any attempt to suggest that we might all sit down and discuss the situation would have been doomed to failure.

I had no option other than to fight. Thus, for the first time since quitting Calais, I unsheathed Gut Cutter in anger and whirled it about me, in the hope of striking someone a mortal blow.

Now your bastard-sword is a mighty weapon indeed and much to be feared. Unfortunately, it is an unwieldy instrument to use a-horseback for, being weighty, you need both hands to swing it, and this leaves no hand free to manage your horse. Now that I look back on it, I am forced to admit that my not being the swordsman I once was constituted something of an advantage for, in swinging Gut Cutter about my head, I neatly lopped the tip off one of Pistol's ears. It was not a grievous wound but it occasioned obvious pain. Pistol reared up mightily, clawing the air with his hooves, and, in so doing, knocked one of the ruffians into the river.

Another villain leapt onto the road directly in front of us and jabbed at me menacingly with a rusty blade. Unfortunately for him, Pistol, doubtless perceiving the said blade to be the author of his wound, rushed upon him and trampled him underfoot. Thus had six buckram rascals become four.

Pistol, by now in an extremity of pain and homicidal fury, bucked and plunged madly and I had to let Gut Cutter fall to prevent myself from being tossed from the saddle. Although I succeeded in reining him in, this manoeuvre left me defenceless, yet, being possessed of the presence of mind of the true warrior, I snatched up my saddle-bag and shied it at the nearest robber.

In truth—and this I would confess to no one—I reasoned that if all these cowardly French dogs were after were my one hundred and fifty *écus d'or*, they could have them gladly if they allowed me to escape.

Now a hundred and fifty *écus d'or* is some considerable weight of coin and when propelled forward with a velocity born of anger and desperation it becomes a most deadly missile. This I did not know when I threw it, but I soon had opportunity to witness its effects for it struck the robber fully in the chest, thereby causing him to follow his colleague into the River Brevenne, which, being a river of great power and celerity, swept him away as quickly as he landed in it.

Six had become three.

Of these three, one—the villain with the billhook—was most cunningly stabbed in the eye by the boy. Thereupon the remaining two took to their heels and were soon lost in the woods.

It had been a magnificent victory masterfully executed. A victory worthy of your Alexanders and Caesars. The boy and I alighted from our mounts, hugged each other and danced in the road for very excess of joy. He is a good lad, if a little stupid.

I dispatched the robber whom Pistol had trampled, who proved to be none other than our host of the previous evening, and the boy retrieved his dagger from the eye-socket of the rogue with the billhook. We consigned their corpses to the care of the River Brevenne.

There was little to be done for the poor secretary for neither of us relished the prospect of binding his body over his horse's back and carrying his head in a bag and so I stripped him of his purse and the silver ring he had upon his finger and gave them to the boy. His body joined that of his murderer in the river.

Sadly we had to squander a good hour or more whilst the boy waded in the rushing flood and poked about in its muddy waters to rescue my saddle-bag. I rewarded him with a few *sous* for his trouble and then we remounted and rode on in peace. Pistol, however, continued to be much vexed by his ear.

We overtook our cowardly spice-merchant at the village of Saint Bel, which lies at the extremity of the valley, where he was calmly refreshing himself at the inn.

Would that I could write that his face paled at our approach, that he trembled and a cold dew fell upon his skin, that he clamoured for forgiveness or, at the very least, showed himself properly contrite.

"Jan!" said he, smiling cheerily. "There you are! Pray take a cup of wine with me!"

I seated myself on the bench and regarded him sternly, which he seemed to ignore entirely.

"You got the better of those *ladrones*, eh?" said he, chuckling. "I knew you would. A man of valour, I said to myself. He'll have no trouble in dispatching a few simpletons."

And so on in like vein. As I quaffed off the cup of wine he proffered me, I could not help but think that he was not worth any of the five men who were presently floating down the River Brevenne and one of them minus his head too. In faith, I bear no ill will to the memory of the robbers who beset us. Thieving is a vocation that brings with it great risks and calls for considerable valour. If you succeed, you may well become rich; if you fail, you are dead.

After an unconscionable deal of further lap-dog ignominy—with nary a question as to the fate of his secretary—Thierry de Royat suggested we pass the night at the inn and continue our journey on the morrow.

This was too much. I confess to this daybook that anger overcame me.

"Messire de Royat," said I, dashing my cup to the floor, which was a shameful waste of good wine. "I would rather spend a month in a lazar-house than share a bed for one night with such an emollient, skulking, white-livered, rat-faced, whore-begotten pig's midden as you! If you say one word more to me, I'll see you embalmed in your own spices!"

He paled most gratifyingly.

I tossed a few *deniers* to the hostess and enquired of the boy who, ungreeted by his master, was loitering by the door, if he wished to accompany me and be my servant. I could see from his face that he liked the idea well enough but he shook his head and fixed his eyes upon the rushes. As I wrote before, he was a good lad, if a little stupid.

Thus did I continue my journey alone and by the hour of nones I reached this fine town of Lyon. Shortly thereafter, I found a room at the *Au Père Burchard* wherein I pen these words.

The sooner I have quitted this land, the better.

At Lyon

On Saint Lucian's Eve.
(Tuesday 7th January 1416)

I have secured a passage for Pistol and myself aboard the barque *Maria*, bound north up the River Saône for Chalon. It is captained by one Thomas Bideau. We leave at dawn.

Finding a boat proved quite a simple task for all vessels go either down the river to Valence and Avignon or up the river to Villefranche, Mâcon and Chalon. Had I wished to travel without my brave Pistol, I might have had my pick of any one of a dozen or so. Even Captain Thomas, who is a short, fat, muscular man with cross-eyes, demurred at ferrying a horse but he accepted readily enough when I produced five *livres*.

He has had a sort of pen built for Pistol in a corner of the foredeck and my good friend has been amply provided with straw and oats.

I dare say it would be swifter to ride to Chalon, for we shall be sailing upstream and progress will be slow, but the weather is still cold and wet and at my age a man prefers to travel in comfort when he can.

Having paid Captain Thomas a *livre* in advance, I went in search of provender for the journey and bought a large cask of Beaujolais wine, two cold capons, a cold leg of boar, a pot of anchovies, a pot of olives and a loaf of *pain blanc*, all of which I had taken to the boat. I asked Captain Thomas if he thought this sufficient for the journey, at which he coughed and spat a great deal and declared that it would be enough for most men but, if it were not, I would be welcome to share their own provisions.

I have often been surprised by the generosity of mariners. Your landsman, who lives surrounded by God's bounty and has only intemperate weather and bad husbandry to blame if he is ill-fed, is often mean and covetous by nature, whilst your mariner will share his plenty as cheerfully as his privations. For myself, I cannot abide avarice in any man; it is a thing I cannot stand. Marry, before the reformation that marked the start of this my pilgrimage, I was something of a crusader in this cause and—I doubt not but through divine inspiration—appropriated the excess and redundant wealth of many a fat caterpillar and distributed it among the poor of Eastcheap.

Having completed my business, I went to an alehouse where I dined on sheep's feet and soup.

As I think I wrote yesterday, Lyon is heavily garrisoned against the Savoyard. This stated, I must add that any advantage they gain in the matter of numbers they as soon squander through lack of discipline. Not since I led my own troops to the slaughter—for which may God forgive me—have I set eyes on such listless, threadbare soldiery. In spite of the cold, there is scarcely a street corner that does not boast its garrison of beggarly pikemen and not an alehouse that is not occupied by bowless archers cadging cups of wine. No sooner had I entered one than the alarums sounded and throughout my dinner I was besieged on all sides. At length, by a strategy of steady attrition, my defences were so weakened that I capitulated and bought wine for the entire company, for which I was roundly cheered. Rarely have I won favour with such ease. There were shouts of *Vive messire le hollandois!* and as many pledgings of health. If they had known me to be English, I doubt that it would have made much difference.

I would gladly have remained in the alehouse and taken my ease with a pint or two of wine but the thought of having to buy yet more wine for my military escort drove me out into the street. I therefore determined to stroll about the town and seek out what pleasures Lyon had to offer.

My mind turned to those two dark-eyed whores that Jehan and Esprit consorted with on Saturday last. It engendered a slight ruttishness in me and thus, the fear of God being absent from my eyes, I sought out a stew. Let me be frank, I mean a leaping-house. Yet it is always simpler to find a stew and in finding the one, you are sure to find the other.

By dint of divers enquiries, I was directed to an establishment in the Rue d'Enfer, which did, in truth, prove to be a very inferno of a place for it was one of the foulest stews I ever sat in. Yet it served its purpose well enough for I was soon in conversation with a sanguine gentleman who was a prominent burgher and—as is the case with prominent burghers everywhere—knew the locations and tariffs of every bawdy-house in the city. I bought him a towel out of gratitude. It was a little cleaner than my own.

The nearest such house was the stew itself, yet the filthy towels and grey, scum-laden water urged discretion. I am not averse to taking French wine and French sausage home with me but the French Disease is another matter entirely. Thus I dressed myself and progressed further up the street into the Rue des Soupirs where, at the sign of *Le Gros Chevreuil*, or the Fat Roebuck, I purchased the favours of a young *demoiselle* who knew what she was about.

Now I am not such a man as Thierry de Royat, for he would have set down the very details of his amours and lent each caress such colour as would have made him seem, in his own estimation, a Titan of the bedchamber. Though indisputably necessary and most enjoyable, the act of love is as banal as any other natural act and I would no more record it on paper than I would describe the *minutiae* of my eatings, drinkings and visits to the jakes. Suffice to state that I left this comely wench well satisfied. With many a sigh, she declared that she had not had one such as I since she quitted her native village.

By the time I left her dusk was already falling and so I returned to the *Au Père Burchard* where I was greeted by a roaring fire of apple-logs. A tapster put before me a pitcher of wine and I made myself comfortable before the blaze to while away the hour before supper in quiet and pleasantly inebriated contemplation.

Supper itself, tasty as it was, was much the same as last night except that there was no salad. This was no great loss to me for I am no rabbit to chew on leaves. In its stead, a tureen of garlic soup was placed on the board.

Fond as I am of garlic and recognising therein divers properties beneficial to the human body, I yet can see no good reason for elaborating a soup thereof, unless it be to employ the resulting concoction as an instrument of defence. I took some all the same, lest the stench of my table-companions become intolerable.

It occurs to me that the eating of garlic is like a man whose countenance is of surpassing ugliness but has never had occasion to gaze upon his own reflection. He may *think* himself the equal of his fellows but only let him present his face to them and he meets with disgust and ridicule, which perplexes him greatly. So is it with garlic. You may eat a bushel of the herb and smell not a whiff of it and yet to others you stink like a poke of devils. I admit that the comparison is somewhat laboured but science is rarely elegant in my experience.

I shall meditate further on this business of garlic and mirrors before I go to sleep.

At Mâcon

On Saint Gregory's Day.
(Saturday 11th January 1416)

I am staying at an inn the name of which I *did* know but seem to have forgotten. I have remembered it again. It is *La Vache Gisante* or The Cow Couchant or The Lying Down Cow With Its Head Raised, if you will. Small wonder I forgot it.

Last night I slept well for the first time since quitting Lyon on Wednesday last and it was the first night I was warm. For all that, the journey has gone well thus far. Today we rest up for it is a Saturday. Tomorrow I re-embark for Chalon.

Pistol is also stabled at this inn and I am sure he is glad of it. I would not have believed that a horse could be seasick—especially on a river—yet it seems to be so.

The *Maria* is a fine vessel: a stoutly-built little tub that wallows through the waters of the Saône like a cart-horse through a marsh. A thick rope joins it to the riverbank where two mules tug it upstream, driven by an equally mulish muleteer. As your mule is not renowned for its sprightliness, and the flood being furious, we make no more than six or seven leagues a day. Yet it is steady progress and less fatiguing than riding a-horseback.

I share my quarters—if such they may be called—with Captain Thomas and the crew, which consists of two men: one on the riverbank driving the mules and the other, Thomas's younger brother, working on the boat itself. The quarters comprise a sort of canvas shelter slung just forward of the steering-oar and under which we spread our palliasses. During the day, by stacking these on top of each other, I construct a tolerable couch and there I recline for all the world like a pharaoh, though considerably colder. At my side I have my cask of wine and a bowl of anchovies and olives.

I am spared the trouble of making conversation with the crew for Captain Thomas, when he is not occupied with sailing, is as silent as an anchorite; his younger brother Martin is a cretin, and the mule-driver Eustache is almost totally deaf and as incomprehensible to me as I am to him.

Where the deck of the *Maria* is not encumbered as mentioned, it is laden with great bolts of cloth covered in canvas. It is thus with only the greatest difficulty that I have been able to comfort Pistol in his seasickness for his pen is situated forwards, near the bows, and reaching it calls for a degree of agility rare even in those who are young, slender and sober. I have learned to eschew the customary route of hopscotching around the gunwales since this constitutes a most unwarranted flirtation with a watery grave. Instead, I now crawl over the bolts of cloth in an ungainly and demeaning fashion, which manoeuvre affords Captain Thomas and his crew the greatest amusement.

It is not even as though my charitable excursions are fully appreciated by Pistol himself, for he watches my floundering approach with a sardonic eye and shows little gratitude when I do comfort him. I think he rather blames me for his predicament.

One notable advantage of travelling by boat is that you stop where you will and your conveyance then becomes your hostelry. In the summer months, which—so I am told—are warm, this must be a happy experience indeed, for I can think of few things pleasanter than falling asleep to the gentle rocking of the boat and the soporific gurgling of the river. In winter it is a different matter. Our rude tent, being devoid of anything even roughly resembling a wall, admits the slightest draught, and despite my heavy cloak and notwithstanding liberal doses of Beaujolais wine, I am nithered to the bone and eventually fall asleep to the chattering of my teeth.

On the first evening of my voyage, I disdained the crew's cabbage soup and dined instead on my two cold capons. This was a grievous mistake. As unappetising as it smelled, the soup was at least hot and provided far better protection against the wind than my cold meats. I awoke several times during the night and cursed Captain Thomas for not having made fast at the quayside in Villefranche, which was less than half a league away. This he had refused to do for it meant paying a moorage levy. To add insult to injury, he and his quarter-wit brother are natives of Villefranche and delighted in telling me of the fine hostelries that abound in that town.

The following night we moored outside the city of Thoissey and I must confess that in so doing Captain Thomas displayed the sort of prudence that is so often found wanting in the young. It appears that Thoissey, being the last town before the frontier with Burgundy, has a small garrison of French troops whose function it is to dissuade the Duke of Burgundy from extending his duchy further down the river. Since Duke John has scant inclination to do this, preferring to gain mastery over the whole of France, if he may, the garrison has little to do but drink and drill. The passing months weigh heavily upon them. Therefore, to divert themselves and subsidise their drinking, they impose unofficial duties on all goods bound for the north, which they do in a manner most disagreeable.

It was thus some relief to me that we waited a mile or so away from the town until it became dusk and then quickly passed by along the opposing bank, to make fast inside Burgundian territory.

As I recount this, it seems a simple enough procedure but as it entailed embarking the mules and poling the boat across the stream and then poling it upstream and back to our original riverbank on the other side of Thoissey and once more persuading two of the most recalcitrant mules as ever bore burden to forsake the safety of the *Maria* and risk a ducking as they jumped ashore, it was a matter of no little difficulty.

At dinner that evening I traded a share of my cold leg of boar for a bowl of cabbage soup and it is certain that all four of us were content with the transaction. I still awoke several times during the night but this owed itself more to the gaseous effects of the soup than to the cold.

Yesterday saw a remarkable change in Captain Thomas. It was as though some divine intervention had restored his powers of speech. Whereas hitherto, with the odd exception, he had broken his silence only to bark an order or give a gruff and highly expectorant answer to my questions, he now appears to play host to a very devil of loquacity.

In truth he has no more conversation than before. His new fluency is limited entirely to invective and the object of his abuse is uniquely the Burgundian people, their Duke, their soldiery, their women, their food and their habits. A fat peasant woman gathering faggots brought forth loud condemnations of the lightness of Burgundian womanhood. A ragged beggar scratching his sores engendered dark grumblings about their love of pleasure. The mere sight of a farmer walking behind his oxen in the manner of farmers the world over elicited curses upon their boundless pride.

Each of these *exempla* served as a point of departure for more general comments about the nature of Burgundians, which were often modified to encompass their supposed allies the English, whom he saw as a sullen, violent, greedy people whose vulgarity is only surpassed by their thirst for gold, blood and ale.

Being temporarily a Dutchman, I was unable to say anything in spite of my rising anger. It suffices to say here that those faults he ascribed to the Burgundians sit equally well upon his own countrymen.

It was with some gladness of heart that I noticed his venom decrease the closer we approached Mâcon, for I had small desire to begin my day's holiday with a brawl on the quayside. For his part, Captain Thomas' witless brother seems to regard his sibling's diatribe as no more than a matter of course and I suspect that it is something of a tradition at this point in their journey.

Today, I lay abed till almost noon when I descended and ate dinner, which was stewed eels most greasy, and visited Pistol, who appears much recovered from the river-sickness. I then bought further provisions for the journey to Chalon, viz.:

A cask of Burgundy wine

Three chickens (cooked)

Two rabbits (dead but uncooked)

A pot of anchovies

A loaf of *pain bourgeois*

Two sacks of oats.

By the time I had accomplished the purchase and delivery of these goods, evening was already drawing in and so I returned to this hostelry for supper.

Supper was better than dinner, which is to say but little. I dined on boiled stockfish. Generally speaking, I prefer your boiled stockfish to your eel stew for there is less grease, which loosens the bowels grievously, and more salt, which improves the thirst wondrously. Truth to tell, I would rather be pardoned fish entirely but that is already a matter of record.

As soon as I was done with eating, I repaired to the upper room and brought with me a large jug of wine and my pot of anchovies, which I appear to have spilt on my daybook. The anchovies, not the wine. I see now that my jug is empty. I shall descend to refill it for I am not yet drowsy.

Captain Thomas sleeps aboard the *Maria* this night. The man is labouring in the wrong vocation. He should truly be an anchorite. Yet for that he needs a desert. Properly speaking, though they also mortify their flesh with hardships, your anchorites do it in deserts and, to the best of my knowledge, there are no deserts in France. This must I verify for I have never seen a desert and a good pilgrim should see one, if he is able.

At Chalon

On the fifteenth day of January, being a Wednesday.

I have had a fortunate escape. More fortunate yet than my combat with that termagent Douglas at Shrewsbury field, which, had it not been for a patch of plashy, blood-soaked earth on which I slipped and fell, might well have been the death of me.

The town of Tournus is visited by the plague. We passed by it on Saint Hilary's Day and I blessed the good Captain Thomas that we did not stop.

We spent Sunday night to the north of Fleurville, having made good time that day, the mules being much refreshed from their holiday in Mâcon. Monday dawned bright and cold. There was still a steady wind blowing but it had weakened since the previous day, the mules plodded on easily, and the *Maria* breasted the flood like a dolphin.

We were about halfway between Fleurville and Tournus, at a place where the River Seille debouches into the Saône, when I heard a knelling in the distance.

Now France and Burgundy abound in bells. Marry, there is scarce a flea dies but there is a bell to mark its passing and thus I accounted it very little. But when we had travelled more than a league without deliverance from the doleful sound, I enquired of Captain Thomas—who was at the steering-oar—if this tolling did not mark some great event.

"Aye," said he, chuckling dryly and spitting into the *Maria*'s wake. "*La peste!*"

Now I was not a little perturbed at this revelation for I had not come this far, braving foul weather, robbers and marriage, to die like a rat of some unseen pestilence. Moreover, since we had quitted Lyon, the wind had blown southwards straight down the river and it was clearly thanks to Providence that I did not have the plague already.[65] And so, without further ado, I tore up a strip of rag, soaked it in vinegar, bound it across my nose and mouth and, from then on, parted my lips only to quaff wine, which I did in great quantity for it is well known that just as pickling preserves onions, so wine preserves people.

I will own that I opened my mouth on one other occasion and that was to remonstrate with Captain Thomas to the effect that, the plague-infested town being called Tournus, we had best turn us with all haste and return to Fleurville. To this Captain Thomas made no answer. He only shrugged and spat. Not since I last saw my erstwhile flatulent accomplice Peto have I met with such economy of language.

Evening was drawing in as Tournus came into sight. I saw it first as a ruddy glow at the apex of the river. As we drew nearer, the Saône and the lowering clouds above it waxed the colour of apple-skin and the silent countryside about us was thrown into pitchy darkness. Here and there, a few solitary objects glowed in the hellish light—a gnarled and naked tree, a gallows and a breaking wheel, a hovel, deserted and forlorn.

I thought at first that Tournus had been put to the torch and was forsaken by its inhabitants but as we neared it I perceived the source of the light to be scores of fires burning in the streets and I knew then that folk still lived in that inferno of a city. Sometimes I glimpsed lone figures silhouetted against the blaze, like demons stoking their conflagrations.

In faith, at night, a city visited by the pestilence is as like any picture of Hell as living man can imagine. The only folk upon the street are those who tend the plague-fires and carry out the dead. All else are shut up in their homes or packed into the churches. Nothing fills churches like the plague.

I know of what I speak. I was no more than four years old when the Great Pestilence ravaged England and in that most damned plague my father, my mother, my sister Mary and my grandmother were all taken from me. In my sixteenth year, when I was living at Mile End, it returned and carried off poor Will Squele and squeal he never did for he had ever a brave heart and died in silence, as a man should.

The clergy said it was God's punishment for our manifold sins and wickednesses and yet my sister Mary had precious little time to be wicked in her short life and Will was as honest a man as you could find anywhere. Those who went untainted and profited from this disaster were the thieves and knaves, whilst those who died in the greatest number were the innocent children and the old.

The pestilence revisited London in my thirtieth year and in my thirty-seventh and in my forty-fifth and in my sixty-first, which indeed was only nine summers ago. And it was not prayer and processions that put an end to it, nor crucifixes, candles and holy water either. It was the winter.

Yet here we were in winter and here too was the plague.

As the *Maria* drew in towards the city walls, I began to smell the dead of Tournus. It was a stench that vinegar could not conceal. I am a townsman born and bred and the stink of rotting meat is as familiar to me as that of new-mown grass to your countryman yet, for all that, there is something in the reek of human flesh that I find particularly loathsome.

Our mules climbed onto the tow-path that divides Tournus from the river and were no sooner on a level footing than a man dashed out of the shadows and made towards the boat. He was bearing a bundle, which he hugged tightly to his chest. Perceiving him, Eustache, our mule-driver, cried out, whereupon the man hesitated and I thought he would turn and flee but this he did not. Instead, he ran up to Eustache, grabbed him by the shoulder and began shouting wildly, though I understood naught of what he said. Eustache, however, pulled his cudgel from his belt and fetched the man two or three sharp blows upon the back, whereupon he dropped the bundle, which struck the earth with a clatter, and darted back into the darkness, followed, for a short distance, by our mule-driver.

Returning to his charges, Eustache paused at the bundle and stirred its folds with his stick. From where I stood, next to Captain Thomas, I could see the firelight glinting on plate—silver or gold, it seemed. But Eustache dared not pick it up and, for myself, I would not have set foot on that tow-path had it been for the crown of England.

Perhaps the man was some honest burgher fleeing from the pestilence with his worldly riches clasped to his bosom. More likely he was a thief.

In such a wise is your pestilence a double menace, for it not only kills without discrimination and in a manner most horrible but also depraves the living, giving licence to the thief and corrupting the souls of true men. Marry, it is wondrous what the fear of death will do to a man. I have seen entire villages given up to such licentiousness as would make Cock's Lane look like a cloister. All to force a little more living into the short space left. The folk will dance and sing and lose themselves in excesses not seen since Trimalchio's Dinner, but they do so to the rhythm of Death's drum.

Captain Thomas did not make fast the *Maria* till well after dark. We ate our cabbage soup in silence and I shared my two remaining chickens with the crew. Behind us, we could still see the crimson glow of Tournus but now the wind blew towards the town and thus we slept easier.

I confess to having been exceeding vigilant since that day but thus far I have perceived naught untoward in my health. If I were back in London, I would have sent my water round to the good Doctor Monks but I have neither trust nor confidence in your French physics and shall have none of them.

Jehan, who knew much of this science of medicine—being afflicted with the gout and the rheumatism besides—was forever cursing these same doctors, saying that they distinguish all infirmities by the weighing of the purse. Belike this is true of their whole race for even the good Doctor Monks, who is the pleasantest and most amenable leech as ever drew blood and uncommon skilled in the corrective use of wine, is inclined to prescribe rest and abstinence if you are too poor for either but cupping, purging, drenching, poking, swathing and every other practice found and not found in Galen and Hippocrates if you look as though you have coin about you.

Thus have I prescribed some rough and ready prophylactic measures for myself, which consist of washing my hands and face in vinegar, saying brief prayers to Saints Roche, Giles and Adrian, and drinking off four pints of excellent Burgundy wine. Sadly the wine has given me the colic.

Thus, with new wine on the inside and old wine on the outside and my immortal soul thoroughly protected by these three worthies, I believe the pestilence may spare me once again. In truth, I know little about Saint Adrian but I have been told that he is useful in this extremity and so I have prayed to him too.

We passed Tuesday night at, or rather near Sennecey, which the inhabitants thereof hopefully call *le Grand*, despite its being pitifully small. Several of these *Senneceyiens* came out of their hovels and walked to where the *Maria* was moored and there attempted to bargain with Captain Thomas over the purchase of some cloth, which they hoped to buy at wholesale price.

Now, I would not bargain with Captain Thomas over the purchase of a gill of pudding-ale, let alone a yard or two of buckram. If you demand naught of him, he is generous enough, but the merest mention of payment will engender the wildest calculations. I am inclined to think that reckoning does not come easily to him and that, to preserve himself from the embarrassment of undervaluation, he will exaggerate any price tenfold.

In the present case, he displayed uncommon forbearance but finally refused to spoil a full bolt of cloth by snipping off odd pieces here and there.

On hearing this, the *Senneceyiens* waxed greatly abusive and cursed him roundly.

Now, throughout the length and breadth of that geographical entity which, for the sake of simplicity, we will call France, your Burgundians are justly famed for their cursing, which reaches heights of blasphemy undreamt of even by Pistol. The man, I mean, not the horse. Captain Thomas, in spite of not being a Burgundian, is no inconsequential blasphemer himself—as I have witnessed daily since we passed by the town of Thoissey—yet he cannot hold a candle to his neighbours, whose cunning and ingenuity in this matter of foul language ranks with those masters who created the shrine of Saint Thomas Beckett or the great door of the church of Our Lady of Paris.

The *Senneceyiens* began their onslaught in a mild enough manner: establishing simple yet solid foundations of profanity in order to test Captain Thomas's mettle. Perceiving that he was unlikely to be demolished by such, they then proceeded to build steadily—imprecation by imprecation, malediction by male-diction—until, having constructed flying buttresses of vulgarity and cunningly wrought gargoyles of expletives, they topped off their edifice of invective with The Burgundian Oath.

Now your Burgundian Oath is as famed as your Burgundian blasphemers yet, to my ears at least, it sounded considerably more moderate than what had gone before. Your Burgundian Oath is no more than *Je renie Dieu*.[66]

On hearing this, however, Captain Thomas was vexed and then, short-ly afterwards, most violent. By the time he had chased these impious villagers halfway back to Sennecey *le Grand*, three were already lying on the riverbank nursing broken pates and another two were heaving themselves out of the River Saône. The good Captain was aided in this by Eustache who, though he clearly had no idea why he was doing so, laid about him with his cudgel with great glee.

On his return, Captain Thomas grumbled a great deal and spat even more and continued to thus grumble and spit all the way through supper and till we four were settled on our palliasses, whereupon he stopped grumbling and spit-ting and snored instead.

I must say that it is little wonder that Burgundian towns are visited by the pestilence when their neighbours blaspheme with such abandon. God's Blood, I marvel that they have not all been levelled by now!

This afternoon we reached the town of Chalon, wherein I now write. I have bade farewell to Captain Thomas and to his witless brother and to Eustache. I have paid the Captain the balance of his five *livres* and bequeathed him the bal-ance of my cask of wine—though of that, I fear, there remains but little. Pistol, whose river-sickness persisted till the very end, was led ashore and most thank-ful he seemed of it too.

I am now quartered in the best room of a hostelry called *Le Toison d'Or*, or The Golden Fleece. It is aptly named for it will cost me double of what I paid in Mâcon.

Still, I have eaten a tolerable supper of meat-filled pastries, goose-livers, thrushes, boiled salt-beef, olives and rye-bread and, considering that today is a fast-day, this is not to be complained of. The inn also serves the most excellent wine, which comes, as the landlord tells it, from a small village not three leagues distant, Mercurey by name. I can think of no better designation for it is of a nimble and ascendant lightness—a fitting tribute to Jove's fleet son who was the god of merchants, travellers and thieves.

Sadly your Mercurey wine does little for the wind or the handwriting and so I must stop here.

At Chalon

On a Thursday, being the sixteenth day of January.

This morning I bought a few necessaries for my journey. I start out tomorrow at cock-crow.

I am not in the best of humours for this afternoon I was cozened in such a manner as left me quite vexed. Seeking to refresh myself before the travails of the road, I repaired to a stewhouse, where I had an eight-*denier* stew and a bath and felt greatly invigorated withal. As oftimes happens, the stew put me in amorous mood and thus I sought out the proprietor, complimented him on the cleanliness of his towels, slipped ten *denier* into his hand and asked him whether he might procure me a good hot wench to cool my blood.

And what did the rogue do? He pocketed my ten *denier*, expressed his satisfaction that I had found my towel so clean and then added—haughtily, mind you—that, whereas in Paris a stewhouse might well provide for the lusts of the flesh, in Chalon they furnished only towels and water!

Towels and water! A man might as well stay at home! That ever such a whoreson knave be yet unhanged! If I were in London and treated with such insolence, I should have chopped the saucy nut-hook into dice and seen him fricasseed in his own boiling-tubs!

How may a man resist temptation in such a damned respectable town as Chalon? Your hypocritical *Chalonnais* will burn in hell-fire for their piety! Was not Sin bestowed on us that we might seek redemption through the doing of Good Works? And what better Good Work can there be than the saving of a Mary Magdalene? Cast out the thieves, whores and beggars and you spurn God's Great Design, which is—or at least ought to be—a most grievous heresy.

And yet so busy are the *Chalonnais* with being virtuous, and constraining innocent travellers to be so, that they utterly ignore the foul abyss of Sin into which they are slipping. And I speak here not only of heresy but also of the Sin of Gluttony! Did not I write yesterday of the luxurious repast that was served me? A feast worthy of Belshazzar! And on a fast-day too! It is well known that the Lord brands the glutton by making him obese, bilious and costive and few could walk the streets of Chalon without marking these signs in its inhabitants. Yet these signs they heed not.

I am well content that my pilgrimage leads me from such a place for it will surely follow the fate of its neighbour Tournus.

Towels and water! I could have disembowelled the rogue! Yet it would have been to render him a service. Let him wax goodly gorbellied and wait on the punishment of the Omnipotent.

I kicked a beggar on the way back and felt somewhat better for it.

At Laconsh (Lacanche)

On Saint Prisca's Day.
(Saturday 18th January 1416)

Today is my birthday. I am seventy-one summers old.

It is said by many that the good die young. This only goes to prove the false-ness of proverbs for those who die young have scant opportunity to be wicked.

Your proverbs are distillations of folly. Consider this: "Trust no man till you have eaten a bushel of salt with him." Now a bushel represents a deal of salt and thus I construe this proverb as: "Trust no man till you have known him for many a long year." However, were I to write of parents deceived by their children, grandparents turned out of doors when food is scarce, husbands cuckold-ed and wives betrayed, it would take more paper than I have in this daybook. Only let me mention one John Bardolph of the carbuncle nose, a man with whom I have eaten Lot's wife ten times over and whom I would no more trust for a single minute than I would learn the bagpipes and live in Ireland.

Consider another proverb of French provenance: *Mieux vault pain qu'écu en paroi.*[67] If bread is worth so much and money so little, why is it that your bakers sell short weight and your millers adulterate their flour? God's blood, I have even heard of them selling bread by night to gull simple wretches out of a few groats!

Nay, your proverbs are a bolting-hutch of foolery and I'll have none of them.

If I could have chosen a place and day to celebrate my birthday, the place would not have been Laconsh and the day would not have been a Saturday. Laconsh is a pitiful group of hovels clinging to the banks of the River Arroux and Saturday is not only a fish day but the day of Holy Innocents last. I am thus constrained to remain here till the morrow.

Laconsh has no church and no inn. I passed last night, and shall doubtless pass tonight, in the hovel of a certain Jean Charon who is a ditcher by trade and occupies the best house in the village, if one room may be called a house. Jean's surname is indeed fitting for the inside of his dwelling is as black as the Styx, being lit only by two rude rush-lamps and a cooking fire, which obscures as much as it illuminates.

Yet Charon deserves his obolus. He is deferential and accommodating. Marry, he even offered me his daughter, and this with many a wink and nod.

But I had little stomach for such an encounter. In faith, since I dined on boiled eggs and turnip soup last night, I have had stomach for very little.

The turnip soup was most miserable. The Charon family called it *ravegout* or *rasgout* or something or other. For wine they gave me that watery slop called *piquette*, which is to your French peasantry what pudding-ale is to your English. For all that, this meagre food seemed to nourish them well enough for they ate no more than a mouse's portion and it was I who tucked in heartily and finished off their leavings.

I slept curled up before the fire on a bed of straw, which was tolerably comfortable, warm and free of vermin. I awoke with parched throat and red eyes, owing to the smoke.

Today I have done naught but sit before the fire. I would have preferred to have put more leagues behind me but it would be foolish to tempt Dame Fortune for she is as capricious a hussy as any of her sex.

Yesterday Pistol was gay and mettlesome. This in spite of the weather, which has turned cold again. We covered a good ten leagues without showing the slightest fatigue. My Pistol is a fine animal and has served me well and faithfully. I shall take him back to England with me, if I may.

This is the first birthday in many a year on which I have neglected to make a will. I have considered it at some length but, despite having pen, paper and time at my disposal, I have not embarked on a new testament. In truth, I cannot think of anyone to whom I would bequeath my few possessions. If I die here in France, they will doubtless go to whosoever finds me. In England, should I finally reach those shores, there is only Doll and she resides in Southwark. And it may well be that before My Lady France claims me, the French malady claims her.

Belike I have escaped the pestilence. It is now five days since I passed Tournus and not so much as a sneeze.

Charon's youngest son is casting pine-cones at me. He is a rascally boy of three years old. I shall set down my pen and chase him a little.

I have taken up my pen again while there yet remains sufficient light. I am sitting near the door, which is always open that the smoke may drift out and the hens drift in. The sky is of a deep blue, fading into rose where it kisses the hills. The first stars are twinkling. It is bitterly cold and the noise of the wind in the pine-trees is like the roaring of the sea. Behind me, Charon's wife Marie is stirring some trouty soup. I can hear Pistol snorting nearby.

What perverse destiny binds Charon and his family to such a plot as this? It is certain that we all have our place in the order of things: we are nourished that we may nourish others, though the nourishment that we ourselves provide is but for worms. Yet these are the mere outer boundaries of life within whose confines we may be joyful for a time. We may laugh, dance, sing, drink heavily, sleep lightly, fight, foin and feed. Why then do folk such as Charon and his family spurn these pleasures and delights to toil upon a few acres of wind-blasted hillside? Why do they make of that their universe?

Perhaps we are all as they are, in our way: like tiny pismires scurrying hither and thither upon a single stone, ignorant of the vastness around them.

Charon's family are staring at me in wonderment as I scratch these words. I shall trouble them no longer.

At Vermenton

On Saint Agnes's Day.
(Tuesday 21st January 1416)

Saint Agnes is the patron saint of virgins. This is comment enough.

I am passing this night at a small hostelry in the village of Vermenton on the River Cure. My excellent Pistol has been trotting along tirelessly and I did have some hopes of reaching Auxerre today. Had the frosty weather which began on Saint Wulfstan's Day persisted, I dare say we might have done so. Unfortunately it turned warmer towards midday today and in the afternoon there was such a downpour as swiftly turned the road into a quagmire.

I slept last night in Avalon.

Now, my late uncle Hugh Falstaff, who assured the upbringing of my brother Tom and I after the pestilence carried off our family, was a man of uncommon learning. Uncommon, that is, for a scrivener, which honourable profession he followed till the day he died—or rather his profession followed him for he would rather have had none of it. It was he who first taught me the French language, and Latin too.

Uncle Hugh, being a man of learning, possessed no less than four books: The Parliament of the Three Ages, Sir Beves of Hamtoun, *Le Roman de la Rose* and the *Historia Regum Britanniae* of one Gaufridas Monemutensis, whom folk generally call Geoffrey of Monmouth. He would often read to us from these books and later, when I was able, I read them myself.

Now according to this Gaufridas of Monmouth, King Arthur, having vanquished the wicked Mordred and his knights at Cambula, was most grievous hacked about and none but two of his men remained to him, it having been an uncommon close-fought contest. Gaufridas writes that, after the battle, Arthur was borne off to Avalon in a boat, there to heal his wounds, there being no physick present in Cambula or its environs.

Now there are certain people who dispute the history of Arthur, saying that it is base invention like the legend of King Alfred and is not worth flea's piddle, but then there are those as would scoff at a tavern reckoning if they did not see it with their own eyes. It is clear to me that no King of Britain who could subdue Scotland, Ireland, Iceland and the Orkney Isles—wherever *they* be—could possibly be a creation of fancy.

It was thus with some excitement that I learned the name of the town in which I slept last night. It was none other that that same town of Avalon of which I read so many years ago! Thus, no sooner was I installed in a convenient inn than I went out in search of some relic of the Great King, and this in spite of the lateness of the hour, the coldness of the weather and my not yet having supped.

The walls of Avalon are massive and truly worthy of a king. What is more, the town possesses a Roman church and all who know their history will remember that Arthur's queen was one Guanhamara—also known as Wenhaver or Guinevere—who was a Roman matron. It was also to Rome that Arthur marched with his host to make war upon the Emperor Lucius.

Sadly, beyond this, I could find little to show for Arthur's stay. The Roman church had much in the way of statuary but naught that pertained to the Great King of Britain, least of all his tomb.

As I wended my way back to the inn, I reasoned that, just as there was certain proof that Arthur had once sojourned in Avalon—the walls, the church *et cetera*—there was equal proof that he had not died there. I imagine that, like any true-born Englishman, Arthur had tired of France, its frivolity and its cooking, and had exchanged Avalon for a place better suited to a hero's repose. I think Jerusalem would have been his final resting place and I doubt not but that one day his tomb will eventually be discovered in that holy city.

At supper I endeavoured to question my table-companions on the subject but was confounded to find that none of them had so much as heard of King Arthur. One or two even seemed to regard my enquiries with suspicion, perhaps fearing that I was a spy. Such simple-minded ignorance never fails to amaze me.

I even accosted the landlord on the same subject. He told me much about Avalon but he too had never heard of Arthur. It now seems clear that since Arthur quitted this town so many years ago, its fortunes have fallen into decline. It is now famed for the making of hats.

Whatever lapses of fortune it has endured, Avalon is truly a Babylon compared with Vermenton, which consists of a single louse-ridden inn, a church and a clutch of hovels and huts, the best of which an English henhouse would put to shame.

At Sens

On the feast of the conversion of Saint Paul.
(Saturday 25th January 1416)

This day is the feast of the conversion of Saint Paul, as I have written above.

Now your Saint Paul was once a traveller such as I. I forget exactly why it was he travelled thus for it is many a long year since I last heard his history. He was no pilgrim—of that I am sure—for there were no saints on active service then and therefore no place to pilgrimage to. Moreover, Paul was a saint himself and could scarcely have pilgrimaged to his own shrine for he was yet alive. I *do* know that he was on his way to Damascus—which lies some leagues distant from Jerusalem—though for what reason I cannot recall. I believe he intended to persecute somebody for some reason or other. The Good Book is full of persecutions.

In any event, Paul was on his way to Damascus when the Good Lord struck him from his horse and turned him into a Christian. Why Paul should be thus blessed is beyond my comprehension for I have fallen from my horse on more occasions than I would gladly own to yet it has never done much for *my* spiritual well-being. He had to change his name too for, up to the moment when the Omnipotent saw fit to cast him from the saddle, he was called Saul. Now I have ever been Jack Falstaff and have little desire to be called Simon or Thomas, and if being chosen by God requires a change of name, I would prefer to remain unchosen, if He wills it otherwise or not.

I now recall that, as if bruising his backside was not enough, the Almighty also *blinded* poor Paul just for good measure.

Yet Paul was a traveller and must be respected for that for it is an arduous profession, divine intervention or not. If I were not so drunk as I am now, I would search out a cathedral and say a prayer to him.

This is the second time I have been in Sens. It was here that I failed to sell my horse—the one I had of the merchant in Charenton. Yesterday I passed through the village wherein I traded her for my most excellent Pistol and, as we approached it, I wondered greatly as to what the manner of his homecoming might be. I am pleased to say that, though he did prick up his ear-and-a-half, sniff the air and whinny a little, he showed scant inclination to forsake my company for his native stable.

The people of Sens have exceedingly strange customs. According to a tap-ster of this inn, which by the by is called the *L'Étoile* or The Star, the *Sénonais* exhibit their infants in the street on midsummer eve, surrounding their cradles with green branches and offering tarts to whosoever may come to look upon them. Try as I may, I can think of no good reason for this tradition, unless it be that the said children are of such signal ugliness that only bald confrontation and bribery can elicit praise, and once a year at that.

This does not fall without the bounds of likelihood for your *Sénonais* are an unprepossessing crew.

The city of Sens is dwarfed by its cathedral and therefore by its archbish-op. Like Saint Paul, the *Sénonais* are thus forever under the eye of God and give less thought to sinning than I do to drinking buttermilk. I would wager a brace of capons that every cut-purse pays his tithes and that there is not one co-ney-catcher hereabouts as does not confess himself twice daily. You may as soon find a maidenhead in an emir's harem as a bawdy-house in Sens.

I have little to note about the journey from Vermenton. I passed Wednes-day night at Auxerre, though I deemed it wise to avoid the *Auberge du Cheval Noir* wherein I stayed with Jehan and Edmond and instead shared a bed with a merchant from Troyes in an inn that stank strongly of cats. Though from Troyes, he was no Trojan for he beheld me as a mouse beholds a weasel and slept with his purse tucked beneath his bolster, though it could not have contained more than a few *denier*. Myself, I carry slightly less than a hundred and fifty *écus d'or* and I sling my saddle-bag over the *perche-manteaux* along with the rest of my clothes. Riches should bring ease and not disquiet and by being so careful with his coin he will but draw greater attention to it. Like the other Trojans, he will be wise too late.

In truth, I have secreted ten *livres* in the hem of my houppeland as an offer-ing to Saint Nicholas.

Thursday dawned bright and cold and the way along the banks of the River Yonne was as hard as any stone. I had not expected to reach Joigny by nightfall but Pistol cantered as if newly released from the stable, sometimes breaking into a spirited gallop, as it seemed, for very joy of living.

In my youth, when it was my pleasure to roam, I often crossed the River Thames to Southwark and walked to the Tabard, an inn wherein pilgrims gather to ride to Canterbury. There you would find all manner of people, young and old, rich and poor, and I often had occasion to observe antiquity a-horseback. They would manage their steeds as a miller's son tickles trout and scarce went above a gentle trot unless some mischievous rascal prodded them on. And here am I—a whelp of three-score and eleven years—clattering along like a farm lad bound for market. I was not overtaken once save for a company of Burgundian soldiery who spurred past as if the Devil himself were at their heels. My Pistol is a brave beast! I wish I had a son worth half of him!

Yesterday I awoke before cock-crow and set out at first light after a scanty breakfast of wine, salt-herring, leek soup and cheese. The weather was yet colder than the day before but the firmament was bright and cloudless and we had a pleasant enough day.

From Joigny to Sens is a mere six or seven leagues yet I thought it wise to exercise discretion and so I provided myself with a leathern bottle of wine and a piece of cold roast pork to keep out the winter chill. The pork was excellent, if uncommon strong on garlic, and I ate in the saddle as a captain should. As for the wine, it was both potent and clear and came from the region of Rheims, or so I was told. At any rate, it dispelled the morning's vapours wonderful well— perhaps a little too well for before I had gone no more than two or three leagues I was in grievous danger of imitating Saint Paul. But without the blindness.

On the way, I entertained Pistol with some singing.

Now, since my infancy, I have always had a tuneable voice and thus no sooner did my melody break forth than Pistol flattened his ears and broke into a joyful gallop.

There is something in the nature of your brutish animals which makes them appreciative of music. I would it were the same with some people I have known. Sadly, it is not, for your whoreson, loutish malt-worm, bawling in his tavern, has less conception of mellifluous singing than a Grimsby flounder.

I well remember singing to my mastiff Snatch who was by so much enamoured of my tunefulness that he often sought to flatter me through imitation, throwing back his head and baying in unison as harmoniously as you please. Indeed, many is the time when, being full merry at the Boar's Head, I have added my chiming bass to some paltry catch and call me a knave if all the cats of Eastcheap did not vie to match my notes.

It is by such precious daintinesses that animals show their esteem of fine singing. As for your common two-legged herd, such as frequent the Boar's Head, they will only stop their ears and shout "Go to!" and heap unjust ridicule upon your accomplishments. This they do out of envy, for my tunefulness merely advertises their discord.

My good Pistol and I are now no more than four days' ride from Paris. We shall proceed thither by way of Montereau, Melun and Corbeil. Weather allowing, I shall sleep beside the River Seine tomorrow night.

It is to my shame that I quitted Paris like a thief two months ago. I shall not enter it so but rather as a triumphant general—nobly caparisoned, his baggage cars laden with booty, proudly saddled on his prancing steed. I quitted that city as a pauper—though unbowed, mark you—yet I shall return a rich man and the delights of that metropolis will be at my feet. Children and beggars will run after me and fight over the coins that I shall throw to them. Maidens will whisper to each other, point and admire. Grey-haired antiquity will gape.

Perhaps I shall pass a leisurely week, sampling the pleasures of Paris, before I progress to England. And then! Aye, a Falstaff returned in glory! Hal will pale at my approach and think himself accursed he was not here! My Hostess Quickly will wring her hands and lament that she squandered her affections—and her tavern—on that braggart Pistol, the misbegotten namesake of my valorous horse.

I shall to bed. The sooner to arrive.

At Corbeil

On the twenty-eighth day of January, being a Tuesday.

I can scarcely write. My head pains me grievously, my hand shakes and these letters dance about the page like tadpoles in a brook. Yet write I must for there are none to whom I can speak. None that would comprehend my pain.

My Pistol, my true and valiant companion and friend, is dead. I slew him with my own hand, cut his veins with my dagger, sat and watched as his blood flowed forth and sank into the leafy earth. I left my friend to rot in the Forest of Rougeau: to rot till his skin and flesh are dust and his bones whiten and become as the dead branches that surround him.

When I read what I have written here above, the words seem void of meaning, mere ciphers that fail to give expression to my grief.

I shall retell the facts alone, without embellishment.

We left Sens early on Sunday morning, my Pistol and I. There had been a hard frost and few people were abroad and so we made good time, following the River Yonne to Montereau, wherein we slept.

It was shortly after quitting Montereau yesterday morning that we plunged into the great forest of oak and beech which swallows up the towns of Corbeil and Melun and extends even to the very gates of Paris itself.

All forests are perilous and the wise traveller will not hazard his life and goods by venturing alone therein but will rather pass through in a company, even if it means attending their arrival.

Not Falstaff. None have ever called Falstaff wise. Nay, Falstaff is an old fool and twice an old fool in that he thinks himself a martial hero—an Alexander of the highway, vigilant, valorous and unvanquished. Yet wherein is he vigilant but in self-regard; wherein valorous but in slicing beef and stabbing capons; wherein unvanquished but in fleeing from danger? Here in France, has it not been Pistol, a brutish animal, who has been the sole author of his bravery and wealth?

Thus did I enter the forest blithe of heart and heedless of danger. Dame Fortune blessed me, for within the passage of a few hours I reached Melun and, before nightfall, had settled myself in the *Cerf du Saint Hubert*—that same inn wherein I diced with Captain Enrico a mere two months ago.

This morning began well. The coldness had abated a little but the road was yet firm under Pistol's hooves and we cantered along easily. We passed through a largish village and thereafter the trees grew denser till they stood close-packed and thickly undergrown on both sides of the road. It was dull and cloudy and, beneath the canopy of trees, it was twilight even at midday. And yet my mood was cheerful and I hummed to myself like some witless cowherd and lost myself in fancies of the lewdnesses in which I would indulge myself in Paris.

Of a sudden a mighty pain blossomed across my shoulders and the road was full of snarling, shrieking men. Someone behind us, unsuccessful at unseating me, swung his cudgel again and fetched me a damnable blow upon the arm. Pistol plunged and whinnied. I fumbled to unsheath Gut Cutter but, as I did so, the whoreson dog on my right slashed with his poignard. A burning pain shot through my thigh and his weapon opened up a great rent in Pistol's flank. Pistol reared high, neighing wildly. I abandoned my sword and clung to his neck.

My memory of what happened then is uncertain. I remember clinging to my brave Pistol as he bounded off the road and into the trees. I remember branches whipping past me, undergrowth ripping at my feet and legs. I remember the forest turning topsy-turvy. I remember nothing.

When I awoke, the world was full of pain. For a time I thought I had died and was gone to Hell for there was an infernal snorting in my ears, as of some demonic bellows. There was fire dancing in my head and thigh and every bone and muscle was racked by devils.

I was lying on my back. I opened my eyes and looked up through a veil of winter branches to the grey sky above. I moved my head and slowly looked about me.

The men had gone. A lance's length away lay Pistol, on his side, his eyes rolling, his nostrils splayed and snorting great gulps of air. Now and again, he raised his head to look at me and then let it fall. His right foreleg was smashed and bent.

I raise myself a little and sat four-square upon the ground—a tun of flesh that, though leaky, still held life. My face was sticky with blood.

I sat thus until I had in some measure regained my senses and then, softly, I knelt and pushed myself to my feet. My leg hurt me devilishly but the blood that had flowed therefrom was already dry and clotted. My feet were naked and the earth was very cold. All was very cold that did not burn like the pit of Hell.

My saddle-bags were gone. The few possessions they contained, other than my coin and wedding gown, were scattered about. I went to Pistol's side and caressed his head, stroked his proud neck, tickled him between the ears as he oftimes liked. Yet I knew what I must do.

My thin dagger of Italian provenance had gone unnoticed. I drew it and cut down through the great veins in Pistol's neck. The blood sprang forth and splashed warm on my hands and pulsed from his black body onto the cold ground.

He did not struggle. He made no movement. He knew, you see, that I did it out of love.

I sat and gazed into his eyes and he looked into mine until his own grew filmy and, at length, there came that change that I have remarked before: a long sigh, a quivering and then a sudden stillness—such a stillness that even a lake at quiet summer's eventide cannot equal.

I sat and watched over him for a good while longer, kissed his noble face, gathered up my possessions, rolled them in my cloak and slung them over my shoulder. I scrambled back through the trampled, broken undergrowth to the road and trudged off in the direction of Corbeil.

As unmindful of peril as I had been before, so was I then. Not through overweening pride, however, but through poverty, for the traveller with empty pockets will laugh in the face of the robber.

A carter overtook me and brought me here, to the hospital of Saint Spire, where the good monks have bound my head and thigh and given me meats and cordials. I shall not stay. I shall leave tomorrow. There yet remains to me the ten *livres* that I secreted in the hem of my houppeland with which I may buy me a horse. A horse, aye, but not a Pistol.

It is said that a fool, when he has taken hurt, grows wise. May this old fat fool yet retain some wisdom.

At Paris

On the last day of January, being a Friday.

A man is unfortunate indeed if he must winter in Paris for never have I known a city to be so cold. It is a cold that could turn a man's blood to ice and freeze him rigid in a single night.

Your Parisians go about swaddled—the rich in furs, the poor in what they can find—and bend their heads against the wind and hold onto their caps with blue fingers. I have scarce ventured from my room these two days past and my room is cold enough already.

I share my lodgings with a vagabond musician—an Italian from Lille. In Paris, all musicians are Italian though the nearest they have come to Rome be singing in the church choir. Guiseppe, he calls himself, though he cannot even pronounce that correctly. And yet he is a merry young fellow who plays the lute passing well and stinks like a Billingsgate fishwife. There is no more flesh on him than you might find on a house brick and it is my opinion that this meagreness serves to concentrate his stench. Marry, if I had the choice, I would rather share a bed with a month-old corpse. But your corpses are cold and Guiseppe has the hotness of youth about him and thus, for some of the day at least, my blood unfreezes.

I arrived in Paris on Wednesday last. There was not a horse to be had in Corbeil. I sent the good Brother Guilhem from one end of the town to the other, till his sandals were worn through. The best he could find was a single, sorry, tick-ridden ass which the owner sold readily for a *livre*, though I would have thought myself cheated had I paid five *denier* for it. Thus mounted, I set off and covered the six or seven leagues to Paris in the same time as Pistol would have covered twenty, arriving at the gates as the cathedral bell rang nones.

Thus did I enter this city not as a triumphant general on his prancing steed, nobly caparisoned and all—I blush to recall my words—but as a dirty, sad old man on an ass's back. The beggars at the gate showed no envy at my passing; young maidens regarded me with indifference; most children had been kept indoors in such cold weather. One aged man, many years my junior, nodded a greeting but belike mistook me for someone else for I knew him not. There were no hosannas. No palm-fronds scattered on the streets.

I confess I had little idea where to go. The *Coq Hardi* was barred to me and I dared not repair to the Rue de la Boucherie lest, by some mischance, I should encounter Jeanne who would doubtless greet me with many a sweet smile while harbouring a vengeful knife in her comely bodice.

At length, as the evening gloom began to fill the streets, I entered in at the sign of *Le Chien Jaune*, or The Yellow Dog, in the Rue des Innocents and was shown into the company of Guiseppe in this miserable upper room. Since then I have scarce stirred. I could afford better lodgings but I must save what coin remains to me or I shall never regain England's blessed shores.

I fear to die here in France. I speak the language well enough now and belike could shake off Mijnheer Jan van Staf and counterfeit a Frenchman. Yet I can never share the life of these people for that would be to be the thing that I am not. The smoke of my own land is clearer than the fire in this.

Oh, my poor Pistol. I grieve for you yet.

At Paris

On Candlemas Eve.
(Saturday 1st February 1416)

This day has seen many a change in my fortunes.

In the morning, I left my room at The Yellow Dog and ventured abroad to sell my ass, which I did to a butcher in the Rue des Deux Boules. He gave me four *denier* for it and told me not to buy his salted beef.

I had thought it would have been well-nigh impossible to have sold my ass at all and that I would have had to abandon it in the stable at The Yellow Dog and hope that nobody would associate me with the poor beast. Since the weather was so cold and the prospect of returning straightway to my upper room so very uninviting, I decided to spend my four *denier* on a stew. I thus repaired to the Rue Courtalon and sought out an inexpensive establishment.

I was relaxing in the vapours and sipping quietly on my third or fourth cup of wine when slender fingers caressed my shoulder and then gripped me tightly by the throat. I spluttered on my wine and tore the hand away. A second hand grabbed my beard and tugged it mightily, which hand I likewise seized. I twisted round in fury and looked into the face of Jeanne.

Now I confess that I was by so much discountenanced that my jaw fell instantly and I am a gooseberry if I did not much resemble a vacant-eyed codfish on a slab.

For a moment I thought I detected murder in her eye but then it softened, her body relaxed and she smiled at me with great sweetness. I released her hands, whereupon she threw her arms about my neck and kissed me furiously, which kisses I returned with a degree of circumspection.

"Jacques!" she sighed. "My own true Jacques! I feared I would never see you again!"

And so on in like vein.

On the occasions when I had called Jeanne to mind since last we saw each other—notably when I was lying up against Agnes in Saint Germain—the image that I had of her was that of a rosy-cheeked peasant girl. The change that a mere two months had wrought in her was worthy of one of your whoreson actors. Her hair was longer, her skin paler, her eyes redder, her lips fuller. She was clad in a shift that the vapours of the stew pressed against her body, thereby revealing every curve and intricacy of her design. She was indeed a very Doll Tearsheet of a whore.

I expected that she would berate me for having abandoned her or perhaps demand monies or even threaten me.

"I have missed you so much, my Jacques," she said, kissing my shoulder and running her thin fingers through my beard.

I told her of my travels, of my brave rescue of Jehan and Edmond, of their rewarding me with my weight in gold which, in turn, had been stolen from me by misbegotten cut-throats who, nonetheless, had paid dearly for their gains. I omitted my marriage and the death of my true friend Pistol for I had no wish to sour our meeting with such unpleasantnesses. If Agnes had possessed a tenth of Jeanne's comeliness, I never would have quitted Burgundy.

I could see that my adventures impressed her deeply, as well they might. She sat in my lap and tickled my neck and allowed me to feel her softness.

"You are a Trojan, Jacques," she whispered. "So you have lost your gold, what of it? Fortune rewards men of good courage. You will regain your wealth."

I felt the rise of amorousness between us. I would fain have enjoyed her there and then but she pressed her finger against my lips and whispered that the owner of the stew would not permit her to bestow her favours *gratis*. Thus we have agreed to meet this evening at the sign of *La Belette*, or The Weasel. There we shall sup together and then hie us to my chamber, there to consummate our reunion till dawn. At least.

Thus do I conclude my daybook for today. I shall wait till Guiseppe returns before I repair to The Weasel for I must tell him that we shall not be sharing his meagre crust this evening. Bread, be it fresh-baked or day-old, has never been Falstaff's staff of life. There is but one of me and ever will be and he needs meat and drink in abundance to stoke the furnace of his wit. If I spend my last *denier* on tonight's pleasure then so be it. My star is rising again.

At Mayrobaire (Mérobert)

On the day after Saint Dorothea's Day.
(Friday 7th February 1416)

Sir Edward Swithun Bevis would try the patience of a congregation of saints! I never yet met a man so wanting in wit and learning! Marry, I have seen better-educated frogspawn! Nay, the stones on which I tread have more about them than he for at least they have the wit to remain silent. Since he sat me in the back of his ox-cart five days past, Sir Edward Swithun Bevis has done naught but chatter and that in a loud voice, in English, in a land infested with Frenchmen. It is a great wonder we live yet!

This Bevis is a soldier from the West Country, a sometime prisoner of war, and, though I blush to write it, my deliverer. Were it not for him I would be lying still in the Forest of Saint Germain—still indeed for I would have been dead and feeding worms for years to come. Thus, though the man tries my patience sorely, I can say little against him out of mere gratitude.

We are now travelling in the direction of Harfleur. This was not always so. Previously, Sir Edward Swithun Bevis *thought* that we were travelling in the direction of Harfleur but then Sir Edward Swithun Bevis also believes in fairies and goblins and that you may find a crock of gold at the end of every rainbow. His geographical imprecision stems from the single fact that Sir Edward Swithun Bevis is quite convinced that your sun rises in the west and thence progresses eastwards. Thus have we been travelling, as he sees it, northwards and as I and the rest of the world see it, southwards.

There is little in the way of reasoned argument that you may offer against such deeply-held conviction and so I have told him that it is well known by scholars that the sun rises first upon Bethlehem, the birthplace of Our Lord, and that since Bethlehem lies in the east, so it is that the sun rises there. At first Bevis countered that, if the sun first rises over Bethlehem, that city must lie in the west. To this I replied that there is naught in the west save ocean and the edge of the world and this he has accepted. He now deems me a man of great learning.

It grieves me somewhat to reflect that I did not earn my banneretcy till my fifty-eighth year while this quarter-wit of no more than thirty summers—and all of them rainy—is already thus honoured simply by virtue of his father's death. May God preserve his tenants.

We sleep this night in a smoky one-room inn and that at my insistence—I shall say more of this anon.

I would prefer not to travel on the morrow for it will be the day of Holy Innocents last and of ill aspect and, at the present time, it would be unwise of us to play fast and loose with Dame Fortune. If we tarry, there is every likelihood that the Watch, if not the entire French army, will soon be at our heels.

The reason for this is surpassing simple—as is its progenitor. Sir Edward Swithun Bevis is possessed of the fancy that all inhabitants of France are soldiers in disguise. Be they frail and aged, juvenile and boisterous, female and delicate or merely clad in sackcloth with more crosses about them than a baker's on Good Friday, he will yet attack and beat them without mercy or discrimination.

Thus, you need do no more than mention that you feel a trifle peckish or that your throat is a little drier than usual or that the icy wind has made you much of a-shiver for this good and exceedingly foolish knight to leap from our ox-cart and belabour some innocent old crone in the interests of rectifying the situation. And this with much shouting of "A Bevis!" and a most disconcerting rolling of the eyes. To my knowledge, he has grievously injured three people during the last five days and only God and the saints know how many before that. If we do not both hang most handsomely for it, I am a Turkish eunuch.

Sir Edward Swithun Bevis speaks no word of French. Many is the time I have wished he spoke no English.

Now, it is commonly considered—why, I cannot say—that the speaking of French is one of the signal indications of a gentleman, just as the construing of the Latin tongue is a needful mark of erudition. I could gladly forgive Sir Edward his ignorance of Latin for he is no clerk and a familiarity with Virgil and Horace will not facilitate the planting of corn or the wielding of the bastard-sword. As for your churches, there are few who truly understand what passes therein, least of all the clergy. But your French is a most necessary accoutrement when it comes to enjoying the company of your peers and a want of it is like to incur as much censure and loss of countenance as hawking in your finger-bowl. Not that your nobility are over-fond of speaking French. When the King was Hal and not Henricus, nary a word of the tongue escaped his lips yet, if the occasion demanded it, he could construe the language as sweetly as the Dolphin of France.

Now, Sir Edward Swithun Bevis comprehends naught of French save *oui* and *non*. Thus far, his lack of comprehension has caused him little inconvenience for even the most loquacious Frenchman cannot say much when he is running away or lying senseless upon the ground. Moreover, until this night, we have slept by the wayside and I have been spared the difficulty of intercession with any Gallic companions.

Now I did not like this business of sleeping in the open for the nights are exceedingly cold. However, Sir Edward is wont to regard hostelries as heavily fortified castles and would no more set foot inside them than ride hobby-horse on his bastard-sword. It was with the utmost difficulty that I persuaded him of the wisdom of sleeping in a bed, saying that he had but to keep his great mouth shut—which, for him, is passing arduous—and counterfeit the idiot—which for him is passing simple—and all would be well.

Thus have I informed the host at this meanest and most nameless of inns that Sir Edward is my imbecile son. As an insurance against his forgetting this—which, being an imbecile, he has done three times already—I have added that he often fancies that he is an Englishman but is otherwise entirely harmless. For my own part, I have donned the alias of one Jean Valstart, a merchant of wherever is far enough away as to be unknown. In this case, Perpignan. Whenever I speak to him in French, as I must, Sir Edward comprehends me not and thus counterfeits the idiot better than ever.

So far this stratagem has proven successful and yet I have still passed a comfortless evening for each time the door of the hostelry has opened, I have much feared the entry of one of Sir Edward's erstwhile victims. It is certain that I must persuade him of the inadvisability of making war on the entire French population yet, in this, I must proceed slowly for Sir Edward's poor brain cannot digest more than a single idea a day, and that an exceedingly small morsel too. I shall say that he suffers from an excess of martial valour, which is a heavy drain upon his youthful vitality. In truth, he sleeps now as I write and has complained of the belly-ache all day.

I shall now record the manner of my coming into the company of this Edward Bevis, for it is a tale of the greatest infamy.

This tale begins last Candlemas eve, when I had arranged to meet that ungrateful wretch Jeanne at the tavern called *La Belette*, or The Weasel. Never was a name more apt or fitting. She was in the company of three whoreson ruffianly knaves whom she introduced as Jean, Nicholas and a certain Didi le Boucher, who was of an aspect most vile. She told me they were clients of hers and also, with much excitement, that they knew that a large sum of coin that had lately been taken from me in the most egregious manner could be had in Saint Germain's Wood, some several miles to the west of Paris. There, at a place well known to these ruffians, was the headquarters of my robbers and, if I vouchsafed them but five *écus* each, they would help me regain mastery over my wealth.

That ever a man was so gulled! Yet, I was greedy for gain—as well I might have been for, truth to say, my lodgings in Paris were not of the best. The rogues had horses ready and thus we tarried not but rode straightway to this Saint Germain's Wood. The bells of Paris had chimed midnight before we reached it.

Now I wish I could lend more colour to this account by writing that Saint Germain's Wood was a dismal and a melancholy place or that the very trees groaned out a warning at my approach or that the wind whispered of dark deeds afoot at this lonely spot. In fact it was a wood like any other and belike less dismal and melancholy than most. I am not one of your whoreson, skim-milk verse-mongerers to make more of it than was its due.

In truth, I was vouchsafed but little time to form an opinion thereof for we had not gone more than a quarter-league within its bounds before I was felled from my horse by a damnable blow upon the head. It was such a blow that would have brained your common, vulgar man and yet it did but stun me somewhat. On my knees, I drew my dagger and turned upon my aggressors, yet the life-blood flowing from my head half blinded me and I could not offer sufficient guard. I was thrust through the chest and arm and thigh and that is all I remember. Marry, I doubt I would remember even that had I not the marks to remind me.

Fortunately, it is one of the several virtues of girth that you ever wear your body-armour about you. Compare, *per exemplum,* your horse and your elephant. A stout thrust of sword or pike will swiftly dispatch the most valiant nag in as little time as it takes to snuff out a candle but your elephant can collect more pricks than a Tilbury doxy and yet continue to advance against the foe—as good King Hasdrubal is known to have used to his advantage.

So is it with humankind. A man of some corpulence may swallow up a goodly length of steel ere its point reaches a vital organ. Moreover, being of great dimension, he must have more blood about him and can vent a good hogshead or two without succumbing. Your starveling is bled dry at the losing of a thimbleful.

Thus it was that Jean, Nicholas and Didi le Boucher did not succeed in their design. For their trouble they gained a fine, though bloodstained, houppeland with my eight remaining *livres* sewn therein, a pair of boots a trifle worn, and my Italian dagger. Not wishing to entrust my saddle-bag to the safekeeping of Guiseppe, I had carried it with me to The Weasel. It had been emptied and stolen, but the contents had been left, including pens and ink and this my daybook. So all in all, my attackers had scant profit for much work. For Jeanne's sake,

I hope she paid them handsomely else were there another murder done that night.

It was as I was thus reposing in a ditch and groaning a little to pass the time that Sir Edward Swithun Bevis happened along in his ox-cart and, on hearing my groans, came to my succour and brought me away. For all my strength and courage, I was grievous sick for two full days and like enough to die. I coughed a great amount of blood and even now, as I write, my chest does me much pain.

Yet I have cheated death once more. I know not what fate or destiny awaits me but it is clear that the Good Lord wishes not that I die here in France. I little thought the Omnipotent was blessed with such good sense.

At Aunay (Aunay sous Auneau)

On Saint Apollonius' Eve.
(Saturday 8th February 1416)

Sir Edward Swithun Bevis' ox-cart may well achieve what Jeanne's hirelings failed to do. This day I have been tossed about worse than a weaver's shuttle. The wound in my chest has opened and has been bleeding somewhat, yet the blood is clean and fresh and there is no pus apparent and no stink thereof. Tomorrow, however, we must have horses. I shall discuss the same with Bevis when he awakes.

Despite this being the day of Holy Innocents last, we have been travelling. We have put three or four leagues behind us and it pleases me much that this was all in the right direction, otherwise I might have visited the shrine at Compostella after all. As befits a day of ill aspect, the weather has been most foul with torrents of rain and a bitter wind, and often our cart was held fast in the mud, axle-deep, and the oxen had great trouble in pulling us free. Happily there were few people abroad and thus Sir Edward's sallies at the foe were infrequent and, owing to the mud and rain, dispirited and desultory. Marry, it was all he could manage to croak "A Bevis!" once or twice and wave his sword about somewhat ineffectually. The enemy fled on all occasions and there were no murders done this day.

I have broached the subject of these forays and, by dint of much persuasion, Bevis is now quite convinced that the enemy host is at our heels and that we have no further time to dally with punitive expeditions.

"I like it not, Sir John," said he, with the air of an infant who has been denied his share of pudding. "I like it not at all. Your Frenchman must be punished for his perfidy."

"He shall be, Sir Edward," said I, nodding sagely. "He shall be! Only not by us, eh?"

"But he does counterfeit piety and womanhood to press home his attack!" exclaimed Sir Edward, quite outraged.

"And most cowardly it is too!" said I. "All the more reason to hie us to Harfleur and inform King Henry's army. Or who knows how many fine men may die at the hands of French nuns!"

"We do waste our energies on them!" declared Sir Edward, with the gravity of a commander-in-chief. "These skipping skirmishes do but delay our purpose."

"In truth!" said I, as if it were his own idea.

"And they make us more remarked upon," said he. "How can we serve our king from a French dungeon? How could our squeals of torment serve his cause?"

"How indeed?" said I, thinking that, if we were taken, we were far more likely to be serving Hal from a gibbet than a dungeon.

"'It would be better," said he, "to choose the fattest among them and make an example of them."

"Or the richest?" said I, for I have some degree of fellow-feeling for the fattest.

"Aye, the richest too!"

"Better yet, the richest only!"

"You say true, Sir John! Let it be the richest only!"

"The richest a-horseback!" said I, valiantly.

"Even so!" said he, doubtfully.

And thus it was arranged. We are now travelling in the right direction and belabouring the right people for the right reasons.

This village of Aunay—or, as Sir Edward has it, "Oh nay!"—squats beside the river of the same name like a heap of horse-droppings. In truth, I was about to write more of the place but this is comment enough.

By the by, it would be best I now record the manner by which Sir Edward Swithun Bevis came to be a captive of the French, and thus my saviour, for it is a tale of surpassing foolishness and I might else forget it.

Sir Edward Swithun Bevis is a captain of cavalry, no less. Hence his fondness for charging about. According to his own version of events, he was patrolling the banks of the River Somme when he espied an enemy village, the name of which was Pauvremon. Believing this to be a garrison-town, he charged it without further ado—as, indeed, he is wont to charge anything, animate or inanimate, in this country. Such was his eagerness to get to grips with the foe that he forgot to give the order to his men who, seeing their captain gallop away with much hallooing, wisely let him get on with it. Thus it was that Sir Edward eventually found himself alone amidst a large company of French soldiery commanded by one Sieur Thomas de Theuville.

I have Frenchified these names as best I can for Sir Edward calls the village of his capture "Povermon" and the French commander "Sir Thomas Turvil".

It is difficult to ascertain exactly what happened next for to grope one's way through Bevis's cloudy vapourings and seize from therein the bright prize of Truth is like wading through a bog at midnight in search of a will-o'-the-wisp. At all events, he was taken from "Povermon" to this French knight's castle where he was vouchsafed every civility. He was given food of the very best, wine in plenty, and allowed his freedom of the house and grounds.

Now, were I, or any man possessed of more than the merest grain of wit, to have found myself in such a favoured position, I would have been quite content to have taken my ease until such time as my ransom had been paid. And if the ransom were never paid at all, you would not have heard much escape my lips by way of complaint or lamentation. God's wounds, I have heard of knights who spent five and twenty years in captivity and regained their freedom quite grudgingly! And who can blame them? Their families had sold their lands to pay the ransom and they returned from a life of luxury to one of extreme paupery.

Alas, this is to reckon without such nice, gaping witlessness as Bevis displays. He sees fit to escape! Having thus broken his bond and made himself the fair quarry of whosoever should hunt him down, does he then procure armour and the swiftest horse to be had? Nay! He commandeers an ox-cart, clothes himself in besmutted dowlas and drives off in the direction of Orleans!

And does he even so much as behave like an ox-driver? Nay! He appropriates a bastard-sword, attacks everyone he meets with much shouting of "A Bevis!" and then, having killed or injured some wholly innocent citizen, and having identified himself beyond any equivocation, he remounts his ox-cart and trundles off again!

So I account Sir Edward's survival thus far a matter of great good fortune. It is not without the bounds of possibility that those lucky enough to witness his deeds and live to tell the tale could not believe that even an English knight could comport himself thus and accounted him a common madman of homicidal intent. In faith, this is not far from the truth.

For one so besotted with valour and knightly virtue, Sir Edward gave himself up most readily at the village of "Povermon". This is the single instance of good sense in all his history, yet it has given me some small satisfaction to tax him with it several times. At first he would give me no answer—his countenance merely grew a little longer than usual. At length, he muttered in his beard something to the effect that the King had ordered his patrolling knights to wear no coat-armour lest, being accoutred for battle, they would refuse to retreat and thus fail to deliver up the intelligence that he wished to have.

Bravo, Hal! Fine boy! At last you have succeeded in knowing idiots when you see them.

Thus, being faced with twenty or thirty men-at-arms and with the prospect of selling his life for a pittance, Bevis cast aside his sword. In his position I would have done exactly the same. Marry, I would have cast it aside a week or two sooner. However, to have admitted that would have been to destroy the little entertainment I have derived from Sir Edward's company and so I have made a great show of tutting and shaking my head sadly, which makes my companion look most shamefaced and quells his jangling for an hour at least.

This inn at Aunay is called *Le Perdrix*, or The Partridge. Above the door is a rude wooden panel with the said bird allegedly depicted thereon. The landlord, a boss-backed churl who stinks most abominably, claims that this avian travesty is indeed truly a partridge but to my eyes, old as they may be, it looks more like a lump of decaying bread-dough with wings. I attempted to question Bevis on the matter but as I had to ask him in French, he understood me not, and when he asked me in English what I meant, I had to reply in French that I understood him not, which he did not understand. This is the most sensible conversation we have had all day.

Supper was smoked eels with bragget and has given me the wind.

At Nogent (Nogent le Roi)

On Saint Apollonius' Day.
(Sunday 9th February 1416)

We have horses! Here follows the manner of our getting them.

I broached the subject of horses soon after we left Aunay this morning. Strange to relate, although quite prepared to rob anyone of anything in this country, Bevis drew the line at stealing horses. When I suggested that we might, he looked properly scandalised.

"Steal?" he said. "Marry, Sir John! Will we not hang for it?"

"If caught," said I.

"But stealing, Sir John! It is a sin! Our souls will be damned for all eternity!"

"Not for a *foreign* horse," said I, calmly. "A foreign horse is the plain booty of war."

"Yea, in faith. I had forgotten that," said he, remembering it again, and set to picking his nose.

"And fancy, if you will," said I, "what destruction we may wreak upon the enemy when we are mounted as knights should be and not condemned to sit behind plodding oxen like common folk."

'Yea, in truth," say he, wiping his finger on his hose.

"It is our solemn duty to commandeer such horses as are needful," said I. "If we shirk from that, are we not most arrant cowards?"

"A Bevis a coward?" said he, suddenly stung. "A Bevis was never a coward! We shall have horses! Here comes a rider now!"

And indeed it was true. Bevis immediately grasped the hilt of his sword.

"Peace, good Sir Edward," said I, staying his hand as the rider passed us. "Let not your courage outweigh prudence!"

"What?" said he.

"What chance has an ox-soldier against a man a-horseback?" said I. "This is, if you recollect, why we need horses in the first place."

"Ah!" he exclaims, setting a finger aside his nose.

"Let us rather devise a plan," said I, "that will permit us to relieve the enemy of a horse or two whilst avoiding getting slashed and slittered into stew-meat in the process."

"I have such a plan!" said Bevis, with an air of great pride.

Truth to tell, I was most amazed at this declaration for I did not think Sir Edward Swithun Bevis capable of planning a visit to the jakes, let alone a robbery.

"And what is this plan, good Sir Edward?" said I, full of curiosity.

"Well," he said, "we take a good stout rope and stretch it across the highway. When your horseman gallops by, we pull the rope tight. Your horseman, taken much by surprise and caught about the neck by this rope, is unseated and we thereby become masters of his steed."

"And if he does not gallop?" said I. "If he merely trots?"

"Then we allow him free passage and wait on a rider who gallops," replied Bevis, smirking a little.

"It is a fine plan, Sir Edward," said I. "That I must concede. Yea, and well-devised. Like all fine, well-devised plans, its greatest virtue is its simplicity. Marry, a simpler plan I have never heard!"

Sir Edward smiled happily and was clearly much flattered by this praise.

"Yet—forgive the foolishness of an old man," said I, "but by what manner do we raise the rope to a sufficient height to unseat the rider whilst leaving his horse unscathed?"

Bevis looks sideways at me, as if disbelieving that the vanquisher of Harry Hotspur could be quite so feeble-minded.

"Why, Sir John! You climb a tree on your side of the road and I climb a tree on mine and we both hold one end of the rope."

"Do we?'" said I, regarding the entirely treeless landscape around us. "And the rope?"

"The rope, Sir John?"

"You did make some small mention of a rope," said I. "I assume you do have a good stout rope suitable for unhorsing galloping riders. Or perhaps my old eyes are playing me false and what I took to be sacks of damp, stale flour in the back of our ox-cart are truly good stout ropes in disguise."

I can say a great deal in Sir Edward's disfavour but one virtue he possesses in abundance is his total imperviousness to sarcasm.

"We might steal a rope," he offered.

"Indeed we might," said I, scanning the deserted countryside. "Yet, I believe I have a simpler plan."

And it was this plan that we put into execution.

Firstly, we needed a crossroads. Now a crossroads, as any competent felon knows, is the best place for a robbery for, if the alarm is raised, your pursuers must choose between three different paths and the chances of your being taken are thereby much reduced. I rightly surmised that we had far more chance of finding such a crossroads than of finding two suitably situated trees. In faith, we had not travelled for more than a league when we came upon the ideal spot—where the *chemin* from Paris to the town of Chartres is bisected by the *route* from Aunay to Nogent. It was a lonely spot, for all around lay the flattest land that ever I saw since my Essex days. Marry, to our left I could make out the spires of a great church, which must have been that mighty minster of Chartres a good three leagues away.

We reined in the oxen and waited by the wayside. I lay down in the back of the cart and gazed at the sky, which was of a dull, plumbeous hue. It began to rain. I spoke not a word to Bevis nor he to me. All was silent save for the distant tolling of bells.

There were few people abroad this day, it being a Sunday. One or two ox-carts rattled slowly by. A group of riders cantered past and called out to Bevis who raised his arm in silent and uncomprehending salutation.

From where I lay, I had a clear enough view of the Paris side of the *chemin* but could see naught of what came from Chartres. In fact, precious little was coming from either direction and I was beginning to wonder if a Sunday was the best day for a robbery when Bevis gave a low whistle and, shortly after, I heard the sound of a single horse trotting along the street.

I raised myself a little and espied a man in a black cloak mounted on a bay stallion.

"Sir Edward!" I hissed. "To your work!"

Now I had spent the morning schooling Bevis in my plan, which was no easy task for he has quite forgotten the beginning of a sentence by the time you have reached the end of it. By dint of much repetition, however, he conned his lesson adequately enough and, as it turned out, later performed it tolerably well.

Thus, as the rider neared him, Sir Edward scampered out into the middle of the road and leaped up and down shouting "Oh suck-oors! Oh suck-oors!". The horseman reined in his steed and surveyed him for a while. "Oh suck-oors! Oh suck-oors!" cried Sir Edward, with much flapping of his arms.

At length the rider spurred his horse forward, pulled up before Bevis and stared at him whilst resting his hand on his sword.

"What's the matter?" he asked, reasonably enough.

"Mon pair!" cried Sir Edward. "Eely mallard! Easy!" and gesticulated frantically to the back of the ox-cart, wherein I groaned most piteously.

"What does he have, your father?" asked the horseman, rightly suspicious.

"Mallard!" shrieked Sir Edward, with much prancing. "Easy! Easy!"

"I can see where he is," said the horseman. "What I don't know is whether it is you who are sick or your father, or perhaps both of you."

"Mallard!" cried Sir Edward. "Tray mallard!"

"God's nails!" muttered the horseman, dismounting. "Show me then."

I groaned more piteously yet and, from the corner of my half-closed eye, I saw the rider approaching.

"Mallard! Mallard!" shouted Sir Edward, dancing in his wake.

"This I know," said the horseman, stopping at the back of the cart and gazing at me. "In what wise is he *malade*?"

"Tray mallard!" explained Sir Edward, shaking his head.

"Dropsy?" said the horsemen, slowly, as though addressing a foreigner or an imbecile.

"Mallard," squawked Bevis.

"The pestilence?" asked the horseman, shrinking back a little.

"Mallard," said Bevis, in a matter-of-fact tone.

I stopped groaning and held my breath. I held it for an unconscionable long time and was beginning to think that Sir Edward had forgotten his instructions when he clutched my leg and cried out:

"Eely more! Eely more!"

The horseman drew a little nearer and examined me critically.

"Dead?" said he, and then shook his head vigorously. "Nay, man, he is not dead. I know the look of death well enough."

"Eely more!" shouts Bevis, with greater conviction still.

The horseman sighed loudly and decided, as any reasonable man would, that the best way to disabuse this idiot would be to prove conclusively that his father was still alive. Thus, he mounted the ox-cart to listen for my breathing. He bent forwards and lowered his face to mine. I opened my eyes. The horseman opened his eyes yet wider. As he did so, I sat upright with great celerity, causing my forehead, which is well-seasoned by age, to connect solidly with his own. The horseman gave a slight groan and fell across me.

"Oh, bravo, Sir John!" cries Bevis, clapping his hands gleefully. "Bravo! Bravo!"

"Practice," said I. "Mere practice, Sir Edward. Now pray remove this black pudding from my chest."

I would have preferred the horseman to have been of wider girth for he had raiment of the best, though it was much of a blackness. Yet Sir Edward profited thereby and I am a little less discountenanced to be seen in his company. In faith, we profited fourfold for besides a horse and a suit of clothes we gained three *livres,* a sword and a good stout rope suitable for unseating galloping riders. Unlikely as this seems, it is nevertheless true. The horseman was a hangman. The rope was his tool and the coin his payment.

We left our client trussed in Sir Edward's old attire and groaning most piteously in the back of the ox-cart. In the town of Gallardon, a league or two distant, Bevis invested two of our three *livres* in the purchase of a dappled mare, which he has named Primrose. This was a source of much gladness to him for he had suffered greatly in keeping up with me on foot.

My own bay I have named Pistol, in memory of a departed friend.

So now are we lodged for the night in a hostelry in the town of Nogent. It is a clean house and passably free of fleas and lice though, for want of a jakes, we must void our water in the chimney or out of the window. We shall have better or I am a villain else.

At Dreux

On the day before Saint Valentine's Eve.
(Wednesday 12th February 1416)

I have been sick of a fever but am now much recovered. It was the wound in my thigh, which is yet inflamed and pains me greatly whenever I walk.

The landlord of this hostelry—which is called *Le Destrier Normand* or The Norman War-horse—sent out for a physick who has tended me these two days. As with all those of his calling, he has bled my body and my purse—or Sir Edward's purse, to be exact—and has given me purgatives and cordials and salts of this and tincture of that and, after payment, has pronounced me grievous sick and like to die. Since then I have felt much better, which owes naught to the skills of the doctor and all to the restorative effects of the ruby-red wine of Aunis.

Since Monday last, I have had much leisure to meditate on this business of physicks and have come to the conclusion that I have been labouring in the wrong vocation, for a good quack, provided with a sufficiency of foul-smelling specifics and painful instruments of health, may rob more worthy citizens in one month than an honest footpad can in a lifetime. *And* it is less fraught with dangers, *and* you do not need to brave foul weather or lose your breath in running from the Watch, and when your victim's gold is chinking in your purse he thanks you kindly for your trouble and whenever he feels his humours disequilibrate he summons you right speedily so you may rob him further.

And what do these learned physicks say when they are standing at your bedside with faces as long as Norfolk eels? With what pithy words of science do they explain your ills? None, in faith. "You are sick, sir!" they say. Or there again, "You are most sick!" Or perhaps, "You are most *grievous* sick!" As for being "like enough to die", so are we all, and a man of threescore and eleven years is more "like enough to die" than most.

And you can say naught against them for, if you make so bold, they will fix you with a superior eye and, with many a sneer and dry laugh, will say that you are unlearned in their craft and know not of which you speak. Any further attempt to pursue your objections will be most condignly punished for they will call in a second quack who will confirm the opinion of the first and for which reassurance you will pay twofold. And in times of pestilence, when fires burn in the streets and the sick and dying are as many as flies on a midden, you may cry in vain for your good and trusty physick for he has been called away to tend the sick of another town and his gold has gone there with him.

Like to die or not, I must quit this town on the morrow for Sir Edward Swithun Bevis draws unwelcome attention by his persistent speaking of English. Our landlord tells me that during my distemperature Sir Edward has been twice arraigned by suspicious townsfolk and it was only thanks to the intercession of our worthy host that he was released.

It is true that Bevis counterfeits the lunatic surpassing well—if counterfeiting it be—and his frequent cries of "Mon pair, eely mallard easy" have done much to add substance to this pretence. Yet we cannot presume too much on the gullibility of these folk for, with Harfleur a matter of leagues away and the prospect of a springtime campaign by Hal on everybody's lips, merely to be suspected of Englishness would be enough to get you most thoroughly hanged. To my mind, anyone who, on looking at Bevis, sees not an Englishman plain and exceedingly simple is bereft of all wit.

We now have a sufficiency of coin about us thanks to a chance meeting with three merchants on Monday morning last. We traded their coin for the good stout rope we had of the hangman on Sunday so it was no robbery but a fair exchange of goods. God's wounds, the rope was such that many a man would have killed for and of a length and stoutness which the merchants must well have appreciated before they escaped its bonds.

It is now night-time and the good Sir Edward lies asleep at my side. So much have I lain abed these two days past that I feel quite awake.

Le Destrier Normand provides a goodly board and I have supped well: leek and onion soup with fat bacon, a boiled hen, roasted mutton and a flan, with many a good draught of Aunis wine to boot.

Having so well supped, I should be blithe and running over with wit and rare conceits, yet I am not. There is ever something in the nature of darkness that engenders melancholia. The candle at my side throws strange shadows upon the wall and sometimes I fancy that I see therein the forms and faces of those I have known and know no longer—Nell Quickly, John Bardolph, the good Sir Walter Blunt, Edward Nym, young Hal himself. If I remain in life, who am less worthy, then what of them? Nay, all's done for Sir Walter for he perished at Shrewsbury in the King's array. I saw his corpse myself. The King could have better spared a fatter man.

If naught befall me between here and Harfleur, I shall surely return to England. And what then? A month or two at most and I shall be in Eastcheap, whoring and drinking and dicing and thieving. And hanging betimes—that I doubt not if riot and disease do not do for me first. What else can I do, landless and penniless as I am? As to advancement, since Azincourt there is many a man deserving of advancement. More brave deeds were done upon that field than I have ever counterfeited.

Aye, counterfeited. I have counterfeited all things: honour, truth, piety, courage, even death itself. I wear my hollow honours with an actor's grace.

Yet for all that it is true, I did have some small thought of reformation. I have ever been mindful of certain words of the poet Seneca that I once read as a lad:

Illi mors gravis incubat
Qui notus nimis omnibus
Ignotus moritur sibi.[68]

Do I know myself? Probably not, perhaps all too well. It is sure that death does not lie heavily upon me. I am no Lazarus to fear it so.[69]

Enough. I shall snuff out my candle and with it the shadows of the living and the dead.

At Passy (Pacy-sur-Eure)

On Saint Valentine's Eve.
(Thursday 13th February 1416)

We have ridden well this day and have put some eight or nine leagues behind us, and this with breaking our journey at Anet—where we dined poorly on cold pork and soup—and with relieving two merchants of an excess of coin that would otherwise have greatly encumbered them.

We have put up at a hostlery called *L'Escus.* In faith, it is indeed a poor Excuse for an inn, yet the word means Shield. There is no sign outside its door but within there is a great buckler hanging from a roofbeam. There being no chimney, this buckler is much blackened and although I have made out the faint lines of a blazonry thereon, I cannot say what it represents. Nor can our host enlighten me for he bought The Excuse with money looted in Paris thirty years ago and the buckler was hanging here then, well-nigh as black and sooty as it is now.

The hotness in my thigh has lessened a little; there is no yellow matter issuing from it and I have had no further bouts of fever. In truth, I feel well enough and, tomorrow being the feast of Saint Valentine when even the smallest birds seek out a mate, I would gladly put my vigour to the trial in the sweet embraces of a fair, lewd wench. Yet in this, as in divers other commodities, The Excuse is piteously ill-provided. And also the village of Passy itself, I fear.

In one particular is The Excuse handsomely provided and that is in fleas. There was never a shoal of tench so beset, never a hedgehog or a master-of-hounds. Marry, I have been worse bitten than ever in my life and I may add, though it do me little credit, that I have slept in some of the lousiest hostelries of England and France. Sir Edward Swithun Bevis is scratching whilst he sleeps and customarily he is as impervious to such discomforts as he is to reasoned argument or wit. God's teeth, The Excuse is a very bestiary! There are bedbugs here as big as penny pieces and I have seen rats that would strike fear into many a good-sized dog.

What more can I write of this day? The weather has been surpassing cold with flurries of snow and sleet yet the way has been firm enough with little mud. The River Eure, which we met with shortly after midday, is in full spate and I much hope that at some point it will be spanned by a bridge, or crossing it will be fraught with danger. That said, the countryside has been as drab and desolate as the Plain of Hell. In faith, had we but met Mad Denys with his arms akimbo and his bloody breast naked to the winter wind, I should have thought myself quite dead already and skirting the stream of Acheron bound for the welcome fires of the Pit.

Now that too is yet another bolting-hatch of nonsense. I cannot deny that being burned is an unpleasant experience but mankind alone has devised far more agonising instruments of torture and Satan must be singularly uninventive if he has not come up with aught better. And is not fire both pure and cleansing? Has it not ever been the boon companion of Man, cooking his food, warming him within and without, cauterising his wounds, forging his iron and his gold? Do not Man's higher instincts mimic its qualities? Is not love of God and Woman likened to a conflagration of the spirit? And what of righteous anger towards an enemy? What of the innocent passions of youth? What of wit and fancy's nimble brightness? What of the blessed sun and moon which warm our days and guide us through our nights? If fire be infernal then are we all damned from birth!

Nay, your true Hell is a place of ice and cold, of bitter winds and constant snow. There our sinfulness is frozen and immobile for all eternity without hope of redemption or comforting fire. All passion and imagination quenched and dead.

God's wounds, I have passed many a Valentine's Eve with happier thoughts. Aye, and with lustier bedfellows too. In my youth, I was the bane of womankind. When I raised my standard and advanced, there was not a blushing maid or saucy wench that did not tremble at my approach. Yet they did not flinch from the encounter but gladly bore the weight of my assault.

It is not so now. Time has done its work. Cares and deprivations have blasted my hair to winter couch and tears have worn deep channels in my cheek. Yet this is but my outward aspect. The wick that is enfolded in so much wrinkled tallow will still burn brightly once it is lit. The trouble is that lighting it requires more labour now and few draw near to proffer a flame if they are not paid to do it.

Perhaps it should be thus. What a devil have I to do with puling maidenhood? Rather give me the bought caresses of a learned whore—one that wastes no time with superfluous d'ye-love-me's and curses with a good grace! Well, the town of Rouen lies nearby and, if I be not taken for an Englishman, there shall I play the satyr royally.

At Tregny (Treigny)

On Saint Valentine's Day.
(Friday 14th February 1416)

I write with some difficulty this evening for I have but a meagre rushlight at my side and its dim flame flickers greatly in the draughts that blow through this house. Yet write I must for there is much to be recorded.

Sir Edward Bevis and I quitted Passy at first light this morning and rode north-east towards the town of Vernon. There had been a sharp frost and the day was exceedingly cold yet bright. We stopped twice before reaching Vernon: once to build a fire and shake our clothes above it and once to distrain a largish quantity of gold coin.

Our clients were two merchants and their attendants or, as Sir Edward will have it, a troop of patrolling hobilars with squires. Somewhat exceptionally for cavalry, they were mounted on ox-carts, by which means they were returning to Paris with full purses. They bore the aspect of folk who were happy to be nearing their destination for there was much laughter and a boy was playing prettily upon the pipe.

Now had we been but base and vulgar thieves, I dare say that the men would have put up a fight for they were ten or so and we but two. Yet this is to reckon without the good Sir Edward who, at a word from me, spurred Primrose to a gallop and bore down on them swinging his sword in great arcs with A-Bev-issing aplenty. I followed him closely to mop up the survivors and, not to be outdone by Sir Edward—who is, when all is said and done, my lieutenant—I brandished my blade and bawled, "Saint George!" The attendants, being men of uncommon good sense, immediately leapt down from their carts and took to their heels, leaving their masters to their fate. These two worthies cowered together and flinched mightily as Sir Edward's sword, directed with more dash than accuracy, cleft the air around them.

It being long since breakfast, and that a poor affair indeed, I had little stomach for serious blood-letting and thus I interposed myself between Bevis and our clients and beseeched him to spare them.

"By God's nails, Sir John!" he cried, in an extremity of frustration. "They are the foe! Would you have them survive and betray our position to their comrades?"

"We are a-horseback, Sir Edward," said I. "Our position changes constantly."

"Oh," said Bevis, looking greatly crestfallen and lowering his blade.

Yet I had to allow him to hack the carts a little and do what further destruction as pleased him for if you do not vouchsafe him such liberties he is wont to be of an ill humour for the rest of the day and will spend much time slashing at nettles. This being the month of February, the nettles are all dead and withered, yet he belabours them all the same.

As I write, we have not yet had occasion to share out the gold thus procured but, judging by its weight, I would put it at some seventy-five to a hundred *livres*. Thus do the bigger fishes eat the smaller.

We reached Vernon around the hour of tierce[70] but feared to tarry there for as like as not the alarm had already been raised and we had no wish to be overtaken by outraged Frenchmen. At Vernon we met with that same River Seine which flows through Paris and greets the sea at Harfleur and we followed the street that runs along its bank for an hour or so till the flood cut away from us and was lost from view.

The sun grew warmer as we rode on and the highway, which had been made harder by the night's frost, grew soft and muddy. Yet, despite that, it was as pleasant a Saint Valentine's Day as ever I saw. The small birds, eager to seek a mate, were all a-twitter in the trees and here and there you could make out the first fresh shoots of springtime. A fox crossed our path and paused to gaze upon us, one foot half raised, before trotting into the forest as calmly as you please. The air was as still as Kentish cider.

Of a sudden, I heard a strange call. It was a high-pitched shriek, like a seagull or some similar fowl but, as we drew nearer to its origin, it gained form and substance and I knew it to be the cry of a woman or child in distress. Without a word to Bevis, I spurred Pistol to a trot. Now that I reflect thereon, I cannot say why I did so. Perhaps it was that natural curiosity that has always afflicted me.

Sir Edward was occupied with hacking at overhanging branches and thus, as I rounded a corner of the highway, he was some yards behind me. It was at that point that a frightful sight met my eyes. The curious shrieks issued from the lips of a young wench with flaxen hair. She was held fast on the muddy earth by two ruffians whilst a third, who wore the chain-mail and iron helmet of a soldier, tore at her raiment and grappled with her white body.

I did not reason or reflect. I think it was the first time in my life that ever this was so. Snarling and unsheathing my blade, I rowelled Pistol deep and he leapt forward mightily. Hearing hoofbeats behind them, the girl's attackers looked round in surprise. The knave in chain-mail, his mouth twisted with lust, sprang to his feet and drew forth his weapon. It was an ancient glaive, worn to half its size through frequent sharpening but, before he could bring its point to bear, my own sword had cut a single glittering arc against the sky, sliced clean through his mail and buried itself deep in his neck. There was a great gout of crimson and a gurgling cry. My arm was jerked backwards by the force of my attack. My foot slipped from the stirrup and I landed heavily in the mud.

In an instant another of the men was upon me. A mighty cudgel-blow fell upon my left arm and I cried out in pain and twisted my bulk upon the ground in an effort to avoid his assault. Yet I still held my blade. Thinking me at his mercy, the rogue darted forwards to press home his attack but, summoning all my strength, I skimmed my weapon level with the earth. It bit deep into his shin. He screamed, began to fall and then halted momentarily as the point of Sir Edward Bevis' bastard-sword transfixed him.

The remaining ruffian ran off into the woods. Sir Edward gave chase.

Meanwhile the girl had scrambled to her feet and, ignoring both myself and her state of half-nakedness, ran to a bundle of rags which lay in the dark bracken bordering the forest. As I stood up, wondering whether my left arm was broken or not, I became aware of a high-pitched wail that had been much obscured by the girl's shrieks but which I now realised had been a constant accompaniment to the battle.

As I drew nearer I perceived the bundle of rags to be a baby in coarse swaddling. The girl lifted it tenderly, cradled it in her arms, cooed to it and stroked its little forehead. At length its tears subsided.

"Are you hurt?" said I.

She looked up at me as though she had forgotten I was there. Now I could see how, in spite of her evident poverty, she might well have excited the lewd lusts of her aggressors on this Saint Valentine's Day.

"No, messire," said she. "A little bruised only."

She looked again towards her baby and began to sob.

"And the child?" said I, laying my hand upon her shoulder.

"I think she be not hurt," said she. "They tossed her into the air as if she were naught."

At this, my rage returned and I strode over to the churl in the chain-mail, drove my sword through his chest and twisted it about. In truth he was well dead already for I never yet saw a man as could survive partial decapitation. Yet it gave me some small satisfaction to slay him twice over.

I returned to the girl, removed my cloak and draped it across her shoulders. She gazed up at me with tear-laden eyes and smiled her gratitude.

"You be a brave and worthy knight, messire," said she. "I be in your debt."

"I am no knight, lass," said I. "Only a man of some years and a little humanity."

It was then that Sir Edward returned and dismounted, his face flushed with excitement.

"He was too nimble for me," said he, panting. "I could not catch him. God's wounds, Sir John! A pretty fight, eh?"

"In truth," said I.

"At last I have had the honour to see a true knight in deadly combat!" said he, fixing me with an admiring eye. "Never have I seen horse, sword and rider in such...in such...er..."

"Harmony?" said I, not wishing to see him suffer so.

"In such harmony!' said he, nodding greatly.

"I thank you, good Sir Edward," said I.

"It was a joy to behold!" he said, raising his eyes skywards. "I never thought to see the great Sir John Falstaff do battle. *There* is something to tell my children!"

"Should you contrive to beget any," said I, under my breath.

I then asked the girl where she dwelled and she answered saying it was in the village of Tregny where we are lodged this night. It lies not half a league from the scene of our battle. On the way, she recovered somewhat and told me that her name was Marguerite—Margery as we have it in England—and that her little girl had been born but two days earlier and was yet unchristened for the village priest had been away on an errand of mercy. She had taken the child to show to her grandparents and had been returning to Tregny when she met with her attackers.

In truth, I wondered greatly that she could have even considered such a journey so shortly after childbed but she told me that the delivery had been an easy one with little pain and that she had been on her feet and attending to her duties within an hour or two.

Though it is true indeed that, being no more than a score of summers old and belike even less, she yet had the vigour of youth about her, I find "an hour or two" a surpassing quick recovery. Tell that to your fine ladies! *They* will pass a week or more in childbed and make great show of weakness and distemperature. Those women who only too well know the clinging grasp of poverty are about their business in a few days at most—weak and distemperate or not.

We drew much attention as we entered Tregny. As is the case with most villages in France, it is but a score of hovels clustered around a church. The folk here are franklins[71] who hold their lands of Sieur Bernard de Gaillon who holds his lands of the County Evreux, who holds his lands of the King.

I was much pleased at having arrived for I had set Marguerite and her daughter atop Pistol and led them afoot. Gallantry is one thing if you be young and nimble but quite another if you be old and a trifle corpulent and my legs are ill-used to bearing my weight for such a distance sanz respite. At first we were gawked at and then a young knave ran up and placed his hand upon Marguerite's foot and asked her if all was well, at which she burst out crying and told him of her adventure and deliverance. At this the young knave waxed grievous angry and then fell to his knees before me, making such exceeding show of gratitude as fair put me out of countenance. I beseeched him to get up.

The young knave's name is Pierre and he is Marguerite's husband of one year.

Bevis and I were straightway escorted to their house and there provided with both food and drink. In truth, the food was bread, salt and garlic and the drink was milk and yet this was well intended and we ate of it heartily. Marguerite was still much disturbed by her ordeal and must be comforted by Pierre and her mother, Constance by name. By and by, their efforts were rewarded in some measure and she recovered herself a little.

As we partook of the food, Marguerite's father, who bears the name of William, questioned me about our travels. As, by now, it was useless to deny that we were English, I had no option but to tell the truth or at least mostly the truth as far as Sir Edward Bevis is concerned. I thought it wise to omit mention of his breaking his ransom-bond and said that he had strayed too far from King Henry's army and had got lost. For myself, I said that I had family in Burgundy and had been visiting there when Hal had inconveniently invaded Normandy.

William then arose and addressed the company in a loud voice—well-nigh all the people of Tregny being crushed within the confines of the small house—and told them that though I and Sir Edward were Englishmen, and therefore enemies, yet in Tregny were we Frenchmen and friends, and that any who dared gainsay that or felt inclined to betray us to Sieur Bernard de Gaillon would have him to reckon with and would surely rue their indiscretion. To this the entire company bawled their agreement and one old crone screeched that she would beat the traitor with a stick.

It was then that the door was thrown wide and a large barrel was rolled into the room and set on trestles. At this, a great many of the assembled multitude departed with much haste and I wondered what noxious brew the cask contained that caused them to quit its vicinity with such speed. Yet in a trice they had all returned bearing cups and bowls and the barrel was broached and from it flowed a golden liquid that perfumed the room with scent of apples.

Now, as a rule, I am no great lover of cider for it is often adulterate and an excess thereof may bring on colic, melancholia and blindness. Marry, the little that has passed my lips has tasted principally of old straw and mouse-droppings and was fit only for scouring tables, and that for want of aught better. And yet this golden liquid was cider right enough but tasted bitter-sweet and clear. It seemed as if you held the whole of summer in a cup and, at each draught, quaffed meadows full of flowers and ripening orchards and warm September sun.

"This is cider!" said Sir Edward brightly, smacking his lips. "I know it full well!"

"Cider! Cider!" cried William, seizing upon the word.

"Yea, cider! Er....tray bon!" said Sir Edward, gaining much applause thereby.

"Tray, tray bon!" crowed Sir Edward, gleeful that he had finally made himself understood to someone. "Mallard!"

At this last remark, the company fell silent and looked much perplexed.

"*Malade* means 'sick', Sir Edward," I explained.

"Sick?" said he. "Yea, so it does. I had forgotten."

I thought it best to rescue him, lest his remark be taken as an insult.

"Mallard is an English word," said I, loudly, "which means most excellent."

The company cheered and raised their cups. Sir Edward laughed heartily and did in like wise. There were several shouts of "mallard".

And thus did we drink off many a cup and the company waxed right merry. There was much singing and pleasantry and Marguerite and the old crone danced for us and Pierre and William offered toasts *à nostres amis anglois* and, at length, Pierre mounted a bench and shouted, "I pray you all be silent!"

"My friends," said he. "Today my wife Marguerite was delivered from certain death and our baby daughter also. It is thanks to these good knights that it be so and they will ever have my gratitude. Therefore have Marguerite and me spoken together and our baby daughter shall be named Jehanne-Edouard Marie in honour of these men and we do invite them to be the child's godfathers."

There was a roar of approval and Sir Edward and I were much pummelled about the back and shoulders, with many shouts of "Mallard". I could see that Sir Edward was growing agitated at this rough treatment from an enemy, albeit a friendly one, and thus I translated the substance of Pierre's speech for him.

"A godfather, eh?" said he, proudly. "God's mercy, Sir John! Yet, do you not think Edward a rare name for a girl?"

"Aye," said I.

"I too. Well, I dare say she will get the habit of it," said he.

As afternoon turned to dusk and rushlights glowed through the fire-smoke, the company dwindled till none were left save Marguerite, her husband and parents, Sir Edward Bevis, little Jehanne-Edouard and myself. We sat around the open fire and talked a little and I told them of the adventures that had befallen me upon the way—or some of them at least. Bevis, having appreciated his cider full well, said but little and of that much less that could be understood in either tongue. Marguerite allowed me to hold Jehanne-Edouard and I let her suck upon my finger till she fell asleep.

And now all are asleep save me. I shall draw one more cup of cider and then curl up near the fire.

At Tregny (Treigny)

On the day after Saint Valentine's Day, being a Saturday.
(Saturday 15th February 1416)

There never was a prouder day in all my life! Jack Falstaff is a godfather!

I would rather the other godfather were not Sir Edward Swithun Bevis but he merits his reward for little Jehanne-Edouard's deliverance was as much his doing as mine.

Jehanne-Edouard is of the rarest beauty. Her hair, what little there is of it, is black like her father's, and her eye is blue like her mother's. Her belly is full and comfortably rounded, like mine. Her skin is as smooth as an eel's and her tiny feet and hands are perfect miniatures perfectly formed. She is a sturdy girl and will grow to be strong and fearless. Already she cries but little and once today she smiled at me.

The name Jehanne pleases me greatly. If you say it quickly enough, it sounds passably like John and, in truth, she shares my fondness for liquor, albeit milk. In England she would be called Joan, which pleases me less. Edouard pleases me not at all yet it is certainly better than Swithun.

The baptism took place at the hour of sexte and was accorded all due solemnity by those present, there being none of the gossiping and shouting that you normally find in churches. Father Jean, the priest of this parish, gave his preamble in Latin, which everybody pretended to understand, and then wetted the child's head with holy water at which she cried a little, bless her.

"Jehanne-Edouard Marie," said he. "I baptise you in the name of the Father, the Son and the Holy Ghost."

Then he turned to Bevis and me and to the two godmothers—one being the old crone with the stick and the other the miller's wife—and said:

"Godfathers and godmothers, I enjoin you with the father and mother to see that this child, until the age of seven years, be preserved from water, fire, the feet of horses and the teeth of dogs and that she does not sleep with her father and mother till she can say 'move aside' and that she be confirmed by the first bishop to come within seven miles of this parish, and that she be instructed in her faith so that she may know the *Paternoster*, the *Ave Maria* and the *Credo* and that you all wash your hands before leaving the church on pain of fasting forty Fridays."

And it was done. Jehanne-Edouard was a heathen no longer, though in truth she seemed singularly unmoved by her redemption. Not so Sir Edward Bevis, who witnessed the ceremony with tearful eye and washed his hands with surpassing thoroughness, and his arms too. In faith, he looked most melancholy and so it was that as we returned from church I asked him what it was that ailed him so.

"Good Sir John!" said he, laying a tight hold on my arm. "How may I protect yon infant when I shall never see her again? How may I preserve her from the teeth of horses and the feet of dogs?"

"It is the feet of horses and the teeth of dogs, Sir Edward," said I, gently prising his arm loose, and rather regretting that I had translated the priest's words for him. "Children are not commonly trampled to death by dogs. In answer to your question, you cannot. Yet no more can you sleep between her father and mother to make sure they do not crush her in their slumbers."

"It is true," said he, dolefully. "But can we not stay a little longer to fulfil our duties in some measure?"

"Why?" said I. "We cannot stay here forever and our parting will be all the sadder for our delay. What is more, the longer we stay here the more we imperil these good people and ourselves. Would you be taken and hanged?"

"Nay," said he, and falls into his old melancholy silence.

Truth to tell, my own sentiments are much the same as Sir Edward's. Marguerite and Pierre have treated me with more true affection than I have ever known, and I feel towards them as a man must feel towards his family. They are grievous poor, as are all the good folk of Tregny, but they share their little with me and face adversity with a merry countenance.

Now there is many a man who counts smiles and embraces as the outward marks of affection yet it is not so. I have known a thousand cozening rogues who would slap your back with one hand whilst the other was busy in your purse, and your whores give smiles and kisses aplenty yet their hearts are often cold and full of hatred. Nay, it is small kindnesses that mark out true affection: such as cost little or naught and are cloyless, and may even go ignored if you receive them too often. This day *per exemplum*, Marguerite discovered that I had been wounded. Now the arm that was struck by the cudgel is only bruised, but my thigh is still red and painful to the touch and the old wound in my chest yet discharges ichor on occasion. Perceiving my afflictions, which I had done my utmost to disguise, Marguerite said not a word but departed the house and returned with divers herbs and simples from which she made a paste and anointed my wounds with it. As I write, the soreness has all but disappeared.

It was a small service and cost her naught but a little time and trouble, and yet I cannot recall anyone else doing the like—not since my poor mother died so many years ago.

And what of little Jehanne-Edouard? It is a hard life that lies before her and the hardest of all will be the next twelvemonth. A pox on horses' feet and dogs' teeth! When death comes to most children, it comes silent and invisible with fevers and agues and the flux, and no deal of care or watchfulness detects its approach.

I wish that I could stay and guide Jehanne-Edouard through the vicissitudes of life. Unlike many a man, I know all its pitfalls, having tumbled into all of them myself. Yet perhaps it is better that I go for I was ever one to debauch the innocent and I am too old to change my feathers now. I have rendered my god-daughter a service in returning to her a life that would have been most cruelly snatched from her. Were I to stay, I would only lose the good opinion I have gained.

There is cabbage for supper. *Crambe repetita*! It is time to taste it.

At Elbeuf

On the sixteenth day of February, being Septuagesima Sunday.

It is now the middle of the night and I am sitting in bed in the upper room of *Le Coq Hardi*. I am sharing this bed with two people, one of whom is Sir Edward Swithun Bevis. The other is a woman. More of that anon.

This has been a day of great moment. In faith, I have some difficulty in penning my thoughts together for they will scamper hither and thither and as often as I pursue one and catch it, the others elude me. I had best begin at the beginning—that is to say, the morning of this day.

It was with heavy hearts that Sir Edward and I quitted Tregny. The villagers had gathered together to witness our departure and all of them with solemn countenances. Bevis and I embraced Marguerite and Pierre and Constance and William and said our farewells, and I managed to hold my tears in check until I came to little Jehanne-Edouard. I kissed her on the forehead and she stared into my soul with her deep blue eyes and I could not prevent the salty drops from coursing down my cheek. For shame. For shame.

Bevis and I pressed ten *livres* upon Pierre. Perhaps it will do to see Jehanne-Edouard through her infancy. At least she is now the richest inhabitant of Tregny. May God preserve her from thieves.

Once the village was hidden from view and Marguerite had waved her last wave and turned homewards, Sir Edward and I spurred our horses forward and kept our own counsel for many a long league. We rode hard, the sooner to leave our memories behind us. At length it was Bevis who broke the silence.

"Sir John?" said he, in a pitiful voice.

"Aye, Sir Edward?" said I.

"These Frenchmen. They are not all the rogues I thought them to be."

"Not all of them," said I, gruffly.

"In truth," said he, "I have not the heart to charge against another one."

"Then do not charge, Sir Edward," said I. "We have money enough and there are nettles in plenty."

And we did not exchange another word till we reached the town of Louviers.

At Louviers we bought a leg of mutton and had it roasted at a tavern. We ate more at one sitting than in the two days past and drank many a cup of Guyenne wine, with the silent deliberation of those who drink not for pleasure but to encourage forgetfulness.

The light was failing fast when we reached the village of Elbeuf, which bestrides a crossroads where the highway from Rouen to Le Mans cuts across a smaller street joining Harfleur to Paris. Owing to its fortunate position, there are several hostelries in this village and of them we chose the best: *Le Coq Hardi*.

I believe that the last *Coq Hardi* I mentioned in this daybook was in Paris and was owned by a rat-faced rascal and his shrewish wife. For all that they provided a grudging welcome, their establishment was always thronged with diners and drinkers from dawn to late in the night. Not so the *Coq Hardi* in Elbeuf. When we entered, there were only two people in the taproom—one a bald-headed man of some reasonable girth who was dozing in front of the fire and the other a slightly thickset girl, of comely appearance, who looked a trifle surprised at our entrance.

The dozing man proved to be the landlord, Claude by name, as a tap on his shoulder soon revealed. He sent the girl out for a chine of pork and ordered it to be roasted for us. Bevis and I found ourselves a comfortable place next to the chimney and were well embarked on our third cup of wine when, of a sudden, I heard the woman's voice behind me.

"Jack?" it said.

I turned about and looked. She was clad in the sort of apparel favoured by serving girls, or at least by their masters. I knew her not.

So convinced was I that I knew her not that I would have sworn the same in any court of law and yet no man of true wit will admit to such a thing lest he be mistaken and cause offence thereby. I thought it best to play safe.

"How now," said I, as if I had seen her last the day before yesterday.

At this she laughed. It was a laugh that is bestowed but once in a generation.

"Jack Falstaff! You know me not!" she shrieked, and laughed the harder.

"Agnes?" said I, looking her up and down and feeling much tempted to finally believe in Pythagorean transmigration.

"The same!" she chortled. "Though I forgive your not knowing me for I am much changed, think you not?"

She was indeed much changed. Lady Agnes Falstaff, when last I saw her, had resembled a large turnip, but the woman whom I now beheld had a waist—a waist, mark you, that a man could put one arm around with ease—bosoms that were independent of her torso and a most inviting rump, which had, I doubt not, felt the touch of many a hand in the *Coq Hardi*. I was quite dumbfounded.

Once more Agnes broke into a shriek of mirth.

"Your face!" she screamed. "It is for all the world like that of some week-old hake."

The mention of hake brought everything back: the manor of Saint Germain, Jehan, Edmond, pigs... I closed my gaping mouth and rose to my feet. At this, there was a sudden change in the pitch of Agnes's laughter and the tears that filled her eyes were no longer those of mirth and she was in my arms with her head pressed against my belly and she grasped me tightly as though she feared I would struggle free.

"I have found you," she said. "At last I have found you."

I knew not what to say. I glanced towards Sir Edward. He too was staring hake-wise.

"My wife," said I, smiling, and his jaw drops another inch.

At that point it occurred to me that if Agnes were here, so might Jehan, Edmond, Esprit and Jean-Baptiste. Having no great liking for being suddenly spitted on a bone-handled dagger, I surveyed the room quickly, but it was as empty as before.

"You are here alone?" said I, stroking her shoulder.

"Aye," came the muffled reply.

She looked up at me with tearful countenance and I saw that there was a hollowness in her cheek that her laughter had concealed. I felt a curious discomfort in my throat.

"You thought my family were with me?' she said, with extraordinary softness.

"Are they?" said I.

"Nay," said she. "They know not where I am."

I eased her from me and we sat down upon the bench and her story came tumbling forth.

She had quitted Saint Germain en Bazois a day after my own departure and had made straightway for Avignon, thinking to find me at the Papal Court. She had travelled for no more than one day before she reasoned that she might never overtake me. Thus she had turned about and headed northwards. There were, she said to herself, but two ports where I might be certain of embarking for England: Calais and Harfleur. Knowing that I must surely pass by Paris, she decided to take up her watch on the road to Harfleur—that being the nearer port—and, if that proved fruitless, would then ride to Calais by way of Rouen.

She confessed that she had entertained little hope of ever seeing me again and that as the days passed, the likelihood grew ever less. Indeed, only last night, she said to herself that she would stay in Elbeuf but two days longer before setting off on the road to Calais.

Divers rare adventures had befallen Agnes upon the way and no little danger. She had commenced her journey ill-prepared and with an insufficiency of coin and had thus gone hungry for days on end. Yet, when all seemed lost, she had outfaced disaster. Sometimes she found work of the humblest kind and had often taken refuge in the hospitals of monasteries and nunneries, or was given food and shelter by such folk as took pity on her.

To say that I was touched by her tale is to say but little. As she recounted her adventures, I found myself holding her hand and this not by way of show, as once was the case, but out of true tenderness and pity. In truth, since quitting Burgundy, I had spared few thoughts for Agnes and of those not one that was not tainted by some measure of contempt and revulsion. Yet now I felt myself humbled by her devotion. It was a devotion that I did not merit and had not sought.

I have known a good many folk in my three-score and eleven years of life—those of the highest and lowest degree—and there were more than several who would take me by the arm and call me cousin and who enjoyed, or feigned to enjoy, my company, and with whom I could drink deep or troll a right bawdy catch, or take a purse. Yet those were not ties of love or friendship, nay, nor respect either, but only of mutual profit and gain, and there was not a man or woman amongst them who, for my sake, would have walked from Eastcheap to London Bridge if it did not benefit themselves in some particular. Nor would I have done the like for them.

There were those, one above all, whose affections I dearly sought, for I saw in them the qualities I admired the most—power, wealth and influence to name but three—and who derived some base entertainment from my contagion. Yet when the play was done, the revels ended and their thirst for pleasure sated, they retired to their lives and vouchsafed me not a second thought.

And here is Agnes, a woman whom I have contemned, ill-used and spurned and yet who, in return, has rewarded me with devotion I have never known.

"I am truly lost for words," said I.

"Say only that you will not abandon me a second time," said she.

"*Abandon* you!" said I, my ears burning with shame. "I never did..."

"Hush!" said she. "I know well what you thought of me and all the divers stratagems that you used to avoid my intimacy. I know that you married me for my father's gold and I do not blame you for it—most men would not have taken me to wife for all the treasures of the Orient. Look at me, John. Remember what I was. Fat. Ungainly. Unaccomplished."

"Unaccomplished?" said I. "Why, you sing better than...than..."

"Any screech-owl you have ever heard," said Agnes, smiling. "And do I not play most prettily upon the rebec? Aye, my father would have done me better service if he had advertised my qualities a little less."

"He did his best for you," said I.

"I doubt it not," said Agnes. "But I fear he only wanted me from his house, and that as soon as might be."

She bit her lip and looked away, and I saw that she felt great bitterness and was struggling to master it.

"But I can wait well on table," said she, smiling, "and draw a cup of wine and bandy words with the most mischievous of customers. I am not a fool. I never was. Unhappy only. I know what my father wanted of me; my mother has ever shown more devotion to her God than to her children; of my brothers, one is a dolt and the other an impetuous coxcomb. I have been the butt of every pleasantry and have had the respect of none. For all your mercenary intent, you alone showed me some small affection—however counterfeit it may have been."

"I am well chastened," said I, and felt it too. "But knowing what I thought of you, why did you follow me?"

"You are my husband," said she. "At first I thought that if you saw me again you might reconsider your resolve. Later, finding you gave purpose to my life. I have thought of little else these weeks past and now that it is accomplished, I know not what I shall do."

For the second time in my life, resolve came quick enough.

"You might do worse than accompany me further," said I. "Life is cruel, Agnes. And crueller yet if you face it alone."

I took her hands in mine and I felt the hot tears prick my eyes and once more was robbed of speech.

It was Agnes who broke the silence. She wiped her face on her apron and glanced from me to Sir Edward, whom I now saw was leaking from the eye, although he had clearly understood not a jot of what we said.

"That man is your companion?" said she.

"Aye," said I, sighing. "He is Sir Edward Swithun Bevis. A woeful foolish knight. He is an Englishman who knows no word of French and thus, for safety's sake, he is masquerading as my lunatic son. He is a very master in lunacy."

"We make a rare family then," said Agnes, "whose son is older than his mother."

I made Sir Edward and Agnes known to each other and that with some difficulty for Agnes has even less English than Bevis has French.

"Good Sir John," said he, sniffing loudly and wiping his eye, "I knew not that you had a wife. She is most beautiful and gracious. Never have I seen so touching a sight as your reunion. But tell me, Sir John. How comes she here?"

And so I gave Sir Edward a shortened and needfully amended account of our marriage and my departure—impressing upon him that Agnes was henceforth to be regarded as his mother. I added that I had intended to return and claim my bride once the King had subdued the French and it was safe to travel. Bevis nodded his head sagely, and smiled and winked at Agnes, who smiled back.

This exchange set the tone for the evening. I would talk to Sir Edward and he would smile and wink at Agnes; I would talk to Agnes, who would smile at Bevis. From time to time, Agnes and Sir Edward would attempt to talk together amidst their smiling and winking. This, of course, to their mutual befuddlement.

It is most apparent to me that the three of us cannot continue together. Foremost is the problem of age. As Agnes has pointed out, Bevis is a good ten years her senior. In faith, I could say that his real mother is dead and that I have remarried but I feel that this story of an English-speaking lunatic son with a stepmother several years his junior is nudging the boundary of likelihood.

There is also the problem of sleeping. Firstly, the *Coq Hardi* is furnished with three beds of which ours is the widest. Secondly, were I to be vouchsafed a choice of bedfellows, Sir Edward Bevis' name would not spring to the fore. This is not to say that he is possessed of any unsavoury or disagreeable sleeping-habits for, in truth, he curls up as tight as any dormouse and is fast asleep before you can slip your boots off. It is just that he is Sir Edward Bevis and I would prefer not to share a bed with him.

Tonight I am constrained to share a bed with both him and my wife. Now for all that she is now deprived of three-quarters of her original mass and her nose has lost most of its Bardolphian quality, Lady Agnes Falstaff yet snores and snorts worse than a cathedral-full of pigs. This affects Sir Edward not a jot. Marry, if the Last Trump were to sound during his slumbers, he would awake ready-judged and consigned to Heaven or Hell without a chance to say aught in the matter. I am not so favoured. Were Agnes and I alone, I would apply dough to my ears and, by dint of much tossing and turning and sheltering under the coverlet, finally prise my way into the arms of Morpheus. Yet nestling together as we do, like three sausages in a pastry, I can scarce scratch my nose without doing mischief to the others.

Furthermore there is the question of propriety. Now, though I am not one of your whoreson hypocrites, I would rather not share my marriage bed with another man. It is true that Sir Edward did offer to sleep on the floor—and I would gladly have let him—but Agnes would have none of it, saying that he must share the bed with us. If she waxes yet more solicitous, you may lead me off to Smithfield and sell me as a milch-cow.

Nay, it is a situation that cannot endure. What is not needful is dear at a penny.

I know not what hour of the night it be. Midnight is long passed. Sleep yet eludes me and it is not the fault of Agnes or Sir Edward. Perhaps it is my age, for it is well known that the more years a man has the fewer hours he sleeps.

I never would have dreamt that I would feel towards Agnes as a man ought to feel towards his wife, and yet I do. I see now that we are of a kind. Though I may be corpulent, my flesh enfolds a spirit that is fleet and nimble, and no matter how ill-favoured my outer facing—and I fear that now the years are accomplishing what licence failed to do—I still defy anyone alive to pass a dull hour in my company. God's blood, it was only my wit that gained me my knighthood! In like wise did Agnes, when fat, bear within her the beauty that she now exhibits. And here I speak not only of her form and countenance, for, pretty though she may be, she is no paragon even now, but of her generous and courageous heart and a spirit that will brook no discomfiture.

It is a bitter perversity that we often despise in others those faults that we find tolerable in ourselves. The chiefest amongst those that I found irksome in Agnes was not the stridency of her voice, her loud snoring or her fawning on me but merely her fatness. She does not fawn now, having no reason to do so, yet she still snores and the timbre of her voice is but little moderated. For all that, I now see that it was the alliance to her grossness—of which these slighter failings seemed a further manifestation—that gave rise to my aversion. And what of that? Should I, the sootiest of pots, have called the kettle black? Marry, when I consider the censure that my own circumference has engendered, I fair blush to recall the insults I have heaped on Agnes. "How long ago is it since you saw your own knees?" said Hal to me. He calls me a bed-presser. He calls me a mountain of flesh, a greasy dripping-pan and much else besides. Cruel words, though meant in jest. As for him, he had the girth of a willow-switch and could speak with impunity, and more impunity yet for being the Prince of Wales. Aye, I have been reviled right royally.

Is it an Agnes reborn that sleeps beside me now? I feel that I met her but today, found her admirable and married her without delay of courtship or betrothal. Perhaps she thinks I shall desert her once again, but it shall not be. We were married in a former life yet this was but a sprinkling of words, and words alone have neither substance nor vitality for they are one with the air and vanish as soon as they are uttered. True love lies in deeds alone.

At Coldbeck (Caudebec en Caux)

On the nineteenth day of February, being a Wednesday.

(Wednesday 19th February 1416)
This journey is waxing ever more perilous. Agnes and I are now no more than a half-day's ride from Harfleur and could have been there now were it not for the French soldiery.

There is trouble afoot for the English. French levies are crowding the fields around Rouen and you cannot travel more than a quarter-league in this direction without being stopped and questioned as to who you are, where you are going, why you are going there and when you are coming back. I pray to God that Sir Edward has taken a safer route or he will be hanging in chains as I write. "Eely mallard" is a poor substitute for "We are going to Coldbeck to visit my wife's father who is grievous sick and like to die and shall return on Thursday next, be he dead or not" and even that mouthful has served us poorly. Perhaps Bevis has returned to his old habits of charging and hacking. In faith, I pray that he has for in that lies his only hope of deliverance.

We parted company from Sir Edward two days ago at the village of Elbeuf. I told him at breakfast that whereas two people might pass through the country-side unremarked, three were well-nigh an army and that it would be in the best interests of all that he continued alone.

This sort of argument finds much favour with Sir Edward for he calls it "learned science" and is much impressed, and bemoans the lack of schooling that prevents him from formulating such ideas for himself. For my part, I think that if Sir Edward had attended both the universities of Oxford and Cambridge, and perhaps those of Paris and Bologna too, he would yet be no further advanced along the road towards a good idea than he is at present.

But that is by the by. He and I repaired to the cow-byre and divided our coin between us and Agnes and I took our leave of him with much sadness. Bevis kissed Agnes as if he had known her for thirty years and then embraced me tightly and blubbered in his beard. The last sight I had of him, as we rounded the corner of the lane, was of a thin, forlorn figure standing at the door of the *Coq Hardi*.

In spite of Sir Edward's absence, I was reluctant to pass through Rouen and thus we set off in the direction of Duclair where there is a ferry across the River Seine. As we rode northwards, I marked that the countryside was visited with the same desolation as I had found in the environs of Calais town four months ago. Last summer's corn was yet unharvested and lay flattened and rotting in the fields. Apple trees remained unlopped and were surrounded with decayed fruit. Fences were unmended, gates left open. Of the few dwellings that we passed between Elbeuf and Duclair, most were deserted and, of those that were not, only the curl of woodsmoke through their roofs betrayed their occupancy for no one showed himself at our approach. Only once did an old man venture forth on hearing the clopping of our horses.

"Messire. Madame," said he, leaning heavily on his stick. "Have you news of the English?"

"The English?" said I, reining Pistol in. "Why, they hold the town of Harfleur and are trapped therein."

"You have seen none on the way then?" said he, anxiously.

"None, in faith," said I.

"And what of our host?" said he. "Know you aught of them?"

"It is said the Constable lies at Rouen," said I, "and has amassed a great army to take Harfleur by storm."

"May God grant him victory!" said the old man, crossing himself. "Else are we all undone."

"Undone?" said I. "Marry, nay! The King of England is most merciful and full of charity...as I have heard. He will do you no harm."

"Maybe he will not," said the old man, spitting on the wayside. "In faith, for one such as I, one king is much the same as another. Yet his men are a different tale. They will lay waste the country and do much wickedness."

"Then God preserve you and give you peace," said I, and I laid my heels to Pistol's flanks.

Indeed it was an argument I could not gainsay for there is many a hound will chase the hare for all its master whips it in. And yet in Paris I heard that Hal had kept his army in good order and that there had been little in the way of pillaging, and much less that went unpunished. This was most wise of him for it is by the winning of hearts and minds that you gain a country. As I surveyed the land around me, I could not help thinking that the French peasantry had despoiled themselves far worse than Hal could have done.

We had gone about two leagues further when it began to rain. There was a strong wind blowing from the south but the day was not cold and, the wind being at our backs, our progress was not greatly hindered. We skirted the River Seine for many a long hour and saw no one on either bank and had no company save each other and the rooks and crows that flapped and wheeled about the sky.

It was early afternoon when we reached Duclair. I have not seen a village half so mean in all my time in France. In extenuation, what we entered was but an outpost of the village proper, which lies on the opposing bank where a narrow stream debouches into the river.

I thought at first that our tiny part of Duclair was entirely empty of people for I saw only one thin dog scavenging in the street. In truth, out of a good eight or so houses, three proved to be occupied for as we neared the water's edge, the good citizens of Duclair left their hovels and followed us silently. There was no sign of a ferry.

"You be wanting the boat?" came a voice from behind me.

I turned in the saddle and saw a square-built man standing a little to the fore of his fellows. I nodded at him. A baby started to cry and its mother, a thin, gaunt woman in a sackcloth shift, hushed it and regarded us coldly through narrowed eyes.

"If you wait a year or so, it will be here," said the square-built man, without a smile.

"Where is it now?" asks Agnes.

The man nodded towards the river.

"Yonder. At the bottom. Soldiers came and stove her in. Said the English might use it to cross."

He gave a dry chuckle and spat at the mud between his feet.

"Where may we cross now?" asks Agnes.

"Rouen. There be a bridge at Rouen, if it stands yet."

"Rouen," said Agnes.

"I heard," said I.

I stared at the swollen river, the deserted hovels and the sorry group of ragged folk crowded about us. We thanked the fellow and quitted Duclair and its sad inhabitants and said not a word to each other until we had covered several leagues.

"Why do they stay when there is naught for them?" said Agnes, at length.

"What else would you have them do?" said I. "They are the wisest who stay. Whither could they go that is better than where they are? If you must starve, it is best to starve at home and die in the company of friends. The highway is a cruel place for folk who are poor and honest."

We were now retracing our path along the riverbank and the wind which had been our ally earlier was set against us. We huddled in our cloaks and the horses plodded head-down through the mire. When we came to the turning that had brought us to the river, we ignored it and continued straightway in the direction of Rouen.

It was night-time before we saw the lights of the city and, though they spelled danger for us, I was very glad to see them for the weather was much worsened. By the time we arrived at the bridge-gate, the curfew had rung and thus we could not enter Rouen proper but were constrained to seek out a hostelry, which, though small, was passing warm and comfortable. The host had meat roasted for us and there was wine in plenty.

Now in truth, Agnes and I had spoken but little that day. This was not for want of aught to say but rather that the desolation about us had imbued us both with the blackest melancholy. Since quitting Duclair, any words that we might have uttered would have gone unheard in any case, so fierce was the wind that blasted us.

Now that we had supped and were seated before the fire with a cup of wine to hand and another three or four in our bellies, I ventured to embark on a tale that had troubled my thoughts since quitting Elbeuf that morning.

"Agnes," said I, laying hold of her arm. "There is something I must say to you."

She gave me the merest of smiles and returned her gaze to the fire and said naught.

"It concerns my degree and my purpose here in France," said I.

Agnes made neither sound nor movement.

"Ahem," said I. "Firstly... By the Mass, I know not how to put this. Squarely then. It is best. Firstly, I am no ambassador of the King's. That is to say, I have no commission of him and thus had no business in Avignon. In truth, I never went to Avignon. Only so far in that direction as was needful until your father and brother quitted my company."

I paused then for I expected a response and yet there was none.

"Thus, you see that I had no reason to quit your father's house. I wished only to return to England with the gold he gave me. Alone."

I paused once more and took a draught of wine. Why did Agnes make no reply? Why did she not rail at me, censure me, smite me with her fists? It would have been less than I deserved. Instead, she kept her silence and her eyes remained fixed on the fire.

"Ahem," said I. "Secondly! Secondly, I am no lord with great estates. My estate is my horse, my saddle-bag here with the money it contains and my accoutrements, such as they be. And of this, there is naught that was not most arrantly usurped—stolen, in truth. Further to that, I have my knighthood—which is real enough though shamefully procured—and my reputation, which is founded upon debauchery and the corruption of youth. I was the boon companion of the King when he was young and I was old and his sire yet held the throne of England. We both sought some advantage from it: he the spiting of the father whom he hated and I the gaining of the preferment I coveted. I went from bachelor to banneret and then no further for Hal—King Henry—was not the fool I took him for and would not advance one such as I to dominion over others."

"When reconciliation flowered between the fourth Henry and the fifth, I should have held my peace and entertained no further expectations and yet I was consumed with base ambition. So sure was I of my future advancement that I borrowed monies on the strength of it and decked myself out with fripperies and waxed fool-large with the wealth of others. Like a true lord, I had my underlings, my retinue of fools attending on my fortunes."

"Yet once Hal was crowned I was dismissed condignly. Like an orchardman who lops off a bough of mistletoe suckling on the life-blood of the tree did he, with cutting words, sunder us apart. And yet he was merciful and just, telling me that I should have his favour if I earned it righteously. That would have sufficed for many men, for honesty is a small price to pay and, some would say, its own reward. It was not so with me. You see, my lady, I have ever had to make my own way in this life. Being too much the commoner, I was denied my noble aspirations and being too much the gentleman, I disdained to learn an honest trade. Being blind to my own foolishness, I saw too well the foolishness of others."

"When I was but ten year old, I learned to lie and cheat and steal and that has been my livelihood ever since. Like any craftsman, I have worked at the perfection of my art—man and boy, apprentice, journeyman and master. For me to be an honest man would be as arduous a task as for a farmer to turn goldsmith."

I paused once more and sipped a little wine and watched the firelight dancing in Agnes's eyes.

"And there, my Agnes, is my apology. I have no fine house and lands to return to. There is not one half-inch of English soil that is mine. What coin I have ever possessed has been squandered on gluttony and whoredoms. I return to England but for one reason and that is that I would rather die there than here. If you yet wish to accompany me, knowing what I have just told you, I will be glad of your companionship. That is all. I tell you this now since it has vexed me greatly and I would do you no further hurt."

With that I ceased speaking and feared the worst. Agnes still gazed into the blaze and the same little smile curled her lips. She remained thus for so long that I began to fear she had been stricken speechless with shock and that her silence was but the uneasy stillness before a storm. Finally, I could brook it no longer.

"Speak, I beseech you," said I. "For I am sick at heart!"

At this, the smile quitted her lips and she looked me in the eye with such calm directness as made me fairly tremble.

"Very well, Jack," said she. "Let us to bed."

And this we did and had the freedom of the upper room and of each other.

I would that I could write that I gave her untold pleasure, that she praised my potency and likened me to a ramping lion or a snorting bull or some such tickle-brained folly. In truth, my passion arose slowly and was spent too soon, as indeed has been the case for two or three years at least. I have much coloured my exploits for the lean-witted.

Though I was greatly pleased at her forgiveness, it grieved me much that I could not honour Agnes as she merited and I grew right vexed thereby and cursed long and loudly. Yet Agnes was most gentle and untroubled and held me close till my anger was assuaged and whispered that it mattered not and that one night was not a lifetime and that a brave assault were as worthy as a victory.

That may well be, yet there will be precious few children born of this marriage if my nether limb learns not patience and rectitude.

We quitted Rouen on the morrow but had to cross the city first.

Now I had feared to come to Rouen lest I be taken and hanged as a spy. The greater part of that fear had been engendered by Sir Edward Bevis, who could not have opened his mouth without betraying us and was incapable of keeping it shut for very long, yet even after parting from him, I was still loath to pass through the city. As it transpired, my fears were groundless for you are never less remarkable than when you are with a thousand others.

We crossed the River Seine by a great bridge that leaps from one bank to an island in mid-stream and thence hops to the other side. There were many boats moored there—amongst them, a goodly number of fighting vessels, heavily armed and in full state of readiness.

In this town of Rouen stands a great cathedral with two lofty towers like those of Our Lady of Paris. Now as majestic as these edifices may be, I would not go far out of my way to behold one—if I had aught better to do—for once you have wondered at the bulk and beauty of its buttresses and gone in and out of the great door and marvelled at how such a mighty portal opens and shuts and have cast your eyes upon the coloured glass, astonished at how the light shines through it, there remains little else to do but go away again.

I had thought, and hoped, that once we had passed under the gate, the quitting of Rouen would be speedily accomplished. Yet I was much surprised to find that the city extended a good half-league beyond the ramparts. There were many fine houses there such as you may see in Paris or in London. Marry, the outlying parts of Rouen are greater and more magnificent than the town itself.

At length, however, we passed into open countryside and yet even there we were not free of dwellings, for a great army was encamped on both sides of the highway. Despite the rain, which now began to fall quite heavily, there was much bustle and activity and the air was full of shouts and woodsmoke, the tapping and banging of the armourer and farrier, the dull thunder of hooves, the bleating of sheep and the lowing of cattle. From time to time, I glimpsed faces staring at us from beneath makeshift tents and I blessed the rain for a brave ally for no one was prepared to endure a soaking to question an old man and a girl.

All went well till we reached the village of Saint Martin, which lies about two leagues from the last house in Rouen. It was there, at the furthest boundary of the village, that we perceived a great tree from which a man was hanging from a rope, swaying and fluttering in the wind. In the shelter of this same tree, a troop of soldiery were drinking and dicing, clad in full panoply of war. As we approached them, a corporal stood forth, sword in hand and raised his arm to halt us.

"God give you good day, messire, milady," said he.

"Good day," said we.

He looked us up and down and I saw his eye linger on my bastard-sword and saddle-bag. His companions stared at us and smirked. The thing hanging from the tree creaked in the wind.

"This way is closed to all but the King's men," said he, leaning on his naked blade.

"I have ever been the King's man," said I.

"Perhaps you have, messire. Perhaps you have," said he. "Though now a little old to do him service, eh?"

"In time of strife, the least of us will do what he is able," said I.

"Well said, messire," said he, sniffing loudly. "Now, what brings you this way? And in such foul weather too."

"My father," said Agnes, quickly.

The Corporal leaned to one side and surveyed the empty road behind us.

"I see him not," said he, idly twisting his sword-point in the mud. "Unless *you* be this lady's father, messire."

"He is my husband," said Agnes. "My father is grievous sick and like to die. We must go and make our peace with him."

"And where lies your father?" asked the Corporal, scratching at his crotch.

"A few leagues hence," said Agnes.

"At Lillebonne?" asked the Corporal, witlessly.

"Aye, at Lillebonne," said I, most readily.

"If your father is like to die, you may save yourselves the trouble of visiting him," sneered the Corporal.

"If the Lord be merciful, he will recover," said I.

"If the Lord be merciful," countered the Corporal, "your presence will be superfluous."

"You will not let us pass then?" I asked, frustrated at encountering such a philosopher.

"Not I," said he.

"Then it is a pity," said I, rummaging in my purse, "for we brought coin with us. To procure medicines."

And I brought forth three silver pieces and tossed them at his feet. The Corporal stooped and picked them up and bit one. Then he raised his sword and wiped its muddy point on his leggings.

"See you yonder man?" said he, waving his weapon at the grinning, eyeless figure on the tree.

"I see him well enough," said I.

"He was an English spy," said the Corporal, "who would travel on this street to Harfleur and there deliver up such intelligence as would have put our intent in hazard."

"Then he received his just deserts," said I.

"Aye, marry, he did at that!" agreed the Corporal. "Know you how he sought to pass us by?"

"I was not here," said I, "thus I know not."

"He offered us a bribe," said he, smiling and chinking my silver in his palm. "I call this a bribe too."

"Nay, in faith," said I. "It is no bribe."

"Jeannot!" called the Corporal to one of his men and held up the three coins. "What call you this?"

"A bribe, Corporal," said Jeannot, and put his bottle to his lips.

"You see, messire," said the Corporal, turning back to me. "Jeannot thinks this a bribe too."

"And I tell you it is not!" said I, somewhat angrily. I glanced at Agnes and saw she had waxed quite pale.

Now, in truth, I was not greatly afeared, for it is my experience that those who kill for money waste little time in idle prattle.

"You have been found guilty of bribery!" said the Corporal, officiously.

"You are a rare magistrate," said I, knowing more than a little of magistrates.

"A magistrate, messire? Nay, in faith! Saving your grace, I am but a mere corporal-at-arms," said he, bending low. "It is Jeannot here who is the magistrate for he can almost read and write."

"Then I bow to your honour's judgement," said I, inclining my head towards Jeannot, who saluted me with his bottle. "And to what pain am I condemned?"

"Distraint of goods," said Jeannot. "To wit, the contents of your purse."

"Your honour is most merciful," said I.

And so the Corporal doffed his kettle-hat and held it up to me and I grasped my purse by its extremity and emptied its contents therein.

"How much has he paid?" shouted Jeannot to the Corporal.

"About a *livre*, I should say," said the Corporal, peering into his helmet and stirring the coins with his finger.

"It will suffice. What say you, Corporal?" said Jeannot.

"He may go about his business," said he.

And with that, he waved his sword towards the road ahead and we spurred our horses forward and passed by.

"God speed your worships!" shouted the Corporal after us. We heard the others laughing loudly.

Now I have often stated that the trouble with Saint Nicholas' clerks is that so few of them are articled. In any profession save that of thieving, doltish incompetence and lack of skill are most condignly punished. Why, having perceived that I was possessed of a bulging saddle-bag, did the corporal not examine it? Had he but done so, he and his rascally cronies would have been five and sixty *livres* the better off. Such men are like moths who, attracted to a candle flame, neglect the moon above.

As a safeguard against further occurrences of this sort, I replenished my purse with another *livre*. Armed with the knowledge that at the cost of sacrificing this money I might save myself much more, I have contrived to get us to this town of Coldbeck. This at the expense of refilling my purse twice further and of much time spent arguing with French soldiery.

Thus far Dame Fortune has remained true to us. And yet she is as fickle a hussy as I ever met and is like to sell her favours to the next French man-at-arms we come across. Lately we have come across too many. I wish I could be sanguine regarding our future but that would mean flying in the face of the naked fact that no one save a soldier, a spy or a fool would be travelling towards Harfleur at this time. If Agnes and I are not swinging on a tree before Saint Lazarus's Day, I am a pot of garlic soup, well-boiled and strewn with breadcrumbs.

At Saint Romain (Saint Romain-de-Colbosc)

On the twenty-first day of February, being a Friday.

Since quitting Coldbeck this morning, we have not journeyed more than two or three leagues and that with the greatest difficulty. So close are we now to Harfleur that we can no longer trust to arguing our way with French soldiery and thus the little progress we have made has been *nec prece nec pretio*[72] but rather by dint of avoiding French patrols and riding northwards and then westwards by the forest paths.

Now it would do untold good to my self-esteem if I could write that this was a faultless and most cunning plan and yet, in all honesty, I cannot. In truth, the sun having refused to shine on so cold and drab a day, and the trees that surrounded us being of such a height as would have obscured it anyway, we neither of us knew where lay the north and thus had no clearer idea of when to turn westwards. Before we had gone no more than half a league, it came to us both that we were right royally lost.

Now you cannot reach the age of three-score and eleven years sanz having got lost from time to time. Marry, when I was first in London, I circumambulated Saint Paul's a good half-dozen times before I arrived in Eastcheap. Thus have age and experience taught me much of this business of losing one's way and they have left me with an adage that I would impart to those of younger years for it is of great usefulness and has saved me much labour and vexation. It is as follows:

When in doubt, turn left.

We did a great deal of turning left this morning. Often we cut across the path we had already taken but there the veracity of this adage showed itself for we knew thereby that we had turned left once too often or that the way had cranked backwards somewhat. Our progress was thus steady but grievously slow and when, finally, we left the trees and trotted out onto the broad highway, we did not know where we were or what o' clock it was. Nor, indeed, was there anyone to ask.

I decided to resolve our problem scientifically, and so I fished a *sou* coin from my purse.

"Heads or tails?"

Agnes looked at me askance.

"*Pile* or *face*," I added, by way of explanation.

"*Pile*," said Agnes.

And *pile* it was.

So, we turned to the right and took once more to the forest yet ignored the paths and worked our way slowly through the timber, keeping the road in view. Only when the way grew so dense that we could no longer pass did we venture again onto the highway and we quitted it as soon as we were able. At length, the appearance of dwellings forced us deeper into the wood.

Thus did we progress with great slowness, though in safety. Yet as the day grew darker, it became surpassing difficult to pick our way between the trunks and branches, undergrowth and thicket and so when at last we came upon a path, we took it and trusted that the good fortune, which had so far favoured us, would not quit us then. We followed the path for a league or so and in time it broadened and gave onto a wide clearing around which were grouped three hovels with lights at their windows and smoke drifting through their roofs. A girl was driving geese into a pen and we rode towards her and stopped. She looked up at us with great dark eyes and smiled.

"Are there soldiers here?" asked Agnes, gently.

The girl shook her head.

"What is this place?" asked Agnes.

"Saint Romain," said the girl.

Agnes asked her where we might find lodgings for the night and thus we find ourselves in the house of her father who is Guillaume by name. Her mother is called Osanne. It is a poor place yet surpassing clean, with a thatch new repaired and fresh rushes on the floor. We have eaten soup and drunk cider and feel much the better for it. Agnes inquired about our location, with suitable circumspection. To my great surprise, we have actually been proceeding in the right direction.

This evening, the sun set above Harfleur, which, though near, is invisible to us. It is queer indeed that a dull day often sees a brilliant sunset—almost as if the sun must remind us that his presence was denied—and I wandered outside to see the great light of Heaven dying behind the trees. All that had been dull, faded, grey and winter-brown was gilded by its light. Thatches waxed wheaten-yellow, walls russet, bare branches bore a blackness that night cannot counterfeit. Above me lay a cold blue sky fretting into palest rose—a presage of summertime in the pit of winter.

It seemed then that time had stopped or briefly paused before stepping forward. Belike it does so every evening at Saint Romain. Kings shall turn to dust and great armies to a mere ink-scrawl on the dry page of history yet there will ever be a light in cottage windows and cows must be milked and chickens fed.

At Harfleur

On Saint Lazarus' Day.
(Sunday 23rd February 1416)

We have now been on English soil for one full day!

Or have we? If the claims of King Henry are true and well-founded, as surely none but the most egregious traitor would gainsay, I have been on English soil since I first disembarked at Calais, save for a brief detour to foreign parts when I visited Burgundy. Being a true-born Englishman and loyal to his monarch, God forfend that I should dispute this claim. Perhaps it is an exterior force—some naughty demon playing truant from Hell and bent on doing mischief to the House of Lancaster—that has sown seeds of doubt in me. Within this doubt, two thoughts predominate. First is that if young Henry speaks the truth, it will be, to my knowledge, the first time ever that he does so. Second, that if the folk of France be truly English, it is passing strange that they speak another tongue, eat other food, possess other temperaments, and little care to lead such lives as ours.

But I am no statesman. It is likely that there is some advantage in conquering France as yet unseen by me. Else would it be a most grievous waste of men and effort. In truth, if you must make war, it is better to make it upon a foreigner than upon your own countrymen. Yet to say that is to say little.

We arrived in Harfleur yesterday at about the hour of vespers, having spent the time since daybreak in much ducking and skulking and toing and froing. I have neither the ink nor the patience to set down the tiresome minutiae of our labours. Let it only be said that we came close to capture and certain death on several occasions.

It is no small irony that the closest we came to capture and certain death was when finally, and quite by accident, we stumbled across an English picket. These men were led by a Welsh ancient, Hywel by name, and they immediately accounted us spies.

Naught that I could say would disabuse them. I described the streets of London in exhaustive detail only to discover that not one of them had ever been there. My description of King Henry's aspect provoked scornful words to the effect that just because I knew what he looked like did not make me any less a Frenchman. Even as deadly a volley of invective as ever left the lips of a Southwark whore could not dissuade them from the belief that I was a particularly foul-mouthed agent in the pay of the King of France.

Marry, it was fortunate for us that they were not as summary in their treatment of spies as your French soldiery, otherwise would our corpses now be swinging from some neighbouring tree. Instead, they brought us to the citadel—and that with much abuse and divers kickings and cuffings—and led us before the Earl of Dorset himself.

Now this earl, Thomas Beaufort by name, commands the garrison and was known to me and I to him, though we had exchanged words on but one occasion and that briefly. I fear I held him in better esteem than he did me, for my judgement of him was founded on his deeds and his opinion of me on base rumour and calumny.

"You?" he said, scowling at me. "What in the devil's name are *you* doing here?"

This put Ancient Hywel quite out of countenance.

"You know this man, my Lord?" he asked.

"I know him well enough," said Dorset, with a most unwarranted sigh. "He is who he said he is. You are dismissed."

"I beg your pardon," said Hywel, with as much humility as a Welshman can muster. "I was but doing my duty, you see. No offence, I hope."

Now for his manifold insults and cuffings, I would gladly have boxed Ancient Hywel thrice round Harfleur and yet it does not behove those who aspire to gentility to descend to base displays of peevishness.

"You are forgiven, good Ancient," said I. "Return to your company, tend to your men and let us say no more about the matter."

And I patted him on the back as hard as I was able.

"As I said," said Dorset, once the three of us were alone, "I little thought to see *you* here, Sir John."

"Marry, I little expected to *be* here, my Lord," said I. "For there is an unconscionable amount of soldiery between here and Rouen, and none that are over-friendly."

"You come from Rouen?" said Dorset, raising his eyebrows.

"Aye," said I. "From Burgundy by way of Paris to Rouen and thence here."

"Burgundy," said Dorset, rubbing his chin.

"Even so," said I. "My wife here is Burgundian."

"And what opinion do the Burgundians entertain of our cause?" asks Dorset.

"Marry, my Lord, for Duke John I cannot speak," said I. "Yet those Burgundians to whom I spoke contemned the King of France most roundly and wished us well in our endeavour. In Paris, the issue is nicer. Some fear us—as well they may—yet others are disaffected and might side with us to oust a king for whom they have no love."

"This news is most welcome, Sir John," said Dorset, smiling for the first time. 'Yet I must know more."

And he bade Agnes and me be seated around the board and called for wine and cakes and questioned me at length about all that I had seen since quitting Rouen: what troops were quartered there, of what provenance they were and under whose command; the strength and dispositions of the soldiery encamped without the city; the number and proximity of the patrols we had encountered around Harfleur. His questioning was as detailed and relentless as any Grand Inquisitor and I answered him as best as I was able, giving no colour to my account and speaking right soberly. In faith, until then I had not realised how much I knew of the French King's preparations.

At length, Dorset was done and he smiled at me in friendly wise and poured us all a cup of wine with his own hand.

"I commend you, Sir John," said he. "You have done your king a great service. You have endured much hardship and danger for a man of your years and the intelligence that you bring is of great value."

"For that you must thank my wife," said I. "Were it not for her, I would not be sitting here now."

"*Je vous remercie profondément, milady,*" said Dorset, smiling a trifle too gallantly at Agnes.

"When think you that the French will make head against Harfleur?" I asked.

Dorset sighed and tapped the board with his finger-ends.

"It will not be tomorrow for they are yet ill-prepared and have learned the price of recklessness. Within the month, that I doubt not."

"And then Harfleur will fall?" said I.

"If it does, there will not be a man alive within these walls to witness the Constable's entrance. Harfleur was purchased at great cost, Sir John and will be sold even more dearly."

And with that Agnes and I emptied our cups and took our leave. Dorset thanked me once again and said that he would tell King Henry of my loyal service and that I might expect some reward. I said naught in return but quitted his company as swiftly as I could. If Hal wants to thank me, he will have to find me first.

Agnes and I recovered our horses and led them through the busy streets of Harfleur in search of lodgings. These we found, but with some difficulty. At last, we were shown to a bed in one corner of the upper room at the sign of *La Sirène*, or The Mermaid as it is now. The other four beds are occupied by soldiery yet they are all honest men and merry and have even moderated their cursings out of respect for Agnes. Gentle as this consideration may be, it is pretty well superfluous since for all Agnes understands they could as well be praying.

It was only when we were comfortably installed in a settle with a cup of wine to hand that the full import of our freedom came upon me. In faith, since our first meeting with Ancient Hywel and his men, I had felt slightly less free than in all my time in France.

And so we drank a toast to our good fortune, and then another, before setting forth for the haven, there to strike a bargain with a Captain Richard Bigelow for the transport of us and our horses to Southampton, sailing on the morrow.

It was as we were returning to The Mermaid that I espied a boy grooming a horse in the yard adjacent to our hostelry. There was something familiar about the animal and thus I approached the lad and enquired as to its owner.

"English *chevalier*," said the lad, grimacing and scratching his crotch.

"And what is the name of this English *chevalier*?" said I.

The boy shrugged and resumed his grooming. Thus, leaving Agnes without the hostelry, I entered and accosted the host.

"Ze 'orse belong to 'im," said he, pointing to a formless heap of cloth, sprawled across a bench and snoring loudly.

"Does it now?" said I.

I approached the heap and perceived that from one end protruded two spindly legs and from the other a single thin arm. I bent down over what I assumed was its head.

"Sir Edward?" I whispered.

"Hummg!" said the heap.

"Sir Edward?" I sang. "It is me, Sir John Falstaff."

"'Sdead," said the heap.

"Not dead, in faith," said I, "but here at your side."

"Nay. Sdead," said the heap.

"Good Sir Edward," said I. "I am alive and here with you."

"Hummg," it repeated.

"Bevis, you tidy pile of stoat's droppings!" I roared. "On your shanks, man!"

At this the heap convulsed, parted company with the bench and landed with a goodly crack upon the flagstones. Sir Edward Swithun Bevis's long face stared up at me, a palimpsest of pain, joy, horror and surprise.

"I thought you were dead!" said he.

"Then belike we all are," said I. "You, me, Agnes, your horse, my horse, Agnes's horse and the Earl of Dorset. Yonder host must be some minor demon demoted to waiting at table."

"Sir John!" cried Bevis and leapt to his feet and embraced me and he was laughing yet his eye was wet, as was my own. At length, I broke free of him and called out the door to Agnes and she entered the taproom and greeted Sir Edward with much bussing and blubbering, and we sat down together and bespoke wine in plenty.

We told Sir Edward of our adventures since leaving him at the village of Elbeuf and, by and by, his own tale unfolded. I shall not recount it fully for it took a damnable long time to tell and is of surpassing strangeness. Let it only be said that, in principle, he had followed the River Seine to its mouth and there had found a town called Harfleur. In truth, its name was not Harfleur but *Honfleur*. Never one to let the difference of a mere syllable come between himself and a fresh bout of protracted foolishness, Sir Edward entered the town and wondered greatly at the singular lack of English soldiery and the large number of heavily armed French troops. He reasoned—if you may call it thus—that Harfleur had been recaptured and the English either driven out or slaughtered to a man.

Those who do not know Sir Edward as I know him, might well ask why a knight who had been present at the siege of Harfleur a few months earlier should fail to mark any difference between that town and the one he now found himself in. They would not be so greatly puzzled if they knew that if Sir Edward did not wear the same apparel every day, he would be grievous hard put to remember what he wore the day before, or that he calls "fox" any wild four-legged beast smaller than a sheep.

As a result of a rare foray into the bright daylight of common sense, Sir Edward asked a passer-by what had become of the English. I for one know not how he accomplished such a feat yet it appears his efforts were successful for he was shown the broad estuary of the River Seine and the town that lay on its opposing bank.

It being impossible to find anyone who would ferry him thither, Sir Edward quitted Honfleur and rode some three leagues back along the riverbank. There he found a ferryman who, on receipt of a largish sum, rowed both him and Primrose across the flood. Thence he reached Harfleur by dint of galloping along the beach and across the dunes and charging anyone who threatened to come in his way. Finally he arrived at an English outpost and was told that Harfleur lay but one half-mile before him, which puzzled Sir Edward greatly for he believed he had just left it.

Bevis entered Harfleur proper the day before we arrived and straightway scoured the town for some sign of us. Finding none and recalling that we had left Elbeuf a full day before himself, he concluded, with much sadness, that we had perished upon the highway. Such was his grief that he returned to this hostelry to drown his sorrows.

Though he did not entirely succeed in drowning them, he did hold them under for a goodly time. In faith, poor Sir Edward had not budged from the bench on which I found him for a full day and had successfully driven away most of the host's regular customers and divers others as were not regular.

"It is a great wonder to me, Sir Edward," said I, "that you contrived to find your way hither knowing no French."

"Marry, Sir John," said he, with a laugh. "I did so with the utmost ease for I knew well that Harfleur lies at the point where the river greets the sea, having been here with King Henry's army. Thus once I had ascertained in which direction the river was flowing, it was a simple matter of following its course. I will own to being a trifle discountenanced to find that the perfidious French have built two Harfleurs and that the Harfleur I sought was on the opposing bank but by travelling contrary to the flow of the river I was able to find my way back upstream and seek out a crossing."

It was most pleasing to mark that some grain of reason, however tiny, had taken root in the fallow space between Sir Edward's ears. I dare say that at some point in time between now and his decrepitude, he may well succeed in finding his way from Exeter to Exmouth without ending up in Edinburgh.

"But what of your French, Sir Edward?" said I. "Was it not needful to speak the language upon occasion."

"Aye, Sir John," said he, setting his finger against his nose. "Yet my French is much improved, as you shall see."

And, of a sudden, he bawled out:

"Mon host! Mon sir! Easy twa vans, silver-plate!"

"Anon, good sir," came our host's reply, in tolerable English.

"You see!" crowed Sir Edward, jubilantly.

How Bevis yet carries a head upon his shoulders is a miracle of biblical proportion.

And so we three fell to drinking to celebrate our reunion and our deliverance and we waxed right merry—so merry, in faith, that sundry of our host's customers, perceiving that Sir Edward was no longer of a morose and bellicose humour, joined us in our carousings. Until, that is, my dear Agnes, who had matched Bevis and me cup for cup, degenerated into song and drove them all out again. And yet I fear it little behoves me to cavil on Agnes's behaviour for I too was dyed scarlet and that most grievously. Thus it was that when an English captain—Challoner by name—suggested that I might further assay my good fortune in a game of dice, I accepted without qualm.

Now the last time I succumbed to such foolishness was at a certain hostelry in the town of Melun where I lost well-nigh all I had to another captain, an Italian who had lately fought at Azincourt. On that occasion, I was constrained to play through fear of mischief done upon my person should I have refused. This night I entered upon my foolishness with a free will and a blithe heart, in spite of the fact that I sat in the company of no less than three Agneses, several Bevises, divers Challoners and a perplexing array of dice. I might just as well have given the good captain the contents of my saddle-bag before we began. As it was, he took them anyway.

"It seems Dame Fortune has deserted you, Sir John," said Challoner, with a sympathetic smile.

"She had another rendezvous this day," said I, dumbly.

Challoner chinked a handful of coin and shook his head sadly.

"You accept your loss with a gentleman's good grace, sir," said he. "And as I would not see gentility reduced to paupery in a single evening, I pray you take these coins as payment for my sport."

And with that he set the handful before me.

Now naught sobers a man quite so swiftly as precipitate disaster. I was now expected to accept Challoner's charity and hazard it on the next casting, which I would most surely have won and perhaps the hazard after that too. Emboldened by the return of my good fortune, I might then have risked a greater main—my horse, my sword, my apparel, belike even this book in which I write—all of which I would as surely have lost.

Thus I took the coin he offered me and dropped it in my purse.

"I thank you for your charity, good captain," said I, "and bid you as much good fortune in trial of arms as you do seem to have at dicing. I wish you good evening."

I arose unsteadily and made my way to a quieter corner of the taproom with Agnes supporting me.

"You have lost all?" said she.

"All save this," said I, patting the few coins in my purse.

Sir Edward approached and, with anxious countenance, gave me a cup of wine, which I quaffed most speedily.

"God's bodkins, Sir John!" said he. "Never have I seen a man so favoured by good fortune!"

"I take it you mean yon captain and not me," said I. "He knew what he was about, Sir Edward. And he carried his good fortune in his sleeve."

"Mean you that he cheated?" said Bevis, in amazement.

I put my finger to my lips.

"Peace, Sir Edward," said I. "He may hear you."

"I care not a fig if he hears me or not!" said Bevis, loudly. "If a man cheat at dice, he is a knave and should be made to rue it!"

"Sir Edward," said I, calmly. "See you those three ruffianly rascals at his side?"

I gestured to the exulting crowd around Challoner.

"The three soldiers?" said Bevis. "The fat one, he who squints, and the fellow with the cudgel?"

"Even so," said I. "They are in his charge and soldier under him. If you accuse their captain of cheating, they will slice you into roundels. And when you are lying in your gore and the Watch is summoned and yon Challoner is searched by them, your very late accusation would be found unfounded for the dice about his person will be of true and equal weight, though those in his corporal's purse will ever roll six-upwards."

"Is there naught to be done then?" asked Bevis, with open frustration.

"Naught, Sir Edward," said I, "save to count up what is left to me that I may pay my reckoning."

With that, I tipped the contents of my purse into my hand and counted out one *livre*, seven *sous* and a *denier*. I know not how much my saddle-bag contained before I began gaming but, by my estimation, I had lost something in the way of sixty-two *livres*.

"Little enough to show for five months in France," said I, replacing the coins.

"At least we have paid our passage to England," said Agnes and she laid her hand upon mine and pressed it gently.

"Fie upon such a rascally knave!" hissed Bevis, glaring at Challoner. "Shall we not make him swallow his own false dice?"

"Two men against four, Sir Edward?" said I. "Poor odds, man. Poor odds."

"Then shall we not lie in wait for him betwixt here and his lodgings and pay him royally for his cheating?"

"We might," said I. "If only we knew where his lodgings were. Nay, good Sir Edward. The highways of France are one thing and the streets of Harfleur quite another. It is bad enough to lose my wealth; to be hanged for murder on that account would be to add injury to insult. Have done. Challoner will be rewarded before long—when once he mistakes sobriety for drunkenness and skill for maladdress."

"But your money, Sir John!" said Bevis.

"I have been penniless before," said I. "Belike I am happier thus. *Post equitem sedet atra cura*, Sir Edward."

"Indeed, Sir John?" said Bevis, vacantly.

"Black care sits behind the man a-horseback," said I.

"But what of Lady Agnes?" he asks.

"Ask her," said I. "I believe she will say that she is my wife and will share my sufferings—as I will hers."

"Nay, Sir John!" said he. "I cannot witness such a scene and do naught!"

And with that Sir Edward left my side and strode across the taproom. For an instant I had a vision of the Bevis bastard-sword leaving its scabbard and lopping off the head of Captain Challoner, as if it were no more than a particularly irksome nettle, yet he marched past my sometime adversary without so much as a glance in his direction and a moment later was in deep colloquy with our host. They vanished into the back-room together but soon Bevis returned and beckoned Agnes and me to follow him.

Our host's private quarters were dominated by a long oaken board, around which were a few stools

Bevis bespoke wine of the landlord and bade Agnes and I be seated and said and did naught till our wine had arrived and our host had departed. Then he coughed loudly and began.

"You see, after I left Elbow..." said he.

"Elbeuf," said I.

"Even so," said he. "After I left Elbow, I met up with a merchant whose name I have quite forgot and who was bound for somewhere or other to buy or sell something though I know not what it was."

I sighed loudly and quaffed off my cup.

"Your tale mystifies and entrances by turns," said I. "Mystifies mostly."

"Now you see, I would gladly have travelled alone," continued Bevis, with the air of one who imparts a great secret. "In truth, I made many attempts to avoid the fellow's company but he was the very devil to dissuade and clung to me more tightly than any leech I was ever bled with. Thus, perforce, we travelled together for a good three or four leagues or more, I holding my peace as best I could for, as you may have perceived, my knowledge of the French tongue, though much improved, is slightly less than perfection."

"Go to," said I.

"And this French chewet jangled worse than three loose groats in an empty tankard," said Bevis, in a rare excursion to the land of simile. "He would say this or that or the other and I could make no answer for I understood naught and had to grunt and cough and ahem in plenty and trust to good fortune that I was making apt reply."

"Indeed?" said I.

"Yet all went well for a few hours at least. Until I believe he required something more than a grunt or a cough by way of answer. It was a great pity for he was a pleasant fellow, yea and a cheerful."

"It was a great pity he required a more reasonable answer?" I asked, striving to rescue some semblance of logic from his account.

"Yea, in faith," said Bevis. "For then I would not have had to blip him and that was a greater pity yet."

"Blip him?" said I.

"Aye," said Bevis. "On the head. With my sword."

"Ah! So you killed him then!" I exclaimed, relieved at having encountered a plain fact at last.

"Nay, in faith!" said Bevis. "Blipped him only, with the flat of my sword. He lives yet—of that I am sure. It was but the slightest blip imaginable. No more than it took to render him senseless."

And with that Sir Edward Swithun Bevis sat back with a smile of satisfaction at an obfuscatory exercise well accomplished and was silent.

There followed a short space of time during which Sir Edward continued to smile on us both and we upon him. Agnes finally shrugged and began to twist her hair. I waited a little longer to make quite sure that Bevis was not going to give vent to a grand declaration that might lend some sort of point to his account of the garrulous and now presumably grievously injured merchant, but he did not.

"Good Sir Edward," said I, at length. "This tale of yours was of great interest and will doubtless keep many a company enthralled on cold Devonshire nights. And yet—forgive my slowness—I quite fail to see what a damned whoreson pox it has to do with the price of herring!"

"Herring?" said he, startled at my outburst.

"Or aught else for that matter!"

"But he had money, Sir John!" said Bevis. "A goodly deal of money."

And he rummaged by his feet, lifted his saddle-bag onto the board, and poured forth a shower of coins: gold, silver and dross, great and small, clipped and whole.

"Well, I am most gratified," said I, "that the few weeks in my company have tutored you in the ways of the highway."

"I thought you would be glad," said Bevis, grinning inanely.

"It seems a considerable sum," said I.

"I am sure it is," said Bevis, "though I have not counted it."

"I thought not," said I. "We had best count it then, do you not think?"

"By all means," said Bevis. "Yet I know not what part of the coin I had before and what part I had of the merchant."

"Well then," said I. "Rather than subtract one sum that you know not from another of which you are ignorant, let us count it all together."

And this I did and the amount came to one hundred and twenty-six *livres*, ten *sous* and three *denier*.

"It is a tidy sum," said Bevis. "Now, if you please, Sir John, divide it into two equal parts."

I shrugged and did as he asked and, before long, there were two piles upon the board, each containing sixty-three *livres*, five *sous* and a *denier*. The remaining *denier* I placed between the two.

Sir Edward picked up the *denier* piece, examined it curiously and placed it in his purse. Then he opened his saddle-bag once more, held it below the level of the table and scooped one of the piles of coin therein.

"The money that remains is for yourself and Lady Agnes," he mumbled, colouring a little and staring at his fingers.

For a moment, I was speechless. I looked at the coins upon the table and then I looked back to Sir Edward who was still regarding his fingers with critical interest.

"Sir Edward," said I, "this money is yours."

"Thus I may dispose of it as I will," said he.

"That's true enough," said I. "Yet it is the fruits of your own labour."

"If labour it was," said Sir Edward, abandoning further examination of his extremities, "it was in a trade that you taught me. Nay, Sir John. It was money ill-gotten and it would bring misfortune were I not to share it with you."

"I shall have none of it," said I, peremptorily.

"Well then," said Bevis. "I will have to seek out Captain Challoner and hazard this money to win back what you lost."

"If you do that, you will lose it all," said I.

"Then that being the case," said Bevis, "spare me the trouble of casting good coin after bad. Accept."

So that I did and yet with much reluctance. To obtain money through gullery or theft is merely to relieve the foolish of what they do not deserve to possess in the first place, yet to receive charity is a source of shame to any honest man. Marry, I would rather swing at Tyburn than hobble at Mile End.

Bevis would accept no thanks and thus I proffered none but once I had told Agnes of his gift, she sprang to her feet and threw her arms about Sir Edward and blubbered mightily into his hair. Bevis was grievously put out of countenance at this assault and coloured as deeply as a virgin in a leaping-house.

"My Lady! My Lady! It is naught, I assure you!" he bleated, flapping his arms in panic. "Sir John, say something, I beseech you! Have her desist!"

"Nay, Sir Edward," said I, chuckling. "I shall not come between a woman and her gratitude. If you have no taste for it, you should never have given us the money."

At length, Agnes left off her thankings and resumed her seat beside me. We three did not return to the confusion of the taproom but settled ourselves around the board and bespoke more wine and such cold meats as our host had in store. After another pint or two of Guyenne, we attained that state of insobriety where foolery is put aside and wit and reason, scoured bright by the action of the wine, illuminate the cobwebbed corners of the soul. Thus did we relive together the joys and hardships of the past weeks and appended our opinions and reflections thereto. All vexation was banished from our talk and we spoke as equals every one.

I have kept a vigil this night for I have had much to record. What I write now shall be the last entry in this daybook.

It is yet dark without but the birds have commenced their morning conversation and Agnes and I must stir ourselves and go down to the haven, there to embark for England.

At Drinkstone Eleigh

On Saint James' Day, in the eighth year of the reign
of King Henry, the fifth of that name.
(Thursday 25th July 1420)

It is a rare delight to write once more in this daybook, in which I last wrote some four years ago. I found it yesterday when I was searching out the deeds to my house.

My neighbour, Edward Nashe, has claimed part of my apple orchard and says it is his own. I know full well that it is not, to which the said deeds bear clear witness. Edward Nashe is known to be as covetous a rogue as ever drew breath. I think I shall have little difficulty in proving my right.

How my life has changed since last I wrote in these pages! Marry, I am an old man now, this being no less than my five and seventieth summer. For all that, I am one of the youngest landowners in this realm for I am but four years old. By way of explanation, lest I read this a further four year hence and understand naught of it, let me state that before I took Agnes de Bazois to wife I was not the Jack Falstaff who shakes and scratches with this pen. Then I was full of vanities and no more would have thought of spending my days in peace and moderation than I would of taking holy orders and squatting on a pillar. In faith, since finding this book yesterday I have read much of it and am sorely ashamed of some of the opinions expressed herein, particularly those concerning the good and kind Sir Edward Bevis.

I have not seen Sir Edward since we parted company at Harfleur, nor have I heard aught of him. Nor do I greatly wish to hear aught of him save to know that he be safe and well for, in truth, and his goodness and kindness aside, he was one of the most foolish men as ever I met.

Also there is far too much thievery in this book. God's wounds, were it not for the fact that such affronts to justice were committed in a foreign land, there is that in here which might hang me. Since my beloved Agnes and I settled here in Drinkstone Eleigh, I have not stolen so much as a flower from a neighbour's garden. Besides, there are more than enough in my own garden. Add to which, if there were robbery afoot in this village, it is I who would be the victim for not only am I a foreigner in these parts, and thus not yet trustworthy, and therefore fair game for the light-fingered, but I am also by far the wealthiest inhabitant. Thus is it that Edward Nashe will have a part of my orchard.

Enough has happened in these four years past to fill this little book twentyfold, yet I lack the patience or the steadiness of hand to recount it all. Suffice to say that my life is no longer governed by the vicissitudes of fortune, as once it was, but rather by the changing of the seasons for I am turned farmer and possess sheep and three or four cows and have ten acres under the plough. Yea, I have pigs too and yet I have not bestowed names upon them and I care more for their weight at market than for their lineage or conduct.

The success of our farming is due in no little part—in faith, in all part—to Agnes. The one quality to which her father gave no superfluous colour was her excellence as an administrator of estates. Never have I seen a sly rogue who could best her, for she is a fine judge of all she buys and sells and, though her English is still not of the best, she can argue a price as well as any. Thus has she earned the respect of all who live nearby and they call her Agnes of Burgundy, as if she were the duchess thereof. Four years ago they called her a French whore.

The King, by the by, is now master of France, or at least he will be when Mad Charles dies. He too—Harry, not Chas—has had the sense to marry a Burgundian but not yet sense enough to buy a farm and live a quiet life, which he would be well advised to do for this French jape of his will cost him much and come to naught. Though I have foresworn kings and princes, yet would I still set eyes once more upon young Hal—not for the sake of advantage or companionship but only to witness those changes that time and care have wrought upon him.

This reminds me of an occurrence that befell me a year or so ago. I had gone to town with Agnes—she to buy seed-corn and I to enjoy the pleasures of the tavern. I was passing the market cross when I was accosted by a beggar with long hair and matted, and clad in rags of surpassing foulness.

"Spare a groat for an old soldier, sir," said he.

Now it is sure that there are ever more old soldiers than young ones and of those said old soldiers there are but few that have not been reduced to beggary. Thus was I about to wave the fellow aside when I paused, for there was something in his voice that sounded familiar.

"Just a groat, kind sir," said he, "to buy me a crust o' bread."

"Peto?" said I.

The beggar started at this and squinted up at me.

"God's blood," said I. "It *is* Peto, in faith!"

Now this Peto was an acolyte of mine in the days when young Hal of Lancaster was a votary of Saint Nicholas. I have put "acolyte" yet "accomplice" is nearer the mark, for his livelihood was the lightening of purses and he was a man of some estimation in that craft.

It is a fact unknown to many that his real name is Tom Bledlow, yet all who knew him called him Peto on account of his being much troubled by the wind. Marry, though he spoke but little, and that seldom, he farted worse than a dog fed on sausages.

"I know you not, sir," said Peto, cautiously.

"Why, man. It is me, Jack Falstaff!" said I.

"Sir John Falstaff is dead," said he, squinting harder. "He died a good five year ago."

"And what did he die of?" said I.

"His heart was broke," said Peto. "And he died unshriven and was carried off by the Devil."

"And was this Falstaff a man of some corpulence, such as I?"

"Aye, but fatter," said he.

"And was his eye not blue, as mine is?"

"Aye, but bluer," said he.

"And his hair? Was it not also as white as snow?"

"Aye, that it was," said Peto. "Though he had more of it."

"And, Peto," I whisper. "Do you not recall a certain business at Gad's Hill near Rochester when you and I and Edward Poins and the King of England himself deprived some honest travellers of coin?"

"Not I," said he.

"Then your memory is as bad as your digestion, Tom Bledlow," said I. "For I *am* Jack Falstaff!"

"I know," said he.

And I took him by the arm and led him to an alehouse but the hostess would not vouchsafe him entrance and thus I bespoke two jugs of wine and had them brought to us without the door. It was a fine day and a warm and so we sat in the sun and I told Peto a little of what had befallen me since quitting Eastcheap and, in his turn, he told me what had become of himself and others.

It seems the Boar's Head stands yet though Nell Quickly is not the hostess of it, having succumbed to the pox in Saint Bartholomew's. Thence it passed to her husband, that feather-brained Pistol, the namesake of my horse. This coward returned intact from France and had much coin about him—profit that he made by misuse of the sutler's office—yet squandered it all, returned to thievery, and swung at Smithfield two years ago.

Edward Poins died of the flux without Harfleur; Nym and John Bardolph were hanged in France; Gadshill hanged in England. My poor, sweet Doll is also dead. Peto himself was arraigned for theft and held three years in Newgate, yet no witness was brought against him and he was released. Since then, he has walked the country from Dover to the Scottish Marches, begging and stealing to keep spirit in his flesh.

So we sat quietly without the tavern and talked and drank until it was time for me to seek out Agnes and wend homewards. I paid the reckoning and gave Peto what remained in my purse, yet I did not tell him where I lived and, thank God, he never asked.

It is a great pity that I shall never have such news of those I left in France. Agnes has had no word from her family since quitting Burgundy in search of me and, upon occasion, she is much saddened thereby. For my part, I often wonder how fares my god-daughter Jehanne-Edouard, but I fear I shall always be doomed to ignorance on that account.

I am sitting in the great hall of my house. In truth, it is not so very great yet it is arrassed finely and is sufficiently warm in the winter months. Before me stands a table whereon rests my daybook and a pot of blackest ink. I have a cup of wine to hand and, when I set the final dot upon this page and close my little book, I shall arise and fill it to the brim and drink the healths of friend and foe, departed and deceased. In faith, it is but paltry gratitude, for all of them, the greatest and the least, have added to the richness of my life.

Endnotes

1   Thomas Mowbray, Earl of Nottingham and Duke of Norfolk. He was exiled for life by Richard II in 1398.

2   King Henry V (1386–1422)

3   Sir Henry Percy (1364–1403), son to the Earl of Northumberland and the "Hotspur" of Shakespeare's *Henry IV Part One*.

4   1403. The decisive battle of the rebellion of the Percys, assisted by Douglas and in concert with Mortimer and Glendower.

5   Restaurant.

6   Although "sack" is associated with Shakespeare's Falstaff, this fortified wine was not widely available until the beginning of the 16th century.

7   The decisive battle of the rebellion of Archbishop Scroop, Mowbray and Hastings.

8   Falstaff's watering-hole in Eastcheap.

9   A widow and proprietor of the *Boars's Head* tavern in Eastcheap, London.

10   A prostitute depicted in Shakespeare's *Henry IV Part Two*.

11   An ensign or lieutenant. The lowest rank of commissioned officer.

12   Bardolph, famed for his rubicund complexion, is another character depicted in Shakespeare's *Henry IV, One & Two*.

13   The Fleet Prison, which once stood in the neighbourhood of the present-day Farringdon Street. Generally, it served as a prison for important people and those condemned by the Star Chamber. Falstaff was temporarily imprisoned there on the accession of Henry V. It served as a debtors' prison from 1640 until 1848 when it was finally demolished.

14   The open drain in the middle of the street.

15   20th March

16   "A name illustrious and venerated by all nations."

17   Timekeeping in the Medieval period tended to be haphazard. A day was arbitrarily divided into 24 hours—12 day and 12 night—regardless of season. In December, one daytime hour had about 30 minutes and in June it had 90. Sexte was the sixth hour of the day and thus noon.

18   A swindler or confidence-trickster.

19   Quartermaster. A position open to many abuses.

20   The *Trinité Royale*. Henry V's flagship.

21   Charles VI of France, known as *Le Bien Aimé*. He was afflicted with madness from 1392. He died thirty years later.

22 Richard, Earl of Cambridge, younger brother of Edward, second Duke of York, and cousin to Henry V. He had been executed for leading a plot against the king.

23 "The traveller with empty pockets will sing in the robber's face."

24 A long, flowing gown. It was the principal garment worn by both men and women until the end of the fifteenth century.

25 An "ale-stake" was a pole with a branch or bush attached, which was fixed outside an alehouse in much the same way as an inn-sign is hung today. In London they were not allowed to be more than seven feet in length in case they injured riders.

26 In fact, the estimated strength of the French army is 20–30,000.

27 In 1414, Holy Innocents Day—the 28th December—fell on a Friday. It was therefore considered unlucky to begin a journey or any new endeavour on any Friday of the following year.

28 Nimble, manoeuvrable.

29 The bastard-sword, often known as the hand-and-a-half sword, was the commonest in use at the time. It was double edged with an elongated hilt that enabled the user to use both hands to wield it.

30 On the following day (8th October) Henry V led his army out of Harfleur. By this time it had been reduced to around 8,000 men. His objective was to march them to Calais.

31 *God zij vervloeckt*: May God be cursed.

32 9 a.m.

33 Probably the River Aa that rises in the Collines d'Artois, passes through Saint Omer and flows into the sea at Gravelines.

34 The name seems unlikely even by medieval French standards. Probably, the inn was either called *L'Epi d'Or*, meaning The Golden Ear (of corn) or *L'Epée d'Or*, meaning The Golden Sword.

35 A cavalry raid. Given that Henry V's army comprised mostly of foot soldiers, this is rather unlikely.

36 Here the page ends in the original manuscript. The following page has been defaced by the action of some liquid, perhaps rainwater.

37 "A thing done, the fool knows."

38 A bathhouse. Most of them doubled as brothels.

39 Bacon rashers.

40 A long, flowing dress that was worn by women until the first quarter of the fifteenth century.

41 "Where one is well off, there is one's country."

42 "But something bitter arises."

43 To have sex.

44 Leonidas of Sparta.

45 They were defeated.

46 The French army numbered twenty to thirty thousand. About twelve to eighteen thousand of them were men-at-arms.

47 10 a.m.

48 "Faith is better put in the eyes than in the ears."

49 In fact, he was taken prisoner. He remained in captivity for 21 years.

50 Whether or not the real Pope slept in Rome is open to some debate. At this time, the Catholic Church was embroiled in what we now know as the Great Schism. This began in 1378 as a power-struggle in the Vatican between the Italian and French factions. By 1415, following the Council of Pisa in 1409, there were no less than three claimants to the papacy: John XXIII, Gregory XII and Benedict XIII. It is still unclear exactly who was the real Pope. John XXIII had succeeded Alexander V who had been elected by the Council of Pisa; Benedict XIII was supported by France and Spain and moved his court from Rome to Avignon. The present-day Vatican recognizes Gregory XII as the official Pope of the day. England tended to support Gregory, while Burgundy, under *Jean sans Peur*, preferred to remain neutral. Given the geographical proximity, however, sympathies still tended to lie with Benedict.

51 The écu was equivalent to three *livres*. The dowry was thus 300 *livres*. It is extremely difficult to compare values with the present day but a skilled artisan could be expected to earn about 30 *livres* a year.

52 Porridge, often flavoured with almonds, raisins and other sweet ingredients.

53 "Pale death, with equal foot, knocks at the hovels of the poor and the palaces of kings."

54 "The die is cast."

55 Skewered meats, often offal.

56 "The fear of death is worse than death itself."

57 On 27th November 1415, this would have been around 8:15 a.m.

58 Falstaff probably means the Conqueror's son William II, who was killed in a hunting "accident" in the New Forest.

59 "War is sweet to those who do not know it."

60 Pope Joan was a mythical female pope who, in the 9th century, supposedly succeeded Leo IV as Pope John VIII, having disguised herself as a man. Of English descent, although born in Germany, she was said to have eloped to Greece in male disguise with her lover—a Benedictine monk. After returning to Rome, she

became a cardinal and eventually pope. According to the story, she died in child-birth during a pontifical procession.

61 1.45 p.m.

62 Richard II, murdered in Pomfret Castle.

63 Holy Innocents Day fell on a Saturday in 1415. All succeeding Saturdays were unlucky.

64 2 p.m.

65 At this time, the real cause of bubonic plague was unknown. Various strange explanations were given for its origin. The plague of 1348–1349 reduced the population of Europe by roughly a third.

66 "I deny God."

67 "Bread is worth more than an écu in the wall."

68 "On him does death lie heavily who, too well known to all, dies to himself unknown."

69 In the Middle Ages it was a widespread belief that, after his resurrection, Lazarus lived in constant fear of dying.

70 10.30 a.m.

71 Franklins were freeholders as opposed to serfs. In general, the peasants of Normandy and Flanders were freemen whilst those of Champagne and Burgundy were serfs.

72 "Neither by entreaty nor bribery."

Acknowledgements

Sometime in the last century I had the bright idea of writing a novel based on the character of Shakespeare's Falstaff. I was aware at the time that I was following in illustrious footsteps – not just Shakespeare's but also those of a host of others. What started out as a literary jape ended up as a daunting task.

I could not have sustained the project without the assistance and support of my dear wife Kjersti Varang and my son Owen Frazer Wray, who occasionally had to put up with a husband and father who was lost in the 15 th century.

I would like to express particular gratitude to my friend Peter Cawley, my first editor, who helped me to curb some of my prolixity and grind the story into a digestible form.

Almost finally, this book would never have seen the light of day had it not been for the courage of Sparsile Books in taking on a project that many had turned down. I would like to thank Lesley Affrossman, Madeleine Jewett, Stephen Cashmore and Alex Winpenny for their faith, praise and peerless professionalism.

Finally, I would like to thank Will Shakespeare for providing me with a ready-made character who has captured the imaginations of so many over the centuries, not least myself.

Further Reading

The Promise

Simon's Wife

The Unforgiven King

American Goddess

L. M. Affrossman

Two Pups

Seona Calder

Comics and Columbine

Tom Campbell

Kindred Spirit

Stephen Cashmore

Science for Heretics

The Tethered God

Barrie Condon

Pignut and Nuncle

Des Dillon

Gamebird

Adrian Keefe

Drown For Your Sins

Dress For Death

Diarmid MacArthur

I Wanna Be Like Me

Kenny Taylor &

Grisel Miranda

Euphorion

Oliver Thomson

www.sparsilebooks.com

Lightning Source UK Ltd.
Milton Keynes UK
UKHW011830151221
395702UK00001B/270